EMMA DARCY

is the award-winning Australian author of over 80 Modern Romance™ novels. Her compelling, sexy, emotional stories have gripped the imagination of readers around the globe. She's sold nearly 60 million books worldwide and Mills & Boon® are delighted to bring you:

Kings of Australia

Nothing will stop this special breed of men from winning the women they love…

D1329036

Dear Reader,

I have always been fascinated by the lives of pioneers – the men who were brave enough, strong enough, determined enough to take on a harsh, dangerous and alien land and forge a future for themselves and their families. To me such men are a very special breed.

In my **Kings of the Outback** anthology last year, I wrote about a family from the Kimberly, who had become legendary in that vast expanse of Australia. Another part of Australia which tested the grit and endurance of pioneers is the tropical far north of Queensland. Instead of drought, they faced cyclones; instead of desert, almost impenetrable rainforest. Yet the land was cleared for profitable plantations – sugar cane, tea, tropical fruit.

I decided to marry one of the King men from the Kimberly to a remarkable Italian woman, Isabella Valeri, whose father had pioneered the far north. This anthology is about their three grandsons – Alex, Tony and Matt – and the women they choose to partner them in the future.

These men are a very special breed. Nothing will stop them from winning what they want. I love reading about men like that. I hope you do too.

With love –
Emma Darcy

Kings of Australia

The Arranged Marriage

The Bridal Bargain

The Honeymoon Contract

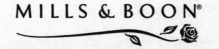

MILLS & BOON®

*First published in Great Britain 2005
Harlequin Mills & Boon Limited,
Eton House, 18-24 Paradise Road, Richmond, Surrey, TW9 1SR*

KINGS OF AUSTRALIA © Harlequin Enterprises II B.V., 2005

The Arranged Marriage © Emma Darcy 2002
The Bridal Bargain © Emma Darcy 2002
The Honeymoon Contract © Emma Darcy 2002

ISBN 0 263 84568 0

062-0805

*Printed and bound in Spain
by Litografia Rosés S.A., Barcelona*

Look out for Emma Darcy's compelling new
novel, *The Ramirez Bride*,
the first book in the exciting new trilogy:

THE RAMIREZ BRIDES

Three half-brothers, scattered to opposite sides
of the globe: each must find a bride in order to
find each other...

Coming next month only in
Modern Romance™.

The Arranged
Marriage

CHAPTER ONE

ISABELLA VALERI KING eyed her niece by marriage, approving the strength she saw in Elizabeth's face. This woman, considered to be the matriarch of the Kings of the Kimberley, understood what family was about—property, heritage, passed from generation to generation.

There had to be marriage.

There had to be children.

Elizabeth had three sons, all of them married this past year and two of them begetting children already. *She* could rest content. Not so Isabella. Of her three grandsons, only Alessandro was planning to marry, and it was not a marriage Isabella favoured.

The woman of his choice was not right for him.

But how to make him see?

How to change his mind?

The wedding date was set in December, after the sugarcane had been harvested. It was May now. Six months Isabella had to somehow show Alessandro that Michelle Banks would never settle happily into his life. She was selfish, that one. Selfish and self-centred. But very clever at wheedling her own way, undoubtedly using sex to seduce Alessandro into indulging her.

How long would that last into their marriage?

And a woman so fussy about preserving her figure...pregnancy would certainly not be attractive to her. Would she agree to have even one child, or would there be excuses, delays, outright refusal?

"This is a wonderful location, Isabella," Elizabeth said admiringly, looking out over Dickinson Inlet to the cane fields on the other side.

They were sitting in the loggia beside the fountain, sharing morning tea, and the open colonnade gave a very different vista to that of the Outback in the Kimberley. Here was the intense green of far north Queensland, and pressing around all the land claimed by man was the tropical rainforest, as primitive on its own unique terms as the vast red heart of Australia.

Isabella remembered how dearly the land had been won; the labour-intensive clearing, the treacherous vines and poisonous plants, the heat, the humidity, the fevers, the deadly snakes. She'd been born amongst the cane fields, to Italian immigrants, seventy-eight years ago.

Apart from the short span of time spent in Brisbane, when she'd met and married Edward King, before he and her brother, Enrico, had gone off to the war in Europe, her home had always been here, on this hill overlooking Port Douglas. This was where she had returned—a war widow—to give birth to the child Edward had given her before he'd gone—their son, her dearly beloved Roberto.

"My father chose the location for my mother who came from Naples," she explained to her visitor. "She wanted to be by the sea."

Elizabeth smiled, appreciating the history. "It's a

very romantic story...your father building this castle for his bride.''

Isabella smiled back at the misnomer. "His villa," she corrected. "Like the ancient villas of Rome. In the old days this place was known as the Valeri Villa. But because my brother did not return from the war, and I married Edward, my son and my grandsons carried the King name. After my father died, the local people came to call it King's Castle and the name has stuck.''

"Is that a sadness to you?" Elizabeth asked quietly. "Having your father's name and what he created passed over for the King name."

She shook her head. "My father's bloodline is here. That is what would matter to him. To have what he built remain in the family and be built upon. You understand this, Elizabeth."

She nodded.

"I am sure you know it is not easy to achieve," Isabella continued, needing to talk her problem through with a woman who would comprehend it. "We have disasters here in the tropics, too. You have drought. We have cyclones. I lost my son to a cyclone. That was a very difficult time...Roberto gone, the plantations flattened..."

A time of loss in every sense.

"I sometimes think it's disasters that forge character," Elizabeth mused. "To rise above them, to endure..."

"To fight. To keep what you have," Isabella strongly agreed.

Perhaps it was the vital conviction in her voice that

caused Elizabeth to look at her consideringly. What did she see—this niece by marriage to the Kings of the Kimberley? They were both white-haired, dark-eyed, and sat with straight backs. Isabella was almost two decades older, but she didn't *feel* old. Her face might be more wrinkled and she probably had more aches and pains than the younger woman, but inside, the fire for life was still there, the fire for more to be chalked up in whatever time she had left before death stole her away.

"You have done your father proud, Isabella," came the quiet summing up. "Holding it all together for your grandsons to grow into men and achieve all they have. The tour of the plantations yesterday…both Rafael and I are very impressed."

"But it can so easily come to an end. The cyclone that took Roberto and his wife…" She shook her head and shot a keen look at Elizabeth. "I want my grandsons married with children to safeguard the future, but they are not obliging me."

"Alex…"

"You met his fiancée, Michelle Banks, at dinner last night. What did you think of her?"

A hesitation, then slowly, "Very charming…very polished."

Isabella grimaced at the careful comment, her eyes flashing a sharp mockery. "Like a diamond, all sparkly, with a heart and will that's just as hard. There is no real giving in this young woman."

"You're unhappy with his choice."

"She will not make him a good wife."

An instant understanding. Appreciation, too, of the dilemma Isabella found herself in. Sympathy. And finally advice. "Then you must find him another woman, Isabella, before it's too late."

"I? How do I do that? It is not as though Alessandro would ever accept an arranged marriage. He has the devil's pride."

"My eldest son, Nathan, was frittering away the years with unsuitable women. His real life was bound up in the land, as I suspect is the case with Alex."

"True. And Michelle Banks does not share it. To her it is a source of wealth. Nothing more."

"I went looking for a woman who could answer Nathan's needs. I found her. And as it turned out, Nathan answered her needs, so it is a very happy match."

"You *found* Miranda for Nathan?"

"Yes. And I put them in each other's paths. I prayed it would work and it did."

"Ah! The paths must cross...with perhaps, some clever angling?"

"Nothing too obvious. Some little pushes to put them together. It's impossible to control everything. If there's no chemistry..."

"Ha! What woman wouldn't want Alessandro?"

"The critical point is...he would have to want her, too. Miranda is quite strikingly beautiful. And Michelle is..."

"Ah, yes. A very artful beauty. Skin-deep."

"Sexually attractive," Elizabeth reminded her.

"Skin and bones. He needs a woman with child-bearing hips and a bosom to suckle the babies. A woman who knows what a proper meal is for a man. And I do not mean lettuce leaves.''

Elizabeth laughed. ''Well, don't forget Alex would have to find her physically attractive, too. If Michelle is any guide, don't choose a woman on the plump side.''

''She can surely have the right curves?''

''You know him best, Isabella. I think someone with the right attitude might be more important. A woman who could be a partner in every sense.''

''A partner. Yes. That's what Alessandro needs. A true partner. Who will be happy to have his children.''

Isabella was highly satisfied with this conversation.

It was good that Elizabeth had come to visit with her new man, the Argentinian, Rafael Santiso. A fine man, too. He reminded her of her father…a man of vision.

Alessandro could also be a man of vision…if he just opened his eyes and saw what had to be seen to make everything right. She would make him see. She would find the right woman to show him.

CHAPTER TWO

"GINA! You're wanted out front!"

It was more a command than a call. Gina Terlizzi quickly set aside the greenery she was sorting for the floral arrangements and hurried from the back room to answer it, wondering why her presence was required *out front*. As the owner of the florist shop, her aunt preferred to deal with the customers herself.

The reason was instantly evident and punched her heart with shock—Marco, her two-and-a-half-year-old son, firmly in the grip of an elderly woman. And not just any elderly woman. Recognition of Isabella Valeri King came hard and fast, doubling the shock.

This shop was in Cairns and King's Castle was in Port Douglas, seventy kilometres further north, but the whole Italian community in far North Queensland knew this remarkable woman and held her in the highest respect. A quiver of apprehension ran down Gina's spine at being put on the mat in front of her.

"Are you the *madre* of this boy?" she demanded, her aristocratic bearing taut with disapproval.

Gina tore her gaze from the piercing dark eyes to look down at her son who was gazing up at his captor with something like awe. "Yes," she answered huskily. "What have you done, Marco? Why aren't you in the backyard?"

He gave her his triumphant achievement look, his brown eyes dancing with mischief, an appealing smile flashing from his adorable little face, his mop of dark curls bobbing as he proudly confessed, "I got boxes an' climbed up an' opened the gate."

Which meant he wasn't safely contained here at work anymore. Gina heaved a deeply exasperated sigh. "Then what?"

"I rode my bike."

"He was out on the street, pedalling his tricycle at wild speed, and almost ran into me," came the telling accusation.

Gina stood very straight, facing the music as best she could. "I'm terribly sorry that his lack of control put you at risk, Mrs. King, and I'm grateful you've brought him in to me. I thought he was playing safely in the backyard."

"It seems your son is an enterprising child. Boys will be boys. You must always keep their very active ingenuity in mind."

This softer piece of advice reduced Gina's tension considerably. "I will. Thank you again for returning him to me, Mrs. King."

She was subjected to more scrutiny, as though everything about her was being meticulously catalogued; her long streaky-brown hair, the bangs that swept across her forehead, her thickly lashed amber eyes, her too wide mouth, the bone structure of her face, her long neck, the obvious curves of her full breasts underneath her sleeveless blouse, the neatness of her waist, emphasised by the belt on her skirt, the breadth of her hips, the shape of her bare legs and her feet, which were simply encased in sandals.

It was embarrassing, as though she was being measured for being a careless creature who didn't have enough interest in looking after her son properly. Which wasn't true at all. Gina prided herself on being a good mother. It was just that Marco could be a little devil at times.

"I understand you are a widow."

The knowing statement surprised her into replying, "Yes, I am."

"How long?"

"Two years."

"Perhaps the boy needs a man's hand."

Gina flushed at the implied criticism. "Marco does have uncles."

"You are a very attractive young woman. No one is courting you?"

"No. I…uh…haven't met anyone I…um,…" She floundered hopelessly under the direct beam of those intensely probing eyes.

"You were very attached to your husband?"

"Well, yes…"

"This is not good for the boy—your working in a shop, unable to supervise him properly. You need a husband to support you. The right man would lift this burden from you."

"Yes," she agreed. What else could she do? Arguing with Isabella Valeri King was far too daunting an option. She could only hope her aunt, who was standing silently by, would not take offence. It was a family favour that she had a part-time job here, and allowed to bring Marco with her.

As long as he didn't make a nuisance of himself!

She would definitely be in trouble once Isabella Valeri King departed. However, no immediate exit took place. Despite having delivered her lecture on Gina's situation, the old lady stood her ground and suddenly took an entirely different tack.

"You are also a wedding singer."

"Yes." How did she know these things about her?

"Your agent sent me a tape of your songs. You have a lovely voice."

Finally enlightenment. "Thank you."

"You are aware that weddings are held at King's Castle?"

"Yes, of course." The most exclusive and expensive weddings!

"I am always looking for good singers and I have found it wise to test a voice in the ballroom. The acoustics are different to those in a recording studio."

The fabled ballroom! Gina had never been there but stories about the castle abounded. Was this a chance to be actually hired as a singer for fabulous weddings? Could she ask for a much bigger fee? Travelling money? It was an hour's drive from Cairns to Port Douglas. Her mind zipped through a whole range of exciting possibilities.

"I would require a trial run. Are you free to come on Sunday afternoon?"

"Yes." It wouldn't have mattered if she'd asked for the moon, Gina would have said yes. This was a huge opportunity for her to earn far more than the peanuts she was usually paid for singing.

"Good. Three o'clock. And bring the boy with you." She looked down at Marco whose hand she still held firmly. Amazingly he hadn't tried to wriggle his fingers free of captivity. In fact, he appeared fascinated by this lady who spoke with such authority to his mother. "You will come to visit me with your *madre,* Marco."

"I could have him minded," Gina quickly suggested, anxious not to have her audition disturbed by any mischievous behaviour from her unpredictable son.

That earned a stern glare. "You will not." As though realising her tone was too sharp, she smiled, firstly down at Marco, then at Gina. "He is quite an endearing little boy. I shall enjoy watching him at play. We will have afternoon tea in the loggia and let him run free in the grounds."

"That's…very kind. Thank you."

"Go to your *madre* now, Marco." She released his hand and lightly patted his curls. "And do not ride your bike in the street again. It is not the place to play."

He obediently trotted over to Gina's side and took her hand.

"How old is he?"

"Two and a half."

"He rides very well for his age," came the astonishingly approving comment. "The tricycle is by the door."

"Thank you."

"Three o'clock Sunday," she repeated imperiously.

"We'll be there, Mrs. King. And thank you once again."

Ten minutes to three…Gina slotted her little Honda Swift under one of the bougainvillea and vine-laden pergolas that flanked the steps up to King's Castle. This was the visitors' parking area, and apart from her own car it was empty, which made her feel all the more nervous.

For the umpteenth time she checked that the backing tape for her songs was in her handbag. It might not be needed. She had no idea if she was expected to sing with or without music for this audition. At least she had it if it could be used. The driving mirror reflected that her make-up was still fine, not that she wore much—a touch of eyeliner, mascara, lipstick. Her hair was freshly washed and blow-dried to curve around her shoulders. She hoped she looked like a professional singer.

Marco had fallen asleep in his car seat. She'd dressed him in navy shorts and a T-shirt striped in red, green and navy—navy sandals on his feet. With his dark curls and eyes, such strong colours really suited him and he looked very cute. For herself, she'd chosen a sleeveless lemon shift with a navy band edging the armholes and scooped neckline. Teamed with navy accessories, it was an outfit that always made Gina feel smartly dressed— a much-needed boost for confidence today.

Having unbuckled Marco's safety harness, she gently woke him then lifted him out. Luckily he was never grumpy after a nap. It was like, "Hi, world! What's new?'' and he was all bright-eyed, ready to go and discover it.

"Are we at the castle, Mama?"

"Yes. I'll just lock the car and we'll walk up to it."

"I can't see it."

"You will in a minute."

As they walked up the steps his gaze was trained in entranced wonder at the tessellated tower that dominated the hill. It was said that Frederico Stefano Valeri, Isabella's father, had built it so his wife could watch the boats coming in from the sea and the cane fields burning during the harvesting.

"Can we go up there, Mama?"

"Not today, Marco. But we will see the ballroom. It has huge balls covered with tiny mirrors hanging from the ceiling, and a wooden floor where the boards have been cut into fancy patterns."

The steps were flanked by rows of magnificent palm trees and terraces with lushly displayed tropical flowers and plants and ferns. At the top of the rise, they moved onto a wide flagstoned path with beautifully manicured lawns of buffalo grass on either side. Ahead of them was a colonnaded loggia which prefaced the entrance to the castle. It covered a very spacious area. In the centre of it was a fountain, around which were casual groupings of chairs and tables. At one of these sat three people and Gina's feet almost faltered at the charge of nervous excitement that ran through her as recognition sank in.

Alex King sitting with his grandmother. Alex King and his fiancée, she quickly amended, identifying the woman she'd seen in the photograph accompanying the newspaper article on their engagement. He's taken, she ruefully reminded herself. Besides which, there never had been a chance of her meeting Alex King on any kind of social level—until this very moment. But if ever there was a man to turn her head and make her heart go pitter-pat, he was *it*—The Sugar King.

Of course she had loved Angelo, her husband. Angelo had been real life. This man had always been—and still was—unattainable fantasy. Yet with his gaze directly on her now as she and Marco approached, Gina could feel her pulse racing and little quivers attacking her thighs. He was so handsome. *Manly* handsome. Big and strong and with that intrinsic air of indomitable authority that seemed to say he could handle anything he was faced with. Definitely a king, measured against other men.

He smiled at Marco who had broken into an excited little skip at Gina's side. The smile transformed the hard angles of his face, emitting a warm charm. His eyes twinkled at her son—startling blue eyes, given his suntanned olive skin and the thick wavy black hair that declared his Italian heritage. The blue eyes had to have come from his paternal line. Somehow they gave him an even more charismatic presence.

Probably Gina should have headed for the end of the table where Isabella sat. She didn't think. She was automatically drawn to the end Alex King occupied. He pushed his chair back and stood up to greet her, making her overwhelmingly aware of just how big and tall he was. Such a powerfully built man, and her head was barely level with his broad shoulders.

Belatedly, Gina shot her gaze to his grandmother, whose autocratic command had brought her here and who should be given her prime attention. *I've come on business,* Gina fiercely told herself. *Business, business, business...* But it didn't stop her from being overwhelmingly aware of the magnetic maleness of Alex King.

"My grandson, Alessandro," the old lady announced with a benign smile that relieved Gina of any fear that she would be judged as ill-mannered.

She flicked an acknowledging glance up at the heart-stopping blue eyes.

"His fiancée, Michelle Banks," the introductions continued.

Gina nodded and smiled and received a perfunctory little curve of the lips in return from the woman seated on the other side of the table. Full pouty lips, *sexy* lips. It was somewhat demoralising to see just how beautiful Michelle Banks was in the flesh—her golden hair sleeked back to a knot at the back, her face so perfectly sculptured it needed no softening effect, big almond-shaped, grey-green eyes, a classic nose, and a swan like neck emphasising her long, model-thin elegance.

She wore one of her signature tie-dyed scarf tops with a halter neckline—a garment that could only be worn well by very slim and small-breasted women—and the artistic pattern of earth colours was complemented by gold hipster slacks which affirmed there was no excess flesh anywhere on the fashion designer's body.

Gina instantly felt fat. Which was stupid because she really wasn't. She was simply built on a different scale to Michelle Banks. However, that common sense argument did nothing to lift the lead that had descended on her heart. This was the kind of woman Alex King wanted to marry. Would marry.

"Gina Terlizzi and her son, Marco," Isabella finished.

"A pleasure to meet you, Gina. And Marco," came the warm welcome from her grandson, the deep timbre of his voice striking pleasure chords right through Gina's body. "A good family, the Terlizzis. Still in fishing boats?"

"Most of the men are," she answered, amazed that he knew of them.

Many years ago his father, Robert King, had financed the Terlizzi family venture into fishing. His great-grandfather, Frederico Stefano Valeri, had begun the tradition of financing Italian immigrants into businesses when the banks had denied them loans. Everyone knew that the Kings would listen to a deal when more conventional financial institutions would not. Judgement was made more on the capability to succeed than on up-front money, and as far as Gina knew, no one had ever failed to pay back the Kings' faith in them.

"And you're Angelo's widow," Alex King went on, his tone softening with sympathy.

She nodded, even more astonished he knew her husband's name.

"I remember reading about him going to the rescue of a lone sailor whose yacht had broken up on the reef."

"The storm beat him. They both drowned," she choked out.

"A brave man. And a very sad loss to you and your son." The caring in his eyes squeezed her heart. "I trust your family has looked after you?"

"Very well."

"Good! My grandmother tells me you've come to sing for her. You must want a drink first. Please…" He gestured to the empty chairs on the near side of the table, opposite to where his fiancée sat. "What would you like…wine, fruit juice, iced water?"

"Water for me, thank you."

"And you, Marco?"

"Juice, please."

"Only half a glass for him," Gina quickly warned as she settled them both on chairs. Her eyes appealed for understanding. "He tends to spill from a full one."

Another warming smile. "No problem."

"So…you're a professional singer," Michelle Banks drawled, focusing Gina's attention on her.

"I do get quite a few engagements—weddings, birthdays, other functions—but I can't say I make a living from it," Gina answered truthfully. No point in pretending to be something she wasn't. In fact, more often than not she was asked to sing by family or friends with no fee offered at all.

"I presume you have had some training," the woman pressed in a slightly critical tone that niggled Gina. What business was it of hers?

"If you mean singing lessons, yes. And I've competed in many eisteddfods over the years."

"Then why didn't you pursue a career with it?"

"Not every woman puts a career first," Isabella dryly interposed.

Michelle shrugged. "Seems a waste if your voice is good enough."

She raised her perfectly arched eyebrows at Gina who bristled at the implied put-down. Why did Alex King's fiancée feel the need to put her on the spot like this. She was a woman who appeared to have everything other women might envy, including the man whose ring she was wearing.

"It wasn't the kind of life I wanted," she answered simply. "As to whether my voice is good enough, I'm here—" she transferred her gaze to Isabella "—for Mrs. King to judge if it meets her requirements."

"And I'm looking forward to hearing it," the older woman said, smiling encouragement. "Indeed, if it is true to your performance on tape…" She looked directly at her grandson. "…you may very well want Gina to sing at your wedding, Alessandro."

Silence. Stillness. For the first time Gina lost her own self-consciousness enough to realise there were tensions at this table that had nothing to do with her. Or perhaps she had become an unwitting focus for them. Very quietly she picked up her glass of water and drank, grateful to be out of the direct firing line.

Michelle Banks glared at Alex, clearly demanding his support. He stirred himself, addressing his grandmother with an air of pained patience.

"Nonna, we have already discussed this. Michelle wants a harpist, not a singer."

"I heard what Michelle wants, Alessandro," came the coolly dignified reply. "Did I hear what you want?"

"It is the bride's day," he countered with a slight grimace at the contentiousness behind the question.

Isabella regarded his fiancée with an expression of arch curiosity that Gina instantly felt had knives behind it. "Is that what you think, Michelle—that a wedding belongs only to the bride, and the groom must fall in with everything she wishes?"

Michelle gave a smug little smile. "Alex is happy for me to have a harp playing."

"I've never thought a harp—indeed, any musical instrument—can project the warmth and emotion that a human voice can."

"It's purely a question of taste," Michelle argued. "A harp is very elegant."

"Undoubtedly. However, to my mind, even within a showcase of elegance, room could be made for some spotlight on love at your wedding." She turned a smile on Gina. "Are you now refreshed enough to sing?"

"Yes. Thank you." She set her glass down and picked up her handbag. "I did bring a backing tape. Are there facilities for it to be played in the ballroom or…"

"Of course." She nodded to her grandson. "Alessandro will set it up for you and give you a remote control for pausing between songs."

Gina's heart fluttered. Was *he* going to listen, too? She glimpsed a V of annoyance forming between Michelle Banks' brows, but said a quick, "Thank you," to Alex King anyway.

"My pleasure," he said kindly, though she couldn't help wondering if he also was annoyed at this manipulation by his grandmother. It didn't make for a comfortable audience. His fiancée, for one, was bound to be judging very critically.

Isabella stood up—a definitive signal for them all to rise from the table. Gina hastily removed the glass from Marco's hands and set him on his feet.

"Are we going to see the balls of mirrors now, Mama?" he asked.

"Yes, we are."

"Come, Marco. Give me your hand," Isabella commanded. "I will show you everything while your *madre* is preparing to sing for us."

He responded without so much as a hesitation, trotting straight over to her and eagerly taking the offered hand, his eyes sparkling with happy anticipation. What was it that made him so pliable to this old woman when he could be quite obstreperous with other virtual strangers? Gina doubted he would have taken Michelle Banks' hand so readily. But Isabella King...was he instinctively drawn to the power that emanated from her...the power imbued by so many years of being the matriarch of this family?

It was definitely there.

Even Michelle Banks was not about to buck it at this point, although Gina could feel the younger woman's hostility as they moved as a group to the ballroom. It made Gina wonder if Isabella King was using her as a pawn in a battle she was subtly fighting against her future grand-daughter-in-law.

She hoped it wasn't so.

She needed this opportunity to be a straight deal between them, one she could count on to lead to a better situation for her and Marco if her singing was approved. It was a big *if*, given the current tensions that were affecting her. Somehow she had to set them aside, concentrate on her singing.

Apart from everything else, she would hate to fail in front of Alex King, hate to have him feel pity for her, hate to give his fiancée reason to sneer at her performance.

She had to sing well.

Had to.

Or she would die a million humiliating deaths.

CHAPTER THREE

"DO WE *have* to sit through this?" Michelle hissed at him.

Alex frowned at her. "Yes."

She rolled her eyes, adopting the air of a martyr as they followed his grandmother and her protégés to the ballroom.

Alex found himself distinctly irked by Michelle's lack of graciousness, particularly towards Gina Terlizzi. He'd taken an instant liking to the young widow and her little boy. Why couldn't Michelle simply wish Gina well, instead of measuring her singing talent against her own drive and ambition? It was perfectly understandable why a single mother—tragically so—wouldn't want to drag her child around the club circuit.

Michelle's single-mindedness needed to be tempered by an appreciation of where other people were coming from. Apart from anything else, it was a matter of respect for different values, different circumstances. And it wouldn't hurt her to compromise a bit on her wedding plans. Cutting his grandmother out of all the decisions was not good. Weddings were family affairs to Nonna. That was the Italian way.

Given his grandmother's none too subtle comments on the harp just now, Alex realised he should start taking a more active role in the arrangements. There *were* other people to consider besides the bride. He recalled Elizabeth King's recent visit, and her account of how involved she'd been in the planning of her sons' weddings. Nonna would certainly be feeling…left out of his. It was not right.

The ballroom was set up in its usual pattern—round tables seating eight forming a horseshoe that faced the stage and enclosed the highly polished parquet dance floor. They'd no sooner entered it than Michelle parked herself at one of back tables, right next to the exit, her unwillingness to be an interested party to this audition all too obvious.

Doubly annoyed now, Alex accompanied his grandmother to the table of her choice, halfway down the ballroom. He saw her and the little boy seated, then escorted Gina Terlizzi up to the stage to familiarise her with the sound system so she could perform at her best.

Her hand was trembling slightly as she held out the backing tape. Nerves? Distress at being virtually snubbed by his fiancée? The unfairness of that slight, and the realisation of how vulnerable Gina must be feeling, drove Alex to take the tape and enclose the trembling hand in his own, wanting to impart both warmth and strength, wanting to give her back the confidence that had been taken from her.

"Don't take any notice of Michelle," he advised, not caring if he sounded disloyal. "Sing to your son, Marco, imagining you are at his wedding."

Colour whooshed into her cheeks. Had he embarrassed her? Her thick dark lashes lifted and her eyes— he'd thought they were a light brown but close up they were a fascinating golden amber—seemed to swim up at him, bathing him in a mixture of relief, gratitude, and a very touching wonder at his caring.

He had the instant urge to draw her into his arms—to comfort and protect—and only a swift charge of common sense deflected him from such unwarranted and totally out-of-place action. The strength of the instinct both stunned and bemused him. He barely knew this woman.

"Thank you. You're very kind," she murmured huskily.

She had a wide, generous mouth. All the better to sing with, he told himself, clamping down on disturbingly wayward thoughts of sensuality and passion. He was suddenly very conscious of her hand, lying still in his now, and gave it a quick reassuring squeeze.

"You'll be fine. Just remember my grandmother would not have called you for an audition if she had not been very impressed with your voice."

She nodded and he released her hand, swinging away to insert the tape into the sound system at the side of the stage. It was unsettling to find himself so aware of her as a woman. It was fine to give her consideration as a person, but the stirring of any sexual interest was out of kilter with his commitment to Michelle. Despite his disaffection with his fiancée's current attitude, this shouldn't be happening.

Having switched everything on, he took the remote control panel to Gina, demonstrated the buttons she would need to press, adjusted the microphone for her, keeping his focus on making sure she knew how to work her performance. Even so, every time he glanced at her, those expressive amber eyes tugged at him, making him feel more connected to her than he wanted to be.

He flashed her a last encouraging smile as he left her on centre stage. The need to put distance between them had him heading back down the ballroom to Michelle. Yet he changed his mind halfway, choosing to sit with his grandmother and Gina's son, rather than placing himself at the side of negative disinterest. It was an action that might just jolt Michelle into reassessing her manner.

The show of support for her protégé earned an approving nod from his grandmother. Feeling slightly guilty, Alex beckoned Michelle to join them, but she waved a curt little dismissal and struck a languid pose on her chair, transmitting a boredom that was not about to be shifted. Alex gritted his teeth. Be damned if he was going to shift, either!

"We are ready if you are," his grandmother announced.

Alex concentrated objective attention on the woman who now commanded the stage. She was younger than Michelle, probably mid-twenties. The rather modest lemon shift she wore skimmed a very curvaceous figure. Her overall appearance was pleasingly feminine, though not spectacular. She would never draw all eyes as Michelle did on entering a room, yet Alex couldn't help thinking a man would feel very comfortable having Gina Terlizzi on his arm.

The music started. Alex noted her gaze was not

trained on his grandmother, but on her son who was seated on the chair next to the dance floor. He smiled to himself realising she was taking his advice, getting keyed up to direct her song to the little boy whose un-critical love would undoubtedly be beamed back at his mother.

Her voice poured through the microphone, a surpris-ingly rich, full-bodied voice that filled the ballroom with glorious sound, nothing wispy or weak either in tone or pitch. He recognised the song as a Celine Dion favour-ite, ''Because You Loved Me,'' and Gina Terlizzi gave it every bit as much emotional expression—if not more—than the original artist.

A touch on his arm directed his attention to the boy who'd been seated next to his grandmother. He'd slid off his chair and moved onto the dance floor, his feet rocking to the beat of the song, shoulders swaying, arms waving in rhythm, his face raptly lifted to his mother who smiled at him in the pauses of the song. He was copying her gestures, her swaying, the two of them joined in harmony with each other.

When the song ended, he clapped delightedly and called out, ''More, Mama!''

Alex couldn't help sharing a smile with his grand-mother who was clearly affected by the little scene, her face softened with the pleasure that old people invari-ably found in the artless joy of little children.

''Yes, we must hear more,'' she called out suppor-tively.

Gina nodded, took a deep breath and started the tape again.

It was certainly no hardship listening to her. As she sang what Alex considered a great rendition of Frank Sinatra's old song, "All The Way," he looked back at Michelle, expecting her to be enjoying it as much as he was. She returned a petulant glare that really riled him. Couldn't she concede Gina Terlizzi was worth listening to?

He looked at the little boy, happily jigging along with the song, and when he clapped at the end of it, Alex couldn't resist joining in the applause. Why not? It was deserved. And he felt a need to make up for Michelle's stubborn stand-off.

"Another one, please," his grandmother requested.

Alex knew most of the popular wedding songs from hearing his grandmother playing them over and over to sort out her recommendations to the couples who booked their weddings here. She'd started the business years ago, determined on maintaining the castle with the profits made—a totally unnecessary decision since the King investments could easily carry any cost to keeping this prime property as it should be kept.

Alex suspected she simply enjoyed planning big occasions and seeing the ballroom put to good use. It also gave her a convenient lead-in to asking her three grandsons when she could expect a wedding from them. She had one now and as Alex listened to Gina Terlizzi sing "From This Moment On," he silently vowed to ensure that his grandmother would have some voice in the planning of it. Michelle could like it or lump it.

Respect was called for.

Respect would be given.

From this moment on…

CHAPTER FOUR

THEY were sitting at the table by the fountain again. A sumptuous afternoon tea had been served. Marco was happily running around the lawn, exploring various parts of the gardens. It would have been the perfect wind-down from her audition, but for the somewhat sour presence of Michelle Banks.

Even so, Gina's inner excitement could not be dampened. Isabella Valeri King had more than approved her singing. She had complimented her on it with open pleasure. So had Alex King. And best of all, she now had Isabella's assurance of a high recommendation for bookings. In future, she would be singing at the castle many times, for a much bigger fee than she had ever been offered before.

It didn't matter that Michelle Banks had more or less removed herself from making even a friendly comment. Perhaps she had wanted Alex to herself this afternoon and resented his being dragged into helping with Isabella's business. Although Alex hadn't seemed to mind the claim on his time.

He'd been so kind and helpful. If he wasn't *taken*, Gina had the funny feeling she'd be head over heels in love with him. When he'd held her hand, and she'd looked into his eyes, there'd been a heart-thumping connection that had energised her whole body.

But she mustn't dwell on that.

He was taken.

It was probably his nature to be kind to everyone. It didn't mean that he was attracted to her, anywhere near as strongly as she was attracted to him. How could he be? She wasn't in the same class as his fiancée.

The home-baked carrot cake with the delicious soft cream-cheese topping kept tempting her. She'd already had one piece. Would it look greedy if she took another? She was always hungry after a performance. It took so much energy. Apart from which, her stomach had been churning with nerves beforehand, making it impossible to eat a proper lunch.

Alex reached out and helped himself to a second slice. Catching her watching his action, he grinned, his blue eyes twinkling a teasing awareness of her own temptation. "It's my favourite cake. Can't resist."

"It sure is the best," she agreed on a pleasurable sigh.

"Like some more?"

He was already moving a serving towards her plate and Gina couldn't resist, either. "Yes, please."

"It's terribly rich," Michelle remarked critically.

"An indulgence in rich food now and then is one of the pleasures of life," Isabella declared.

"If you want to pay the price," Michelle mocked, her gaze flicking over Gina's well-rounded arms.

"Oh, some people burn off the calories easily enough," Alex drawled, then smiled at Gina. "I imagine keeping up with a highly active little boy like Marco gives you plenty of exercise."

Her heart fluttered at the support he was giving her against his fiancée's opinion. She wasn't *fat* in his eyes. He liked her. He had to like her to be defending her weakness for the calorie-laden cake. Or maybe he didn't care if she put on weight. Why would he? She wasn't the woman he was going to marry.

"Marco does keep me busy," she replied to Alex, then wrenched her gaze away from him, bypassing the fashionably thin woman he *loved,* to excuse her appetite for rich food to Isabella. "It's Sunday. I've always considered it a day to relax a bit on rules and simply enjoy."

"That is the Italian tradition," the old lady approved. "Besides, I like my cooking to be appreciated."

"It really is a superb cake," Gina instantly responded.

"Thank you, my dear."

Gina wasn't into the game-playing of scoring off people, but she couldn't help taking considerable satisfaction in Isabella's benevolent approval. Strict dieting could be taken too far. When people took the trouble to provide special treats, unless there was some medical problem forbidding any indulgence, it seemed impolite not to partake of anything. It was like ignoring the efforts to please. Possibly Michelle felt no need to please in return. She had only taken black tea with a slice of lemon, disdaining all the food offered.

Not that it was any of her business how these relationships worked, Gina told herself, but she had the strong feeling Isabella wasn't overly fond of her grandson's choice. Neither was she. Although it could be jealousy prompting the dislike that was growing in leaps and bounds.

Marco provided a fortuitous distraction, pelting across the lawn with his hands cupped together to contain something. "Look what I found, Mama!" he crowed excitedly.

"Come and show me, Marco," Isabella called, turning in her chair to beckon him to her.

Her encouraging smile—or her natural air of authority—drew him to the other side of the table and he came to a triumphant halt between Isabella and Michelle. His eyes danced delightedly at the older woman and Gina knew he was basking in her indulgent interest, wanting to show off to her.

"It's a surp'ise!" he told her, beaming sheer mischief.

"I like surprises," Isabella assured him.

"Look!" he cried, uncupping his hands like a master magician.

A small cane toad instantly leapt from his uncovered palm, straight onto Michelle Banks' lap.

She jumped up from her chair, shrieking with horror, her hands moving in frantic, scissor-like slaps to get the creature off her. Perversely it hopped onto her arm before escaping to freedom, and Michelle shuddered all over at having suffered its touch on her skin.

"You filthy child!" she flung at Marco. "Bringing that slimy thing up here and letting it jump on me!"

She stepped towards him, her face screwed into venomous fury, her long lean body bending forward, arm outswinging.

The realisation that she was going to hit Marco had Gina leaping to her feet. But she was too far away to stop it, too shocked to even call out "No!"

It was Alex, surging from his chair, who caught Michelle's arm, halting it in midair, his fingers closing around it with warning force and lowering it her side. Virtually in the same instant, Isabella acted, reaching out and scooping Marco back from the line of fire.

"There is no harm done, Michelle," Alex stated, his voice hard with command, the power of the man literally shimmering from him in such strong waves, Gina instinctively held her breath, her heart thumping wildly against the constriction in her chest.

He was defending her son...saving him from the physical abuse his fiancée would still deliver, given half a chance.

"No harm!" Michelle screeched, her body snapping upright, her gaze slicing daggers at Alex for intervening. Frustrated in one act of violence, she bared her teeth at Marco who shrank back, not understanding his offence. "You've ruined my trousers with your filthy careless-ness," she accused, her rage unabated.

"Hardly ruined," Alex bit out, his jaw tightening at this further outburst.

"Boys will be boys." Isabella's tone was deliberately temperate but she flashed a quelling look at Michelle as she put her arm around Marco in a comforting hug. "All living creatures are fascinating to them at this age."

"Cane toads!" Michelle raved on, her revulsion still volatile. "Ugly, creepy cane toads!"

Marco was cowering back in the protective circle of Isabella's arm, fright stamped on his face as he stared, goggle-eyed at his attacker.

Gina shook herself out of the gut-knotting tension. Her son needed her help, her reassurance. Alex and Isabella King were protecting him but she was his mother.

"I'm sorry the toad accidentally leapt on you, Michelle," she said quietly, "but please don't blame my son for it. Marco thinks catching toads is good. He sometimes helps one of his uncles do it and he's used to being praised for bringing them to him."

Blazing outrage was swung directly on her. "You let him help his uncle catch these disgusting things?"

Gina nodded, keeping her composure very calm for her son's sake. "To Marco, it's a great game. His uncle organises toad races for tourists. He gives them names like Fat Freddo, Forest Lump, Prince Charming..."

"Prince Charming?" Alex cocked an eyebrow at her, his tone amused, although there was no amusement in his eyes, more a wry appreciation of the distraction she was offering. Anger at the ugly scene simmered behind it.

Gina forced a smile at him, grateful for his help in easing the tension and the shock for Marco. "What's more..." she went on, determined on giving her son more recovery time, "...if Prince Charming wins the race and it's been bought to win by a woman, he tries to chat the woman into kissing it."

"Kiss a toad?" Michelle gagged at the thought.

"It causes great hilarity amongst the spectators. They

enjoy the mad fun of it. No one has to go through with the kissing but some do, getting their friends or family to video it so the story will be believed when they go home,'' Gina patiently explained.

''I'll bet it makes a great story,'' Alex chimed in, sealing her account with pointed approval, then turning to deal more directly with his fiancée. ''It's all a matter of perspective, Michelle.''

''Ugh!'' was her jeering response. ''If you don't mind…'' She tore her wrist out of his hold. ''…I'm going to wash the slime off my arm.''

She swung on her heel and with a haughty disdain of every effort to rescue the situation, marched off to the closest rest room. Her snubbing departure left a silence loaded with spine-crawling embarrassment. Gina glanced quickly at Marco who looked as if he was still teetering on the point of bursting into tears, despite the soothing-down process.

Alex moved to crouch in front of him. ''Hey, Marco! How about we go look in the fish pond,'' he suggested cheerfully.

''Fish?'' her little son repeated on a slight wobble.

''Yep. Big red ones, gold ones, spotted ones. Let's count them and see how many there are.'' He plucked Marco out of his grandmother's protective hold, swung him up in the air and perched him on his chest so they were face-to-face. ''Can you count?'' he asked, waggling his eyebrows as though in doubt.

''Yes.'' Marco nodded gravely as he counted, ''One, two, four, ten…''

"Good! Then off we go to the fish pond. If your mother permits?"

They both turned to Gina. She was momentarily transfixed by the burning need to make reparation being transmitted by Alex King's vivid blue eyes. The intensity of feeling bored straight into her heart, forging an even stronger connection between them.

"Mama?"

The hopeful appeal from Marco forced her attention to him. The threat of tears had been effectively wiped out with the exciting flush of further achievement to be pursued.

"Yes, you may go," she said, submitting to the need of the man and the moment, though she wasn't at all sure this was the best action to take.

She watched Alex King carry her son away on a new adventure, grateful for his initiative in one sense, yet feeling hopelessly ambivalent about where this was leading. She *wanted* to believe...all sorts of wild things...yet surely the better solution would have been for her and Marco to leave, allowing these people to sort out their differences in private. Being the meat in their sandwich was not a happy place.

"Alessandro has a fine affinity with children," Isabella assured her, intent on dispelling any worries she might have. "He looked after his younger brothers well when they were little boys."

Realising she was still standing, Gina dropped back onto her chair to show she accepted Isabella's assurance that Marco was safe with Alex. That wasn't the problem.

"He's very kind," she replied, pasting a smile over her inner turbulence.

Michelle's rage had been defused but the memory of it was not about to miraculously lift. She hoped Alex would bring Marco back soon enough for them to leave before his fiancée returned.

Though how he could marry a woman like that was beyond her comprehension. Especially if he wanted children. Admittedly, Marco wasn't Michelle's own child, but such a blaze of temper over a little toad, and the urge to hit...

It was wrong.

Terribly wrong.

And everything Alex King had stirred in her this afternoon made his connection to *that woman* feel more wrong.

The fat was in the fire and definitely sizzling, Isabella thought with deep satisfaction.

She had struck gold with Gina Terlizzi and her delightful little son. No doubt about *her* feelings for Alessandro and the attraction was definitely mutual. Best of all, Michelle had shown her true colours this afternoon. In fact, the manner in which both young women had conducted themselves provided such a striking contrast, her grandson would have to be deaf, dumb and blind not to appreciate the differences.

He was most certainly feeling considerable discontent with Michelle.

And it wasn't just *kindness* towards Gina.

But what had been achieved this afternoon could all

slide away if Gina wasn't thrust right under Alessandro's nose again and again in relatively quick succession. The big hump was the diamond ring on Michelle's engagement finger. Alessandro didn't give a commitment lightly. Nor would he lightly withdraw one. It had to be broken.

Determined to strike while the iron was hot, Isabella quickly formulated a plan which she could surely manipulate to serve her purpose. "To return to business…" She let the words linger for a few moments to give Gina time to get her mind on track. "…are you free next Saturday night?"

Surprise at the early date, but eagerness to clutch at it, too. "Yes, I am, Mrs. King."

"I've been thinking…a friend of my grandson, Antonio, is holding his wedding here next Saturday. I would like to do something special for him. It has been arranged for Peter Owen to play and sing. You know him?"

"Not exactly *know*. But I have seen him perform. He's quite brilliant on the piano and a very professional crooner. He really sells his songs."

"Yes. He's very popular. But it would, I think, offer a very interesting variety if you sang a few duets with him."

"Duets?"

"You must know 'All I Ask of You' from *Phantom of the Opera*."

"Yes…"

"I'm sure the two of you could do that song justice. Peter could also do the backing and harmony for your

'Because You Loved Me.' And 'From This Moment On' can also be sung as a duet.''

"But…" Gina frowned uncertainly "…would he want to share his spotlight with me?"

"Peter Owen will do what I ask of him." Whatever the financial persuader was, Isabella would pay it. "You would need to make time to rehearse with him during the week."

"If you're sure he…I mean, compared to him, I'm an amateur, Mrs. King."

"Oh, I don't think he'll find you so." She smiled her confidence. "Leave the arrangements to me. I'll call you after I've contacted Peter. Are we agreed?"

"Yes. Thank you."

She looked somewhat dazed but determined to pursue the opportunity. She had grit, this girl. Give her the chance and she'd go the full mile on what she believed in. At the present moment, she thought Alessandro was out of her reach, but put him within reach…

More importantly, put *her* within *his* reach.

Proximity, natural attraction, the continual contrast between what he had and what he could have, temptation…

"Peter Owen always wears white tails for his act. You would need a formal evening dress," Isabella cautioned, hoping Gina's wardrobe extended to something…fetching. A woman with a fine bosom could afford to show some cleavage.

"I do have one I think would be suitable," Gina assured her.

"Good!" Isabella smiled. "All three of my grandsons will be at the wedding. I must confess I like showing off my finds to them.''

She flushed, her thick lashes sweeping down to veil a rush of anguished emotion in her eyes, but not before Isabella had glimpsed it.

''I'll do my best to make you proud of me, Mrs. King.''

''I'm sure you will, my dear.''

And not least because Gina now knew Alessandro would be there.

Probably Michelle, too…unfortunately.

Though Isabella was counting on Gina outshining Michelle next Saturday night…in her own very appealing and extremely suitable way.

CHAPTER FIVE

"LADIES and gentlemen…"

The formal call on their attention reduced the buzz of conversation in the ballroom. Heads turned to look at Peter Owen who commanded the stage, along with the white grand piano which was currently adorned with an elaborate candelabra reminiscent of Liberace's style. A deliberate affectation, Alex thought, as were the white tails Peter Owen wore. Still he was certainly a consummate showman, and much liked by the ladies.

"Tonight we have a very special performance for the bride and groom…" He made an expansive gesture towards the bridal table where Tony, Alex's youngest brother was also seated—best man to the groom. "…courtesy of our wonderful hostess, Isabella King."

His other brother, Matt, was sharing a table with him and the rest of their party further down the ballroom. Matt instantly leaned over and whispered, "So what has Nonna cooked up?"

"I don't know," Alex answered, curious himself as he watched his grandmother give Peter Owen a nod and a smile.

"May I introduce to you…" The singer/pianist stepped back, his arm swinging out to one side of the stage, his head turned in the same direction. "…Gina Terlizzi."

"Well, well, your little songbird, Alex," Michelle drawled, causing the hair on the back of his neck to prickle.

They'd had a blazing row last Sunday over Gina Terlizzi and Alex didn't want one provoked tonight. The trouble was, Michelle's arguments had tapped a guilt in him he couldn't deny. He wasn't sure what to do about it, either.

"*Your* songbird?" Matt picked up teasingly.

"Nonna's," he answered with a curt, dismissive gesture.

Gina was coming out on stage, her hand reaching for Peter Owen's. He took it, pulling her to his side, making a cosy pairing that instantly raised Alex's hackles. What was his grandmother thinking of, coupling Gina with a well-known womaniser of highly dubious charm? The man was already twice divorced, and putting a woman as attractive and as vulnerable as Gina Terlizzi in his path could easily bring her grief.

"Gina and I have been rehearsing all week..."

All week!

And she was positively glowing beside him, a big smile lighting her face, the amber eyes very sparkly, her toffee-coloured hair swinging loose around her bare shoulders, her curvy figure shown to stunning advantage in a bronze, body-moulding lace top, sashed at her waist with a piece of the darker bronze filmy fabric that formed a long skirt featuring a rather provocative side ruffle.

"Hmm...very sultry and sexy," Matt murmured.

Alex found himself thinking the same thing and was

extremely discomforted by the bolt of desire that was sizzling through his system. Michelle was sitting right beside him, dressed in a slinky, metallic-red gown that was braless and virtually backless, so blatantly sexy she'd had every male eye at the wedding giving her the once-over. And she was *his!* Why on earth would he suddenly feel even a trace of lust for another woman?

The thought struck him that Michelle's sexiness was artful.

Gina's was…something else…like a celebration of the woman she was. And Peter Owen was basking in it. No…*gloating* in it!

"I warn you, this lovely lady's voice will grab your heart," he announced fatuously. "So sit back and enjoy the beautiful duet from *Phantom of the Opera,* a song that strikes every emotional chord there is between a man and a woman—'All I Ask of You.'"

Alex found himself tensing as the seasoned performer put his arm around Gina to draw her closer to the piano. The man was altogether too smooth with the liberties he took.

"Wonder if he's got her into bed yet," Michelle said snidely.

Alex frowned at her.

She returned a knowing little smile. "Give Peter Owen a week…" Her eyes mocked any other result.

It was what Alex had been thinking himself, though he hoped Gina had more sense than to fall victim to a flattering seduction. The guy was in his late thirties, not much more than average height yet with a lean elegant air, raffish good looks, longish dark hair with enough curl to flop around when he performed with the charismatic energy that captivated audiences. Gossip had it he never went home to a lonely bed. There was always someone willing—wanting—to share it.

He oozed charm from every pore and Gina was getting a liberal dose of it as he positioned her by the piano, handed her the microphone, held her gaze with a stream of smiling banter while reseating himself at the piano, flicking his tails theatrically. A showman, Alex thought savagely, willing Gina not to be taken in by tricks of his trade.

There was a flourish of notes on the piano, then Peter Owen was leaning forward, crooning up at Gina, pouring an all too believable sincerity into the words he sang, maintaining eye contact as he softly pleaded his cause. Alex's teeth clenched. It was an act…only an act, he fiercely told himself.

Gina's voice came in, soaring with a yearning that eclipsed everything else. There was absolute silence in the ballroom, the whole audience captivated by a purity of sound that projected a high charge of emotion. Of course, the act demanded she aim the words at her duet partner. It didn't mean she was *asking* anything of him. They were simply performing together. She couldn't possibly feel these feelings for Peter Owen.

Despite this forceful reasoning, Alex could not relax and simply enjoy the duet for what it was. In fact, it took all the pleasure out of the evening for him. He was even annoyed with his brother afterwards when Matt commented, ''Wow! What a find!''

And Michelle for adding, "Peter did provide the perfect foil for her. They worked extremely well together."

Fortunately the duet was the lead-in to the formal speeches so Alex didn't have to listen to much more on the successful pairing of the singers. He was grateful for the distraction since it took his attention away from the stage, though he found it a struggle to focus his concentration on what was being said.

Tony did himself proud as best man. He'd always had the gift of the gab and he had everyone laughing with droll little stories about the groom and the changes to his life wrought by his beautiful bride.

It gave Alex pause to think about the changes he'd made in his life to fit in with Michelle, spending less time at the plantations and more on financial management in town, taking an interest in how the fashion business worked. Impossible not to since Michelle was so committed to it. And it *was* a different and intriguing slice of life—colourful people, exciting activity around the creative process. He'd been quite dazzled by it, dazzled by Michelle.

The speeches over, Peter Owen announced another duet—"From This Moment On"—which covered the cake-cutting ceremony. This time Alex deliberately kept his gaze away from the stage, smiling at the happy bride and groom and their posing for photographs. The singing finally came to a halt and conversation picked up again.

"Just a few more months, Alex, and we'll be seeing you and Michelle cutting the cake," Matt commented.

Michelle laughed. "I want at least a triple-decker."

I want…

She wanted to wait at least three years before thinking of having children, too. That had come out during their row last week. In fact, Alex wasn't convinced about Michelle wanting a family at all.

He did. He definitely did. A little boy like Marco Terlizzi…

His train of thought was broken by the announcement of yet another special song— ''For the newly wedded couple's first dance together…''

It was the first song he'd heard Gina sing—''Because You Loved Me,'' and his gaze was inexorably drawn to the stage as her voice seemed to reach out to him, just as it had last Sunday afternoon. She wasn't directing the words to her singing partner who was providing the background harmony. She was facing the couple circling the dance floor, pouring the heartfelt words out to them.

Her body moved in a graceful sway, accentuating her lush femininity. The expressive gestures she made had almost a mesmerising come-to-me invitation in them. The shining curtain of her hair glided over her shoulders with a kind of sensual freedom as she tilted her head to deliver the high notes, and Alex found his hands clenching, wanting to feel swathes of it running through his fingers.

It was crazy…this strong attraction that had him questioning everything he'd ever felt with Michelle. One afternoon's short acquaintance…one professional appearance on stage…what did it amount to? How could Gina Terlizzi affect him with such compelling intensity? He didn't want this happening, putting him at odds with decisions he'd made, giving him the disturbing sense of losing control.

The song ended to a round of applause. Peter Owen moved into DJ mode, inviting everyone to join the couple on the floor and switching the sound system on to play the dance tracks he'd chosen. Alex instantly stood up, determined to get himself *on track* by drawing Michelle into his arms for a dance. He needed to feel close to her again, to feel completely engaged by all she was.

It didn't work.

Michelle chose to dance apart from him, creating a spotlight on herself, much appreciated by the men looking on. She was *his,* Alex told himself, so it shouldn't matter, didn't matter. Let other men envy him. Let Michelle enjoy being the focus of lustful attention. Hadn't Gina Terlizzi drawn the same attention up on stage just now?

Before he realised what he was doing, his gaze was travelling around, searching her out. Gone from the stage. So was Peter Owen. He spotted them both at the table where his grandmother sat, Gina smiling happily at her new employer as Peter chatted, no doubt eliciting praise for their performance.

The strong gut urge to leave Michelle to her admirers and tear Gina Terlizzi away from her slick companion and sweep her onto the dance floor and into his arms threw him completely out of step with the rhythm of the music.

"Alex, get with it!" Michelle protested, continuing to gyrate seductively.

He stopped dead, too unsettled to even try to follow her movements. "I'm not in the mood for this kind of dancing," he stated bluntly.

Her eyes glittered a challenge. "Then I'll get another partner."

"Do that," he said, not rising to the bait, not even caring about it. "I'll go and have a word with my grandmother."

He was asking for trouble. He watched Michelle testily pluck another partner from a group of unattached males and knew with absolute certainty he was courting *big* trouble. But the need to sort himself out with Gina Terlizzi was paramount.

CHAPTER SIX

STRANGE how flat she felt now her performance was over. Gina knew she should be feeling exhilarated at how well it had gone. Peter Owen was delighted with her, suggesting they do more gigs together. Isabella King and the other people at her table had showered her with compliments. Yet she yearned to get away and be by herself.

Stupid to let seeing Alex King leading his fiancée straight onto the dance floor affect her like this. They'd been the first to join the bridal couple there after she'd finished her last song, Michelle shimmying seductively in a slinky red knock-out gown, Alex's attention riveted on her. And why not? she fiercely berated herself. What else could she have expected?

"Peter, bring one of those empty chairs from the next table over for Gina," Isabella directed. "She can sit with me while…"

"No, no, I really must be going now," she quickly protested.

"Going?" Isabella frowned at her. "I intended for you to stay and enjoy the party. Marco is perfectly safe in the nursery quarters with Rosita watching over him."

Isabella had pressed the invitation to stay overnight in the castle and Gina had been tempted into accepting it, not really admitting to herself that the main attraction had been the possibility of some further connection with Alex King. With that barely acknowledged fantasy now revealed as hopelessly askew, she sought a quick escape route.

"The surroundings are strange to him, Mrs. King. Should he wake…"

"If there's any problem…"

The words floated past her, not sinking into her consciousness. She'd caught sight of Alex King carving a path through the crowd on the dance floor, heading straight for her. The couples seemed to roll aside like the Red Sea letting Moses through, reacting to a strength of purpose that willed them away from him. And she was the end destination. His eyes told her so. He didn't so much as glance at anyone else, not even his grandmother.

Gina had the weirdest sense of her whole body being attacked by pins and needles. Her heart seemed to catapult around her chest. Her breath was caught in her throat. She stood absolutely still, waiting for him to reach her, hardly believing this was really happening and nothing was going to stop it. Did he really want to be with her? Did he want…

She didn't dare finish that thought. Her mind was trembling with an anticipation that had shot beyond the real world. But his gaze *was* trained exclusively on her, projecting a need—or a desire—that was triggering all these wild responses, and every aggressive stride he took towards her made them clamour with a compelling intensity, shutting out everything else.

He looked incredibly handsome in his formal dinner

suit. Somehow it made his tall, powerful physique even more imposingly male. She felt her inner muscles quivering and knew she was very much at risk of making a total fool of herself with this man. He struck at everything female in her, igniting a sexual chemistry she had never experienced before, not even with her husband.

As he skirted the table where his grandmother sat, Gina instinctively turned towards him, the people close to her fading into a grey area that held no importance. She wasn't even aware of them anymore. He dominated, his brilliant blue eyes holding her captive to whatever he intended.

"Come with me," he commanded more than asked.

"Yes." The word spilled from her lips, more a submission to his will than any decision on her part.

He reached out and took her hand. Maybe she lifted it in response to his invitation. All she really knew was her hand was captured in his and her feet followed him towards the dance floor. The moment they were clear of the table and chairs, he gathered her into his embrace and they were together, hard muscular thighs pushing hers, the arm around her waist pressing an electric intimacy.

Her free hand rested on his shoulder. She stared at it, fighting the urge to slide it around his neck, to touch…where she shouldn't if any sense of decorum was to be kept. Bad enough to be so aware of his physicality—and hers—with the barrier of clothes between them. To nakedly touch the nape of his neck, his hair…no. It was begging trouble. Bigger trouble than she already had. A struggling strain of common sense insisted a line had to be drawn somewhere.

Michelle was on this dance floor, too.

Michelle could be watching them.

But Alex didn't seem to be caring about what his fiancée might think. Did he hold all his dance partners like this? She was close enough to smell the intriguingly attractive cologne he'd splashed around his jaw—an intoxicating scent that made her head swim with the wish to be even closer to him, to know what it might be like if only she had the freedom to pursue the wild desires he evoked in her.

Could he smell her perfume? Did he like it? His head was bent towards her ear, near enough for his cheek to be brushing against her hair. What was he thinking…feeling? She had the sense of him breathing her in, absorbing all he could, wanting more.

He didn't speak. She was hopelessly tongue-tied. The silence seemed to magnify all the sensations of dancing with him, the rhythmic matching of every movement, the heat of friction making her thighs and breasts tingle with almost unbearable excitement, the possessive pressure of the hand on the pit of her back, denying her any release from him. Not that she wanted to be released. Yet every beat of the music heightened the sheer sexuality of their togetherness and she was not the only one aroused by it.

She felt him stir and harden and secretly revelled in his inability to hide the effect she was having on him, though he did loosen his hold on her, easing slightly away. Not quickly enough though. Reluctantly. Or perhaps that was wishful thinking.

Gina fiercely wanted this evidence of desire to mean more than a simple response to stimulation. It was madness…forbidden pleasure…dangerously seductive…yet she couldn't stop herself from hoping he couldn't help himself, either, that this overwhelming attraction was mutual.

The rather slow track they'd been dancing to came to an end. The music continued almost seamlessly into a much faster number. The couples around them responded to it, but Alex remained still. A sharp stab of panic cramped Gina's heart. Was it over? Would he let her go now? Take her back to his grandmother and return to Michelle?

The turbulent questions forced her to look up, to read whatever the expression on his face revealed. She caught an air of grim decision, his jawline tense, his mouth slightly compressed. Then his eyes were blazing into hers, seemingly demanding answers he didn't have and the need for them was just as intense as hers.

"Let's get some air," he bit out.

He didn't wait for a reply, taking her agreement for granted as he scooped her with him, hugging her to his side while he carved another path from the dance floor. Gina fixed her gaze on the exit he was making for, the exit that would take them out to the loggia. Her heart was skittering nervously. She was letting him sweep her out of the ballroom, away from watching eyes, and she probably should be stopping him but she couldn't bring herself to listen to caution.

The hand clamped on the curve of her waist and hip insisted he wanted to keep her with him. She had to know what this was leading to. There was no turning back from it. If he wasn't worrying about what other people thought, why should she? Maybe he did simply want a breath of cooler air.

Certainly there was a sobering pause, once they had emerged from the ballroom. Had the fever of the moment passed for him? A quick glance at his face showed it turned towards the fountain. He set off again, still apparently intent on getting her away from the crowd of guests and having her to himself.

The few people who had stepped outside remained close to the ballroom. No one had wandered as far as the fountain. Although there was lighting in the grounds, this section of the loggia was in shadow, and Gina was extremely conscious that Alex was seeking privacy. Yet once it was attained, he seemed to hesitate over what to do next. Having come to a halt, he audibly dragged in a deep breath, then gestured jerkily towards a bench seat.

"Best sit down."

He watched her settle on it but made no move to sit beside her. He stood barely a metre away, his tension so palpable Gina found it impossible to relax. Every nerve in her body was in taut waiting for what would come next. She had the eerie sense of being at the edge of something momentous to her life, yet she felt powerless to take any step on her own.

The silence stretched…seconds, minutes…as he brooded on his decisions, his gaze slightly hooded, yet burning a trail over the bare roundness of her shoulders and the slight swell of her breasts above the line of the lace bodice. She could feel herself blushing although the neckline was not daringly low. In fact, a band of the bronze organza under the lace was joined to shoulder straps that stopped any slippage. There was only a hint of cleavage.

"How old are you, Gina?" he gruffly asked.

"Twenty-six." It was a husky whisper. Her mouth was completely dry.

"I'm thirty-four. Thirty-four," he repeated, as though it was some critical indictment of his behaviour with her.

Age had nothing to do with feelings, Gina thought. Yet he shook his head as though the eight-year gap between them mattered in some way. She didn't understand the inner conflict that chased across his face as he moved to put more distance between them, walking to the space between the next two columns of the colonnade and standing in profile to her, staring out at the grounds.

"Tell me about your life."

Again it was a command, yet the need to know was strained through it. What answers he was looking for Gina couldn't even guess. She could only relate the truth and hope it satisfied him.

"I was brought up on a cane farm. My parents still own and run it."

"Where?"

"Near Edmonton, just the other side of Cairns."

"Their name?"

"Salvatori. Frank and Elena."

He nodded. "I know of your father."

"My older brother, John, and his family live on the farm, too. My younger brother, Danny, works in the tourist trade."

"The toad races."

"Yes. Amongst other things."

He turned to look quizzically at her. "No sisters?"

She shook her head. "Just the three of us."

"Where did you go to school?"

"The local primary at Edmonton. Then to St. Joseph's in Cairns."

An ironic curl tilted his mouth. "A convent girl."

Gina held her tongue, unsure how to take that comment.

He continued the inquisition. "Did you hold a job before you married?"

"I worked in a florist shop. I've always loved flowers." Not exactly a high-flying career but it had satisfied her so she wasn't about to apologise for it.

"How old were you when you married Angelo Terlizzi?"

"Twenty-two."

"Very young," he muttered.

"It felt right," she asserted, needing to justify the decision in the face of this far stronger attraction that seemed to just reach out and seize her. She had loved Angelo for many, many reasons. There was no reason at all behind what she was experiencing now with a man she barely knew on any personal level. Yet his compelling tug on her had a vibrant life of its own, impossible to ignore or deny.

She should be asking him questions. But would any more knowledge of him make any difference? Why was he asking these questions of her? Was he trying to reason away an attraction he didn't want, that he found inconvenient? Maybe he was trying to convince himself she was totally unsuitable for him anyway, that Michelle was a much better match.

An angry pride stirred in Gina. She hadn't asked for this. She wasn't *chasing* him. He'd made all the moves, stirring what shouldn't be stirred if he didn't want to explore it further.

"Did you go on working after you were married?" he went on.

"Not in the florist shop. I used to do the lunches for Angelo's deep-sea fishing charters."

And I was more a helpmate to my husband than Michelle Banks will ever be to you, she thought on a wave of fierce resentment over whatever judgements he was making.

"You played hostess to his clients on board?"

"Yes. I enjoyed that, too," she said on a wave of belligerence. "Until I fell pregnant and started getting seasick. Then I did the lunches at home and Angelo served them on board."

Most work was about service to other people, she argued. Even dress designing catered to clients. She didn't see that what she'd done was any more lowly than what his fiancée did. It certainly didn't make as much money but so what? She had nothing to be ashamed of.

"So you've been a stay-at-home mother since you had Marco."

"Not completely."

She didn't want to recall the time of empty nothingness—the shock, the grief, the numbness about any future at all—following on from Angelo's death. Only Marco had been left from the plans they'd made for a big happy family, her wonderful little son who was both a comfort and a reminder of what had been taken away from her. She didn't try to foresee a future anymore, perhaps from a fear of tempting fate.

In a way she'd been drifting, just taking each day as it came, coping more than making opportunities for herself. Isabella King had opened another door for her. Peter Owen might open up more, but suddenly they didn't seem important. Alex King had taken centre stage and she couldn't think of anything else, yet she still had no real idea of where she stood with him. This fever in her blood probably *was* madness.

"You mean your singing engagements," he prompted when her silence went on unbroken by further explanation.

"I'm also working part-time in my aunt's florist shop," she answered slowly, realising the job formed a pleasant stop-gap rather than a step to some reason for being. "I can take Marco there with me," she added, acknowledging what an advantage such a situation was for a single parent who didn't want to surrender the care of her precious child to anyone else, not on any regular basis.

"Who's minding him tonight?"

It burst upon her that she'd completely forgotten what she'd been about to do before he'd taken control of everything. "Rosita. Your grandmother's house-keeper." The reply tripped out as she rose to her feet, agitated by the sense of having selfishly indulged what was beginning to feel like a stupid flight of fantasy, instead of sticking to the reality of a life with her son. "I should go and check on him."

"He's here? At the castle?"

Alex swung on her, his surprise and the sharpness of his tone halting any further movement. Her heart skittered again, setting her pulse leaping haphazardly as the full force of his personality was aimed directly at her. Her mind skittered, too. Did he find something wrong with this arrangement? Wasn't she good enough to be his grandmother's guest?

Instinctively her chin tilted, defying any negative opinion he might hold. "Mrs. King kindly invited us to stay overnight to save disturbing Marco's sleep with travelling."

"So you'll be sleeping here, too."

Tension poured from him, swirling around her like a tightening net, holding her captive. "I've been given the nanny's room in the nursery quarters," she said, then wished she hadn't told him that. Although the arrangement was most suitable for her and Marco's needs, it sounded as though she didn't rate a proper guest room.

This status thing was really bothering her. "Why are you asking me all these questions?" she burst out, her inner anguish demanding some satisfaction. "Why don't you say what's really on your mind?" Her hands jerked out in an emphatic gesture of appeal. "This isn't fair!"

"I know it's not!" he retorted in a darkly savage tone. "I wanted you to help me out of my dilemma but there is no help. I have to make the choice myself."

It fired all the resentments she'd been silently nursing. "Well, how very lucky you are to have a choice. Seems to me I didn't get one. But that's okay. I can walk away."

It was like dragging her body out of a magnetic field to take a step backwards, to force her legs to turn aside from his powerful presence, to will herself into some dignified retreat.

"No!"

He caught her wrist and with a strength that had her stumbling off balance, spun her back towards him. In almost a blur of motion he loomed much closer, releasing his grip to take a far more comprehensive hold, his arms wrapping around her so fast, her hands slammed against his chest in an instinctive warding off action.

"Don't play with me!" she cried, her gaze lifting to his in a torment of protest at his arbitrary use of her.

A dark blue fire blazed down at her. "Does this feel like play?" he demanded harshly. "Did it feel like play on the dance floor?"

Her resistance instantly weakened. There was no stopping his intensity of feeling from flooding through her, re-igniting all the powerful sensations of wanting him, a very immediate primitive wanting that craved action. It wasn't enough to be held in this close contact. It was nothing but a tease, a torment, a prolonging of conflict that begged at least some resolution.

One of his arms clamped her more tightly to him as he lifted the other to touch her face, light fingertips sweeping her hair from her forehead, trailing down to her cheek, feathering the line of her lips, flowing over her chin, her neck, under the long flow of her hair, stroking her nape. The tingling skin-to-skin contact was so mesmerising, Gina couldn't think. The challenge she might have made melted from her mind. Feeling filled it…and the raging desire for more.

His chest heaved against her breasts as he dragged air into his lungs. "I have to do this," he murmured, the low words carrying a deep throb of need that was echoed in the thundering of her heart.

The kiss came hard and fast—an explosion of pent-up passion from both of them, a stampede of tasting, tangling, an urgent assault on any inhibition, a fierce giving and taking that flowed into an all-consuming sense of merging.

Gina was barely aware that her hands had flown up around his neck and were clutching his head to hers. Her body was arched against his, exulting in the imprint of his hard masculinity, straining to indulge the rampant desire to feel all of him. Everything within her yearned to be immersed in total intimacy with this man.

It was as though she had never known what could be…and here it was…the promise of how it would be when the chemistry was perfect, and the recognition of it was singing through her entire body, pulsing from her heart, jamming her brain with a host of needy signals.

Even when he pulled out of the kiss, the promise was still there, gathering a momentum of its own. His cheek rubbed against her hair as he regathered breath, the pressure of his embrace almost crushing as though he couldn't bear to release any other part of her.

"Believe me...this is not play, Gina," he rasped. "But it has to stop now because...you're right. It isn't fair."

The feverish burst of words floated past her consciousness, tapping on the door of a mind that was too full of more compelling messages to admit them. It was not until he stiffened away from her and the squaring of his shoulders caused her hands to slide from his neck, that the sense of what he'd said began to sink in.

Stop?

Not fair?

He dropped his hold on her, his arms falling to his side as he took a step back, watching her with keen concern as she swayed on her feet. With her hands so abruptly dislodged from his shoulders, all physical support removed, still giddy with sensations that had been given no time to abate, Gina instinctively wrapped her arms around her midriff to hold herself steady. A shivering started, cold attacking heat, the sense of loss growing sharper and sharper.

She stared at him in paralysed disbelief, not understanding how he could *stop* this. Or why he would want to. It felt as though everything inside her was churning around in frantic futile circles, finding only emptiness because the promise of fulfilment had been broken and there were only jagged edges left of it.

She didn't know what he saw in her eyes—the open wound of rejection? A devastated heart? A truth he didn't want to face?

His brows dipped into a pained frown. His mouth moved into a vexed grimace. "I'm sorry," he said.

Sorry...

It was unbearable.

A fierce surge of pride gave her the strength to turn and walk away, blindly at first, the need to flout his belittling apology driving her legs to put a decisive distance between them. The entrance to the castle was straight ahead of her and her focus gradually zeroed in on it.

Marco slid into her frayed mind.

Marco was real.

Her little son loved her unconditionally.

There was a big difference—*huge*—between love and sexual lust.

Best to be with Marco.

CHAPTER SEVEN

MICHELLE felt a rush of elation as Peter Owen tapped the shoulder of her dance partner. "My turn, dear boy," he drawled, one eyebrow wickedly cocked. "I claim old friendship."

She couldn't help laughing. More *intimate* friendship than old. "It's okay, Chris," she assured the guy she'd snapped up. "Thanks for dancing with me."

He grinned back at her. "A pleasure. Any time."

Which was what Alex should be telling her instead of choosing to smooch around the dance floor with *his singer*. Still, darling Peter could make up for that slight. She gave him a simmering look of seductive possibilities as he moved in on her, his long, supple body instantly capturing and projecting the beat of the music. He was definitely the sexiest dancer she'd ever known—both in bed and out of it.

"Deserted by your precious fiancé, sweetie?" he mocked.

"Not quite a duet with your duet singer?" she retorted.

"A promising prospect. But I suspect...more the marrying kind. Want to watch that, darling. Seemed to me Alex was quite hot for her."

"I'm holding the cards, Peter."

He sighed, his eyes running over her salaciously.

"Pity it's the wrong hand. You know I appreciate you more than he does. Do you fancy a quickie in the bushes?"

She laughed. "Too much of a risk."

His eyes twinkled a tempting challenge. "Ah, but the delicious spice of danger…"

"Not worth it, Peter," she said, though her eyes flirted with the promised pleasure of it.

He performed a provocative bump and grind to push the idea further. "He's taken the delectable Gina outside with him. Tit for tat?"

"I doubt they've gone as far as the bushes."

He shoulder-shimmied around her, suggestively murmuring, "Probably headed for a bedroom."

"Alex is far too straitlaced for that."

"How boring for you! Nevertheless, he probably is heading for a bedroom. Gina wanted to check on her son, Marco. Apparently Isabella invited them to stay at the castle overnight."

"Old witch!" Anger surged. "She's trying to make trouble between me and Alex."

Peter exulted in stirring the pot. "No doubt he'll be leaning over the little boy's cot, all choked up by the sweet innocence of a sleeping babe, thinking about how it'll be with his first child…"

"Shut up, Peter!"

He grinned—the devil incarnate. "While we trot the light fantastic, darling."

Grabbing her hand, he led her into an intricate sequence of steps that took them right down the dance floor. He was so light and clever on his feet, it was exhilarating matching him, and Michelle couldn't help thinking how much she missed having this kind of fun. Of course, with Peter, nothing could be taken seriously, but that was his charm. Sheer fun with nothing else attached to it. Free fun.

They stopped at the stage end of the ballroom. Still holding her hand, Peter drew her towards a side exit, whispering in her ear, "Let's snatch a bit of memory lane before the King family noose is around your lovely neck."

It wasn't wise to go with him.

But she did.

Alex knew he should return to the ballroom, if only for the sake of appearances. Michelle would have her nose out of joint at his prolonged absence. He didn't want any sly gossip arising from his exit with Gina. It certainly wasn't fair to have her reputation tainted in any way.

Yet he couldn't bring himself to rejoin the party, couldn't bear the thought of being forced into small talk. It would be easy enough to explain away his actions, but he didn't want to. He was deeply uncomfortable with the thought of skating over what he'd done with Gina. What he'd felt with her...

The restraint he'd imposed upon himself was still a physical pain. Every muscle in his body seemed to be aching, wracked with a tension that hadn't been released. Best choice was to walk it off, he decided. He needed time alone to think anyway.

*   *   *

"You can't be wearing anything under that dress," Peter remarked slyly, dropping her hand to hang his arm around her waist and feel the unbroken line of fabric curving over her hipline with his usual sensual expertise.

"Stop it," Michelle chided, though she did nothing to halt the wandering hand from sliding down under her buttocks to check the lack of underwear.

It was typical of Peter's outrageous little liberties with women and she secretly enjoyed the sexual kick of feeding his lust for her. Besides, there was no one else in this courtyard. Most people who wanted to smoke or get some fresh air chose to go out to the loggia on the other side of the ballroom.

"Absolutely nothing," Peter declared after his cursory examination. "Which means you're all naked and ready for me."

"Hardly naked."

"Where it counts, sweetie. Where it counts." He led her around a hedge of thickly leafed and flowered hibiscus trees to a garden bench behind it. "Now how spicy is this? You can lean against the back of the bench. The hedge hides us to above our waists. You can watch over my shoulder for anyone coming out of the ballroom while we have a lovely little…"

"You really are incorrigible, Peter." But it was a titillating scenario.

"Mmm…and weddings make me so randy."

"I don't need you for sex. Alex is very good at it," she protested, though she stopped where he had suggested, leaning against the back rest of the wooden bench, her arms casually spread to rest her hands along the top plank. The cooler air—or the excitement of the game—had hardened her nipples and she was very aware of their obvious thrust.

So was Peter who lightly fanned them with his palms as he seductively teased, "Nothing like a bit of stolen infidelity, is there?" He dropped his hands and started gathering up her skirt. "I bet you're all hot and wet for me."

"I don't think I should do this."

"Then you just stand there and chat to me. I'd like that. Quite a challenge operating on two levels." He grinned wickedly as he slid his hand between her bare thighs. "Don't know why you want to get saddled with Alex King. He's a terribly worthy person."

Michelle had to catch her breath before she could speak. "That's the problem with you, Peter. You're terribly unworthy. Can't count on you for any backing if I need it."

"Are we talking money here?" he lilted over the telltale unzipping of his fly.

"Alex has solid wealth. And his family has the kind of prestigious status that adds more class to my standing as a designer. They're assets you can't give me, darling."

"But I *can* give you this…"

Alex didn't know how he made it through the rest of the wedding reception. It was a torturous length of time before the bride and groom finally took their leave. Maintaining a semblance of geniality in the face of

Michelle's high spirits had stretched his self-discipline to the absolute limit. The moment the honeymoon car drove off, he forcefully led his very soon-to-be *ex-*fiancée towards his own car.

"The party isn't over," she protested.

"We're going," he stated curtly.

"What is the matter with you, Alex?" she cried in exasperation. "You haven't been any fun all evening. Are you sick or something?"

"Yes, I am."

"Well, you could have told me."

"I'm telling you now."

She huffed her annoyance at this unsatisfactory end to her *good time.* Alex contained his own inner seething until they were both seated in his Jaguar SL—evidence of his *solid wealth*—and on the road, heading for Michelle's apartment. It wasn't far, just down the road from the marina where her Port Douglas boutique was situated. Rather than be distracted from driving, he did the short trip in silence.

"Since you're feeling sick, I take it you won't be staying with me tonight," Michelle sniped, probably regretting that she hadn't set something up with Peter Owen.

"No, I won't. Nor any other night," he bit out, bringing the car to a halt outside her apartment building.

It drew a sharp look from her. "What's that supposed to mean?"

"It means I'm breaking our engagement. As of now." He switched off the engine and turned his head to look at her with very clear cold eyes. "Our marriage is off, Michelle. We're not really suited to each other."

"And what made you suddenly decide that?" she flared back, incensed by his flat announcement.

"Several things. But I'd have to say your intimate encounter with Peter Owen tonight capped the decision. And hearing how you viewed my assets as a husband."

Her mouth gaped momentarily. Her recovery was fast, though she spoke in a fluster. "That was just silly chat, Alex. Peter is so superficial, it's pointless talking about feelings." Her hand flew across to squeeze his thigh. "You know I love you."

He picked up the all too experienced hand and dropped it back in her lap. "I was taking a walk around the castle. Voices carry on the still night air, Michelle. So do other sounds. I didn't want to create a scene so I left you to it and walked back the way I'd come."

Her chin tilted in defiance as she saw that denial was futile. "Peter and I were lovers before I met you, Alex. There's been nothing between us since and there'll be nothing more. It was just a…"

"Reminder of old times? A fond goodbye?" he shot at her cuttingly.

"It was meaningless," she lashed back.

"Like any bit of infidelity stolen here and there whenever the urge takes you." He shook his head. "That's not the kind of marriage I have in mind, Michelle. Better we go our separate ways."

"Why? So you can hit on Gina Terlizzi without having a guilty conscience?" she jeered.

It wasn't far off the mark and his grim silence lent Michelle the ammunition to fire again.

"Don't be stupid, Alex. Have her if you want to. Get it out of the way."

"And that would neatly excuse your peccadillo, wouldn't it?" he flung back at her, hating her casual dismissal of any honour and integrity.

"Oh, for God's sake! It's like having a brief binge on chocolate. You do it because you're tempted. Once the taste is satisfied, you go off it. You know what diet suits you best and that's what you keep to in the long run. It's all a matter of perspective."

"Thank you for giving me that point of view. It just so happens I don't care to share it," he returned icily, reining in his anger. She was displaying an attitude that absolved him from any concern about her feelings, making it easier for him to walk away.

"At least I'm honest," she went on jabbing at him. "What I did with Peter is over and done with. You're still sizzling for the singer, aren't you? Nothing like frustration to screw up your head, not to mention other parts of your anatomy. I bet that was what you were trying to walk off. And now you're angry because I did what you wanted to."

Her eyes gloated with a derisive certainty in her assumption.

She was wrong.

He would not have used Gina Terlizzi like that.

Never.

He unclipped his seat belt, alighted from the car,

strode around the bonnet and opened the passenger door.

"I'm not getting out until we talk this through," she declared, furious at his action.

"We're finished. I have nothing more to say to you, Michelle," he clipped out, giving her no room to manoeuvre a different situation between them.

She stared up at him in hard-eyed challenge.

No way was he about to budge.

With a doleful sigh she unclipped her seat belt and slithered her way upright beside him, probably trying a reminder of how sexy she could be, given some incentive.

"You'll think better of this, Alex," she purred huskily. "I'm not going to give you your ring back."

"Keep it," he replied carelessly. "Consider it the spoils from the game. But don't think for one minute the game isn't over. It is." He closed the car door to punctuate the point.

"Pride is a poor bedfellow, Alex."

"I can live with it more easily than I can with a string of Peter Owens." He gestured to the apartment building. "Do you want me to see you to your front door?"

She gave him a mocking little smile. "No. I think I'll see you off instead. Who knows? You might change your mind halfway down the road."

It was her choice to reject the courtesy. Alex didn't argue with it. He nodded a cold acknowledgement, said "Goodbye," and returned to the driver's seat, closing Michelle Banks out of his life.

Halfway down the road, he didn't even glance back.
He wasn't consciously driving towards Gina Terlizzi.
She just happened to be in the castle tonight.
He was simply going home.

CHAPTER EIGHT

A CRY from Marco snapped Gina awake. She rolled out of bed in automatic response, then still groggy from the sleep she had finally fallen into, found herself completely disoriented in unfamiliar surroundings. It took several moments to get her bearings. A dim night-light came from a half-open door. It triggered the memory of where she was—the nanny's bedroom in King's Castle—and Marco was in the adjoining nursery.

She started to move towards the connecting door, then stopped, realising it was quiet now. Marco must have cried out in his sleep, then resettled. A bad dream? Since she was up, Gina decided she might as well check on him, make sure he was all right.

A soft murmuring made her hesitate. Was someone else attending to him? Had he been crying for some time before she woke? Rosita's rooms weren't far away. Frowning over the thought of the kindly housekeeper's sleep being disturbed, Gina snatched up the dressing-gown she'd tossed on the end of the bed and thrust her arms into the sleeves. Best for her to sit with Marco for a while, relieving Rosita of any sense of responsibility.

She grimaced over the sensual slide of silk and lace on her bare skin. The coffee-coloured gown and nightie from her honeymoon trousseau were more luxurious than practical garments. She'd put them away...hadn't worn them for years. It had been a silly impulse to pack them for tonight, yet when she'd chosen to, a night spent at King's Castle had seemed special enough to warrant wearing them.

And Alex King had made her feel…well, she'd wanted to feel like a woman again, not just a mother. He'd certainly made her feel it when he'd kissed her. Now she wished he hadn't. It was too disturbing. Better not to have needs aroused when they were never going to be answered. She savagely fastened the tie-belt around her waist, calling herself all sorts of a fool for indulging in fantasies that had nothing to do with real life.

Alex King wasn't for her.

She'd known all along he wasn't for her.

She was a twenty-six-year-old nobody with a child by another man, and he was engaged to be married to a glamorous dress designer who was experienced in leading a high-class, sophisticated life. Dressing herself up in expensive silk and lace didn't change anything.

Having achieved a reasonably modest appearance with her very non-motherly wrap-around, she tried to shove the weight of misery in her mind aside as she moved to the doorway and stepped into the nursery. Expecting to see Rosita, she was stunned to find her son being cradled and softly crooned to by the very man who'd caused her so much heartburn.

She hung on to the doorjamb while the shock subsided. Alex King had his back turned to her but there was no mistaking his identity. His head was turned in half profile, his gaze fixed on the face of the child in his arms. Marco's mop of curls was nestled just above the crook of his elbow and it was obvious her little boy had been calmed and was lying contentedly still, being gently rocked back to sleep.

The scenario her eyes were taking in made no sense at all. Alex King was still in his formal dinner suit. The covers on Marco's bed were flung right back, though she remembered having tucked them in. What had happened? Why was Alex here with her son and not with his fiancée? What time was it?

She spotted a seahorse clock on one of the nursery walls. The hands showed almost half past one. The wedding reception had been due to end at midnight. As far as she could hear, the castle and its grounds were completely quiet. Alex must have taken Michelle home and returned, yet that didn't answer why he was in the nursery. Perhaps he'd heard Marco cry out when he was going upstairs to his quarters, but hadn't she closed the door to the corridor?

It was open now.

Totally perplexed she watched as he slowly lowered Marco back onto the bed, settling him gently on the pillow, then carefully lifting the covers over him, tucking them in at shoulder level. He stood for a moment, visually checking his handiwork, then bent over and pressed a soft kiss on Marco's forehead, apparently satisfied all was well now.

It was such a tender, paternal action, Gina felt her heart turning over. Angelo would have done this if he were still alive. It wasn't fair that Alex King was emitting the same fatherly caring, striking chords that jangled hopelessly in the barren spaces of her widowhood. He made too intimate a connection, too painfully intimate when it could never *mean* anything.

He turned from the bed, a serious, reflective expression on his face, and started towards the door to the corridor. Either he caught sight of Gina out of the corner of his eye or something made him suddenly aware of her presence. An abrupt jerk of his head had him looking directly at her and his forward movement froze.

Her whole body was instantly tremulous. It was lucky she was still hanging on to the doorjamb. It felt as though she was trapped in an earthquake and any chance of escape was irretrievably gone. She shouldn't have lingered—watching him. It had been stupid, dangerous.

Now he was watching her, and even across the room the intensity of his gaze was utterly riveting. It seemed the very air between them was charged with an electricity that had them both locked in a force-field that couldn't be broken.

How long they stood in a transfixed state, Gina had no idea. She noticed his bow tie was hanging loose and the top studs of his dress shirt were undone. He was undoubtedly aware of her bed-tousled hair and the skimpiness of her attire, although the mid-thigh-length gown did cover the more provocative lace edging of her very short nightie.

He took a step towards her, then checked himself, glancing back over his shoulder to assure himself Marco was sleeping peacefully. His gaze swung swiftly back to Gina. She hadn't moved, hadn't thought of moving.

As Marco's mother, it was her right to be here. It was Alex King's presence that begged an explanation.

Apparently he thought so, too. As he stepped closer to her, he whispered, "I'm sorry you were woken. I think he's all right now."

"What was wrong?" she whispered back, maternal concern over-riding the inner turmoil raised by his proximity.

He grimaced apologetically. "When I came in, there was only a lump at the bottom end of the bed. He'd burrowed down under the covers and I was worried about him smothering."

"It's okay. He does that sometimes. Like a little possum snuggling into a safe pouch."

He gestured helpless ignorance. "I thought I'd better check he was breathing and lift him back on the pillow. I didn't mean to startle him into crying out."

She managed an ironic little smile. "Well, you did a good job of soothing him down again."

He returned her smile with a wry twist of his own. "At least, he didn't mind my nursing him. Maybe he remembered me from last week."

It was more than that, Gina thought. Marco instinctively responded to him in some elemental way, just as she did. The pain of their earlier encounter tonight suddenly gripped her heart.

"Why are you here?" she cried, louder than she meant to.

"Ssh..." he warned, once more glancing back at Marco, his brows lowered in concern.

Confused, disturbed, she didn't resist when he proceeded to bundle her back into the nanny's bedroom, following her in and pushing the door to barely a crack ajar, diminishing any sound they made, yet still allowing them to hear a cry from her son. She ended up against the wall beside the door and he was much closer to her, heart-thumpingly close, his hands lightly, hotly curled over her shoulders, burning through the thin silk.

She stared at his throat, frightened to look up at the face she found too attractive, the eyes that might see her quivering vulnerability and the wanton desire for him clawing through it.

"This probably won't make sense to you but I just wanted to look at him," he pleaded in a low voice, gravelled with needs she had no way of understanding.

"What can he mean to you?" she asked, shaking her head in non-comprehension.

His chest heaved as he drew in a long breath. "I was thinking...of how it might be...to have a son."

A curiosity? A yearning? She looked up, compelled to see exactly what he was expressing and he lifted a hand to cup her cheek, holding the tilt of her head while his eyes bored into hers, playing havoc with her own secret yearnings.

"He is a beautiful child...like his mother."

He was wrong. Marco was more like his father. But any thought of correction was swallowed up by the raging need to believe he really did find her beautiful. Her throat was so dry and constricted, she could barely make the protest that her sense of rightness demanded.

"You shouldn't say such things to me."

"Why not? It's the truth."

She forced herself to say, "What about Michelle?"

"Forget Michelle. It's you I want."

You I want...you I want... The words pounded through her heart like a drum roll of anticipation that couldn't be muffled. It was impossible to tear her eyes away from the raw desire in his, impossible to deny her own wanting for him. It surged like a torrent through her bloodstream, screaming for satisfaction this time, needing it with such blind force she couldn't think of anything else. Michelle *was* forgotten. Her mind was driven into a wild chant—*Make it true then. Make it true...*

Maybe his mind picked it up or the same refrain was beating through him, demanding action. His mouth crashed down on hers and a hunger for knowledge of each other erupted—an intense, intimate knowledge that recognised no barriers at all. There was a barrage of deeply passionate kisses, a craving for every possible sensation, an urgency that feared frustration and fought against giving it any chance to break into what was happening.

Action...action...action... The tie-belt of her gown wrenched apart, the silk being slid from her shoulders, sleeves pushed down, off, out of the way...hands skimming her curves, clutching them...kisses, trailing down her throat, over the swell of her breasts, his mouth finding her nipples through the thin fabric of her nightie, drawing hotly on them, unbelievably exciting...helping him get rid of his coat, his shirt, her hands greedily exulting in the ripple of his muscles, his naked shoulders, his back, the dark nest of male hair on his chest.

Touching…with a total abandonment of any inhibition. Touching because she wanted to, needed to, making this intimacy with him so real she was giddy with the intense pleasure of it. More kisses…wonderful intoxicating kisses…her pulses pounding, her heartbeat raging, her mind swimming with the awesome knowledge he was removing his trousers, the rest of his clothes, stripping himself naked, wanting flesh to flesh, wild for the same earthy reality of feeling all he could with her.

And the raw power of this new touch of him had her falling apart, a sweet disintegration that begged for the fulfilment he promised with the hard strength he could bring to her. He lifted off her nightie—a fever of impatience now—his body rubbing against hers, letting her feel, *making* her feel his readiness, *and* her readiness for the ultimate joining. More than readiness. A compelling yearning to give and take all a man and woman could experience together. It was so strong, so immediate, when he swept her off her feet and carried her to the bed, it was like soaring towards a climax and she was spreading her legs for him even as they landed on the mattress.

No waiting. He came into her with all the urgency she felt, and instinctively she locked her legs around him, rocking, rocking hard, harder, needing to capture every sensation, the deepest essence of this blissful merging. Blindly she clawed his back, arched her hips, intensifying the connection, and he more than met her need, increasing the beat of their primitive dance, driving a savage joy through it, injecting an exultation that peaked again and again and again, penetrating every part of her as she came and kept coming until she was sated with the sheer ecstasy of it and he lay limp inside her.

They collapsed together, drained, breathless, slipping into an aftermath of paralysed silence, lying side by side, still touching...but the time of mindless union was over.

Gina felt stunned on many levels. Sexually, she had never experienced anything like this. And it was with Alex King. *Alex King!* Who was stretched out beside her, as naked as she was, and probably equally stunned by this sudden intimate development. Yes, the desire had been there—*mutual* desire—but neither of them had planned this encounter in the middle of the night, nor such an explosive outcome to it.

But it was done now. They couldn't take it back. And in all honesty, given the choice, Gina knew she wouldn't have it any different. If this turned out to be a once-in-a-lifetime experience, then it was certainly worth having. No regrets on that score. So strange— even loving Angelo had not brought this intense all-invasive pleasure, nor such a frenzy of passion.

Alex King...

Alex...

Her mind lingered over his name, silently lilting it as though it had to contain some secret magic. She almost spoke it out loud, wanting to taste the sound of it in her mouth, revelling in it as she had revelled in the taste of him.

Did he have this sense of wonder over how it had been?

Or was he now remembering Michelle?

Forget Michelle!

How fiercely he had spoken those words!

And she had forgotten. In the heat of their coming together, any thought of the other woman had been burned away. What's more, she didn't feel guilty about what had happened. Alex wasn't married to Michelle Banks. Though he was cheating on her, Gina sternly reminded herself.

Was he regretting it? Feeling guilty?

How much did this intimate sharing with her tonight mean to him? Had it just been a surge of lust that was now exhausted? Would he go back to Michelle, having purged the desire that had disrupted his commitment to her?

Gina's heart fluttered anxiously. Lying here in the darkness with him, remembering their tumultuous mating, her body still so vibrantly alive from being aroused to heights she'd never known...it just didn't feel right for it to have no meaning beyond this one night.

"Gina..."

Her name, coming deeply from his throat, sounded like a velvet purr, so soft and sensual it sent tingles all over her skin. His hand slid over hers, interlacing their fingers, gripping possessively. Her pulse instantly leapt with wanton excitement. He could not intend to part from her. Not yet.

"I won't say I'm sorry this time. I'm not sorry at all," he continued, slowly lifting her hand to his mouth and grazing his lips over it as though savouring the femininity of its shape and texture, or paying some homage to what she had given him as a woman. "Tell me you're not sorry either, Gina," he murmured gruffly.

"I'm not sorry, Alex," she answered truthfully, the hope for more from him galloping through her heart.

He sighed, as though venting deep relief. "At least that's all right then. Problem is…I didn't use protection. How does that sit with you?"

It almost blew her mind that she hadn't thought of it herself. There hadn't been any reason for her to be using any means of contraception, so she wasn't. Even nursing a secret desire for Alex King hadn't spurred her to such a practicality because she hadn't really believed anything would come of the attraction. Certainly not this…here…tonight!

Frantically she counted up the days since her last period. Having a regular cycle made it relatively easy to work out her *safe* times. It was over three weeks, which meant she was past the fertile span. Relief whooshed through her.

"It's okay. No risk," she assured him feelingly.

"You're not on the pill," he deduced from her long hesitation.

"No. I never have been. And I wasn't expecting…"

"I wasn't, either." He squeezed her hand, reinforcing the mutuality of their acting without any premeditation. "But I can't say I haven't been thinking of you, wanting to know…" Another sigh. "Earlier tonight…"

"I wanted you, too," she acknowledged quickly, seeing no reason to let him take responsibility for a desire

she shared. There was no denying how much she'd
craved knowing what it might be like with him.

He lowered her hand, released it, then hitched himself
up on his side to look directly at her. She braved meeting his gaze, knowing she couldn't hide from this situation and needing to see what was on his mind. It was
too dark to read his expression with any accuracy but
his face didn't seem to reflect concern. More a gentle
bemusement.

"So here we are," he murmured, as though it were
some amazing trick of fate that he hadn't quite come to
terms with, although it was certainly to his liking. The
burr of pleasure in his voice was unmistakable.

As much as Gina wanted to hug his pleasure to her
and blot out everything else, her mind circled his
words—*here we are*—and latched onto the big tormenting question… *Where was Michelle?*

Wasn't he thinking of his fiancée at all?

The temptation to keep it that way battled with the
urge to ask. Earlier this evening he'd declared kissing
her wasn't fair. Had *fairness* now lost all meaning in
the face of what they'd felt together?

His gaze travelled slowly over her nakedness and his
hand followed the same path, lightly tracing and caressing her soft curves, making her skin tingle again—
too seductive a distraction to keep fretting about
Michelle Banks.

"You are addictively beautiful…every part of you
lushly perfect," he murmured, and although Gina knew
it wasn't true, it was so sweet to hear, coming from
him, she wasn't about to point out any faults. Besides,

the way he touched her *was* making her feel voluptuously beautiful, and it was wonderful to bask in the sense of being absolutely desirable—here and now, when she most wanted to be with this man.

It gave her the courage to explore his magnificent maleness with far more sensual pleasure this time since there was no longer the urgency that had driven both of them earlier. To her mind he really was perfection and she savoured the freedom to touch and exulted in the positive responses that revealed he was still excited by her and every contact she made delighted him.

It wasn't just sex, she thought. They were making love to each other, and her whole being was gradually caught up in a world circumscribed by sheer sensation—the flow and ebb of it, erotic ripples, huge waves of pleasure, exquisite peaks—nothing forbidden nor unwelcome because it was all part of an ever-deepening journey of intimacy that drew them into doing whatever took their fancy long into the night.

No words were spoken. None seemed quite right. It seemed there was a continual flow of communication on a far more elemental, instinctive level…something that words might spoil because they couldn't really express this kind of sharing. Better simply to feel and keep going with the feeling.

It was, for Gina, an entrancing revelation of how it could be with both partners so physically enthralled with each other—a potent mixture of awe and tenderness and passion and sensuality. She was mostly conscious of an amazed joy in the intense pleasure of their sexual harmony, and how incredible it was that it could go on and on. Satiation came slowly, accompanied by a contented languor that soothed them into sleep.

An end or a beginning?

Neither of them even thought of asking that question. Only time would resolve it.

CHAPTER NINE

"MAMA?"

Marco's whisper and his touch on her arm brought Gina instantly awake. She looked straight into big-eyed wonder. Her son's highly expressive gaze flicked beyond her and back again, the unspoken question bringing a sharp clarity to her mind and a shock wave to her heart.

Alex King in bed with her!

She lifted a finger to her lips to keep Marco silent, then quickly whispered, "Go back to your own room and Mama will be there in a minute. Okay?"

He nodded reluctantly, curiosity obviously rife. Gina was intensely grateful he did her bidding without arguing. At this point she had no idea what answers to give him. She needed time to think but there was no time right now. Fast action was required if Marco wasn't to be drawn into a situation that was too complicated to be presented to a little boy who saw things in very simple terms.

Mama had been sleeping with Alex King.

Hopefully Marco hadn't taken in they were both naked. As Gina carefully slid out from under the bedclothes, she was intensely grateful that fact had been mostly hidden from her son. How she was going to explain what he had seen was difficult enough and she certainly didn't want Alex disturbed and contributing anything she hadn't had the chance to monitor first. The situation was highly sensitive, given his engagement to Michelle Banks—was that still on?

She looked back at him as she donned the clothes she'd set out on a chair before going to bed. His thick black hair was mussed, a five o'clock shadow darkened his jaw. Neither factor lessened the impact of his strikingly handsome face. Even with his eyes closed, he could still stir the desire that had engulfed her last night. His wonderfully muscular shoulders, the satin smoothness of the skin stretched over them, the tempting hair on his chest…

She wanted to touch him again, but was he really hers to touch? Was it stolen pleasure? She forced herself to keep on dressing, hands busy pulling on the T-shirt printed with blue butterflies, buttoning the denim skirt, strapping on brown leather sandals. It made her feel like a thief, creeping around the room, collecting her belongings, but she felt too uneasy about the consequences of waking Alex to do anything else.

The need to remove herself and Marco to their own home ground pressed urgently. She didn't want to be involved in *a scene* here. Let Alex sort out his life and come to her if last night held any real meaning to him.

The morning after…

The enormity of what they'd done shivered through her as she slipped out of the nanny's room, closing the door as noiselessly as possible on the intimacy they had shared. Would he pursue a relationship with her or…she shook her head, her mind shying from contemplating any other outcome.

Alex could find out where she lived and worked from his grandmother if he wanted to. A man chased if he was truly drawn to a woman. His arrival or non-arrival on her doorstep would tell her where she stood with him soon enough. Best to concentrate on Marco now.

He was sitting cross-legged on the nursery bed, patiently waiting for her to give him permission to speak, his big brown eyes agog with interest. Gina smiled warm reassurance at him as she crossed the room, setting her overnight bag down close to him and laying the plastic bag containing her evening dress at the foot of the bed.

"Have you been to the bathroom?" she asked softly.

He nodded.

"Let's get you dressed then." She pulled his clean set of clothes from her bag. "Can you manage these while I go to the bathroom?"

"'Course I can. But, Mama..."

"Ssh! Other people in the castle are still asleep, Marco. We'll talk when we go downstairs."

He frowned but started pulling off his pyjamas. Satisfied her instructions would be followed, Gina hurried off to use the ensuite facilities, acutely conscious of the need to achieve a respectable appearance as fast as she could. Although it was early morning, and a Sunday, someone would undoubtedly be astir in the castle and she couldn't depart without leaving a thank-you message for Isabella King. Such kind hospitality demanded courtesy in return.

Nevertheless, she didn't want to be caught up in any long conversation, didn't want to risk any kind of embarrassing situation, not in front of Marco. Bad enough that he'd witnessed what he had. If he blurted out the truth to Isabella King... *Please let it all stay private,* she willed frantically.

It was almost seven o'clock when she led Marco downstairs. Having persuaded him to stand guard over her bags in the huge foyer, she went in search of castle staff and was relieved to find Rosita in the kitchen. The housekeeper's welcoming smile was swiftly replaced by an anxious frown as Gina made her leave-taking speech.

"But you are expected to stay for breakfast. At the very least, breakfast," came the pleading protest.

Gina poured out apologies and excuses and was profuse in her gratitude for the kindness extended to her. Remaining firm about going was difficult in the face of the pressing entreaties to stay, especially as Rosita trailed her back to the foyer, insisting Mrs. King would be most upset not to have Gina's and Marco's company this morning.

"Please tell Mrs. King it's family business. I'm sure she'll understand," was the best exit line Gina could come up with, quickly bustling Marco outside and determinedly heading for her car.

Thankfully they were beyond earshot before Marco's questions started. "Who was the man in your bed, Mama?"

"It was the man we met at the castle before, remember? He showed you the fish in the pond."

"I 'member. The nice man."

"Yes. And the castle is his home."

"Doesn't it have another bed for him?"

"Yes, but last night he came to your room to see if you were all right. He found you snuggled up under the bedclothes and thought he should lift you back on the pillow. It woke you up, remember?"

He shook his head.

"Well, you cried out and I heard you. When I came into your room, there was Alex—the nice man—giving you a cuddle. He put you back to bed and tucked you in. Then he wanted to talk to me so we went into my room. He waited to make sure you went back to sleep all right and we both got tired and fell asleep ourselves."

Marco thought about that for a while, then nodded. "The bed was big enough for him, too."

"Yes." A child's simple logic was wonderful, Gina thought, hoping her explanation would fully satisfy him.

"He *is* a nice man, isn't he, Mama?" came the stress-free conclusion.

"Yes," she heartily agreed.

Too nice for Michelle Banks! But was Alex thinking of ending his commitment to his fiancée? How could he be unfaithful to her and not change his mind about his future course?

Hope moved swiftly into a churning sickness.

Last night had to mean something.

It had to.

Since she could not keep Gina Terlizzi and her son from leaving, Rosita decided she might as well tidy their rooms and take the bed linen to the laundry. Isabella had announced she would not come down to breakfast until eight o'clock. It was always so when she attended an evening wedding reception. There was time to spare.

She entered the nanny's room and came to a shocked halt. The bed was still occupied. By a man! And it looked like…Rosita took a deep breath and tip-toed to a better vantage point for recognition to be unmistakable…Alessandro! A bare-chested Alessandro! And there were his good clothes strewn carelessly around the floor!

It could mean only one thing.

Rosita now had a clear understanding of Gina Terlizzi's early departure. She tip-toed out of the room, not wanting to disturb the sleeping Alessandro. It could be a big embarrassment to do so. Besides, this was Isabella's business and her employer would want to be told at once that her grandson had not spent last night with Michelle Banks.

Over her many years of employment at the castle, Rosita had listened sympathetically to the concerns Isabella had voiced about her family and its future. She was proud of being a trusted confidante and she was very aware that Michelle Banks was not a wife Isabella favoured for her oldest grandson. The plan to put Gina Terlizzi in his way had worked. Although how far it had worked with Gina now gone…

Rosita shook her head worriedly. She wasn't sure it was wise to interfere in other people's love-lives. Strong attachments could stir dangerous passions. But this *was* family business. Isabella would know what to do. She had to be told. At once!

Alex woke slowly, conscious of a deep sense of well-being he didn't want to lose. It was only as he vaguely searched for the reason behind it that the memory of being with Gina filtered into his mind.

Gina…

Hadn't she been nestled against him when he'd fallen asleep? Suddenly aware of being nakedly alone in the bed, he whipped around to check where *she* was, his eyes very sharply open.

Gone. And not one sign of her left in the room anywhere he could see. A glance at his watch showed a few minutes past nine o'clock. No wonder she was gone. Her son would have woken hours ago. And what had felt so very right to both of them in the darkness of the night might not have felt so right to her in the light of the morning. If Marco had found them together…highly probable in the circumstances…how had she explained it?

Alex frowned over that thought. He wished she hadn't excluded him from any responsibility over what had happened. Easier, perhaps. Less awkward. But he *was* responsible. More so than she, since he had come to her. Though not intentionally. After the break-up with Michelle, he'd been brooding over what kind of marriage he did want—a wife who shared his values, children…

Shock hit him. Had he told Gina his engagement was over? What had he said in the heat of the moment? He remembered her protesting his presence in the nursery, more or less asking why he wasn't with Michelle...and he'd replied...

Forget Michelle!

Damn it! That wasn't enough. God only knew what Gina was thinking this morning but it wouldn't be good. His fault. His blind fault for not communicating his situation clearly. He'd lost himself so fast in the seductive promise of all he'd sensed coming from her—all she gave—nothing else had mattered to him.

But it mattered now.

Alex hurled off the bedclothes, galvanised into action by the hope that Gina was still at the castle, lingering over breakfast with his grandmother. It was an outside chance. The doubt instantly arose that she would have stayed on in these circumstances, yet maybe the need to gauge his reaction to what had happened was strong enough to hold her here.

He grabbed his clothes and sprinted to his own quarters, reasonably confident he wouldn't meet or be seen by anyone along the corridor at this hour on a Sunday morning. A quick shower and shave, fresh clothes, and he was downstairs by nine-thirty, his mind having raced through various scenarios and his responses to them, though he could be faced with something entirely unpredictable.

Trying to reduce his inner tension before he reached the breakfast room was difficult. He didn't want his grandmother latching onto the situation between him and Gina before he had resolved it himself, or at least gone some way towards sorting out where they stood with each other this morning.

An upfront announcement that his marriage to Michelle was off seemed the best way to soothe any distress Gina was feeling on that score, as well as distracting his grandmother from the more sensitive area he'd have to negotiate with her guest and protégé. There was Marco to consider, as well. Had the little boy seen him in bed with his mother?

Keyed up to meet and deal with multi-level problems, Alex's mental train was thrown off course again when he reached the breakfast room and found only his grandmother occupying it. He paused in the doorway to re-gather himself. Luckily her gaze was turned towards the windows at the end of the room. They faced east to give a view of the sunrise over the ocean, if one was up early enough to watch it.

The sun was long risen this morning but the rolling ocean sparkled in its endless movement, almost a hypnotic view if one looked long enough. A coffee cup sat on the table by her hand which was resting idly next to it. Breakfast had obviously been cleared away. His grandmother wouldn't have been expecting him to join her. His usual practice was to stay with Michelle on Saturday nights. If Gina and Marco had been here, they'd eaten and gone before he'd even woken.

Caught in the dilemma of what best to do now, he was still standing in the doorway when his grandmother drew herself out of her private ponderings and looked at her coffee cup. As she reached for the bell to summon Rosita, Alex knew the option of simply absenting himself at this point was gone. Before he could move, her sharp gaze flicked to him.

"Alessandro...this is a surprise," she said with an air of expectation that couldn't be denied.

"Good morning, Nonna," he replied, forcing himself into a casual stroll forward and an even more casual inquiry, "Your guests are gone?"

"If you mean Gina Terlizzi and her son...?" A raised eyebrow because she had not given him that information.

"Gina told me last night you had invited them to stay overnight," he quickly supplied.

"Ah! I did expect them to stay for breakfast but they left early this morning."

Her displeasure was obvious. Guilt knifed through Alex. It was clear now that Gina had fled the castle, fearing major embarrassment. Or worse, humiliation. She had even risked offending his grandmother in her need to escape any unacceptable reaction to their intimacy. He had unwittingly put her in a highly equivocal position and it was up to him to make some amending move.

His grandmother rang the bell and gestured to the chair directly across the table from hers. "Would you like Rosita to bring you some breakfast?"

Odd that she didn't immediately inquire what he was doing here. Needing information, Alex sat down, prepared to chat long enough to find out what he wanted to know. "No breakfast." That would take too much time. "Though I'd welcome a cup of coffee if you're having one."

Rosita promptly appeared and his grandmother ordered coffee for two, not bothering to try pressing any food on him, which was also odd. For some reason she always assumed Michelle never fed him properly and she must be thinking he'd just come from his fiancée's apartment.

"I thought the wedding went off very well last night," his grandmother commented while they waited for the coffee.

"Yes," he agreed. To him it seemed like a lifetime ago—a blur he didn't even want to remember.

"Antonio made a fine speech."

He nodded, belatedly remarking, "He enjoys entertaining an audience."

Tony was an extrovert, always fun company. Alex sometimes wished he had his younger brother's bright *joie de vivre,* his ability to simply let go and move with the flow. *You try to keep control of too much, Alex,* Tony often teased him, but control had gone right out the door last night.

"And my new find—Gina Terlizzi—sang beautifully," his grandmother went on.

"I thought so, too," he muttered, turning his gaze to the view, not wanting his grandmother to see how deeply her protégé affected him.

Her ensuing silence gave him the strong impression that she knew and was waiting for him to comment further. Of course she had seen him sweep Gina into dancing with him and probably watched their exit from the ballroom. Not exactly the action of a disinterested man. But she couldn't know what else had transpired between them.

Certainly he had to inform his grandmother that *his* wedding was now cancelled, releasing the date for a booking by some other couple. There was no possibility of any reconnection with Michelle. Even without the attraction to Gina, no way would he reconsider marriage to a woman who could be so blithely unfaithful.

Which brought him straight back to the impression Gina must have taken away with her—of him having cheated on his fiancée. It was intolerable. Never mind that the desire which had exploded between them last night had been mutual. He'd pushed it and taken what he wanted without clearing the way first.

Rosita returned with freshly percolated coffee and the accompaniments. He turned to smile his thanks but the smile wasn't returned. She seemed to evade looking at him, busily laying everything out on the table. It was not like the usually voluble Rosita to remain silent, and skipping out of the room the moment she was done.

Something was very wrong here. Rosita had been working at the castle since he was a boy and always had a smile for him. Alex directed a quick searching look at his grandmother. Her eyes were half veiled as she poured out the coffee, her facial expression giving nothing away. It struck Alex she appeared too calm, too composed, which was invariably her manner when faced with trouble.

''What's the problem, Nonna?''

She finished pouring, set the coffeepot down, then

met his probing gaze with a very sharp directness. "You are the problem, Alessandro," she stated unequivocally.

He realised instantly that they knew—both Rosita and his grandmother *knew* he'd slept with Gina. Damage control leapt to the fore.

"I'm sorry you are distressed by my actions. I'll redress any problems I've caused very shortly," he promised.

"And just how do you propose to correct the situation?" came the pointed demand, her eyes biting with reproof. "I might remind you…"

"I broke my engagement to Michelle last night," he interjected. "As soon as the wedding was over. The parting was decisive before I came home."

Her eyes flashed some other strong feeling before she sat back with an air of relief. "It is good to know you have not acted entirely dishonourably."

"Nonna, I assure you…"

"Let me put it quite plainly, Alessandro," she interrupted, determination blazing at him. "Gina Terlizzi was my guest. She was entitled to the safe privacy of the suite given to her and her son. I do not believe for one moment that she invited you into it. Her hasty departure early this morning speaks volumes to *me*…if not to *you*."

He frowned. "Did she say anything?"

"Do you expect a young lady of any dignity to blurt out that my grandson had seduced her?"

"There was no seduction," he curtly protested.

"That he used her on the rebound from breaking up with another woman?"

"No!" His fist crashed down on the table as he pushed up from his chair. "Just stay out of this, Nonna! I'll fix it!"

"See that you do, Alessandro," she fiercely retorted. "I do not like to feel ashamed of my grandson."

Ashamed?

It stung him more than anything else she could have said, stung him into a more sober re-appraisal of his conduct, stung him out of the anger that had surged at her accusatory assumptions. His grandmother was trying to see through Gina's eyes, read her reasons for leaving as she had. The reasons weren't right. But it was clear his grandmother's sympathy was very much on Gina Terlizzi's side.

He stood still, understanding the attack on his character, though to his mind it wasn't warranted. "You like her," he said quietly.

"Yes, I do. She has solid worth. It pains me that she should be hurt through any association with my family."

He nodded. *Solid worth.* His grandmother had never really taken to Michelle. He'd excused it on the grounds that she was old, old-fashioned, not in tune with today's world and Michelle was very much the modern woman. As it had turned out, perhaps he was old-fashioned, too. Certainly *solid worth* now had more appeal to him than superficial glamour.

"It wasn't seduction, Nonna. Nor was it a rebound reaction on my part. It was mutual attraction. Which I intend to pursue," he declared, wanting the murky air between them cleared.

His grandmother closed her eyes and breathed a deep sigh of relief. "You'll find Gina Terlizzi's telephone number and address in my office diary."

"Thank you. If you'll excuse me?"

She nodded. "Please take care, Alessandro." Her lids lifted, her eyes delivering an eloquent look of warning. "No one can sing like that without a feeling heart."

"Do you think I don't know it?" he answered with considerable irony. "My judgement may have been astray with Michelle but I'm learning, Nonna. I'm learning."

He left the breakfast room, intent on learning more.

CHAPTER TEN

GINA stood at the kitchen sink, idly washing the breakfast dishes as she watched Marco through the window. He was wheeling his little trolley around, pausing at chosen places to set a plastic block on the lawn, creating a pattern that satisfied his eye for whatever game he had in mind.

It was a good backyard for him to play in, securely fenced, with a small vegetable garden adding the interest of watching things grow and picking them when they were ready to be picked—tomatoes, capsicum, cucumbers. Gina grew the flowers she loved in the front garden, ensuring they wouldn't be damaged by bouncing balls.

The house itself was an old wooden Queenslander, built high to catch breezes, verandas providing shade from the hot sun. It was nothing grand or flash—certainly no castle—but it was a home, a home of their own which both Angelo's parents and hers had helped them buy to start off their marriage. Except she no longer had a husband and Marco didn't have a father.

Was it a wild fantasy that Alex King might fill those roles?

Last night…caring for Marco…loving her…

She heaved a sigh loaded with all the inner miseries that had been building up over his connection to

Michelle Banks. Maybe Alex and his fiancée had been at odds with each other at the wedding, ending with a big argument, passions erupting. People could go off the rails at such times, but given a day or two to cool down...

The telephone rang.

Gina lifted her hands out of the soapy water and hurriedly dried them on a tea-towel as she moved to pick up the receiver. It was probably her mother calling, wanting to know how the gig had gone at the castle—such an honour to be asked to sing by Isabella King.

Gina grimaced at the need to sound bright and cheerful, pretending nothing of a disturbing nature had happened...like having taken a lover in the middle of the night and not knowing whether he'd even want to remember it in the morning.

"Hi! Gina here," she announced, forcing a lightness into her voice she didn't feel.

"Gina, it's Alex King," came the strongly spoken reply, instantly spinning her into emotional turmoil.

The shock of hearing from him so soon when she'd been thinking she might not hear from him at all, left her totally speechless. Her gaze darted to the kitchen clock. It was only a few minutes past ten. Had he just woken and found her gone? Was he calling to say it had been a *mistake?*

Her heart seemed to be thundering in her ears. Her chest was so tight, she could barely breathe. Her hand gripped the receiver with knuckle-white intensity. Her mind willed him to say something good, something that would ease this awful tension and give her back the sense of peace and pleasure that had been eaten away by doubts and fears.

"I understand you felt it was the discreet thing to do…leaving early this morning," he went on, his deep voice seeming to throb in time with her pulse. "But can we meet today?"

Meet…today…

For the life of her she couldn't get her tongue around a reply. She was dizzy with shock and joy. It seemed he didn't want to forget that last night had ever been. He wanted to be with her again. But…for what purpose? He might be feeling the need to explain himself, excuse himself…

"Gina…?"

She tried to work some moisture into her mouth. Her heart was screaming *yes* to the meeting, no matter what, but her sense of rightness cried out for more from him. If he was still tied to that woman, why go so far as to ask for a meeting? Did he mean to test his feelings? Or…her stomach cramped…was he hoping to have a fling on the side?

"Gina, I'm no longer committed to the relationship I had with Michelle," he stated in a rush. "I broke my engagement to her after the wedding, when I took her home. There's no barrier to…" He paused, obviously hunting for inoffensive words. "I mean there's no reason for you to be concerned about my playing anyone false. Please believe that."

He was finished with Michelle Banks! This news was like a star burst going off in Gina's head.

"I should have told you so last night," he said regretfully. "And I apologise very sincerely for any grief it's given you this morning."

Her relief whooshed out in a heartfelt sigh. "Thank you, Alex. It did worry me." *Understatement of the year,* but it didn't matter now. The weight of misery had lifted and her blood was zinging with a bubbling fountain of hope.

"I would like very much to spend some time with you today," he pressed. "Could I bring a picnic lunch and take you and Marco out somewhere?"

Such an invitation, including her son, surely meant he anticipated enjoying their company. "I'd like that," she answered, trying not to sound over-the-moon eager. "Crystal Cascades is a lovely place for a picnic, and it's not far from here. I live at Redlynch, on the outskirts of Cairns."

"I know. My grandmother gave me your address."

Another shock, mixed with a surge of pleasure at this proof there was nothing hidden about his intentions. "You spoke to her about me?" The words spilled out, artlessly revealing her need for any relationship between them to be openly acknowledged.

"A little while ago. If I pick you up at twelve o'clock, will that suit?"

"Yes," she answered dazedly, unbelievably happy at this train of events. "We'll be ready."

"Good! I'll see you then."

A picnic with Alex King! Gina hugged the telephone receiver to her heart. It was really happening. Not a completely wild dream. Alex wanted to be with her and Marco!

*   *   *

A picnic! Alex set the receiver down, a triumphant sense of achievement sliding into bemusement over the meeting he'd arranged. When was the last time he'd been on a picnic? He couldn't remember. Yet the idea had popped straight into his mind…Gina, Marco, family picnic. It formed a seductive picture. Which gave him pause for thought.

Was he reacting against Michelle?

Reacting against the pattern of Sunday brunch at some fashionable waterside restaurant…idle chitchat with fashionable acquaintances?

He certainly felt a strong desire to remove himself from that entire scene, to move towards something else. Right now, Gina Terlizzi and her son formed the focus of a new direction, but maybe he should move forward with more caution, more consideration, instead of plunging headlong into another serious involvement.

He'd made a bad mistake with Michelle.

Could he trust his instincts with Gina?

His grandmother's warning came sharply to mind—*Please take care, Alessandro.*

He should.

He would.

Control was the key.

Yet with Gina…did he want to control the feelings she stirred? Was he even able to? All he knew was the need to see her, be with her, know more of her, was compelling, and no way was he about to deny himself this course of action.

* * *

Gina was still floating on a cloud of happiness when her mother telephoned a half hour after the call from Alex. There was no need for any pretence to be cheerful. A natural joy lilted through her voice as she answered the flurry of questions about the wedding.

"So the duets were well received," her mother concluded with satisfaction.

"Absolutely," Gina enthused. "Mrs. King was delighted with the double act, and Peter Owen said he'd contact me about doing more with him."

"Well, that is a compliment, coming from a real professional. Not that your voice isn't lovely," she added with a warm ring of pride.

Gina laughed. "I know what you mean, but I don't know how serious he was. Peter Owen is the kind of guy who pours out flattery."

"You must come over for lunch and tell me all about it."

"Mum, I really have no more to tell," Gina quickly protested, though she hadn't mentioned the most important development from last night. A deep residue of fear and doubt seeded a reluctance to speak of Alex King to her mother. Not yet, she argued cautiously. Not until she was sure of what Alex actually wanted from their meeting today. "Actually, I've promised Marco a picnic so I can't come anyway," she excused. "Though thanks for the invite."

"Oh! Well, I'll catch up with you during the week. Give Marco my love. No, put him on the 'phone. I'll have a chat to him myself."

She couldn't risk Marco blurting out about the man

who'd slept with Mama. "He's outside playing. Leave it 'til next time. Okay?" Hopefully he'd forget that highly sensitive information in the excitement of more recent events before he did speak to her mother.

"Of course. I'm so glad you've had this opportunity, Gina. I'll go and tell your father you were a big success."

"Thanks, Mum. Bye for now."

Gina put the receiver down more thoughtfully this time, having reached the sobering realisation that while she certainly *matched* Alex King in bed, he might not see her as his match in other areas of his life. She remembered all the questions he had asked about her family and background after they'd danced, before he'd kissed her and then declared he wasn't being fair.

Not fair to kiss her while he was committed to marry Michelle Banks, or not fair, given her life would never meld with his? Sexual attraction had nothing to do with either. She'd had proof enough of that reality. In the darkness of the night, hadn't their desire for each other overridden every other sensibility? It was true of her, and most probably true of him, too.

Detaching himself from Michelle Banks might not mean anything in the long run, except he'd decided he didn't want to be married to the glamorous designer. It didn't mean he'd prefer Gina as his wife. She had to be very careful not to assume too much from Alex's wish to spend time with her today. The intimacy they had shared last night was fresh in his mind. He could be feeling guilty about it, simply wanting to clear himself with her.

On the other hand, he could have done that with his phone call, so it seemed more likely he did want to pursue the attraction. Besides, there really was no point in stewing over where it would or could lead. Gina knew in her heart, however reckless and wanton it might be, she was not about to deny herself the chance of any kind of relationship with Alex King. As far as she was concerned, it was a once-in-a-lifetime chance.

The plain truth was she didn't want to talk it over with her mother or anyone else, didn't want to hear doubts and fears and cautions. She could think up enough of them herself. Whatever the consequences, she was going to listen to her heart, first and foremost. Surely instincts were more important than opinions shaped by other factors.

Twelve o'clock. Gina had decided not to change the clothes she'd dressed herself and Marco in this morning. A picnic was a picnic, and she liked the outfit she'd planned to wear for breakfast at the castle, though ironically enough, there were more butterflies in her stomach right now than there were on the top that went with her denim skirt.

They turned into a wildly fluttering flock when Marco charged down the hall, yelling, "He's here, Mama! He's got a big cruiser like Uncle Danny's."

A four-wheel-drive vehicle, not a flash car. The thought instantly zipped into her mind that he'd undoubtedly driven something else on his dates with Michelle Banks. *Stop it!* she fiercely berated herself. This was a picnic, not a fancy outing. Besides, she couldn't imagine he'd have a child-safety seat for Marco, so they would have to go in her car anyway.

She picked up the all-purpose bag she had prepared to cover all contingencies for her son—Alex could hardly be expected to know a little child's needs or the accidents that could occur—and took a deep breath as she headed for the front door, pulled along by a highly excited Marco who was determinedly leading her out to "the nice man."

They stepped onto the veranda just as Alex started up the steps to it. He paused, looking at them both, as though taking a moment to assess what he was doing here. He was dressed in blue jeans and a royal-blue sports shirt, making the blue of his eyes so vivid, Gina couldn't tear her own gaze away from them. All her insides were helplessly aquiver, waiting for his judgement. Then he smiled and the nervous flutters melted in a wave of warm pleasure.

"Hi! It's good to see you again," he declared, including her son in the greeting. "Remember me, Marco? My name is Alex."

"Yes, I 'member. You weren't scared of the cane toad and you showed me the pretty fish," Marco smugly informed him.

Alex laughed, delighted by the recognition given. "Well, maybe we'll find something exciting to do this afternoon. I'll just carry your mother's bag for her and off we'll go." He acted on his words, remarking ironically, "You didn't need to bring anything, Gina."

"It's just stuff for Marco. I wasn't sure…"

"I figured all little boys like barbecued chicken, bananas and ice blocks." His eyes twinkled teasingly. "Right or wrong?"

She had to smile at his forethought. "Right enough." They were down the steps and following the path to the front gate before she remembered the transport problem. "You won't have a car seat for him. I thought..."

"Yes, I have. Got one installed at a hire-car place."

She stopped, amazed at the trouble he'd gone to.

"I did ask you both out with me," he gently reminded her.

"Yes. Thank you," she mumbled, blushing like a tongue-tied schoolgirl. Having a man outside her family care about her and her son's needs—a man as sexy and desirable as Alex King—simply hadn't happened to her since she'd become a widow. Up close like this, close and very personal, with the memory of their physical intimacy flooding through her mind, Gina found herself floundering in the situation instead of breezing through it with womanly confidence.

Alex simply took charge, ushering them to his big Land Cruiser, helping Marco into the hired seat and doing up the safety straps with practised ease, putting her bag in the back of the vehicle, then opening the passenger door for her. It was a big step up into the high cabin. Gina was trying to work out how to accomplish getting to her seat gracefully, acutely aware of Alex watching. He took the decision from her, scooping her off her feet and lifting her in.

"There! No problem," he said, the grin on his face tilting slightly as he looked into her eyes and saw she was remembering the passion that had triggered a similar action last night. "Couldn't resist," he murmured, and for an electrifying moment his gaze dropped to her mouth.

"Are you going to do up Mama's strap, too?" Marco asked.

Alex's swift intake of breath mirrored Gina's own breathless state. Her whole body was poised for a kiss, aching for it, but he pulled back and grabbed the safety belt, making much of stretching it across her and clicking it into its slot. "All strapped up now," he directed at Marco. "It's important to follow the rules."

He closed her door, and in the time it took for him to settle in the driver's seat, Gina managed to recover some semblance of composure, though inwardly she was buzzing with the excitement of knowing he was still as affected by her as she was by him.

"You didn't follow the rule of picking up your clothes," Marco stated critically. "Didn't your mama teach you that, Alex, like my mama did?"

Her heart stopped. There could be no mistake about what her son was referring to. No avoiding it, either. She felt Alex glance sharply at her and she rolled her eyes at him, expressively pleading for some innocent reply.

"Yes, my mother did lay down that rule, Marco, but I was so tired last night I forgot. I picked them up when I woke up this morning."

"So you were a good boy," Marco concluded with satisfaction.

"I was a bit late getting to it, but better late than never."

A strong hand reached across and squeezed Gina's. She squeezed back, grateful for his discreet and sensitive support. It forged a sense of togetherness again, as did the deliberate physical link. An exultant energy coursed up her arm and danced all the way to her heart.

"Okay?" he murmured.

She smiled at him, impulsively teasing. "You were very good."

Wicked pleasure leapt into his eyes. "So were you."

Three little words, delivered with feeling, and Gina's sexual awareness zoomed to a new high, coloured vividly by all she had experienced with Alex last night. She forgot about Marco sitting in the back seat, forgot to give directions to Crystal Cascades, even forgot they were going on a picnic.

Alex drove and she watched him drive, remembering how his hands had felt on her, the very male muscular strength of his thighs, the sheer perfection of his body, the sensations it had aroused in hers. She wanted to feel it all over again, and her mind sang with the certainty...so did he.

So did he!

CHAPTER ELEVEN

CONTROL....

Alex held on to the need for it with grim concentration as he drove Gina and Marco home from the picnic. It had been a good afternoon. He'd enjoyed being with both of them. He'd probably talked too much about his life, warmly encouraged by Gina, her interest even drawing him into reminiscences about his childhood, but at least talking had kept at bay the rampant desire to touch her, to recapture the incredibly intense sensuality that simmered in his memory.

Just the scent of her, right beside him in this cabin, was making it difficult to keep his focus on the road. Friendship was important, he told himself. It was more important than sex for any lasting relationship. But the very fact he'd felt she was in tune with everything he'd told her about himself this afternoon—understanding, appreciation, amusement so clearly in her eyes—made him want to leap into a deeper intimacy all the faster.

Not in front of the boy, he'd cautioned himself and that stricture still held true. Better to wait until Marco was more used to having him around, accepting him naturally as the man in his mother's life, the man who shared her bed. *And picked up his clothes!*

An ironic smile twitched at his lips. He'd give anything right now to be able to tear off Gina's clothes and

118

his own, to have all the pleasure of being naked with her, making love. She wanted it, too. Her body signals had been positive towards him all afternoon. He was sure it was just a matter of reaching out, taking…

No!

It could wait. She'd invited him to dinner on Wednesday night. A return of hospitality for the picnic, she'd insisted. Marco would undoubtedly be put to bed at a reasonable time. He would have Gina to himself— a situation she must be thinking of, as well—the two of them alone together in a private place.

Anticipation spread a treacherous excitement. He tried to block his arousal by rushing into speech. "I'll bring a bottle of wine on Wednesday evening. My contribution to dinner."

"If you like. But you didn't let me contribute to the picnic, Alex."

"That was my penance and my pleasure." He shot her a smiling appeal. "All worries gone now?"

Her sigh expressed happy satisfaction. "I've had a lovely afternoon. Thank you."

The warmth in her voice left him in no doubt of it. As he brought the Land Cruiser to a halt in front of her home, he told himself to be content with having established a good rapport with her. And with her son, who had nodded off in his car seat. If Marco stayed asleep as Alex carried him inside…

No! Don't start something you'll want to finish!

The circumstances were still risky.

Just see them to the door and take your leave while the going is good.

With fierce control over almost-irresistible temptation, Alex went through with his plan, aided by Marco's waking up the moment he was lifted out of his seat. The little boy's bright chatter made cheerful goodbyes relatively easy, and Alex was congratulating himself on not having transgressed his own ruling as he walked back down the path to drive away.

A white sports convertible pulled up behind his Land Cruiser as he opened the front gate.

Peter Owen stepped out of it.

Alex paused, tension spiralling through him like a wire spring being compressed, wanting to be released with explosive action. He didn't want Peter Owen with his rotten smarmy ways anywhere near Gina. And what the hell was he doing here? Not content to screw Michelle, he had to try his luck with Gina, too?

"Hi! Been visiting my new partner?" came the casually confident greeting.

Alex unclenched his jaw. "Partner?" he grated out, barely containing the violent feelings this man stirred.

"Gina of the fabulous voice," he rolled out with relish. "Wasn't she marvellous last night? Your grandmother certainly made a great find with her."

"Yes, she did," Alex agreed, but not *a find* for the likes of Peter Owen.

"Thought I'd drop in and line up some gigs with her."

"On the off chance she was here?"

"Well, she is, isn't she?" He nodded to the veranda where Gina and Marco were still standing, waiting to see Alex go…or find out what Peter Owen's arrival meant. "Luck is running with me."

The claim riled Alex further. Owen had the habit of seizing opportunity and turning it into his playground. "Don't press it too far, Peter," he warned. "My grandmother wouldn't like having *her find* diverted. She's taken quite a shine to Gina Terlizzi."

Amused eyebrows were raised but the eyes beneath them were hard and cold. "Oh, the Kings don't own everything around here, Alex. People can make choices. It's up to Gina what offers she decides to take."

True, Alex privately conceded, and he'd have to trust Gina's judgement on this, but he hated the thought of this slime oiling his way into her life. He remembered she'd said a career singing on the club circuit did not attract her, and hoped Owen could not persuade her otherwise.

"Of course, the choice is hers," he agreed with a shrug, realising to play too protective a hand might well represent a stimulating challenge to a man who thrived on any stimulation to his ego. "Just make sure she knows what you're offering."

A cynical amusement accompanied his retort. "I never promise more than I deliver."

And that was short and sweet in Peter Owen's book. Alex hid his contempt, not wanting to reveal what he'd witnessed the night before. "Fair enough!" he granted. "Though I hope you keep her situation in mind. She's got it tough, being a young widow with a child."

"Well, maybe I can give her a bright spot or two."

Alex had to resist the savage urge to smash his face

in, wiping out the raffish charm he used so successfully on women. "I'll leave you to it then," he bit out.

Owen raised his hand in a mock salute. "See you around, Alex."

He had to leave. He had no right to block the path to Gina's door, nor forcibly turn Peter Owen away from it. As he moved to get into the driver's seat of the Land Cruiser, he glanced back to the veranda and was surprised to see no one there. Gina had obviously decided to take Marco inside the house, not waiting for his conversation with Peter Owen to end. Perhaps she thought Owen had simply been catching up to him and wasn't here for her. Whatever the reason for Gina's absenting herself from his departure, he still had to go.

It was up to her to decide on any further connection with Owen. It *was* her choice. Just as Michelle's little peccadillo last night had been a choice, too. People did what they wanted to. He'd find out on Wednesday night what Gina wanted. In the meantime, he had to curb his protective and possessive instincts and wait.

One thing was certain.

He was not going to be part of a triangle with a man he despised.

"Which video would you like? *Jungle Boy?*" It was Marco's favourite, and Gina hoped it would keep him occupied while she spoke to Peter Owen.

"Yes, *Jungle Boy*," he agreed, settling himself on the lounge in ready anticipation.

Despite his nap in the Land Cruiser on the way home, he was still tired from all the excitement and activity of their picnic and it was highly probable he would doze off in the TV room while watching the video. Which would wreck his usual bedtime. Better that than giving Peter Owen fuel for gossip, Gina decided.

He was a gossipy kind of man. During their rehearsals last week, his conversations with her had been peppered with titillating bits about people he knew. Amusing but with a slight touch of malice in them. Gina didn't like the idea of being his newest bit of news, speculation running rife since he certainly knew of Alex's engagement to Michelle Banks. Being branded "the other woman" would be horrible.

It was disturbing enough that he'd turned up just as Alex was leaving. She had the strong impression Alex hadn't liked the coincidence, either. His back had gone quite rigid as Peter Owen had stepped out of the car and from what Gina had observed of their conversation, it hadn't relaxed him one bit.

It worried her what had been said. No doubt she'd find out soon enough. Her own urge to keep her relationship with Alex King private had driven her into the house, firstly to settle Marco out of the way, and secondly to put her bag out of Peter Owen's keen sight. His curiosity would be stirred enough at finding Alex here.

The doorbell rang just as the video came on. "Stay here, Marco," she firmly instructed. "Mama has to talk about singing with Peter Owen. It's business, okay?"

"Okay." His gaze was already glued to the screen.

Gina did her best to control her nervous apprehension as she went down the hall. This was nothing but a professional call, she told herself, though Peter Owen's decision to visit without telephoning first, didn't seem properly professional. In fact, she didn't like it at all. It was downright presumptuous of him to think he would be welcomed at any time. In fact, she didn't feel inclined to ask him into her home. It felt like an intrusion.

As a result, when she opened the door, she stepped straight out onto the veranda to do whatever talking was needed. "This is a surprise, Peter," she started off. "What brings you here?"

"The sweet smell of success," he answered rather grandly, accompanying the words with a smile full of charming appeal. "We were a hit last night, you know."

"I'm glad you think so, but…"

"Oh, I was lunching in the area and it occurred to me I should strike while the iron is hot, so I carried on here to lay out some ideas to you," he rolled out, explaining his presence and holding out the bait of future work with him.

Somehow the idea of being paired with Peter Owen—even professionally—made her feel uncomfortable. Last week she'd been focused on performing at the castle, in front of Alex King. Right now…maybe she was foolish to turn down a connection like this. Probably the more sensible course was to put the whole issue off until she could give it more consideration.

"I'm afraid this isn't a good time," she said apologetically. "Marco is tired and about to become fractious. I've settled him in front of the TV, though it may not hold his interest for long and…"

"Alex just brought you home from the castle?" Peter interjected, avid curiosity underlining every word.

"It's been a long day," she replied with a weary sigh, leaving the question unanswered.

"And you're feeling frayed," he chimed in understandingly.

She offered an ironic smile. "I am a bit. Was there anything urgent you had in mind, Peter?"

He reached out and ran a finger down her cheek as he pressed his interest. "Just don't forget how good we are together. I think we can capitalize on our duet act, Gina. Think about it. I'll call you during the week."

"All right," she agreed, though she didn't care for the over-familiar gesture.

His smile beamed approval. "Good girl!"

Inwardly she bridled, feeling she was being patronised, which of course she was, since he was the professional singer and much older than she was. All the same, *he* had come to her, not the other way around.

"I think I should tell you I only do weddings, Peter," she blurted out. "Performing in clubs is not for me."

"Ever tried it?" he bounced right back.

"No."

"You have a great voice, Gina Terlizzi. Time you let more people hear it." He slid out the understanding smile again. "I realise you're tired right now and your son takes up a lot of your day, but *you* have a life to live, too, and a gift that shouldn't be squandered." He raised his hand to ward off any further protest from her. "Sleep on it. I'll be in touch."

His argument carried the same attitude held by

Michelle Banks. Gina pondered this as she watched Peter return to his car. A gift…wasted. But was it really? She enjoyed singing, and she couldn't deny a good performance in front of an audience gave her a buzz. It was nice to be applauded, nice to give people pleasure.

Nevertheless, she had no delusions about how much work would have to go into pursuing and forging a career, and from all she'd read about the music business, there were far more lows than highs in it. Even with the step up Peter Owen might be able to give her, wouldn't he want favours in return for any success he brought her?

He drove off in his dashing white sports car—a status symbol proclaiming how successful he was? But how happy was he with his life? Two divorces behind him…

Gina shook her head as she went back inside her home and closed the door on an afternoon which had been more eventful than she could ever have imagined. She might have been more open to listening to Peter Owen, if not for Alex King's advent in her life. The chance of a relationship with him was more important to her than anything else and she didn't want to mess it up by not being available when he wanted to be with her.

Hardly a feminist viewpoint, she thought ironically, walking down the hall to the TV room. Marco had fallen asleep on the lounge. As she looked at her sleeping son, she saw Angelo in him so clearly, her heart turned over.

He deserved to have a father.

She wanted a husband.

Was Alex King the man who could give them the love and caring they'd lost?

Or was she chasing rainbows?

CHAPTER TWELVE

ALEX found Gina in the kitchen, mixing a dressing through a garden salad. "Marco wants you to kiss him goodnight," he informed her, grinning over the fun he'd had, reading a bedtime story to the little boy.

Her face lit with an instantly engaging smile. "I take it that Mr. Frumble has crashed everyone's boat in 'Busytown Regatta'?"

"With a vengeance."

She laughed. "Thank you for doing that, Alex. I must say, from what I heard, you put marvellous expression into it."

He thought how marvellously expressive she was—eyes, mouth, voice, shoulders, hands. Even her hair swayed as she spoke or gestured. Poetry in motion, vibrant, evocative, intensely emotive.

And he found her clothes very, very sexy. A soft blue clingy top moulded the lush fullness of her breasts, its wide scooped neckline giving a tantalising accessibility. The long swinging skirt she wore wasn't quite transparent but through the blue and pink and green floral pattern he could see the shadows of her legs. It was a tiered skirt, ribbons and frills—very romantic, very feminine. Michelle wouldn't have been caught dead in it but on Gina it looked beautiful, flimsily frivolous, emphatically female.

128

She wiped her hands on a towel and gestured to the kitchen bench. "Everything's ready. You could open the wine while I kiss Marco goodnight."

"Will do.".

He wanted to catch and kiss her as she swished past him, but contented himself with watching her, the natural sway of well-curved hips and a very provocatively rounded bottom, silver strappy sandals on bare feet. He imagined her wearing only a G-string underneath the skirt—definitely a blood-stirring thought!

A corkscrew lay next to the bottle of red wine he'd brought—a fine Cabernet Sauvignon which went well with most Italian cooking. It was, of course, an assumption that she would cook Italian, but the old heritage was strong, even though both he and Gina were born Australians.

He opened the bottle and took it into the dining room to fill the glasses she'd put out for them. He was struck by how much trouble she'd gone to; pretty tablemats, sparkling cutlery and china, scented candles, an artistic centrepiece of tropical leaves and little sprays of Singapore orchids, which reminded him that Gina worked part-time in a florist shop.

A pity she sang, as well.

The thought slid into his mind and Alex instantly pulled himself up on it. Her glorious voice was an integral part of Gina. She sang from her soul. To even wish to silence that would be a heinous crime against the person she was. He just didn't want her to be sucked in by guys like Peter Owen, used because of her talent.

All the same, a special talent such as hers should be

used. It would be wrong of him to get in the way of any chance she might want to take with it. But if she did choose to partner Peter Owen…

"Ready for dinner now?"

Gina swept in, carrying two salad bowls.

He was still holding the bottle of wine. Her sparkling warmth instantly evoked a smile. "Anything else I can help you with?" he asked, setting the bottle down on the table.

"The bread. I popped it into the oven to make it warm and crusty. It's a pull-apart loaf with cheese and herbs and bacon, but if you'd prefer plain…"

He shook his head. "Sounds great!"

Everything was great; the superb lasagne she'd cooked to her own special recipe with eggplant and mushrooms added to the usual mix, the tasty salads, the wine, but most of all her company. He loved the artless spontaneity of her responses to him, the entrancing lilt of her voice, the innate sensuality that flowed from her. It was a pleasure simply to watch her enjoy the food and wine. Not a word about watching her diet, not even when she served a deliciously rich chocolate mousse with coffee, happily relishing her own serving.

His gaze kept fastening on her mouth. Its softness and mobility fascinated him, its generous width when she smiled, the occasional lick of her tongue. He remembered its uninhibited passion, the incredible pleasure it gave moving over his body, its sensitivity, its instinctive eroticism.

Restraint was wearing very thin, the desire she aroused in him beating constantly at the gate of control

he'd imposed upon himself. Surely she realised by now
that this was a serious attraction, not just a physical lust
he wanted satisfied. Though there was no denying the
strength of the sexual element. It had seized his mind
to such an extent he wasn't even aware he'd fallen silent. The anticipation that had sizzled all evening was
surging into a burning need, searing away any other
thought.

Her amber eyes seemed to have turned into warm
liquid gold. Her mouth was slightly parted, but no
words came from it, either. Her lips trembled. She
scooped in a quick breath. Her eyelashes flickered as
she jerked her gaze away from his to stare at the table.

"More coffee?" she asked huskily.

As though sitting still had become unbearable, she
rose from her chair, reaching for his cup.

"No!" The word exploded from his throat. He was
on his feet, halting her action, grasping her wrist, drawing her into facing him.

Her gaze lifted to his, questing, wanting the same
answers he did. His heart drummed a fierce *yes* as he
gathered her into his embrace and she lifted her hands
to his shoulders, sliding them around to link behind his
neck. He pressed her closer, his whole body exulting in
the soft womanly feel of her, craving more.

Any last barrier of reserve was smashed by their first
kiss. The fuse of passion was instantly lit and swiftly
running, fuelled by taste and touch and the erotic scent
of her, the real and intense ardour of her response. He
needed the collision of flesh, needed her breasts bare,
her legs open to him. His hands pulled the stretchy top

from her skirt, scraped up the curve of her back, urgently seeking a bra clip.

She tore her mouth from his. "Not here, Alex," she panted.

"Gina…" It was groan of protest from every taut nerve-end in his body.

"I feel it, too." For a moment she laid a palm on his cheek, transmitting her own physical need as her eyes swam with the same yearning. "Come with me."

It was like a siren call, singing through his blood. Her hands glided down his chest, a lingering promise before she broke away from him, moving towards the door into the hall. Already she was lifting off the clingy top, her long hair being tossed carelessly as she drew it over her head. Her bare back gleamed enticingly, satin skin, broken by the white lines of a bra, being deftly unfastened.

Alex's feet were moving, following her bewitching lead. His hands tore at his shirt buttons. His fevered mind recalled Marco's chiding about dropped clothes. Gina was carrying hers, stepping out of her skirt as they headed down the hall. It floated around her thighs, her legs, and only a silky strip of nothing much left on her body, highlighting the soft curves of her naked bottom.

It was more erotic, more exciting than any striptease he'd ever seen. He unfastened his trousers, acutely aware of his erection straining against the frustrating fabric. He almost tripped, getting them off. She was trailing her skirt through the doorway of a dark room, soft lamplight switching on. Good…he wanted to see her, wanted every sense of her to be his.

She'd dropped her clothes on a chair and was facing him when he finally entered the room, her body lustrously silhouetted by the bedside lamp behind her. She looked like some wild pagan goddess, proud and primitive and breathtakingly beautiful. It made Alex stop to stand straight and tall himself, momentarily driven to match her naked dignity, to measure up as worthy of her choice.

It was a strange kind of respect but it felt right, like the squaring up of equals before meeting...and mating. He walked forward slowly, his gaze locked on hers, the desire charging through him gathering an extra vibrancy, a power that went beyond the ordinary. He dropped his clothes on top of hers, covering them as he wanted to cover her.

He rested his hands lightly at her waist, loving the feminine indentation above the flair of her hips. She ran hers up and over the muscles of his arms and shoulders, revelling in his male strength. He edged closer so that her large dark nipples brushed against his chest, closer, bringing her aureoles into contact, closer to savour the soft pressure of her lovely full breasts. He wondered if she could feel his heart pounding against them.

Her eyes seemed to glow with all the mysterious pleasure of being a woman, drawing him into her world, showing how it was to give this pleasure to a man. She swayed her lower body, rolling the hard length of his arousal across her stomach, moving closer herself to press her thighs against his. It was like having his whole body exquisitely electrified. Never had he been so acutely conscious of his own masculinity and the complementary nature of their separate sexualities.

This time he kissed her without all the pent-up need of waiting for days. He kissed her, wanting to explore every nuance of sensation she evoked, each seductive graduation of passion, of tantalising intimacy. Her mouth was like a treasure cave of rich, wondrous rewards every time he entered it. He moved her onto the bed, wanting to kiss every glorious part of her, feast himself on her femininity.

He wallowed in the lush feel and provocative taste of her magnificent breasts, grazed his mouth over her stomach, revelling in the erotic spasms of muscles responding to the trail of warm kisses and the sensual sweep of his tongue. He reached the apex of her thighs, felt the quiver of her legs as he moved in to savour and caress the most hidden parts of her sex. The moist heat of her was intoxicating, her responsive excitement addictive.

"Alex, please..." Fingers tugging at his hair, her body arching, yearning. "I need you now...now..."

Her words were like trumpets ringing in his ears as he surged up and over her, bringing himself to meet and answer her plea, elated by her need, and with the first exultant plunge deep inside her, the soar of his own pleasure was intense. They moved together in a rhythm that focused all his energy on feeling this sweet innermost part of her, the melting waves that clutched at him, squeezing, releasing. He concentrated on taking himself as far as this union would allow, revelling in the sheer ecstasy of pushing her to climax after climax, rolling through them, loving the throaty little cries, the erotic sounds of her pleasure, until finally, finally, he could not contain the driving rush of his own need, the fierce seizure of muscles that demanded release.

He heard himself cry out as he buried himself deeply inside her in the last ultimate act of mating, a climactic burst that spilled from him like tidal waves of explosive sensation, breaking into a warm haven that welcomed him and held him safe until he was entirely spent. Then the glorious contentment of simply lying with her, still intimately joined, embraced by the softness of her legs and arms wound around him, the lovely cushion of her breasts, the scented silkiness of her hair.

What more could a man ask?

She had given him—was still giving him—the most perfect pleasure he'd ever known…incomparable to anything else.

Words alien to his usual thinking slid into his mind— a state of bliss. He smiled over them…no exaggeration at all. Absolute truth. Then for a while, he didn't think at all. Basking in bliss with Gina Terlizzi was the best possible use of time.

It was she who stirred first, sighing, shifting her head so as to look at him, her face expressing a languorous satisfaction, her smile reminiscent of a thousand sensual delights, her eyes a darkly gleaming amber trapping sparkles of golden joy.

"You are amazing, Alex. Thank you for being so…so generous in your loving."

Generous?

He smiled, thinking how much he'd indulged his own

desires, yet it was Gina herself who had inspired them, the woman she was and how she made him feel.

"No, you are the amazing one," he murmured, lifting a hand to trace her lips with his fingertips. "You invite the freedom to give instincts full play and you let me follow them without any drawing back."

"Why would I? You gave me more pleasure than I could dream of."

"Then I'd say we're very well matched."

Her smile tilted ironically. "In bed."

"Oh, I wouldn't limit it to bed." He grinned teasingly. "If that lasagne was a fair sample of your cooking I'd be happy to share a meal with you anytime."

She grinned back. "I'm glad you enjoyed it."

"I enjoy everything about you."

Her head tilted as though she didn't quite believe him. "I'm not very sophisticated."

"Sophistication…" *if she was thinking of Michelle's superficial glamour* "…can be vastly over-rated. I love being with you, Gina. No false images."

She frowned over that last phrase and he wished he hadn't said it. A sour note. Yet in the next instant it led his mind straight to even more acid thoughts on Peter Owen and a pertinent remark tumbled out of his mouth.

"I hope you realise Peter Owen is a user, particularly where women are concerned. I wouldn't want to see you hurt by him."

. Her frown deepened. "Do you mean personally or professionally?"

He grimaced at his urge to interfere, knowing it was seeded by a jealous possessiveness he didn't even like in himself. "I was just concerned when he called on you so casually last Sunday afternoon."

"I wasn't expecting him, Alex."

"Hey...you don't have to answer to me," he asserted. "I know he can be very charming."

"I meant...there is nothing personal," she went on earnestly. "He came about work. Some singing engagements."

He couldn't stop himself from asking, "Are you interested in taking on more engagements with him?"

"I don't know. I put him off. It was the wrong time to talk business. Marco was tired after the picnic. I'm to meet Peter tomorrow after I finish work." Her eyes held an anxious query. "I thought there was no harm in listening to what he has to say."

"No harm at all," he assured her, suppressing his own dislike at the whole idea. Peter Owen didn't have one moral bone in his body. On the other hand, if his professional interests were being served, maybe he would keep his hands off Gina, especially if she made it clear they weren't welcome.

"If he offers you a deal tomorrow, make sure it's a fair one to you, Gina. You could become a very strong drawcard for his act, so don't undersell yourself."

She gave a self-conscious little laugh. "Alex, he's the professional. Compared to him, I'm an amateur."

"You have a wonderful voice. I'd rather listen to you than him any day."

"Well, thank you, but..."

"No buts." He cupped her cheek and chin, fixing her gaze on his as he assured her of her true worth. "When you sang together last Saturday night, you were the star, Gina. It was your voice that enthralled the audience.''

"That could be prejudice speaking, Alex.''

"Then ask my grandmother. She'll tell you. Don't make a quick decision with him. That's all I'm saying."

"I won't,'' she promised, though her eyes seemed to be searching his for other reasons not to make a connection with Peter Owen. "Do you think I should pursue a career with my singing?''

"Only you can make that choice, Gina. You know best what's in your heart.''

She said nothing. Her eyes seemed to be wanting him to say more yet what more could he say? He'd been as fair as he could. He wasn't about to plead Peter Owen's case for him. In fact, what he wanted most was to wipe Owen right out of her mind.

He leaned over and kissed her. She welcomed him so fiercely, the desire to have her again charged through his entire body. Yet subtly, persuasively, Gina pressed her wish to make love to him this time, and Alex found himself so entranced by her kisses and caresses, he didn't want to take over.

It was quite awesome, the many ways she excited him; watching her, feeling her body move around his, the incredible sensitivities she aroused and played on. In some deeply possessive sense, it was as though she was imprinting herself on him—*her man*—and Alex couldn't help revelling in being so intensely desired.

Finally she straddled him, controlling the rhythm herself this time, voluptuously magnificent as she teased and took him to exquisite peaks of excitement, holding him there, holding him as though she never wanted to let him go. Her hair swayed over her breasts, a tantalisingly primitive picture, and it stirred the caveman in him. In a surge of wild energy, he swept her back onto the bed and took her, wanting to be the possessor, needing her to feel his imprint, and there was a savage joy in bringing them both to a triumphant climax.

She evoked so many feelings in him—more than he'd realised could be felt. Even as he lay with her afterwards, he was aware that the tenderness she drew from him was all-encompassing, an emotional level that no other woman had ever tapped. He didn't want to leave her, but time ticked on and common sense insisted it was a weeknight and they both had work to go to in the morning.

"Are you free on Saturday, Gina?" he asked, looking ahead to the weekend, wanting all the time he could get with her.

"Not really." Her sigh sounded rueful. "I'm booked to sing at a church wedding on Saturday afternoon, then later at the reception. I'll be taking Marco to my parents' home beforehand."

"What about Sunday?"

"It's free."

"Will you spend it with me?"

She hesitated. "Marco, too?"

He'd forgotten the little boy asleep just down the hallway in his own lovingly decorated little boy's room. As much as he wanted Gina to himself, he knew instinctively she was not the kind of mother who would let her son be ignored. Besides, he really liked Marco.

"Of course," he answered easily, his mind leaping ahead for some activity that would involve the boy. "I meant to check on the cane plantation. We can have lunch with the manager and his wife. They have a couple of young children. Marco might enjoy playing with them. How does that sound?"

She snuggled happily. "Sounds great!"

He smiled, thinking he'd take her on a long walk.

He'd never made love in a cane field.

There was a first time for everything.

CHAPTER THIRTEEN

"WHAT has made you so happy?" her aunt inquired, cocking her head assessingly as she watched Gina select precisely where to place a flamingo lily in the floral arrangement she was working on. "You sing, you hum, and your face is wreathed in smiles."

Gina grinned at her, brimming over with the wonderful pleasure of being desired by the man she desired. "Oh, I just feel life is looking up for me."

Her aunt arched an eyebrow. "Might it have something to do with Peter Owen?"

Gina sighed. "Has Mum been speculating with you?"

"Well, I know you're meeting with him this afternoon. And your brother, Danny, has just called to say he's on his way to pick up Marco."

"Danny's going to have a look at white-water rafting and he thought Marco would enjoy watching it, too," she quickly explained.

"Leaving you free…"

"It will be easier to talk business with Peter on my own. But that's all it is, *Zia*. Just talking."

"Ah…" She rolled her eyes expressively. "…who knows where it might lead. It's time you spread your wings, Gina."

Luckily, an incoming customer drew her aunt back

to the showroom at the front of the shop, cutting short the personal conversation. Gina was discomforted by the obvious gossip sessions running hot within the family circle. Of course, Isabella Valeri King's interest in her had set the tongues wagging, then singing the duets with Peter Owen at the castle had added to the brew of speculation. Neither had anything to do with how she felt today…after last night with Alex.

Should this new involvement be mentioned now?

She still shied from giving out such a highly personal piece of information. Even though Alex's invitation for Sunday assured her he really did enjoy her company— beyond the bedroom—she wasn't sure how deeply the attraction went for him. What if she simply had a novelty value, given his disenchantment with *false images?* Was that phrase a pertinent link to his break-up with Michelle Banks?

The urge to keep this part of her life private remained strong. One afternoon and two nights of being together could hardly be a called *a relationship,* not in any decisive terms. Maybe after Sunday…

Danny arrived in his usual rush and cheerful hustle. He was so accustomed now to working with tourists, his professional manner overflowed into everything. He collected Marco from the backyard of the shop and carried him off on his shoulder, both of them whooping excitedly about going on an adventure.

For the rest of the morning a steady stream of customers kept Gina and her aunt busy. Orders came in for deliveries to the maternity ward at Calvary Hospital— Gina always liked doing those happy arrangements, giving new mothers pleasure—and she was occupied in the backroom choosing the flowers for them when her aunt came to the door with a shock announcement.

"Alex King's fiancée wants you out front."

Gina was stunned speechless.

"Michelle Banks, the fashion designer," her aunt prompted.

"But..." She barely caught herself back from blurting out the engagement was broken. Yet if Michelle was claiming...or maybe her aunt was assuming...

"Apparently Miss Banks attended the wedding at the castle on Saturday night," her aunt went on, "and wants to discuss songs with you for her own wedding over lunch." Her smile was lit with delight at her niece's sudden rise to fame. "Your voice is now in demand, Gina. Better get going."

"But..." she spluttered again, totally flummoxed by these further statements. Michelle's wedding was supposed to be *off!*

"Don't worry about the maternity deliveries. They can wait until you get back." Her aunt actually rounded her up, thrust her shoulder-bag into her hand, and gave her a push, urging, "You can't miss out on singing at a King wedding."

Had Alex lied to her?

Her mind buzzing with heart-wrenching questions, Gina forced her legs to carry her towards a confrontation with the woman who shouldn't belong in Alex's life anymore, who shouldn't be calling herself his fiancée, nor planning a wedding with him.

Michelle Banks was idly glancing around the display

arrangements designed to catch the eye of passers-by and hopefully draw them into the florist shop. Her highly polished beauty instantly put another knife into Gina's heart. She wore a silk slacksuit in a shimmering grey-green pattern that picked up the striking colour of her eyes, and her golden hair was piled on top of her head, drawing immediate attention to her long, swanlike neck and the classic bone structure of her face.

She bestowed a lofty, slightly patronising smile on Gina, making her feel lowly, despite her average height, and definitely *common* in her little lime green shift. "There you are!" she said, as though she'd had to go to tedious lengths to find her. She waved her left hand in an eloquent gesture of frustration as she added, "You disappeared from the ballroom before I could speak to you on Saturday night."

The glittering diamond engagement ring on her third finger was as mesmerising to Gina as the swaying head of a cobra. And just as deadly to the hopes she'd been nursing. Alex had taken her out of the ballroom. Alex had kissed her, made passionate love to her, had told her…but his ring was still on Michelle Banks' hand.

"Your employer informs me you're free to come to lunch and I'd very much like to discuss my wedding plans with you," Michelle went on, exuding supreme confidence in Gina's falling in with her wishes. "Shall we go?" She headed towards the door. "I understand there's quite a pleasant little coffee shop just along the street."

Michelle opened the door, pausing to give Gina a look of arrogant expectation. It made Gina want to dig her heels in and flout the other woman's preset plans, but the painful need to clear up the situation drove her forward. She caught a glittery satisfaction in Michelle's eyes as she stepped past her to the sidewalk outside and gritted her teeth against the surge of sickening hatred it evoked.

Alex couldn't love this woman, she argued fiercely.

False images.

Her frantic mind seized on the phrase he had spoken last night. Maybe he had let Michelle keep the ring when he'd broken the engagement. Maybe...yet why had she come, talking about her wedding to him? Who was lying? For what purpose?

Michelle prattled on about the duets with Peter Owen as they walked along to the coffee shop. Gina barely heard a word, too consumed by turbulent emotions to concentrate on listening. Michelle selected a table in a corner and quickly commanded the attention of a waitress. She didn't bother looking at a menu, ordering a Caesar salad and black coffee for herself.

Gina found herself automatically ordering a cappuccino and a Foccacio melt—ham, tomato and cheese. It was doubtful she'd be able to eat a bite of it but that was irrelevant. This meeting with Michelle Banks wasn't about having lunch. The order simply got the waitress out of the way. The moment she moved off, Michelle dropped her *social* mask and floored Gina with a sly sardonic punch.

"I take it you and Alex are still hot for each other."

Gina felt her jaw drop with shock.

Michelle sighed. "Good old lust. It does raise its

wicked head now and then. I hope you're not getting yourself into some serious twist about it. It only ever runs a brief course.''

"You know? About Alex and me?'' Gina choked out, reeling from this revelation.

Michelle laughed, her eyes dancing with cynical amusement. "Of course I know, darling. It was perfectly obvious on Saturday night that Alex couldn't keep his hands off you. I don't really fancy him making love to me while he's thinking of someone else so I told him to go and get it out of his system with you.''

Gina's stomach cramped. They had discussed her as an object of desire before Alex had come home, come to the nursery suite and...she felt sick. The sex that night hadn't been unplanned. It had been premeditated. Her mind jolted through the train of logic Michelle was spelling out.

"But...you expect him to come back to you,'' she managed to say with a semblance of calm consideration.

"Naturally. We have a great partnership going.'' Michelle shrugged off the infidelity as though it were nothing. "A bit of bed-hopping makes no difference to the more solid things we share.''

"And do you...bed-hop...too?''

Another shrug. "If someone tasty comes along. Actually, Alex was well aware I fancied someone else on Saturday night and was a bit peeved because he was frustrated over not feeling right about taking you. Had some attack of conscience because you're his grandmother's protégé. I told him you were a grown woman and if you wanted him, why not satisfy each other?''

"Get it out of the system..." Gina repeated, feeling she was dying inside.

"Exactly. We're just taking a bit of time out from each other at the moment, letting things swing."

"Why are you telling me this?"

Michelle gave her a pained look. "I just had the feeling I might have made a bad judgement call with you. A widow, wanting a bit on the side, seemed right, but Alex is a prize in any woman's book, and it occurred to me you might think you can get your hooks in and end up making trouble that could be embarrassing for everyone."

"So you want me to understand it's just a little fling that will burn itself out. Enjoy it while I can."

"Well, looking at it sensibly...what do you think? I don't mean to be offensive, but...Alex King and you?" Her eyes mocked any image of lasting togetherness. "Can you really see it, Gina?"

That was the crux of the whole issue.

And the diamond ring on Michelle's left hand kept winking its devastating reality at Gina.

Time out.

It made more sense than anything else.

No future with her...just time out for now.

Peter Owen sat in the Coral Reef Bar, sipping a whisky as he waited for Gina Terlizzi to join him. Normally it would amuse him to think of Alex King having it off with some woman other than Michelle. And serve Michelle right, the two-faced bitch. But Gina Terlizzi?

He shook his head. For all his cynicism about

women, Gina was different. Just a sweet kid really, open-hearted, devoted to her little boy, not the kind to play around with. Even he recognised that. What the hell was wrong with Alex King's vision? Blinded by lust? Peter frowned, never having considered the highly controlled Alex King that kind of guy.

Still, difficult to doubt Michelle's version of events since he himself had seen the man leaving Gina's house last Sunday. All uptight he'd been about Peter calling there, too. And no doubt about Michelle being totally peeved last night, coming to his apartment and spilling her anger out to him after finding Alex's car outside Gina's house.

"He's taking it too far," she'd stormed. "I'll spike his guns. I'll lay it out to her it's just a payback for my little dalliance with you, Peter."

"You keep my name out of it, Michelle," he'd retorted with very deliberate menace. Gina Terlizzi was serious business and he didn't want her turned off him by something that was utterly meaningless.

He took another sip of whisky, thinking he'd rip a few mats out from under Michelle's slippery feet if she screwed up the deal he wanted to make with Gina. He had plans for that girl. Not only might she give his career a new shot in the arm, but...if he took the job as director of musicals for the Galaxy Theatre in Brisbane and he could produce a new star...the birth of two new careers...

He caught sight of Gina entering the lounge and swivelled on his bar stool with a warm smile of welcome to put her at ease. She didn't smile back. She aimed herself at him and moved forward like a sleep-walker on automatic propulsion, no vivacity at all in her body, blank face, dull eyes.

Michelle had done a real number on her, Peter thought savagely, and for once in his life, felt a deep shame for even being loosely connected to this conse-quence. The slaughter of innocence was a miserable thing. He rose from his chair to meet her, to gently steer her to an armchair and see her safely seated.

"I'll get you a drink. What would you like, Gina?"

Her name focused her gaze on him, but in her eyes was a struggle to come up with an answer.

"A gin and tonic?" he offered, thinking she needed a good slug of alcohol.

A relieved nod and a huskily whispered, "Thank you."

Gina tried to pull herself together as she watched Peter Owen go to the bar for drinks. He might offer her some kind of positive step into a real future. Not dreams. Not fantasy. Something she could do for herself. It was im-portant to listen.

Alex didn't like him.

But what did it matter what Alex thought now?

What she decided to do wouldn't intrude on his life. Not his real life. And however much she wanted to, she couldn't go to bed with him anymore, not knowing it was just a lustful fling on his part. That was too sham-ing, too humiliating.

Anger boiled up in her as she recalled Alex saying Peter was a user of women. How did he see himself?

Of course, he could undoubtedly defend his actions on the grounds it was *mutual* desire, and where was the hurt in that? None at all if she was like Michelle.

So what if Peter Owen was a *user!* Having learnt such a salutory lesson from this experience with Alex, she wouldn't be so stupid as to think there was any caring for her beyond the talent she had for singing. And even Alex had conceded Peter could be helpful in establishing a professional career with her voice.

If it didn't interfere too much with being a proper mother for Marco, she would try it. At least it would be something to focus her energy on, something that might lead somewhere good in the days, weeks, years that stretched so emptily ahead of her right now.

Don't undersell yourself, Alex had said.

How could someone who was worth nothing undersell herself?

Totally soul-sick, Gina watched Peter carrying their drinks back to the table. Whatever he offered her was better than nothing. Listen to him, she fiercely told herself. If Peter had a proposition that was workable within her circumstances, not neglecting Marco's needs, she would say *yes*.

As to what terms would be fair, how could she judge? She would have to trust Peter on that. The end result had to be more money for her anyway. So best to say yes. Go home with something positive to think about, something positive to look forward to.

The dream of Alex King wanting to share her life, be her husband and the father of her children, was gone, and she couldn't see any other man ever filling that role.

Time to start building a different dream.

"Here we are!"

Peter set the drinks on the table and settled himself in the chair opposite hers. No sexy flirtatiousness in his eyes today. He seemed to be viewing her with sympathetic concern. Was her inner distress so obvious?

"One thing I want to get straight first, Peter," she blurted out, realising there were some terms she had to enforce if she was to be comfortable working with him.

He nodded encouragingly.

"This is business, right?"

He nodded again.

"You have a...a sexy manner. I don't want you to come onto me in any shape or form. We sing together. That's it."

He heaved a sigh. A cynical disillusionment settled on his face. "If it's there, and I feel like it, I take it." His shrug dismissed that aspect of his life as non-consequential. "My experience is I'm no good at personal relationships, but a celibate life doesn't appeal, either." His eyes bored directly into hers. "I know it's not there with you, Gina. Nor do I want it to be there. It would interfere with business. So, believe me, no amount of randiness would make me risk losing your voice."

Could she believe him?

He leaned forward, forearms resting on the table, his hands spread in open appeal. "In this business, a sexy manner helps to sell a performance. It creates an intimacy with the audience. I'm not about to tone that down. On the other hand, should we come to an agreement, and I very much hope we can, at all times off-stage I shall treat you as my little sister. I don't want any friction between us. I want us to work in harmony to produce the best act we can. Okay?''

He looked sincerely intent on persuading her this was so. ''A little sister,'' she repeated, not quite seeing the very raffish Peter Owen in the role of big brother.

His mouth tilted ironically. ''I've never had a family. You'll have to teach me how I should behave.''

''No family?'' That was unimaginable to Gina.

He grinned. ''I'm just an orphan boy making my own way in the world.'' The grin winked out and a very focused energy was aimed at her as he added, ''I have learnt how to protect my interests and you come under that umbrella, Gina. You won't get any grief from me. In fact, I'll be the first to stand between you and anything that might have a negative effect on your performance.''

He was telling her that above everything else he was a professional. She could count on the success of their singing partnership being his prime consideration where she was concerned.

''Fair enough,'' she murmured gratefully. ''What do you have in mind?''

He explained.

She liked the plan.

It was easy to agree to it.

It felt good to have something to look forward to.

CHAPTER FOURTEEN

DANNY was helping himself to leftover lasagne and feeding Marco at the same time when Gina arrived home from her meeting with Peter. The congenial understanding between uncle and nephew reminded her that Marco had more than enough male relatives to take the place of a father—her brothers, her own father, Angelo's family. Her son was certainly not deprived of male influence and interest.

"What did you think of the white-water rafting?" she asked, managing a smile that projected interest.

"It was fun, Mama," Marco instantly piped up.

"Sure was," Danny agreed. "I think I'll get my finger in that tourist pie."

"Not too dangerous?"

"Not if it's properly run. They had a good operation going on the Tully River." Danny, who was whip-lean despite the mountains of food he consumed, pointed to the lasagne left on his plate. "Better than Mum's."

"Different recipe."

He grinned. Even at twenty-four, he was still very boyish, though very attractive with his sun-bleached streaky hair and bright brown eyes which were dancing at her with a teasing twinkle. "Did you cook it for Alex King?"

Gina froze. Any connection now to Alex King was

153

anathema to her, and everything within her recoiled from having to answer questions about him.

"Oh, come on. Spill the beans," Danny coaxed. "Marco said he was here last night and read him a bedtime story."

"He called by," she returned stiffly. Impossible to deny his presence with Marco listening. "I'd left something at the castle," she added in explanation...*like Alex King in her bed there,* her mind mocked. "You know Marco grabs anyone he can to read him a story. Alex was kind enough to oblige."

"Alex now, is it?" Danny commented stirringly.

She grimaced at him. "Get off it, Danny. He's engaged to Michelle Banks."

He shrugged. "Not married to her, though. There's many a fall twixt the cup and the lip."

"Not likely in this direction. Now if you don't mind..."

"Okay, okay! So what happened with Peter Owen?"

"I'm doing a gig with him at the Coral Reef Lounge tomorrow night."

He whistled appreciatively. "Fast work! And classy venue!"

"Yes. Top of the line. Which means I have a lot to prepare tonight."

"I'm off!" He stood and ruffled Marco's curls in passing. "Be good for your mum, chum." He gave her a brotherly smooch. "Knock 'em dead tomorrow night. Got my own gig with the cane toad races so can't be there cheering you on, but I'll be thinking of you."

"Thanks, Danny. For today, too."

"No worries. Marco and I are buddies."

He left on that cheerful note, the Alex King visit brushed aside and dropped as inconsequential, much to Gina's relief. She needed to close the door on all her treacherous feelings for Alex and pretend the whole shameful affair had never happened.

Which was much easier decided than done.

Nevertheless, with determined purpose, Gina kept herself very busy for the next couple of hours, making sure her clothes and Marco's were ready for tomorrow, bathing her son and putting him to bed, making calls to her aunt and her mother, both of whom were atwitter at the news of Peter Owen's offer.

Her aunt insisted Marco stay with her tomorrow night since her mother was taking him on Saturday. Gina felt a stab of guilt at her very young son being shuttled around the family while she pursued her own course, but how could he come to any harm amongst people who loved him? She would always be the main constant.

Gina was still salving her conscience on that point when the telephone rang, no doubt an afterthought or extra piece of advice from her mother. Wearily she picked up the receiver, girding herself up to once more sound reasonably excited about her forthcoming debut on a stage that had nothing to do with eisteddod concerts or weddings. Never mind the dark misery dragging on her heart. She had a bright step ahead of her.

"Hi! What did you forget?" she rattled out.

"Gina…"

Her leaden heart came to a dead halt.

Alex King's voice!

She closed her eyes, trying to shut out a thousand haunting images of him.

"I've been thinking of you all day," he went on.

Likewise! her mind snapped. Though not on the same scale of pleasure as his tone told her his thoughts had been. Her heart revived and started catapulting around her chest, gaining painful strength as anger took over from shock.

"I don't want to wait until Sunday," he purred. "I was wondering if you were free tomorrow night."

Still hot for her and wanting a system overload before going back to Michelle! Gina gritted her teeth against the bile that rose at that thought.

"No, I'm not free, Alex," she bit out. "I have an *engagement*...singing with Peter Owen."

Proving there was life after him!

A pause, a sigh. "So you liked the deal he offered you."

"Well, let me put it this way. I know where I am with Peter. I didn't with you, Alex."

Her hard tone gave him more pause for thought. A tense puzzlement answered her. "What do you mean, Gina?"

"I had a visit from your fiancée today," she stated with pointed emphasis.

"I told you I'm no longer engaged to Michelle," he shot back.

"She was wearing your ring, Alex."

He cursed under his breath. "I let her keep it. Since

I was ending the relationship it seemed...ungentle-
manly...to demand its return.''

Ungentlemanly?

A rocket of rage exploded in Gina's head.

''Was it gentlemanly to discuss your attack of lust
for me with her? To plot a course of getting me out of
your system with your fiancée's permission? Just a bit
of time out to slake a temporary passion?''

''She said that to you?''

His voice rose in shock—shock at having his duplic-
ity revealed, no doubt. Gina bored in, fury overflowing.
''Yes, she explained about her own *lustful* fancy for
another man on Saturday night, and how such urges
meant nothing in the big picture. A bit on the side for
her...a bit on the side for you...''

''The bitch!'' he thundered, a mountain of outrage in
his voice rolling over her.

It was just noise, Gina told herself. Nothing but distracting noise.

''Actually, she wasn't bitchy at all,'' she said with
commendable calm. ''It was really quite kind of her to
let me know how matters really stood, stopping me
from getting foolish ideas that might embarrass everyone. A pity you hadn't been more honest, Alex.''

''Honest! Michelle wouldn't know honesty if she
tripped over it.''

''What a splendid marriage the two of you will have,
bed-hopping wherever the fancy takes you...''

''You think I want that?''

''I don't know. I don't know anything about how you
lead your life or what you want from it. If you were

excusing what you did with me on the basis of mutual desire, let me state here and now I am no longer *hot* for you, and I am not *free* for you, not tomorrow night nor any other night.''

"Gina, she was lying, manipulating…''

"For what purpose, Alex?'' Ice dripping off her tongue.

"God knows!'' Much heat from him. "Possibly malicious spite because I preferred you to her.''

"For a novel bit of sex?''

"No! In every way!'' he asserted even more heatedly.

"Like you can't wait to get in my bed again. That's why you're calling me, isn't it?'' she bitterly accused.

He hesitated, possibly a bit of honesty catching up with him, Gina thought savagely.

"And you meant to keep calling until the passion burnt out,'' she mocked.

A swift intake of breath—quick, tense speech. "I appreciate—believe me—how clever and convincing Michelle can be when she's serving her own interests. For a long time she played a very appealing role for me, with only the occasional slip of the mask—a few discomforting moments that I overlooked because she dazzled on other fronts. But that's over, Gina. She might think she can draw me back to her if she gets rid of you, but she can't. She used the ring to cover her lies with a semblance of truth.''

"A few hard truths, wouldn't you say, Alex?'' she challenged, not prepared to shift from the ground she'd so painfully reached.

"Michelle's truths are not mine," he claimed with vehement force.

"Well, why don't you go and sort them out with her? I don't care for the role of meat in the middle, thank you very much."

"I'm sorry you were cast in that role, Gina, but it wasn't by me. And I will most certainly sort it out with Michelle," he stated grimly.

"I wish we'd never met. I've never been made to feel like…like a disposable person before."

"Don't say that. It's not true."

"The truth is…you came onto me too fast for me to believe anything else. A widow from the backblocks of Cairns…and Alex King—*the prize*. That's what Michelle called you and she's right. What else could a man in your position want from me except…"

"A woman with heart, Gina," he cut in. "Something Michelle never was."

"Then find someone who fits all your requirements if you're not happy with her. Goodbye, Alex."

"Wait!"

She'd already moved the telephone receiver away from her ear. Even so, his command came over the line loud and clear, making her hesitate for a moment. The instinctive tug towards him had a power that almost swamped common sense, but today's pain erected the barrier that had to be maintained. A brittle but determined sense of self-worth forced the receiver down— disconnection firm and absolute!

Before going to bed she took a sleeping tablet, telling herself she needed a good deep rest if she was to perform well tomorrow night. It didn't work as quickly as she hoped it would. For a long time she lay in the darkness, the memory of sharing this bed with Alex King last night too vivid to block out.

There was no denying she'd wanted him. He wasn't entirely to blame for what had happened between them. She had invited him here, madly bent on keeping him in her life despite the perspective Michelle had hammered home today.

False images...

The tormenting little phrase applied to so much.

The diamond engagement ring could be one of them. Michelle might very well have lied, aiming to get rid of any threat to achieving her own ambition. Gina wanted to believe Alex had at least been truthful on that score, though she felt he had come to her on some kind of swinging rebound, triggered by Michelle's desire to dally with someone else.

It could be the contrast that had drawn him—a woman with heart—but other things were just as important to the success of a relationship. Gina knew she wasn't his social equal. And as kind as he'd been to Marco, her son wasn't his. The Kings were like a dynasty. When it came to marriage, they would want their own children.

It had been utter madness to dream of something different.

She had to fill her mind with something else—the songs to be sung tomorrow night. The words were all about love...memories, hopes, yearnings, loss. Easy for her to feel them, she thought with bleak irony. Did a professional singer sell her soul? No, music was simply a way of expressing it.

The music of the night…

CHAPTER FIFTEEN

THE Coral Reef Lounge was packed, much to Peter Owen's satisfaction. Friday nights were always good business, but he'd plugged this evening's special performance on local radio this morning, organised the billboard to catch the interest of passers-by, and the response was even better than he'd hoped. The greatest songs from favourite musicals appealed to all ages—a sure drawcard—and he'd given Gina Terlizzi's voice a big wrap, as well. A star of the future.

He hoped Gina wasn't having an attack of nerves in the dressing-room. They'd rehearsed most of the afternoon and she'd been on fire, ready to sock the songs to the audience with all the voice power she had. Now all geared up in the bronze evening dress she'd worn for the wedding duets last week, she looked every bit a star.

The question was whether to tell her that the King family was here in force, Isabella herself with her three grandsons, notably Alex looking moody and magnificent.

Would it put Gina off or turn her on?

Once she was on stage and in the spotlight, she might not see them. The audience could remain a blur to her. It might be better to keep her focused on the songs— no distraction. On the other hand, the urge to *show* Alex King she could be a star in her own right might just push her to that extra edge of performance that created magic.

Alex King checked his watch again. Time was crawling. Gina's debut on stage here was scheduled for nine o'clock and there were still six minutes to go. Peter Owen was doing his thing on the grand piano, warming up the audience, but Alex was incapable of appreciating the man's talent in these circumstances. His whole mind was bent on projecting to Gina that he was here for her.

Very publicly *here for her,* with his entire family in tow to witness where his heart lay, and it sure as hell wasn't with Michelle Banks. As far as he was concerned, Michelle had ceased to exist. He'd told her so in unequivocal terms last night. And threatened her with legal consequences if she used his ring to make false claims again. His fury over that deceit put an even finer edge on his taut nerves as he waited for Gina's appearance.

She had to realise he didn't view her as a bit on the side. Nor would he treat her as one. He'd introduce her to his brothers, make sure she understood that his grandmother was aware and approved of a relationship between them. Surely such a public statement would have its impact on the sleazy doubts Michelle had planted in her mind.

Isabella Valeri King sat very comfortably, listening to Peter Owen's virtuoso performance. He really was an excellent pianist. She was looking forward to the act he'd worked out with Gina Terlizzi. Though, of course, the highlight of the evening would come after the performance.

She was very aware of Alessandro's tension. And her other grandsons' curiosity. Their older brother's request for their support on such a personal matter was extraordinary. And the sheaf of red roses he'd brought with him had certainly raised their eyebrows.

Although both Antonio and Matteo had heard Gina Terlizzi sing last week, neither of them had known of any attachment formed between the wedding singer and their brother. The news of his broken engagement to Michelle Banks had come as a thunderclap, let alone this sudden piece of family stage management to impress a woman they hadn't even been introduced to. Tonight was certainly shaping up as of prime interest to all of them.

It gave Isabella intense satisfaction to know that Michelle Banks had completely obliterated any chance she might have had of retrieving a relationship with Alessandro. And her malicious meddling yesterday had vindicated Isabella's own meddling in this affair. It had also fired up so much feeling in Alessandro, Isabella could only hope now she'd done right in bringing Gina Terlizzi to his attention.

What if Gina was persuaded to pursue a career in singing?

Would she still be a good wife for Alessandro?

Marriage…children…it was still a worry, but not as big a worry as it had been with Michelle Banks. Tonight, Isabella was content to count that blessing, and hope for more.

*   *   *

Gina stood in the wings, waiting for her cue from Peter. She took deep breaths, needing to calm the tremulous state of her nerves. Her parents were out in the audience. Her older brother and his wife had come, too. The whole family was excited about this chance for her, and she was determined they should be proud of her singing tonight. No mistakes. No going blank on the lyrics or wavering off the note. Total focus on delivering the best she could give.

Applause followed Peter's last flourish on the piano. He stood and bowed, then strolled to the apron of the stage, carrying his microphone with him, ready to woo the audience with words which she had to live up to. With an ease Gina envied he jollied them into a buzz of anticipation, then held out his hand to her and with an encouraging smile, called her on-stage.

Her heart was pounding but she managed to reach his side without any mishap. Peter gave her waist a squeeze as they waited through another round of applause. "Isabella King is here with her three grandsons," he whispered in her ear, electrifying every nerve in Gina's body.

Alex…with his family?

"That's hefty support, Gina, so break a leg!" Peter urged.

The old theatrical expression for good luck barely penetrated the daze of shock. No way in the world could she have anticipated such a move from Alex—such a *public* move! What did it mean?

Or had Isabella King commanded her grandsons' presence here?

But why?

Why?

"One of the great musicals of recent times is *West Side Story*," Peter announced. "And what more fitting song to begin our program than Maria's and Tony's heart-lifting duet. Ladies and gentlemen, we give you… 'Tonight!'"

Heart-lifting.

No time to sort out the chaos in her own heart. Somehow she had to rise above it. Peter was moving back to the piano. He'd handed her the microphone she was to use. This was the kind of moment that separated amateurs from professionals. *The show must go on!* Never mind Alex and the King family. Her own family was out there, willing her to pull this off.

Pretend she was Maria in *West Side Story*—the modern remake of *Romeo and Juliet.*

Pretend Alex was Tony.

Pretend they'd just met and it was wonderful…a dream come true…before it was destroyed.

Peter played the introduction and Gina didn't have to pretend. She remembered how it had felt with Alex before it was destroyed and she poured all that feeling into her voice as she lifted it to sing, to soar to that ecstatic place where for a little time, everything had been perfect.

It worked.

She was fine.

Better than fine if the audience response was anything to measure by.

They moved on to the duet, "All I Ask of You" from

The Phantom of the Opera, then two of the most poignant songs from *Les Miserables*: "On My Own" and "A Little Fall of Rain." There was absolute silence throughout the lounge while these were sung, which was surely some kind of tribute to the touching lyrics and how they were interpreted. Even Gina thought her voice had never been so true and powerful in its delivery.

Maybe it was the spur of having Alex listening, or maybe it was the need to prove to herself that Peter's faith in her talent was justified. Whatever was driving her, she knew she was giving the performance of her life as they followed through the program Peter had plotted. Her last solo, "Love Changes Everything" from *Aspects of Love,* was an absolute show-stopper, much of the audience rising to their feet and even calling out "Bravo!"

Peter grinned at her, giving her an exultant thumbs-up signal as he waited for the acclaim to die down. Clearly his ego wasn't on the line here. He was delighted with the reception they were getting. He literally purred into the microphone as he acknowledged it.

"Thank you, ladies and gentlemen. To complete our very special program tonight, we take you back to *West Side Story,* to the song that encompasses what we most want from life. It's entitled "Somewhere"—that mythical place where even impossible dreams become possible. And so, I would like to invite you all to join Gina Terlizzi and myself in spirit on the magical journey that takes us… 'Somewhere.'"

It was amazing how quickly the audience quietened to listen, and their expectation was well and truly met when Peter started with no musical accompaniment, his voice crooning the words with such husky emotion, a lump rose in Gina's throat. She had to swallow hard before following his lines with hers, echoing the yearning and building on it. The piano came in, adding its spine-tingling notes. Then together, and in thrilling harmony, they drove the song to its soul-stirring climax.

For several moments after all sound ceased, the silence held, as though everyone in the lounge had been gripped by the song's heart-wrenching impact and didn't want to let it go. But it was over. The whole performance was over.

A single hand-clap started a storm of applause. Peter rose from his piano stool and joined Gina at centre stage. It was like being bathed in waves of pleasure. People called for encores but they had no more to give tonight.

"Let them remember the high and they'll come back," Peter murmured. "Just smile and nod."

"Is it always like this?" she whispered.

"No. You were superb. And it looks like Alex King thought so, too. Accept the gift gracefully, Gina. You're on show."

Gift?

She'd been trying to search out her parents from the crowd, deliberately evading any glance at the King group, not wanting to appear as though she was asking for anything from them. Her heart leapt skittishly at

Peter's prompt. Before she could begin to monitor her response, her gaze zeroed in on the man who should have no business approaching her unless…unless…had she hopelessly misread the situation between them?

He was in a formal black dinner suit, commandingly tall and stunningly handsome. As in the ballroom at the castle, people automatically moved aside for him, giving a clear passage to the stage. She could feel the power of his presence coming at her, squeezing her heart, raising flutters in her stomach, sending quivers of weakness down her legs.

Too frightened to let herself believe everything between them would ever be happily resolved, Gina couldn't bring herself to look directly into his eyes. She fastened her gaze on the sheaf of flowers he carried across her arm. The gift…it was the kind of tribute people gave to a singer at the end of a show, yet he must have thought of it beforehand, must have anticipated…what?

That her performance would be worthy of it?

Or had he intended to seize this opportunity to get close to her again anyway?

Glittering gold cellophane encased the flowers. A satin red and gold ribbon made a bouquet of them. As he mounted the steps at the side of the stage, she saw that he was bringing her roses—masses of red roses!

Her mind dizzied with feverish thoughts. The songs she and Peter had sung had been about love. Did Alex think red roses were appropriate for the occasion? Or could they possibly represent a more personal statement from him? *Love changes everything.* The words of that song were so true in so many ways...but she mustn't let herself get confused by wild hopes.

Somewhere a time and place for us... That was a hope, a dream. The impossible didn't really become possible. She had to accept the gift gracefully. That was all. Smile. Nod a thank-you. She was on show. No need to look directly at Alex. She didn't want him to see what her eyes might tell him.

"For you," Alex said in a deep velvet voice, presenting the roses to her.

She smiled and nodded. "They're lovely. Thank you," she murmured, keeping her gaze fixed on the perfect blooms. Dozens of them.

"May I invite you both to our table?" he went on smoothly. "My grandmother would like to congratulate you personally on a truly marvellous performance."

"For Isabella, anything," Peter declared. "I have always admired her judgement of quality and she certainly picked it in Gina. If you'll wait a moment while I deliver our exit line..."

"Of course."

"Thank you, ladies and gentleman, and goodnight. We hope to see you here again next Friday evening...for the encores," he added with that touch of wicked promise he did so well.

Laughter and more applause. Peter tucked Gina's free arm around his, gestured for Alex to lead the way and they followed him across the stage to the steps leading down to the lounge.

"Does my little sister want protection from the big

bad wolf?'' Peter murmured in her ear. "I can run in-terference for you."

She threw him a startled glance.

His mouth tilted ironically. "Alex King is not here to give you accolades, darling girl."

"What then?"

"To win you." He cocked an eyebrow. "Are you winnable?"

"I don't know. It depends…"

"Shall I step aside and let him have his chance with her?" he half-sung from *My Fair Lady.*

"Yes," she decided in a wild rush.

"Just remember you're quality. Real quality, Gina Terlizzi," he insisted on a sharply serious note. "Don't undersell yourself."

Amazing to hear Alex's warning about dealing with Peter Owen coming now from Peter's mouth and di-rected at Alex's interest in her. Clearly Peter had guessed something from having seen Alex leaving her house last Sunday.

She looked down at the extravagant sheaf of roses resting in the crook of her other arm. The cost of so many might not mean a lot to Alex King, but to Gina's all too impressionable mind, it meant he did not hold her cheap. But was he trying to buy her? Win another night in her bed?

She wanted him.

It might be a terrible weakness in her but…she lifted her gaze to the man leading them towards the table where he had his family gathered and she ached to touch him; to run her fingers through the hair at the nape of his neck, to curve her hands over the muscles of his broad shoulders, to lose herself in the strong masculinity he exuded from every pore of his magnificent body.

Was it only lust driving him?

Her instincts cried that it had to be more.

Surely the roses said it *was* more.

All she knew was…she had to find out.

CHAPTER SIXTEEN

SHE wouldn't look at him.

Alex pressed the introductions to his brothers. They responded admirably. His grandmother said all the right things. Gina had to know he was not intent on pursuing some hole-in-the-corner affair with her. She had to know. But she wouldn't look at him.

She laid his roses on the table. Her hands were trembling, revealing an inner agitation that he desperately wanted to soothe. She addressed his grandmother. "Will you please excuse me, Mrs. King? My family is here…"

She was going to walk away. His roses meant nothing. She wasn't going to keep them. Only courtesy to his grandmother had brought her this far.

He was seized by a wild primitive urge to grab her, hold her, preventing any escape from him, carry her off to someplace where they could be alone together, where he could…

"Your family?" his grandmother picked up. "I would very much like to meet them. Alessandro, please ask if they will join us."

"Of course," he plunged in, grateful for the lead. Control, he fiercely told himself. Meeting her family was good. Best it be accomplished right now, so Gina would be forced to acknowledge him, to introduce him

173

to those closest to her. It forged a bond she couldn't ignore.

"Thank you," she replied to his grandmother, then hesitantly, "I'm not sure..."

Alex instantly appropriated her arm and tucked it around his. "Let's ask them," he said, forcefully denying her the chance of refusing on their behalf.

For a long, tense moment she stood absolutely motionless, staring at their linked arms, still not looking at him. Her face took on a set determination. He could feel her thinking, "Well, let's see how he deals with this!" Alex was equally determined to meet any challenge she put in his path and come out the winner.

For the next few minutes he focused on winning the regard of the Salvatori family; Gina's parents, Frank and Elena, her older brother, John, and wife, Tessa, all of whom seemed somewhat bemused by his personal interest in Gina and the invitation to join his family in a celebratory drink. To his intense relief they were happy to comply with the sense of *occasion,* pleased to be included in Isabella Valeri King's party, which meant Gina had no ready excuse to evade his company.

Nevertheless, he was acutely aware of the mental and emotional barriers that remained—silent but very powerful barriers of pride, humiliation, raw wounds that needed urgent attention.

He could count on his grandmother to play gracious hostess to the Salvatoris. He could count on his brothers to make them feel welcome. He could even count on Peter Owen to entertain them. A sense of civility forced him to wait through this last round of introductions, but waiting any longer was beyond him. Impossible to sit down and pretend a party mood in this situation.

Gina's arm was still tucked around his. He clamped his other hand over the connection to reinforce it, bent his head close to hers and poured all his willpower into a quiet command.

"Come with me!"

She didn't reply.

He didn't wait for a reply.

"Please excuse us. I'll bring Gina back soon," he announced to the rest of the party.

Immediate action, removing her from their midst, heading for the doors that led to the outside deck beyond the lounge. His heart beat an exultant tattoo as she came with him, not even a tug of resistance. Her fingers clenched under his grasp—a fighting impulse?—but her feet followed his.

The deck overlooked the channel to the marina downriver; rows of boats as far as the eye could see. The Terlizzi fishing boats were undoubtedly amongst them, boats his family had helped to finance. It reminded him that Gina was too conscious of such things, considering herself an *unsuitable* match for him, which was nonsense. Absolute nonsense!

Nevertheless, the fresh salty air and the imminent prospect of the fight ahead of him, blew away the heat that had driven him this far. To win this woman, it was reason he needed, not passion. Yet the dictates of his mind were lost in a surge of need as he drew her over to the deck railing and he swung her into his embrace, the desire to hold her to him overwhelming everything else.

"For God's sake! Look at me, Gina! I don't know what else to do to prove to you Michelle lied."

Finally, finally she dragged her gaze up to his, her golden amber eyes darker than he'd ever seen them, dark with an anguish that tore at his heart.

"Does it really matter, Alex?"

"Yes. It matters."

"Because you're still hot for me?" Her hands pressed against his chest, her body straining away from contact with his, her eyes sadly mocking the desire they had shared. "You had it right when you first kissed me. This isn't fair."

"I won't let you go, Gina."

"You will…eventually," she said with dull certainty. "I think Peter read it correctly. Your family…the roses…tonight is about winning. You don't count the cost. You just want to win."

"Owen!" A red haze of anger blurred any clear judgement. "He has his own barrow to push, just as Michelle did."

"At least it's a barrow I can fit into." Her mouth took on a wry twist. "Where do I fit in your world?"

"With me."

"The Sugar King? The chief executive of what amounts to a private bank? The heir to the castle?"

"I'm a man with the same needs as any other."

"More needs, Alex. You're no ordinary man. You may not have noticed when you barged in on my family, but they are in awe of you. How could they refuse a

King invitation? Your family represents a power they
have never personally known. They don't understand
this is about proving you didn't lie to me. You've pulled
them willy-nilly into a situation that I'll have to explain,
and what answers am I to give them?''

"I'd say the situation is self-explanatory. I'm aiming
to have a serious relationship with their daughter, their
sister, you, Gina!''

"An ordinary canefarmer's daughter.''

"You're not ordinary!''

"An ordinary fisherman's widow. With a child. Who
isn't yours.''

"I'd be proud to have Marco as my boy. He's a wonderful child.''

"Yes he is! But he's not yours!'' Her eyes flared a
poignant despair at his stubborn rejection of her pro-
tests. "What you want with me…it will never progress
to you actually taking Marco on as your son, will it?
You'll want your own children.''

Had Michelle fed her these lines?

Or had Peter Owen?

Michelle and Owen together, pursuing their own selfish interests, not caring what they destroyed as long as
the destruction served their purpose. Thursday…
Michelle doing her damage first, Owen following up
with his proposition. Then tonight, feeding her the poi-
son about winning…

Gina's hands suddenly curled into fists and beat at
his chest. "We're not toys you can pick up and put
down when you find something more attractive.''

"Neither am I!'' he retorted fiercely, dropping his

embrace to catch her clenched hands and contain the violence of feeling they emitted. "Why don't you listen to me, Gina, instead of the people maligning me? Michelle wanted to get rid of you. Owen wants to use you. You're letting them screw us both over."

Shock, agonised confusion.

"What of all you felt with me? Did that mean nothing?" he pressed.

Pain in her eyes. A desperate searching. "What did you feel with me, Alex?"

He took a quick deep breath, harnessing all his energy to answer her in convincing terms.

"Enter the villain," Peter Owen drawled, stepping out onto the deck and closing the door to the lounge behind him.

It startled them both into turning towards him, Gina tearing one hand free of his as she swung aside.

Owen gave her a crooked little smile as he strolled forward. "I know I promised no interference, but it just occurred to me that Alex might colour me black, which doesn't suit me at all."

"What do you mean?" she shot at him.

He paused to light a cigarette.

Alex was sorely tempted to smash Owen's face in but Gina had left one hand in his and he was not about to release it. Holding her with him was more important than anything else.

Owen exhaled a stream of smoke, then cocked his head consideringly. "Has he told you it was me in the garden with Michelle last Saturday night?"

A shocked "No!"

Owen shrugged. "Well, he knows it anyway. And he probably thinks I was in on Michelle's plot to undermine your relationship with him so you'd see my offer as an alternative road to take."

"Oh, Peter!" Disappointment…pain…

Owen shook his head at her. "But that part isn't true. I may not have many morals, but I can see the difference between a woman like Michelle and a woman like you. I meant it when I said I'd treat you as my little sister and I'm telling you with absolute honesty, the mud Michelle slung at you was not mine."

"But you knew she was going to do it," she said flatly.

He nodded. "People do what they are bent on doing. I had no power to stop her. Michelle doesn't care for anyone but herself."

"Neither do you, Owen," Alex sliced in bitingly.

Another crooked smile. "Funny thing about that. I would have agreed with you last week. But I now find myself caring about Gina getting hurt. By you or anyone else. She has a great voice. It should be heard. I can do that for her. So don't use your opinion of me to rubbish what I can offer. That will hurt her, Alex. Her singing is an expression of all she is."

Alex hadn't expected that perception from Owen, nor the sincerity with which it was delivered. Had Gina touched something in his heart…tugged on his soul? It was certainly possible, Alex silently acknowledged, his contempt for the man shifting as a measure of respect weighed in.

With his usual air of flouting any criticism of his

behaviour, Owen took another drag on his cigarette, then flicked it into an ashtray left on the deck for smokers. His gaze held Gina's for a moment before moving a hard mocking challenge to Alex.

"The thing is…" he drawled. "My offer to Gina is genuine…and would be good for her. Can you say the same of yours?"

The caring was definitely there. Alex's mind was still adjusting to this incredible fact as the man raised his hand in a salute to Gina.

"Exit big brother," he said ironically. "I'll call you Monday. Okay?"

She nodded. "Thanks, Peter."

They watched him return to the lounge, the challenge he had thrown down—*will you be good for her?*—gathering a silent force that Alex knew was very much the enemy in tonight's battle with Gina. Yet in a roundabout way, Owen had given him the one weapon that might open her heart and mind to the truth that had brought him here.

Her singing is an expression of all she is.

Truth.

She had to recognise it.

"Those words you sang tonight…*love changes everything*…" Gently he pulled her around to face him. "You have to believe them to sing as you did," he pleaded with all the passion she stirred in him. "You have to believe love does change everything."

CHAPTER SEVENTEEN

LOVE?

Gina's mind struggled through the morass of thoughts that had kept her in torment since...since Alex had presented her with the red roses.

Red roses for love?

The wild hope that had hit her then...Dear God, could it be true? Please...?

With the helpless sense of surrendering her soul, she lifted her gaze to the man whose love she yearned for with all her heart.

A vivid blue blaze instantly seared away any doubts about his holding anything she'd said against her. An intense caring came at her like a tidal wave, crashing through the apprehensions and uncertainties that had been clinging on, fretting at a truth he was forcefully laying bare to her.

"What are you saying, Alex?" she whispered, not quite daring to believe.

"I'm saying I love you, Gina Terlizzi. And that definitely changes everything you've said against being with me."

Her whole body tingled with the energy he poured at her, carrying with it the determination to heal any breach, to prove the way was clear for them, no barriers, not even shadows of barriers.

Did it change...*everything?*

"I'm sorry I...I listened to Michelle," she choked out, shamed by the strength of his feeling for her.

"I'm sorry I ever became entangled with her in the first place. It was never right. Not *right*..." He lifted a hand to her face, stroking her cheek tenderly as he softly added, "...as it is with you, Gina."

She took a deep breath and asked, "How do you know it's right this time, Alex?"

No hesitation for thought. "I guess you could say I knew it in my bones the day we met. And the recognition just keeps getting stronger."

Instinct? Chemistry?

"I've never been hit like this before," he went on. "There have been other women I've found very attractive—obviously." An ironic edge there. "But what I feel with you goes much deeper. It's like you're in my blood, Gina, and you make it sing."

Yes, she thought, it *was* like music...big and overwhelming at times, soft and sweet, always emotional, passionate, tender, joyful, stormy and sad, as well.

"One thing I'm sure of...it's not going to burn itself out," he said very emphatically. "This isn't some brief candle. It's something essential—elemental—that goes right to the core of the man I am. Call it the fire of life. That's what you've lit in me, Gina. You are the woman it revolves around. And I'm not about to let it go out."

The fire of life... It seemed to Gina a perfect description of love—the magic spark that brought a man and woman together, making the heat that eventually gave birth to children, the source of heart-warmth that made life so much worth living. Yesterday, it was as though she'd been left with dead ashes, cold chilling ashes, and singing could never really take the place of the fire. All it did was reflect it in music. It could never match living it.

"I don't want it to go out either, Alex. I more or less plunged into a deal with Peter Owen because...because I was frightened of the emptiness...with you gone."

"I'm right here. I'll always be here for you."

Tears pricked her eyes. "I'm sorry I didn't believe. Michelle said things...things that struck true to me...like our lives were at odds with you being who you are and me being..."

"Perfect! You are everything I want, Gina. Everything! And don't ever let anyone tell you any different. Their vision might be messed up by things that are totally irrelevant to me, but my vision is very, very clear on what counts in my life. And you count one hundred percent. Have you got that?"

She nodded, the joy and the wonder of it momentarily robbing her of speech.

"As for the deal you've made with Peter Owen..."

"I don't know that I want to go far with it," she rushed out, not wanting anything between them spoiled. She heaved a long shaky sigh and laid out the dearest dream of her life. "The truth is...I mostly wanted to sing to my babies. Angelo and I had planned a big family."

Alex's hands slid around her waist, drawing her closer. "We'll have as big a family as you want. And I *will* have Marco as my son if you'll allow me to adopt him. I want to. I may not be the father Angelo would have been to him, but I'll do my best to fill that role, Gina. He makes me feel…'' His smile held a whimsical appeal. ''…I wish he was mine.''

Her heart turned over. ''You're…you're thinking of marriage?''

Burning certainty in his eyes. ''I want you as my wife and the mother of my children. That's where we're going, Gina, if you're happy to come with me.''

A fountain of happiness exploded inside her.

''But that doesn't mean I want you to give up professional singing,'' he went on seriously. ''Your voice is such a powerful gift, I think the world should hear it. Owen's right about that. And I was wrong about him. I have no doubt now he'll do the best he can for you, Gina.''

''I don't want it to interfere…''

''It won't. We'll fit around it.''

His confidence, his absolute self-assurance about handling anything where she was concerned, held Gina in silent awe. Was it possible for every dream to come true? It seemed the brightest of bright futures was shimmering before her eyes and it was difficult to take it in, difficult to believe that the groundwork for it was being laid right now…with Alex. Alex King!

She felt such a huge swell of love for him, it lifted her onto tip-toe and her hands flew up to curl around his neck. ''I was afraid,'' she confessed. ''I thought you were bulldozing everything in your way, just to have your way. Even using my family…''

"I was glad to meet your family. I wanted them to know. Mine, as well."

"I love you, Alex King."

His eyes glowed with blue fire. "There *is* a place for us. I promise you we'll make it together, Gina."

"Yes," she breathed ecstatically.

And that place—*somewhere*—was suddenly here and now as they kissed, pouring out all the passion in their hearts, touching, holding, hugging the fire they'd lit in each other, determined on nurturing it through all the years of their lives.

CHAPTER EIGHTEEN

Dear Elizabeth,

I am pleased to announce that a wedding is now arranged between my eldest grandson, Alessandro, and Gina Terlizzi, a young woman who has my warmest approval. She is from a good Italian family, a widow with a child, who is the dearest little boy you could imagine. His name is Marco and Alessandro is soon to adopt him legally so I am almost a very delighted great-grandmother already.

You must be wondering how this has all come about since Alessandro was planning to marry that other woman when you were here with us. Following your very good advice, I proceeded to engineer a meeting between Gina and Alessandro, and a most fortuitous meeting it turned out to be.

As you so wisely said, nothing more could be controlled. Yet it is quite eerie, seeing them together, how right they are for each other. I am reminded so strongly of how it was with Edward and myself all those years ago. I feel very sure this will be a good and fruitful marriage, the kind of marriage I wished for Alessandro.

I hope you will be able to come to the wedding. I

enclose a formal invitation for you and Rafael. I will also be sending invitations to your three sons and their families. Perhaps their successful marriages will inspire my other grandsons, Antonio and Matteo, to think seriously of finding themselves a wife who will bring the gift of love into their lives.

It's been brought home to me that it really is a gift, and one that cannot be ordered or chosen. It simply happens when the right people come together. Nevertheless, in future, I shall certainly be on the lookout for any young women who could be right for my other grandsons. Having found Gina for Alessandro, I cannot be too far wrong in my judgement.

Thank you once again for your very good advice.

With sincere respect and affection,
Isabella Valeri King.

The Bridal Bargain

CHAPTER ONE

JOB day!

Hannah O'Neill rolled out of her bunk in the youth hostel, collected the necessities and raced for the shower block, needing an early start this morning. She had to prime herself up for the interview which would win her the job she wanted. Of course, there were probably other jobs she could get, and certainly her financial situation demanded that she snag one this week, but chef on board a luxury catamaran doing day-trips to The Great Barrier Reef was definitely a plum position.

It was to be hoped that whoever was doing the hiring had been so impressed by her brilliant résumé of previous experience, they hadn't checked every minute detail. Not that she'd actually lied. Kitchen hands did assist chefs so saying she'd been an assistant chef was a perfectly reasonable statement. And a take-away fish and fries shop was a seafood restaurant—more or less.

All she needed was the chance to talk her way into being given the opportunity to prove she was as good as her word. It was her one great talent—convincing people she could do anything. Lots of zippy energy and confidence—that was all it took. Plus being a nice person to have around; cheerful disposition, ample tolerance, ready smile, never too proud to appeal for help.

On her two-year journey of discovery around Australia, these well-developed qualities had won her work whenever she had needed to replenish her bank balance. There was only the east coast left to explore now. She'd come across The Top End to Cooktown and down the Bloomfield Track to Cape Tribulation. Next stop, Port Douglas, where she hoped to stay for the main tourist season—May to November—provided she got a job.

The job, if luck was with her.

As she showered and washed her hair, Hannah gave herself the pleasure of remembering the wonderful days she'd had here at Cape Tribulation; hiking through the fantastic Daintree Forest which was as primeval in its own way as the ancient Kimberley Outback, then the incredible contrast of Myall Beach, surely the most beautiful beach in the world with its brilliant white sand and turquoise water.

It was sad to be leaving, but needs must, she told herself. Her shoestring budget was running out of string. Besides, Port Douglas and The Great Barrier Reef would undoubtedly prove a great new adventure. And it was time to get in touch with her family again to let them know she was still alive. Not that they worried overmuch about her. All the O'Neills had been brought up to be resourceful. But it was always nice to call in and catch up on the family gossip.

It would be interesting to find out if the faithless Flynn was still happily married to her ex-best friend, for whom he'd virtually jilted Hannah at the altar.

Two years on…the honeymoon period would definitely be over by now. Some darkly malevolent
thoughts skated through Hannah's mind. It was easy
to say forgive and forget, move on. She'd certainly
moved on, and on, and on, but forgiving and forgetting…not easy at all!

Nevertheless, today was a day for looking ahead
and that was what she was going to do. The past was
gone. No changing the Flynn-and-Jodie blot on the
landscape of her life but it was a long way behind her
now and she'd enjoyed a lot of bright and shiny days,
weeks, months, since then. And if she got the job on
Duchess, that would be as good as being a duchess.

Having towelled herself dry, she pulled on her
clean jeans and the stretchy, no-wrinkle midriff top
striped in green and blue and black and lipstick pink.
It was a brilliant little top. Not only did it go with
everything she carried with her, it showed off the
great tan she'd acquired and picked up the green in
her eyes.

Her long, crinkly blonde hair always took ages to
dry, but the road trip to Port Douglas would probably
consume the whole morning. She would have plenty
of time to put it into a neat plait before the interview,
which wasn't until three o'clock this afternoon.
Couldn't have lots of hair flying around if she was to
look like a professional chef.

Having checked that she'd packed everything into
her bag, Hannah said goodbye to her fellow back-
packers and headed off to The Boardwalk Café, needing to pick up some breakfast and hoping to beg a
lift from someone going her way. One good thing

about being on the tourist track. People were usually generous about giving help. It was fun chatting about where you'd been and what lay ahead.

Optimism put a happy smile on Hannah's face. Today was going to be a great day. It was lucky she'd seen the job advertisement in the Cairns newspaper two weeks ago, lucky her résumé had won her an interview. If her luck held good—and why wouldn't it?—by tonight she would be the new chef on the top cat of the Kingtripper line.

"The phone. It is Antonio. For you," Rosita announced, carrying the cordless telephone to where Isabella Valeri King was enjoying morning tea by the fountain in the loggia.

Yesterday Isabella had celebrated her eightieth birthday. She did not feel eighty. Her hair was white, her skin more wrinkled than she cared to notice, but she could still sit with a straight back and her dark eyes missed very little of what was going on around her. Rosita, who had taken care of her needs for the past twenty years, had insisted she rest today, but Isabella's mind never rested.

Antonio…her second eldest grandson, thirty-two years old and too footloose and fancy-free for Isabella's liking. Something had to be done about that and soon. Time was the enemy as one got older. The young thought they had all the time in the world, but it wasn't so. It had to be used wisely and well, not frittered away.

"Thank you, Rosita." She smiled at her most

trusted confidante and lifted the telephone to her ear. "What is the problem, Antonio?"

A call during the day invariably heralded a problem.

"Nonna, I need your help."

"Of course."

"I'm at Cape Tribulation. There's a management hitch at the tea plantation here. I'll have to fly down to the other plantation at Innisfail and fix things at that end. The problem is, I had today earmarked to interview three people who've applied for the job of chef on *Duchess*…"

Isabella's interest was instantly sparked. "And you would like me to do that for you and select the best?"

A huge sigh of relief. "Can do? I'll have them redirected from the office at the marina up to the castle for you."

"It will fill in my day very nicely, Antonio."

"Great! They're all young women…"

Splendid, Isabella thought. Perhaps one might be a possible wife. Antonio would need someone who liked being on a boat.

"…and according to their résumés, which I'll have brought up to you, they've had years of experience in the catering business. What I specifically need is a chef who can cook fish really well. That's expected on *Duchess*. So make sure you question them on that, Nonna. Test them out."

She smiled at his confidence in her ability to do so. And why shouldn't he respect her judgement? She'd been supervising the catering for the weddings at the castle for many years and never had there been a complaint about the food served. Isabella had always insisted on the best and knew how to get it.

"You can safely leave this matter in my hands, Antonio. Go and sort out your management problem with a clear mind."

"Thanks, Nonna. I'll catch up with you this afternoon."

"Hannah O'Neill?" Speculative interest in the receptionist's eyes. "Lucky you're early. Unfortunately, Mr King is tied up with other business so I'm to redirect you to King's Castle where Mrs King will conduct the interview."

"Fine!" Hannah flashed an agreeable smile. "If you'll just point the way…"

Surprise in the receptionist's eyes. "You don't know King's Castle?"

Was she supposed to know? "I only arrived in Port Douglas a couple of hours ago. Still getting my bearings," Hannah quickly explained, throwing in an apologetic shrug. "Must say I headed straight for this marina. Great place…"

"Oh! Well, keep going along Wharf Street, on up the hill and you can't miss it. You'll see the visitors' parking area. The steps there will lead you to…"

A real castle! Hannah could hardly believe her eyes as she reached the top of the steps some fifteen minutes later. It even had a tesselated tower! Positively medieval! Although the colonnaded loggia that fronted the massive building could have been lifted straight from ancient Rome. A simply amazing place, set here overlooking the ocean in far North Queensland. A very commanding place, too.

Hannah's curiosity was instantly piqued. What kind of people owned it, lived in it? Only great wealth could maintain it like this, she decided, eyeing the manicured lawns and magnificent tropical gardens. There had to be some really interesting history behind it all, too. Maybe she could winkle some of it out of Mrs King during the interview. People did enjoy talking about themselves and the less talk focused on Hannah, the better.

It surprised her to see an elderly woman seated outside in the loggia. She looked perfectly relaxed, in command of a table placed near a very elaborate stone fountain. In front of her were several manila folders and a tray holding refreshments; a jug of fruit juice, another of iced water, a plate of cookies, three glasses. As Hannah approached, she realised the woman was subjecting her to a very thorough scrutiny. She also noted her autocratic air, the black silk dress and the opal brooch pinned at her throat.

Hannah had anticipated meeting a much younger woman, but she suddenly had no doubt that this was *Mrs King,* and while she might be a white-haired old lady, the mind behind those brilliant dark eyes was razor-keen. Hannah felt she was being catalogued in meticulous detail, from the wavy wisps that invariably escaped her plait, to the cleanliness of her toe nails poking out from her sandals.

She was suddenly super conscious of her bare midriff and wished she'd worn a skirt instead of the hipster jeans which might or might not be showing her navel. Looking down would be a dead giveaway of an attack of nerves. Hannah held her head high, shoulders back, spine straight, and blasted any negative judgement with her best smile.

"Hannah O'Neill?" the woman inquired, a slightly bemused expression on her face.

"That I am," Hannah replied, employing an Irish lilt for a bit of friendly distraction.

A nod, a half smile. "I am Isabella Valeri King."

Which was definitely a mouthful of name, underlining a heritage that probably had royalty in its background. Being hopelessly ignorant of any useful facts, Hannah maintained her smile and warmly replied, "A pleasure to meet you, Mrs King."

Another regal nod. "Please sit down, Miss O'Neill, and help yourself to any refreshment you would like."

Hannah was glad to put the table between her and any possible sight of her navel. She wasn't usually self-conscious about her body, but then she wasn't usually in the presence of a woman who exuded aristocracy and was dressed like a duchess. Certainly not in these tropical climes.

She poured herself a glass of fruit juice, managing not to spill a drop, and determined not to be intimidated out of putting her best foot forward, even if it was only shod in a brown leather sandal. After all, hadn't the old Roman senators worn leather sandals in their villas?

"Quite fascinating the list of places where you've worked, Miss O'Neill," came the first leading com-

ment. "Have you been travelling around Australia
alone?"

"Well, not all alone. I've made friends here and
there and sometimes journeyed on with them. It's
good to have company on long trips."

"And much safer for a young single woman, I'd
imagine. Or are you attached to someone?"

"No." Hannah grinned hopefully. "Still looking
for Mr Right."

"With an eye to marriage?"

The highly direct comeback floored Hannah momentarily. "Well, I guess that's what Mr Right is for,
Mrs King," she recovered, understanding this woman
was highly unlikely to view the more casual live-
together relationships in a kindly light.

"Unfortunately he's not all that easy to find these
days," she rattled on, feeling she had to give a proper
explanation of her failure to find him. "It's not only
a matter of him being right for me. I've got to be
right for him and then the timing has to be right..."
She heaved a rueful sigh. "Here I am, twenty-six, and
the whole combination has not yet occurred for me."

A sympathetic nod. "It's true one cannot order it.
As you say, there has to be a combination of auspi-
cious circumstances."

Got out of that one, Hannah thought triumphantly.

"Would you mind telling me something about your
family, Miss O'Neill? I take it you are of Irish descent?"

Hannah laughed. Good humour covered a multi-
tude of shortcomings. "Irish on both sides," she replied. "My mother's name was Ryan. Maureen Ryan.

I'm the middle one of nine children, all of us very much wanted and loved.''

"Nine? That's a very large family these days."

"I know. It amazes most people. Some disapprove, calling it breeding like rabbits. I can only say I've never felt like a rabbit and it's always been great having the ready support of a big family."

"You haven't missed them on this long journey you've taken?'' was asked curiously.

"Well, we were brought up to be independent, too. To follow our own star, so to speak. Besides, they're all only a call away. I noticed an Internet café here in Port Douglas when I arrived. That makes it easy to stay in touch."

The old lady nodded, seemingly pleased with Hannah's portrayal of her family background. "Are you keen to have many children yourself when you do marry?'' she asked.

Why was this important? Hannah sensed it was. "At least four," she answered truthfully, then shaved the answer with practical issues. "*If* I can get my husband to agree, *and* I'm not too old when I find him."

"Twenty-six, twenty-seven," the old lady said assessingly, as though she was totting up how many babies Hannah could fit in. "Perhaps you need to stay in one place for a while, Miss O'Neill. How long do you plan on staying in Port Douglas?"

"Oh, definitely for as long as the job lasts, Mrs King."

A warm approval was now coming from the older woman, which boosted Hannah's confidence. Family was obviously a key factor here. Hannah didn't care why as long as it was working for her. Her instincts were shouting—*Play it to the hilt!*

"I notice you spent the last tourist season working at King's Eden Wilderness Resort in the Kimberley," came the next tack in the interview.

King's Eden...King's Castle...oh wow! Was this another branch of the same family? More legendary stuff—the Kings of the Outback and the Kings of the Tropics?

"What did you think of it?" Isabella Valeri King ran on.

Hannah's enthusiasm did not have to be feigned one bit. "The resort was a fantastic slice of the Outback. A great experience. And so was working with the head chef there, Roberto," she popped in judiciously. "I swear no one can cook barramundi like Roberto. Absolutely superb. It has to be the best-tasting fish in the world. Whenever the guests at the homestead brought in a catch..."

"And you learnt to cook it as he did?"

"Mrs King, give me a fresh barramundi, and I'll give you a meal to remember."

"I may take you up on that, Miss O'Neill."

Enough about cooking! That hook was in. Better to get back to family. She projected eager, bright-eyed interest. "Is there a connection between the King family here and the Kings of the Kimberley?"

"We are related," came the proud acknowledgment. "The older brother of my husband, Edward, carried the family line on at King's Eden."

Remembering the wonderful homestead on the

great cattle station, sited like a crown on the top of a hill overlooking the river, she had to ask, "Did your husband build this castle?"

"No. My father did. It used to be known as the Valeri Villa in the old days. After my father died, and my son took over the plantations, the local people started calling it King's Castle, and so it is today."

"Plantations?" Hannah prompted.

"It was all sugarcane then." She waved to the view. "Look across the inlet!"

Cane fields stretching from the sea to the mountains.

"My mother used to watch the burning of the cane from the tower here. But they do not burn the fields now. The cane is harvested green with special machinery. My grandson, Alessandro, looks after that business. His brother, Antonio, manages the tea..."

"Tea?" Hannah remembered seeing a tea plantation at Cape Tribulation.

Isabella nodded. "Though I suspect Antonio is more interested in his Kingtripper Company. The new boat, *Duchess,* is his pride and joy."

So Antonio would be her boss if she clinched the job. Antonio, Alessandro...a very strong Italian influence here. Maybe that encompassed the thing about family.

"Your résumé says you worked on a boat at Fremantle in Western Australia," Isabella went on, getting back to tricky business for Hannah.

She nodded. "Catering for Sunset Cruises around the harbour." If you could call drinks and nibbles *catering!*

"So you're used to working in a galley."

"Oh, yes. Absolutely."

"And you don't get seasick?"

"Never have been."

True, but she hadn't been tested much on that score. Better buy herself some travel-sickness pills to be on the safe side.

"Matteo supplies a selection of exotic fruit for exclusive use on *Duchess*," Mrs King informed her. "You will have to learn about their qualities. Matteo is my youngest grandson. He looks after the tropical fruit plantations."

Three Kings, Hannah thought, and wondered if they had wives. "Do you have any great-grandchildren, Mrs King?"

She smiled, delight twinkling in her dark eyes. "A little boy, Marco. He is the son of Alessandro and Gina, who is now expecting another child."

"Well, congratulations!" Hannah said heartily.

"Thank you. Unfortunately, my other two grandsons have not yet found..." Her mouth quirked. "...Miss Right."

"It's not easy," Hannah said with much sympathetic feeling.

"Love is a gift," Mrs King murmured, with a look of satisfaction that stirred Hannah's curiosity again.

Before she could inquire what was meant they were both distracted by the noise of a helicopter zooming very close above them.

Mrs King looked even more satisfied as she explained, "That will be Antonio, coming in to land on the helipad. He said he would join us here if he could.''

Uh-oh! Hannah's stomach did a little flip. She'd been doing so well with Mrs King, establishing a really warm rapport that would surely have led to her being given the job. Now she had to face the boss-man and win him over, too.

Double jeopardy!

At least she had his grandmother onside, which was some consolation, but undoubtedly the boss-man would have the last say.

Antonio…

Not married.

Did this mean he was hard to please? Or just too busy with his plantations and boats to care too much for any woman? Obviously a high-flyer in his helicopter, Hannah fervently hoped Antonio King would still have his head in clouds of tea business, at least until she could get a handle on him.

CHAPTER TWO

HANNAH'S heart did a hop, step, and jump as one of the great entrance doors to the castle swung open and *the man* came striding out towards the table by the fountain. Her wits went flying off to limbo in scattered little fragments. Her stomach contracted as though all her female muscles were twanging red alert. It was lucky she was still sitting down or her knees might have melted.

If this was Antonio King he was a king-size ten on the male Richter scale! Tall, dark and handsome did not sum it up. Dynamic energy came from him in waves. It had a magnetic effect that glued Hannah's gaze to him. She did manage to keep her mouth closed which stopped any danger of drooling.

He was dressed in light grey tailored shorts and a grey and white striped business shirt, collar open, sleeves rolled up. Both arms and legs seemed to bristle with athletic muscle power. He wasn't Mr Universe, but he was very, very masculine, the kind of masculine that made any woman want a bite of him. As many bites as he'd allow. Major sex appeal here! Major!!

"Nonna..." Arms out ready to embrace his grandmother, a smile full of straight white teeth, a squarish jawline, strong nose. "Thank you so much for filling in for me."

19

"My pleasure, Antonio," she said, rising from her chair to receive him with affection that was amply returned.

He enveloped her in a hug and planted a kiss on her forehead while Hannah was occupied admiring the taut cheekiness of his very cute backside, as well as the glossy thickness of his black hair and the neatness of his ears. Flynn's ears, she remembered, had stuck out, and she'd actually planned on giving her children plastic surgery to pin theirs back if they inherited Flynn's ears. Not that she had to worry about that anymore, but she couldn't help thinking Antonio's ears were quite perfect.

He swung aside from his grandmother, gesturing towards Hannah, a dazzling smile accompanying the question, "And this is...?"

"Miss Hannah O'Neill," his grandmother supplied. "Your third applicant for the job of chef onboard *Duchess*."

"Hannah..." He stepped forward, offering his hand, grey eyes with intriguing bits of hazel in them meeting hers with the impact of an atom bomb, blowing apart the long-held shield around Hannah's heart. "...I'm Tony King."

Tony, Tony, Tony..., some wild voice in her head sang as she stood up to greet him properly.

Hannah O'Neill sure had a body, Tony thought, noting her eye-catching curves as she rose from her chair. Didn't mind showing it off, either, the clingy midriff top outlining breasts that would very sweetly cushion a man's head, hipster slacks laying bare a highly feminine waist and a peek-a-boo navel with…was that a butterfly tattoo around it?

No time for a closer examination, though Tony found himself fancying precisely that. Satin-smooth skin, honey-tan, a nice soft roundness to her flesh, no bones sticking out, definitely the kind of feminine physique that appealed to him.

Her choice of clothes had probably turned his grandmother off, but they were a turn-on for guys. No question. A clever piece of calculation for this interview? Misfiring in these circumstances. A black mark against her would have been instantly notched in his grandmother's mind.

She lifted her hand to meet his and he automatically grasped it, actually feeling a little jolt of pleasure at the touch of her—a slender hand, long fingers, warm and soft. She smiled and he was momentarily fascinated by the dimples that appeared in her cheeks. Very cute effect.

Her eyes were green, like the green of forest pools. Thick fair hair waved from a centre parting and was pulled back in a plait, although she hadn't been able to trap it all. Fuzzy little tendrils gave her face a rather endearing frame that went with the little girl dimples.

"I'm very pleased to meet you, Mr King."

Nice voice, sort of musical.

"Tony," he corrected, without pausing to think if giving her his first name was appropriate.

"Tony," she repeated in a soft sensual lilt that put a tingle in his groin.

And those green eyes were dynamite, projecting a pleasure in him that could scramble his brains if he wasn't careful. Already he was thinking he'd like to taste the mouth that had spoken his name like that. He was still holding her hand. He clamped down on the urge to hold more of her—not the right time or place—though he had a strong desire to pursue this woman once the job issue was out of the way.

Good thing he could blame his grandmother for selecting someone else for the position of chef. Which he had no doubt she would do. It neatly separated business from pleasure. And he could probably wangle some other job in town for Hannah O'Neill if she wanted to stick around.

"Miss O'Neill is your new chef for *Duchess*."

"What?" The word spilled out before Tony could catch it back. He instantly released Hannah's hand and spun around to face his grandmother, frowning over her shock announcement. "You've chosen already?"

She smiled serenely at him. "You did leave the decision in my hands, Antonio. Miss O'Neill and I had been chatting for some time before your arrival. There is no question in my mind she will suit you very well."

"Oh, thank you, Mrs King!" Hannah flew past him and grabbed his grandmother's hands, pressing them effusively. "I promise I won't let you down. And any time you'd like me to cook a barramundi for you, just say the word and…"

Cook? Tony stared at the thick plait falling down to the delectable curve of her spine, which led to her even more delectable bottom, and couldn't see

Hannah O'Neill in a galley at all. He could only see her in a bed...with him!

Yet, here she was, dressed in positively provocative clothes, somehow getting on like a house on fire with his grandmother who was smiling at her as though she was the apple of her eye, not minding at all being pounced upon and gabbled at by a woman showing her naked navel with a butterfly tattooed around it!

Tony was still trying to get his scrambled mind around this incredible state of affairs when Hannah turned back to him and grabbed his hand again, squeezing it in both of hers.

"I'll be the best chef you've ever had on *Duchess*," she gushed, her eyes lit up like Christmas trees, lots of electricity sparking at him and pumping up his heartbeat. "I'll learn everything that needs to be done double-quick. I promise you won't be disappointed in me, Tony."

Tony... She was doing it again, making his name sound like something she savoured on her tongue. It was almost a French kiss. And he sure as hell *was* going to be disappointed if she was working for him. Mixing it with an employee would only lead to trouble. Right now, with her hands clasping his, he had a mental image of her body clasping another part of his anatomy which was already giving him trouble.

"I think we should sit down and talk about this," he said quickly, deciding that putting a table between them was fast becoming mandatory. Not only would it hide his physical discomfort but it would give him enough distance to view Hannah O'Neill in a business-like light. If that was possible.

"Oh, yes!" She released his hand to clap her own. "I need to know when you want me to start and..."

"All in good time," he instructed, waving her to the other side of the table.

She virtually skipped around to the chair he'd indicated, her exuberant spirits totally irrepressible and almost mesmerising. Tony had to wrench his gaze away from her to get himself settled on a chair and his mind properly organised to deal with this problem.

He shot a glance at his grandmother who had resumed her seat. Her complacent air niggled him. She should have taken more time over this, should have consulted with him first before handing the job to Hannah. That bemused little smile on her lips...had she been mesmerised into an impulsive decision? His steely-willed grandmother?

"Ah! Here is Rosita with afternoon tea!" she announced with warm satisfaction, obviously happy now to turn this into a *social* situation.

Tony gave up. Hannah O'Neill had somehow wormed her way into his grandmother's good books and she was now being given the ultimate seal of approval—afternoon tea with Isabella Valeri King in the loggia. He was going to have to run with this ball, whether he liked it or not.

His grandmother proceeded to play grand hostess, aided and abetted by Rosita who fussed around, making sure everything was to their liking. She even produced the carrot cake with the cream cheese and walnut topping—a sure sign the company rated five stars. He was definitely down the mine here without a tin hat to protect him.

Having accepted the inevitable, Tony pulled over the manila folder that contained Hannah O'Neill's particulars, and focused his mind on getting down to business. Pleasure was now out. Regardless of how strong the temptation, it was utter madness to get sexually involved with an employee. He had to keep Hannah O'Neil at arm's length. Though even the width of the table didn't feel far enough.

"I see we addressed our reply to your application, care of Mason's Shop at Cape Tribulation," he started off, needing to establish a properly serious vein to this meeting.

"Mmm..."

He looked up to find her licking cream from her lips, and his stomach instantly contracted, hit by a bolt of desire so hard his mind was out for the count.

"I was picking up my mail there," she explained, once she had her sexy mouth composed for speech. "I spent a couple of weeks exploring the Daintree. Such an amazing rainforest. Being in the midst of it was like being plunged back in time to when..."

"Yes," he snapped, cutting off her disturbingly lyrical voice. He picked up a pen and jabbed it at the form she'd filled out. "So where are you staying at Port Douglas?"

She took a deep breath.

Her breasts rose distractingly.

"I haven't found a place yet. I only came down from Cape Tribulation this morning. For the interview. But I'll find somewhere before tonight. I've noticed there are loads of accommodation places here."

Tony was gaining the fast impression Hannah

O'Neill operated on a wing and a prayer. She wasn't *prepared* for taking on this job.

"*Tourist* accommodation," he pointed out. "If you intend to stay the whole season…"

"Absolutely," she assured him. "I'll look for something appropriate."

"Where have you left your luggage?"

"I put it in a locker at the marina." She leaned forward, smiling an eager appeal for understanding. "You see, it did rather depend on whether or not I got this job what I did next, so…"

Definitely a wing and a prayer, Tony thought sternly, battling not to drown in her eyes.

"You will need an apartment with a well-equipped kitchen," his grandmother inserted authoritatively. "Antonio, until Miss O'Neill gets her bearings here, I think it best you put her in one of the guest apartments Alessandro keeps in the Coral King block."

"A guest apartment?" Tony eyed his grandmother, wondering if she'd gone stark raving mad. Hannah O'Neill was not family or friend. She was an employee, and hardly a highly valued one at this juncture! She hadn't even been on trial yet.

"I'm sure there'll be one that's not being currently used," came the unshaken reply. "It will give Hannah the chance to settle into her new job and time to look around for suitable accommodation."

So, it was *Hannah* now!

"This is very kind of you, Mrs King," the fair-haired witch chimed in, her dangerous green eyes obviously casting spells in all directions.

"A simple resolution to immediate problems," his grandmother declared.

"Right!" Tony agreed, knowing he was outgunned before he'd fired a bullet. Feeling constrained to fire other bullets before they could be diverted, he fixed a steady gaze on Hannah O'Neill and stated, "Please understand you start this job on a trial basis. The people who pay for a trip out to the reef on *Duchess* are promised the best of everything. Any failure to deliver it, in any area of service on that boat, cannot be tolerated."

"You mean...no second chances?" A touch of anxiety.

"That depends on how large the blunder is. The odd mistake can be glossed over. Anything that spoils a day out..."

"Would be terrible!" she exclaimed, looking appalled at the thought. Like quicksilver her expression changed, her eyes filling with eloquent earnestness. "Any little problem I might cause, I swear I'll make up for it a hundredfold. I've never had any complaints lodged against me, Tony."

He could believe it. She could probably get anyone to forgive her anything. In fact, before they knew it, they'd probably be helping her out of whatever fix she got herself in. Here was his grandmother, *giving* her prime accommodation, and every time she called him by his name, his heart did this weird curl which took his mind off what he should be concentrating on.

Was she going to be a hazard for the male members of his crew? What if the dive team lost concentration?

She'd better stay in the galley where she belonged. No straying out on deck. At least his current chef on *Duchess* was gay, so she shouldn't disturb him while he familiarised her with the job she'd be taking over.

"Chris, the chef you'll be replacing, wants to leave at the end of the week, so it would be good if you could start tomorrow, learning everything you can from him before he takes off. He's been a top chef for us and I'm sorry to be losing him."

"Why is he going?"

"Personal problems." He sighed, giving vent to some of his frustration. Then with an ironic grimace, he added, "His partner is yearning for the more so-phisticated scene in Sydney. Paradise has its limita-tions."

"I'm sure I'll be *very* happy here."

She twinkled so much happiness at him Tony's chest tightened against the barrage. He forced his gaze down to the papers in front of him. He couldn't even hope she might start yearning for city lights and fly out of his life. It was clear from her résumé she'd been working in tropical climates for some time— Broome, Darwin, even a six-month stint at King's Eden in the Kimberley. Port Douglas probably was a paradise to her.

"So what time am I to be at the marina tomor-row?" she asked eagerly.

"Eight o'clock. *Duchess* leaves at eight-thirty and returns at four-thirty. You'll be provided with a uni-form which is to be worn onboard at all times." Which should cover up her most distracting assets. He glanced at his watch. "If we leave now, I can introduce you to the crew when they disembark this afternoon.''

She immediately leapt up from her chair.

The butterfly pulsed at him.

Tony closed his eyes for one tight moment and rose to his feet, turning to his grandmother and lining up his vision on her.

"Always in a rush, Antonio,'' she sighed. ''You didn't eat anything.''

"Sorry, Nonna. Had a big lunch,'' he excused, stepping over to kiss her cheek. ''Thanks again for doing the interviews.''

"Perhaps Hannah will tempt you with her cooking.''

Her culinary expertise was very low on the list of temptations where Hannah O'Neill was concerned. ''As long as she tempts our trippers, I'll be happy,'' he said, hiding his dark thoughts.

"Mrs King, I can't tell you how much I appreciate your kind consideration and the chance to do my best for *Duchess*,'' came the fervent flow from the seductive voice, working some more magic on his grandmother who bestowed her most benevolent smile.

"I hope everything works out well, my dear. You must have afternoon tea with me again one day. I did enjoy our chat together.''

"I'd like that, too, Mrs King.''

Oh, great! Tony thought in high exasperation. Next thing you know she'd be invited to family functions and she'd be in his face all over the place. Apart from which, he now had to contend with Alex's and Matt's reactions to her being put into one of the Coral King apartments, free of charge. *His* employee!

Nonna had boxed him into a very uncomfortable corner. Somehow he had to work his way out of it without upsetting her and without getting himself into big trouble with Hannah O'Neill.

CHAPTER THREE

"COME this way. We'll take the jeep down to the marina," Tony instructed, setting a brisk pace along a path that led around to the other side of the castle.

Always in a rush, his grandmother had said, and Hannah could see what she meant. Her legs were working overtime keeping up with him. Her heart was racing, too. She hoped she hadn't bitten off more than she could chew with this job. Living up to Tony King's standard of excellence was a scary prospect. She was going to have to learn fast, even faster than he walked.

The jeep was parked next to the helipad. Hannah was used to the small bubble helicopters that transported guests at King's Eden Wilderness Resort. The one Tony King flew was a very sleek machine in comparison. Big money. Big money everywhere she looked. Could a million-dollar-man fall in love with a cook?

Her mind fuzzed with the thought of happy miracles. She shot him her best smile as he opened the passenger door of the jeep for her. Unhappily he didn't see it. His gaze seemed to be trained on watching her legs swing in before shutting the door again, and he frowned all the way around to the driver's side.

Business worries? she wondered. It was probably a

31

bit forward to ask, so she held her tongue as they rode down to the marina. He maintained a grim-faced silence until they reached the Kingtripper office where he handed her over to the receptionist with an efficiency that left Hannah feeling somewhat deflated.

"Sally, this is Hannah O'Neill," he said with almost curt haste. "She will be our new chef on *Duchess*."

"Hey! That's great! Congratulations!"

Hannah didn't even get time to reply.

"Supply her with a uniform, give her all the information about our cruises, and let me know when the crew comes in. I need to catch up on the latest figures."

"Will do," Sally more or less said to his back as he headed towards a door that opened to a private office. His abrupt manner hadn't dimmed her brightness. She had a pretty, vivacious face, a very short bob of dark brown hair, and blue eyes that danced lively curiosity at Hannah as she aimed a grin at her. "Welcome onboard the Kingtripper line."

"Thanks." Hannah grinned back, then nodded to the now closed door, whispering, "Does he always move this fast?"

"Well, the chef situation is getting fairly urgent with Chris all upset about Johnny leaving," Sally confided.

"Who's Johnny?"

"His partner. Who threw an ultimatum at him last week and took off to Sydney. Follow him or else." A roll of the eyes. "Chris would be better off without Johnny, if you ask me, but I guess gay relationships are just as demanding as any other.'' She grimaced. ''I took this job as therapy after divorcing my overbearing husband. What about you?''

''Me?'' Hannah's mind was still buzzing through all these new bits of information.

''Well, you're obviously a stranger in town since you didn't know about King's Castle. Are you escaping from something?''

''More looking around,'' Hannah said blithely, realising Sally was a gossipy person and it paid to be wary of giving out too much before she knew the lay of the land. Besides which, the ex-love of her life had receded into the far distance since she had met Tony King. She could almost wish Jodie well of Flynn. Almost.

She pasted a smile over the niggling sense of betrayal and elaborated on her carefree theme. ''I wanted to get work here and stay awhile. It's a beautiful part of Australia.''

''Sure is,'' came the ready agreement. ''And the perfect base for bouncing off to other great places. Have you got accommodation?''

''Yes. All fixed up.'' A strong sense of discretion told her to keep quiet on that front, too, so she rushed on, ''What I need now is all the info on *Duchess* and...''

''A set of uniforms,'' Sally said obligingly. ''Come on. I'll fit you out and feed you facts.''

They only had ten minutes before *Duchess* glided in to dock at the marina. They watched it from the double glass doors that opened out to the promenade deck. Even to Hannah who'd seen many expensive boats in Fremantle, it looked fabulous; a sleek, stylish, black and white catamaran that exuded power and luxury.

"By far the best," Sally said proudly. "Only launched last year. Air-conditioned saloon and bridge, the most up-to-date entertainment systems, walk-in easy water access for diving or snorkelling, and for you, a fully equipped galley, including an espresso coffee machine and a dishwasher." She gave Hannah a droll look. "No plastic plates on *Duchess*. It's all top class."

Hannah nodded, observing the stream of day-trippers emerging onto the wharf—the clothes they wore, the bags they carried, all classy casual gear. These were moneyed people who paid for the best and expected it as their right. They looked happy and satisfied, which meant the five-star service had not fallen short today.

She took a deep breath, refiring her determination to ensure her service didn't fall short of the standard Tony King wanted maintained. The strong need to please him—more, to delight him—went far beyond what she should feel for her employer, but there was no point in trying to deny he'd put a new zing in her life. She got an electric charge just bringing his image to mind.

"Does...uh...Mr King ever go out on *Duchess*?" she couldn't stop herself from asking.

"Oh, yes! He skippers it most Saturdays and Sundays. And also when it's chartered by a special party. We've had a few celebrities with their entourage wanting *Duchess* to themselves for a day. Tony likes to take personal care of VIPs. He's a terrific host, and of course, they spread the word to their friends. Best publicity we can get.''

Tony… Sally spoke the name so familiarly, Hannah reasoned it must be okay to use it in front of the staff. It was silly to suddenly feel awkward about it. It had felt right when they'd been at the castle. He just seemed to have distanced himself from her since they'd left his grandmother. But she was probably being over-sensitive where he was concerned, not wanting to put any foot wrong.

Today was Wednesday. She had two days to learn all the ropes, practise her cooking and have everything down pat before *he* came on board. Tomorrow she would bring a notebook with her and jot down everything Chris did, everything she had to know about the galley and how it worked. Once the overall routine was fixed in her mind, she could add her own special touches, show Tony he'd really got a prize in his new chef. Then he'd give her that heart-buzzing smile and…

''Crew's coming off now,'' Sally announced, jolting Hannah back to the immediate situation. ''Eric and Tracy and Jai do the diving. They're the first three. Next comes Chris and his assistant, Megan, then the skipper, David, and the first mate, Keith.''

Five men, two women, all of them young and looking very fit and full of vigour. Soon to be four men and three women, Hannah thought. She saw Chris—hair very peroxide blonde—hurrying past the others, an urgent intensity driving him as he headed for the office.

"I'd better get Tony," Sally muttered, and made a dash for his door.

He emerged just as Chris bounded in, clearly pumped up with his personal problems, his frown lifting as he saw Tony. "Did you get someone?" he burst out, so intent on his own needs he didn't even give Hannah a cursory glance.

"Calm down, Chris." The strong, authoritative voice warned the chef he was out of line. "You have just walked past the person I've hired as your replacement."

"Sorry, sorry…" He spun to face Hannah, relief breaking a smile through his anxiety. "Hi!"

"Hi!" she returned with smile inviting fellowship.

"This is Hannah O'Neill," Tony introduced. "Chris Walton, who'll show you precisely what's expected of the chef on *Duchess* over the next two days."

Which jerked Chris's head back to Tony. "Do I have to? Can't Hannah…?"

"No." Very firm. "You stay till the end of the week. As agreed, Chris."

"But Megan could show her everything."

"It's your responsibility." The grey eyes were very steely as he added. "Don't let me down, Chris."

Me, too, Hannah thought on a panicky note, her nerves instantly protesting the prospect of being thrown in at the deep end without a life raft.

"You now have a cut-off day," Tony went on. "You can book a flight to Sydney on Friday evening. You'll forfeit your pay and a reference if you leave before then. Understand me?"

Chris crumpled. "Yeah, yeah. I just thought..."

"I want a smooth changeover, Chris."

"Okay!" He sighed and turned back to Hannah. "Don't get me wrong. It's a great job. I just need to be elsewhere."

She nodded sympathetically. "I will appreciate your staying on to show me how to handle everything, Chris."

"No sweat," he muttered, but it obviously was. The absent Johnny definitely had the screws on him.

The others streamed into the office and having settled the departure issue with Chris, Tony proceeded to introduce her to the rest of the crew. They seemed a cheerful bunch and Hannah felt only good vibrations coming her way, no reservations about her fitting the role she'd taken on.

She was very conscious of Tony watching, and hoped he was pleased with the quick and easy connections made and the positive mood engendered by them. In any tourist business, it was important to promote an air of friendly approachability. Keeping a happy face was second nature to Hannah and today it was very easy for her to exude happiness.

A lovely new place to explore.

A new job to keep her going.

A new man who might just be Mr Right...if her heart was telling her true!

"Hey! Great dimples!" David Hampson, the skipper remarked. He was the last one to be introduced, the senior man on the crew, and very good-looking with bright brown eyes and a charming grin which he swung from her to Tony. "I think you've picked us up an asset here."

It earned a frown. "What we need is great cooking."

"Granted," David cheerfully agreed, returning a sparkling gaze to Hannah. "But give it to us served with dimples and it'll put a fine edge on our appetites."

She laughed, liking his good-humoured teasing.

"Are you ready to move now, Hannah? Got everything you need?" Tony shot at her, cutting off the laughter.

"Yes." She quickly picked up the plastic bag which contained her uniforms and a pile of print-outs on the Kingtripper cruises.

"Right!" He addressed the crew. "I expect you all to look after Hannah tomorrow, without her becoming a distraction to what you should be doing. Just keep everything running smoothly. Okay?"

They chorused assent.

His gaze sliced to her. "Let's go. I'll take you to your accommodation now so you can get settled and ready for work in the morning."

"See you all tomorrow," she tossed at everyone and quickly accompanied Tony out to the walkway through the shopping mall, her heart fluttering at his rush to be on the move again.

"Where's your luggage?" he asked.

"This way." She waved to the left and he was off at a stride that demanded she keep up. A glance flashed at his profile told her his mouth was grimly set again. "Thanks for your support back there," she said tentatively, grateful for his stand with Chris.

"I hope you're not going to be trouble, Hannah," he grated out.

"Trouble?" she echoed, flustered by this negative reading which she hadn't been expecting.

He beetled a warning look at her. "David Hampson is married. He's got two children."

"Well, that's very nice for him," she replied, still mystified by the almost accusing manner.

"Yes. Let's keep it that way." His chin jutted forward, along with his gaze as they walked on.

It took a while for his meaning to filter in. Tony King saw *her* as a threat to David Hampson's marriage? Why on earth would he think that? Because David had made a comment about her dimples? That was ridiculous...wasn't it?

"You know, it's not my fault I've got dimples," she said testily. "I was born with them."

"And a lot else, besides," he muttered darkly.

It was too much for Hannah. "Do you have a problem with me?"

"No." His chin jutted even more forward. "Why would I have a problem?"

"I don't know." She frowned over the puzzle. He'd been distant towards her ever since... "Maybe if you'd been making the choice, I wouldn't have been given the job."

"I have the utmost faith in my grandmother's judgement," he declared as though not the slightest doubt had ever entered his mind.

"Well, that's a relief!" She heaved a sigh to get

rid of that bit of unnecessary tension. "It's not a good feeling working for someone who doesn't want you."

"No question that I *want* you," he said very dryly.

"That's okay then." She felt much better, and to relieve any worries he might have about her, she said, "Generally I get on very well with people."

"So I noticed."

"And I don't believe in messing with anyone's marriage." *Not even Flynn's and Jodie's.*

"I'm glad to hear it."

"I certainly wouldn't enter into any flirtation with David."

"Fine!"

"Sally filled me in on Chris's situation so I understand about that, but is there anything else I should know about the crew so I don't put a foot wrong?"

"Nothing that springs to mind."

"You're not going to warn me off Eric or Jai or Keith?"

"Tracy might well throw you to the sharks if you get your teeth into Jai." A sharp glance. "Do you fancy him?"

How could she fancy any of them with *him* around? Didn't he know he outshone them by about a million megawatts? "I thought they were all attractive people, but they didn't ring any special bells for me," she answered honestly.

"Who knows when the bell might toll?" he said with heavy irony.

It tolled the moment you walked into my life, Hannah thought, but she wasn't sure Tony King was ready to hear that, particularly when he seemed to

have some funny ideas about her…like she was some
kind of honey-pot who drew men from other women.
Which was really strange, because no one had ever
cast her in the role of femme fatale before. She wondered why he saw her that way?

A happy thought struck. It had to mean he found
her attractive. Maybe more than just attractive if he
thought other men could be tempted out of their relationships because she was there.

No question that I want you.

What if he actually meant *he wanted her* in a man-
woman sense, not a job sense? Excitement pumped
her heart faster. It almost put a skip in her step as
they exited from the mall and headed towards the row
of storage lockers outside another booking office.
Hannah quickly found hers, unlocked it, and lifted out
her backpack.

"Is that all?" Tony asked as she closed the door
on the emptied locker. He looked amazed at the eco-
nomical amount of her possessions.

"It is easier to travel light," Hannah explained
matter-of-factly.

He stared down at the bag near her feet as though
it represented a life he couldn't quite bring himself to
believe in. His gaze shifted to her well-worn sandals,
then slowly travelled up her much-washed and somewhat faded jeans. He was probably realising she had
few clothes with her and they were in frequent use,
but this direct re-appraisal made Hannah super-
conscious of her body again.

Her knees quivered. Muscles below her stomach
spasmed. By the time his scrutiny reached her bare

midriff, she could feel her nipples hardening in some wild anticipation of his liking the shape of her breasts, even wanting to touch them. His gaze certainly lingered on them long enough to take her breath away. She couldn't think of anything except how much she wanted him to really *want* her, and her temples were pulsing with an exhilarating excitement when he finally looked into her eyes.

But there was no suggestion of desire in his.

No flirtatious twinkle.

What poured out at her was an almost savage intensity of feeling. It gripped her heart like a vice, squeezing it as though he wanted to extract her life essence, everything she was made of. Not because he wanted it. He just wanted to know. And he was angry at the need to know.

Hannah could feel herself shrivelling inside. She didn't understand what he found wrong with her, why he was angry. In sheer self-defence, she broke the shattering flow from him by bending over to pick up her bag. He beat her intention by grabbing the straps ahead of her.

"I'll carry it for you," he said gruffly.

She didn't argue. In fact, she snatched her hand back from making any contact with his. When he set off for the parking area where he'd left the jeep, she lagged a pace behind, struggling with a mountain of emotional confusion. She wasn't sure she wanted to go with him or be connected to him for any length of time.

Rejection hurt.

She'd been there before.

All those months with Flynn…then to find him cheating with her best friend. It had made everything—absolutely everything—feel wrong.

She'd only just met Tony King but…anger started to burn, searing away the hurt. He had no right to treat her as though she was some kind of unwelcome intruder in his life. He could have vetoed his grandmother's judgement and taken on one of the other applicants for the job of chef. She shouldn't be fretting over what he might perceive as *wrong with her.* The fault obviously lay in him.

She was fine.

His grandmother thought she was fine.

The crew of *Duchess* thought she was fine.

So there had to be something wrong with Tony King if he didn't think she was fine.

CHAPTER FOUR

TONY tried to get a grip on himself as he drove the jeep up to Macrosson Street. He'd never felt jealous over any woman in his entire life. Just a harmless comment about Hannah's dimples and David Hampson could have been a dead man back there, which was a totally over the top reaction.

The effect Hannah O'Neill had on him was getting close to disastrous. Even when she had set him straight in an upfront reasonable manner that should have forced him to be rational about the crew situation, he couldn't get over the hump of the feelings she stirred in him. He told himself it was stupid to transfer those feelings to every guy who met her. She wasn't so...stunningly captivating. She was just... very attractive.

Yet when he'd checked her over again with that one modest backpack from the locker telling him she was certainly unique amongst all the woman he'd known—living with so little—bells had definitely been ringing for him, a whole host of physical bells that still had his body buzzing with demands he had to dampen, not to mention the alarm bell in his head that told him he was in danger of losing it, along with all the common sense he'd learnt from past experience.

Remember Robyn, he savagely recited to himself as

he spotted a place to park and pulled the jeep into it. He'd taken the tempting bait, fallen into the Robyn trap, then found she was claiming special privileges from the crew on the grounds of being *his woman,* lording it over them and even being rude to the day-trippers because *she* didn't have to please anyone as long as she was pleasing Tony King in bed.

No more of that.

Employees could not be playmates.

Never!

He switched off the engine and steeled himself to look at Hannah O'Neill with no more than polite consideration.

"I have to pick up the apartment key from my brother. It will only take a few minutes." He pointed to the building he was about to enter. "That's the control centre for King Investments. Alex runs it. Are you okay waiting here?"

She nodded, her attention turning to the building so he only caught a glimpse of the bewitching green eyes. He got himself moving, determined on swift practical action. The sooner Hannah was delivered to an apartment, the sooner he could get her out from under his skin.

A pity he wasn't involved with anyone at the moment. That was probably half the problem, missing the intimate company of a woman he liked. There was a hole in his life to be filled, but that was no reason to fill it with Hannah O'Neill. It was just a matter of looking around, putting himself in the social swim. He'd find a woman who attracted him and maybe she'd be right for him. Like Gina was for Alex.

Now there was a marriage he could envy. His brother had hit the jackpot with Gina Terlizzi. And made a lucky escape from the woman who'd thought she had Alex right where she wanted him—a user like Robyn. Self-centred sexy women could be very dangerous. A man definitely needed to keep his wits around them.

He just caught Alex as he was about to leave. Five o'clock. No working overtime now he had Gina to go home to. "Hold on a moment! I need a key to one of the guest apartments," Tony told him, blocking the doorway out of the executive office.

His big brother backtracked to his desk, throwing him a questioning look. "I didn't know we had anyone arriving."

"We don't." He heaved a sigh and rolled his eyes. "Nonna, in her wisdom, has offered an apartment to my new chef for *Duchess* until she gets herself settled in Port Douglas."

"She? You're replacing Chris with a woman?" Raised eyebrows. "I thought you preferred a male chef."

"Chris has worked very well, but he did put me in a bind to get someone fast and there were only female applicants." Sighing his vexation over the whole pressure situation, he went on to explain, "I asked Nonna to interview them and she seems to have taken a real shine to this Hannah O'Neill. Gave her the job before even consulting me about the others."

"Accommodation, too," Alex remarked, smiling at Tony's obvious chagrin.

"I just hope she's not a free-loader who'll prove

difficult to shift once she's in,'' Tony muttered
darkly.

"Oh, I'd trust Nonna's judgement on that. Very
astute when it comes to character,'' Alex drawled,
fishing a key out of a drawer.

"Character has nothing to do with the overall picture,'' Tony argued. "I don't like *any* of my staff
getting preferential treatment, let alone a newcomer.''

Alex shrugged. "If it's only a stop-gap…''

"Nonna even invited Hannah to afternoon tea in
the loggia. And asked her to come again.''

"So?'' Alex's sharp blue eyes were highly amused
at this preferential treatment. "Aren't you always telling me to relax and go with the flow?''

Tony heaved a sigh of exasperation. Alex had always been into controlling things. It seemed that being the oldest brother he'd been over-endowed with
a sense of responsibility and he was big enough and
tough enough and smart enough to carry through anything he thought should be done. Over the years Tony
had tried to lighten him up. Turning those tables on
him now was simply not appropriate.

"This is work, Alex, not play,'' he tersely reminded him.

"If Nonna thinks it will work out fine, I'm sure it
will,'' he blithely returned, tossing over a key attached to the Coral King tag. "I take it this Hannah
O'Neill is…uh…very appealing?''

"As far as I'm concerned she's completely out of
bounds. Thanks for the key.'' He turned to leave, then
hung back on a strong afterthought. "Don't mention
this to Matt.''

"Why shouldn't I mention it to Matt?"

"Because..." He didn't want his younger brother sniffing around Hannah. She wasn't Matt's employee. He'd feel free to pursue an interest in her and...

"Well?" Alex prompted, looking quite intrigued.

The conflict he was struggling with could not be voiced. "Just leave well enough alone. As Nonna should have." Holding the key between finger and thumb, he shook it at Alex. "She's gone too far with this."

"I imagine she was just trying to give you a smooth changeover, Tony," came the bland reply. "Do you have Hannah O'Neill parked downstairs?"

"Yes, she's waiting in the jeep."

"Then I'll walk out with you and meet her. Give you my opinion."

"That isn't necessary," Tony grated, wishing he hadn't run off at the mouth.

"I'm curious. As you say, it's not every day Nonna takes such a personal interest in someone she's just met."

At least Alex didn't have eyes for anyone but his wife, Tony reasoned, giving up on arguing. This brother probably wouldn't even notice Hannah's dimples. He certainly wouldn't look as far as the butterfly!

Hannah noted the display window of a real estate agency just along the street. As soon as she had some spare time, she'd inquire there about available accommodation for residents. She was tempted to do it right now, but it would probably be a black mark against her if Tony King returned and didn't find her waiting in the jeep. Besides, her backpack couldn't be left unattended in this open vehicle. It was not a good move to risk losing what she had, including her new job.

Tony King's confusing attitude towards her was very unsettling. She wished she hadn't accepted his grandmother's offer of the Coral King apartment, even with the understanding it was only on a very temporary basis. While it was too late today to change her mind on that issue, she would certainly assert her independence as soon as possible.

Her nerves tightened as she saw him emerge from the building in step with another man who was undoubtedly his brother, coming to check out the unheralded *guest* his grandmother had insisted on accommodating. Alessandro…Alex…

He was bigger and taller than Tony, though there was no mistaking the family likeness in their strong facial features. Same thick black hair, too. The way they carried themselves held an innate confidence that somehow exuded success in whatever they did. Both very striking men, Hannah thought, yet it was Tony's presence that made her heart slip beats.

Sure she was about to be introduced, Hannah opened the passenger door of the jeep and hopped out, feeling the need to stand her ground in the face of being judged again. The action instantly drew attention from Tony's brother who took one sweeping glance at her and then smiled, apparently seeing no wrong in her at all.

"Hannah, this is my brother, Alex. Hannah O'Neill."

Alex's eyes were a vivid blue and Hannah felt warmth and kindness flowing from them as he offered his hand. "Welcome to Port Douglas, Hannah," he said in a deep pleasant voice that contrasted sharply with Tony's curt tone.

She smiled back, relieved at *his* ready acceptance of her. "It's good to be here." The touch of his hand was nice and warm, too, comforting. "I hope I haven't caused a problem," she added earnestly. "I can find some other place to stay."

"As I understand it, Tony's rushing you straight into work, so I'm perfectly happy to go along with my grandmother's arrangements."

"Thank you." Needing to establish she had no intention of becoming a problem, Hannah quickly added, "I promise I won't impose on your generosity for long."

"Don't worry about it."

Alex withdrew his hand and clapped his brother on the shoulder, grinning widely as Tony shot him a sharp look. "You've got the key. I'll leave you to handle everything. Happy days!" he added, saluting both of them as he moved off about his own business.

"What a nice man!" Hannah remarked on a sigh of pleasure in the meeting.

"Alex is married."

The emphatic warning tightened up her nerves again. What did Tony think she was? Some kind of man-eater? "I know that," she stated, glaring considerable impatience at him. In fact, enough was enough on this point. "Mrs King told me so. She also told me he has a son and his wife is pregnant. Should that stop me thinking he's a nice man and she's a lucky woman?"

He grimaced at her irritation, looking quite irritated himself. "I was merely giving you information which I didn't think you had."

"Thank you," she bit out, reminding herself he was her new boss and while he might be the most exasperating man alive, she didn't really want to get on the bad side of him, so she climbed back into the jeep, vowing to keep her mouth firmly shut in his presence except for saying "Thank you," when it was appropriate.

He settled himself beside her and said, "I'll drive you down to the apartment now."

Hannah wondered where it was but limited herself to replying, "Thank you."

It was only a three-minute drive. The jeep pulled up outside an apartment block situated on the lower side of Wharf Street. She'd walked past it earlier this afternoon on the way up to the castle. The apartments were terraced down the hill to the waterfront and all of them would clearly have a fantastic view of incoming and outgoing boats, not to mention the sunset which would start happening soon. Great location!

Despite her earlier misgivings about accepting this very hospitable offer, Hannah couldn't stop her spirits rising at the thought of spending her first few days in Port Douglas at a place that had such marvellous advantages. It was close to the township, close to the marina, and being a "guest' apartment, it would un-

doubtedly provide pure luxury after her weeks of
bunks in back-packer hostels.

She followed Tony down a path which led straight
to one of the top floor apartments. He was carrying
her bag with no visible effort which showed just how
strong his muscular arm was…and his muscular back
and muscular buttocks and muscular legs.

She sighed, wishing he wasn't such an enigma.
Was he *off* women for some reason? He'd been curt
with Sally, too, so maybe it wasn't just her.

If he'd had a bad experience—and Hannah certainly knew how *bad* experiences felt—well, being
sour on women in general could be quite understandable. It did wear off after a while. Though learning
to trust again was difficult if one had been brutally
let down by someone near and dear. The shields went
up and no one was allowed close.

A wounded man, Hannah thought, feeling a rush
of sympathy for Tony King as he unlocked the door
and waved her to enter ahead of him. "Thank you,"
she said warmly and smiled to show she harboured
no ill feelings about his manner towards her. After
all, he didn't know her very well…yet.

He stiffened into a very upright stance as she sailed
past him. Hannah kept going, giving him some space
to feel more comfortable with her. A galley kitchen
led to a big open living area, furnished with a dining
and a lounge setting—all cane with brightly coloured
cushions in a cheerful tropical pattern.

"This is lovely!" she cried, forgetting to limit her
speech to "Thank you' as she beamed her pleasure
back at him.

He lowered her bag onto the floor. Refraining from any comment on her comment, he pushed the Coral King tag attached to the door key into a slot on the wall. "This turns on your electricity and the air-conditioner."

"Thank you," she said, clasping her hands gratefully and hoping he didn't think she'd been too effusive about a place which was strictly temporary.

He stared at her for several seconds and Hannah caught the sense he was in some fierce conflict with himself. "Right!" he finally snapped. "I'll leave you to it then. Don't forget it's an eight o'clock start tomorrow."

"I'll be there on the dot. Probably earlier just to be sure. You can count on it," she assured him.

"Good!" He nodded but his head was the only part of him that moved. He seemed stuck there in the doorway, his gaze still locked on her, like he was trying to burn his way into her mind to see if she could be trusted.

"I'll keep everything here spick-and-span. You don't have to worry I'll make a mess of it."

"I'm not worried," he asserted, frowning over her supposition. "I'd better give you my card so you can contact me if you run into any problems. The mobile phone number can always reach me."

He started forward, taking his wallet out of his back pocket and opening it to extract a business card. Hannah also moved forward to meet him halfway, anxious not to hold him up since it was clear he wanted to get away. He was looking at the card, stuffing his wallet back in his pocket and walking so fast he almost collided with her.

Shock on his face.

His hands instinctively grabbed her upper arms to steady her as she rocked back from him.

"Sorry..." The word rushed out of her mouth, just before her throat completely choked up as shock hit her, as well.

His face was so close his eyes seemed to blaze into hers, and the fingers pressing into the soft flesh of her arms...they seemed to burn, too. She felt invaded by an electric current that was playing total havoc with her entire body.

Heat was swarming through her like a giant tidal wave, making her senses swim, filling them with a huge awareness of the man holding her, the over-whelming maleness of him tugging at her own sex-uality, the strength he emanated, the power, even the masculine scent of him was flooding through her nostrils, an intoxicant that jammed all thought.

She stared back at him, her mouth still half open though incapable of emitting sound. Her ears seemed to be roaring with other messages...a million bells exultantly ringing that he wanted to do far more than hold her arms, far more than tunnel into her brain to find out who and what she was. There was no reason at all in what sizzled from him but its sheer physical blast held Hannah totally captivated.

His gaze dropped to her parted lips and the cer-tainty he was going to kiss her clutched her heart. His head started lowering towards hers, then unaccount-ably jerked up. For one shattering moment she saw horror in his eyes. The hands on her arms sprang open, releasing all contact. He shook his head, stepped away, bent and scooped up the card that had fallen on the floor.

Hannah was too dazed to move a muscle. He lifted one of her hands and pressed the card onto her palm, actually curling her fingers around it. "There!" he said on a heavy expulsion of breath. "Must go now. Must go. Number's on the card if you need me."

His fingers brushed her cheek as though driven to draw her out of what had happened between them and into the immediate *now*. "Okay?" he asked, the horror in his eyes replaced by anxious alarm and a need to paste something else in place.

She nodded, still unable to get her throat to work.

"Okay," he repeated, backing off, swivelling around, heading straight for the way out.

He was gone with the door closed behind him before Hannah could even blink. She found herself touching her cheek as though his fingers had left some imprint there.

She'd never felt anything like this before.

Not even with Flynn, whom she'd loved.

Tony...Tony King.

CHAPTER FIVE

SHE hadn't called.

Tony brooded over this absence of any contact with Hannah O'Neill as he drove to the marina on Saturday morning. For the past two days and three nights he had been more conscious of having his mobile phone on hand than he'd ever been, waiting for Hannah to test his response to her, anticipating her voice almost every time it rang. Part of him had wanted it to be her voice. At least then he could have dealt with a real problem instead of being subjected to this continual inner restlessness.

He'd even taken his mobile to the party he'd attended in Cairns last night—just in case she called—and fully intending to let her hear the party sounds in the background so she'd know he was out enjoying himself and not thinking of her. And he'd meant to enjoy himself, too. Except he couldn't stop thinking of how *she* made him feel and not one woman at the party had lit the slightest spark of interest in him.

The inescapable truth was he wanted *her*. Only her. It didn't matter what his mind dictated, his body was in full rebellion against all restrictions where Hannah O'Neill was concerned. He'd barely caught himself back from kissing her on Wednesday afternoon, and he strongly suspected he wouldn't have stopped at kissing, given they'd been in the apartment with a bed handy.

Unless, of course, she'd said no.

Which she might have.

She certainly hadn't called.

Tony kept telling himself he should be pleased about that. It proved she did not intend to take any advantage of her power to get at him. Or maybe she was simply waiting to check out his behaviour towards her today. Which should be exemplary—treating her as he would any other staff member, making a few allowances for her newness on the job—except he wasn't sure how far he could trust himself to act as he should.

He could only hope she wouldn't have such an undermining impact on him today. The surprise element was gone. When he saw her again, he might very well wonder why he'd got himself into such a twist about her. He'd probably been blowing the whole thing up in his mind because…well, he wasn't used to being struck so strongly by any woman. It had never happened before.

Tony decided he didn't like it.

A guy was supposed to be in control, knowing exactly what he was doing and why. He had to stamp his authority on this situation. Be captain of his own ship.

This resolution burned in his mind as he parked his jeep and checked his watch. Five past eight. The whole staff should already be on board *Duchess,* preparing for the day ahead of them and their passengers. He strode down the wharf, feeling a swell of pride in his newest acquisition to the Kingtripper line. This cat left all the others for dead, not only in speed but in looks and amenities.

And Hannah O'Neill had better live up to his grandmother's judgement when it came to cooking seafood! If she didn't dish up the best barramundi he'd ever eaten, then nothing about her could be trusted.

He greeted the catering people who were just leaving *Duchess,* having delivered the day's order of fresh salads and bread rolls. At least that much of the guaranteed sumptuous lunch was reliable, he thought, stepping on board to more greetings with the dive team who were checking equipment against a passenger list.

"How many coming with us?" he asked.

"Thirty-six," Tracy answered. "Almost a full complement."

The limit was forty. Thirty-six meant a busy day for all hands, especially Hannah's as people drifted in and out for lunch.

"How's our new chef fitting in?"

"Hannah is amazing!" Tracy declared with a little shake of the head denoting awed admiration.

"Doesn't miss a trick, that girl," Jai remarked with a nod of agreement.

"It's the energy she gives out," Eric said more consideringly. "Lots of positive vibes. Gives everyone a good buzz while she gets 'em doing what she wants."

Aha! Tony thought triumphantly. So that was how she'd got his grandmother in! Hannah O'Neill was a witch weaving spells and she'd caught him in her magic trap before he'd built up any objective immunity. *Amazing* was right. Everyone was giving her what she wanted—the job, free accommodation, approval all around, and she'd probably wanted to be kissed, too.

"What about her cooking?" Tony asked.

"Don't know," Jai answered. "Chris was doing it yesterday."

"I think she was helping until she started the exotic fruit thing," Tracy chimed in.

"Yeah! Now that's what I mean," Eric said pointedly. "She got everyone having fun tasting all that stuff. I reckon Hannah could sell anything if she put her mind to it."

"No worries, Tony," Jai assured him with a grin. "Even if her cooking isn't great, she'll sell it to them with her smile and they'll *think* it's great."

"I hope you're right," Tony bit out, feeling he'd been an all too easy victim of that smile.

"Hey! Don't forget that scrumptious salad she brought along yesterday," Tracy reminded the other two divers. "Anyone who can create a salad as good as that is sure to be a fine cook."

Tony frowned. "She doesn't have to bring salads with her."

Tracy shook a finger at him. "Don't discourage it. I sneaked back for seconds it was so yummy. And I wasn't the only one. The stuff we get delivered didn't rate in comparison. Wait and see, Tony."

"Okay. I'll wait and see. I'm glad you're all happy with Hannah. I'll go and have a word with her."

"A lot more cheerful to be around than Chris has been the past few weeks," Eric tossed at him for good measure.

All of which formed a very positive picture, Tony acknowledged as he moved on into the saloon. The need to be fair-minded about Hannah O'Neill, particularly where this job was concerned, bore down on the personal prejudice he'd been nursing. There was not a hint of envy or anything negative coming from Tracy, and while Jai and Eric obviously *liked* Hannah as a person, neither guy had given any indication of hot sexual interest.

Was he the only one turned on by her?

Energy…chemistry…all he really knew was that some compelling force was being generated and he needed to get a hold on it so it didn't mess him up. Captain of his ship, he thought again as he approached the L-shaped bar that enclosed the galley. Consciously relaxing, he was ready to smile at both Hannah and Megan who were busily setting out cups and saucers for the first rush on tea or coffee by the incoming passengers.

"Good morning, Tony!" A bright greeting from Megan who spotted him first. She had a very short crop of brown hair and was into ear-piercing in a big way—at least a dozen studs and rings hanging off her lobes—but Tony didn't mind her taste in fashion. Nothing about Megan distracted him.

"Good morning," he echoed, barely managing a glance at her. His attention was riveted on Hannah, who was very slow to raise her gaze to him.

There was tension in her sudden stillness. Her

shoulders squared as her chin lifted, eyelashes at half-mast, veiling her feelings until she had them guarded enough to deflect any probe from him. He caught the wary expression instantly. And more. A flash of vulnerability that made his stomach flip.

She was as unsettled by him as he was by her.

No devious plan.

The thoughts flashed through his mind and a wild satisfaction surged over the questions that had nagged so infuriatingly. It wasn't one-sided. He wasn't her victim. A bite had been taken out of her breezy confidence with that almost-kiss on Wednesday, which surely meant she'd been left in some sexual turbulence, too. *Over him.*

It put a grin on his face.

"Hannah…" he said with an encouraging nod, not stopping to consider whether *encouraging* was a good move.

She had her hair braided again. Such long, thick wavy hair had to look fantastic when it was not constricted, even more fantastic spread across a pillow. Funny how both she and Megan wore the same uniform—white T-shirt and shorts with coral cuffs and the Coral King insignia on the pockets—yet it simply looked neat on Megan. Hannah filled it with luscious curves. Tony had a mental image of the hidden butterfly and wondered if it was fluttering.

"Got here in time!" a triumphant voice declared behind him.

A voice he instantly recognised.

Matt's voice!

His younger brother swung past him and dumped

two trays of fruit on the wide counter of the bar. "Hi, Tony!" he tossed over his shoulder, the barest acknowledgment before concentrating the full blast of his big personality on Hannah. "You must be the new chef. I'm Matt King. I supply the exotic fruit you ran out of yesterday. And from what Chris said, if you want a job change…"

"Stop right there, Matt!" Tony cut in. "Hannah is mine!"

"Hannah…" Matt rolled her name off his tongue with obvious pleasure and completely ignoring Tony, thrust his arm over the bar, hand extended. "Glad to meet you!"

She took his hand, looking at him somewhat dazedly. Matt was almost as big as Alex and always a hit with women, an uninhibited talker with the gift of the gab, not to mention his good looks, curly hair, and dark chocolate eyes that apparently had the power to induce swooning.

Tony unclenched his jaw and bit out, "If you think you can come in here and poach on my territory…" He stepped right up to the bar in belligerent challenge, which served to unhook Matt's hand from Hannah's so he could hold it up to Tony in a gesture of peace.

"I know you need her right now with Chris leaving," he said reasonably. "But…"

"No buts. You've delivered your fruit. Now beat it, Matt!"

Both hands up now, warding off the fire-power Tony was in no mood to tone down. "Okay, okay," Matt soothed. "Didn't mean to make waves. Just letting Hannah know I appreciate her talent for getting people to try something new. Not many people have that kind of entrepreneurial skill, Tony. It takes..."

"What does it take to get you moving out of here, Matt?"

He huffed. "You're not listening to me."

"You're out of line."

Lowered brows, eyes shooting some private meaning. "Alex said..."

"I don't care what Alex said," Tony snapped, wishing he hadn't implied to his older brother that Hannah was more Nonna's choice than his and he didn't like being boxed into a corner.

"I thought..."

"Think again." And Alex should have kept his mouth shut!

"Fine!" Matt slanted an appealing smile at Hannah. "Just keep up the good push on my exotic fruit. Could tap into new markets with the kind of people who go out on *Duchess*." He clapped Tony on the shoulder. "Got the word. No poaching!"

He swaggered off in such apparent good humour, Tony knew he'd just been baited. His younger brother was too damned clever, and he enjoyed nothing better than getting a rise out of Tony or Alex. It probably came from having been bossed around by them when he was little, but Matt really needed being taken down a peg or two. In the meantime, he'd better stay clear of Hannah if he didn't want to get thumped.

With a sense of having settled something important, Tony swung his gaze back to the woman who'd triggered this territorial battle. In his mind she now belonged to him. It had been a swift transition in his thinking about her but Tony didn't pause to ponder reasons or gather doubts. How they were going to get over the employer/employee hump was still a complicated issue. Nevertheless, there had to be a way.

The green eyes were opened wide, staring at him as though she didn't know what to make of his sharp exchange with Matt. Hot colour in her cheeks indicated a fast pumping of blood. Had she picked up the inference that he'd complained to Alex about their grandmother's arbitrary choices?

"First day without Chris," he rolled out, using business to remove the personal element from her thoughts. "Let me know if you run into any problems and I'll do what I can to ease them for you. Don't try to go it alone. Teamwork is always better. Okay?"

She nodded, still wide-eyed and looking totally confused.

He moved off to greet the passengers now streaming onto *Duchess,* a new zest for life leaping happily through his veins. His confusion had smoothed out into an understanding he found both exhilarating and highly challenging. It was great to feel captain of his ship, master of his fate, the holder of knowledge he could use as he saw fit.

He wasn't expecting to be rocked again.

Fate decreed otherwise.

CHAPTER SIX

HANNAH is mine!

The possessive ring of those words had been so loud and strong, nothing else had really penetrated Hannah's mind during the brief meeting with Tony's brother, the tropical fruit plantation King, Matt... Matteo...more Italian-looking than Tony or Alex, his eyes so dark they were almost black, reminding her of his grandmother.

Tony had cut him off so fast, she'd only had an initial impression of big vitality, then... *Hannah is mine!* Was it simply a territorial demarcation, brooking no interference with his staff placement? Or was it as personal as it had sounded? Intensely personal.

She'd been incredibly nervous about coming face-to-face with Tony this morning. Having watched and assisted Chris for the past two days, she was reasonably confident of handling the job. That wasn't the problem. It was the feeling that Tony King had the power to stir things in her she had no control over which really threw her into a loop.

Physical attraction was fine. It was natural. Mutual attraction made it all the more exciting. But chaos had never been acceptable in Hannah's world. She liked to plan, to have her life proceeding in an order that made sense to her, that resulted in foreseeable outcomes. Of course, one had to make reasonable allowances for the unpredictable, and she'd always been able to adjust quickly to external surprises. But she'd been well and truly rocked by the internal shocks Tony King had left her with on Wednesday afternoon.

Hannah is mine!

Did he sense he could just take her if he wished?

It was a terribly disturbing thought. She wasn't just a body that responded willy-nilly to his. She needed to get some respect going here. There was a little matter of freedom of choice, too. Tony King did not *own* her, not even as a chef. Being on trial went both ways. She could leave if she wanted to.

Though when it came to *wanting,* she couldn't help thinking he looked stunningly handsome in his white and navy captain's uniform. Most of the incoming female passengers obviously thought so, too, glowing as he greeted them on entry to the saloon, then casting an interested second glance at him as they advanced to the bar for tea or coffee.

"A terrific host," Sally had said, and certainly he was giving out pleasure as though he had an endless well of it to give. In fact, Hannah was beginning to feel quite jealous of the smiles he bestowed so easily on other women. She remembered his first smile to her up at the castle, before his grandmother had declared her the new chef for *Duchess.* Definitely pleasure. But he'd withheld it from her ever since. Which begged many questions and didn't make her feel good.

Nevertheless, she put on a happy face for the people she was serving, automatically feeding their anticipation of having a wonderful day ahead of them and fully intending to contribute to it every way she could. It wasn't her fault that the smile froze on her face at the sound of a voice she'd never wanted to hear again.

"Hannah! I can't believe it! What on earth are you doing here? I thought you must have taken some top-flight job overseas…"

Jodie! Her ex-best friend, Jodie Dowler. Who was now Jodie Lovett, Flynn's wife. Which meant… Hannah's heart dropped like a stone at the thought of Flynn being on board, too.

Here was Jodie almost at the bar, her long black hair still styled into a sexy tousled look with artistic strands hanging around the darkly pencilled blue eyes, bright red lipstick matching a bright red shirt, gold belt, tight white slacks—gorgeous Jodie, babbling loudly about Hannah having completely dropped out of *the scene*. Had she always been so *loud?*

Tony was frowning, his gaze darting between the two of them, and Flynn was bound to appear next—Flynn, the dazzling dynamo of the money markets, whip-lean in his city elegance, sharp, witty, one of the few men Hannah had ever known to carry off chestnut-red hair with distinction, with an arrogance that somehow made it highly individual to him, setting off his high forehead, but not hiding his ears, Hannah reminded herself. Though that detraction didn't help to lower the rush of inner agitation. She wished there was a hole in the ground for her to drop into.

"Not a word of you from anyone for the past two

years," Jodie complained, as though Hannah had committed a crime against *her*.

"Tea or coffee?" she asked through gritted teeth.

"Hannah?" It was an exasperated appeal for some personal acknowledgment to be made.

"Fruit juice…soft drink?" The words tripped out in stubborn denial that Jodie *Lovett* had any claim on her apart from the service she was paying for.

"Oh, coffee then," she gave in petulantly. "Make it two cappuccinos. Flynn will be here in a minute. He just stopped to chat to the dive team."

Hannah concentrated on using the coffee machine, fiercely cursing the fact she was a captive audience here in the open galley, but be damned if she'd give Jodie or Flynn any response that wasn't related to her job. She didn't care if it appeared rude. They'd lost any right to demand anything more personal from her two years ago.

"Hannah, for God's sake! We were best friends…"

It hadn't stopped her from having sex with Flynn behind Hannah's back.

The coffee whooshed into the cups.

"We didn't plan to hurt you," Jodie hissed.

"Help yourself to sugar." Hannah nodded to the sugar bowl as she placed the order on the counter in front of Jodie, determinedly keeping her hands steady. She was shaking inside, hating being cornered like this, hating Jodie for confronting her so publicly, hating herself for not being able to deal with it better.

It was like ghosts walking over her grave—the grave of the life she'd had before it had been killed by Jodie and Flynn. She didn't want to remember it. It was gone. Long gone. They had no right to come back and haunt her with it. She'd moved on.

"Damn it! I'm not going to let you block me out!"

Selfish. Totally selfish. What Jodie wants, Jodie gets. Except she'd coated her selfishness with lots of sugar in the old days, so sweetly cajoling Hannah had been fooled into closing her eyes to that truth. Much easier to go along with Jodie's plans, to fit in. But not today. Not anymore. Ever.

"Flynn and I are only human, Hannah," came the slimy defence. "If you hadn't been up on your high-flying pedestal, not making time for us..."

"Please excuse me. There are other people to serve."

"The other girl can serve them," was snapped back at her.

Hannah ignored that argument, skirting Megan to move to the other end of the L-shaped bar where there were people waiting, wonderful strangers who had no axe to grind. She bestowed her best smile on them.

"Tea or coffee?"

"Tea, please."

Thank heaven she didn't have to move back to the coffee machine. The urn for tea was at this end. "Is this your first visit to The Great Barrier Reef?" she asked brightly, picking up the woman's very English accent.

"Yes. Though we have dived in the Caribbean," her husband remarked.

Hannah grinned. "Ah...but what we have here is

one of the seven wonders of the modern world. I'm sure you won't be disappointed."

They laughed and took their tea. "I'll report back to you," the man tossed at her as they left the bar.

"You do that," Hannah cheerfully invited, wishing they'd stayed to chat longer. It was easy to give out to strangers. She had a desperate need to surround herself with them. Then she could keep operating on a surface level that didn't hurt. But Megan was serving the only other person waiting.

"Flynn, Flynn…"

Jodie's call was like a nailfile scraping her spine.

"…look who I've found! It's Hannah!"

She would not turn around. No way. She picked up the bowl of used teabags and emptied it in the garbage bin.

"Hannah?" Flynn's voice sounding puzzled and disturbed.

Hannah hoped a load of guilt was hitting him like a freight train and he'd want to get out from under the weight of it as fast as he could.

"Come and say hello to her," Jodie commanded, a note of sweet malice in her tone now, determined on breaking Hannah's guard against them.

"Ah, Jodie, isn't it?" Tony's voice. "I was just inviting Flynn up to the bridge to watch us take *Duchess* out now that everyone's on board. You have your coffee? Yes, I see you have. Good! Do come and join us."

A very smooth rescue mission.

Hannah hated his awareness of a problem blowing

up with her at the centre of it, but was intensely grateful for his interference.

"Thank you," Jodie crooned. "But Flynn must say hello to Hannah first. We haven't seen her for so-o-o long."

Putting her on the spot in front of her boss!

No ready excuse to deny a simple greeting.

No escape.

Flynn had to be faced.

Get it over and done with, Hannah savagely reasoned.

Her stomach was curdling with rebellion as she swung around, her gaze instinctively targeting Tony, the green blaze of her eyes warning she was not going to play Jodie's game, come hell or high water.

"It's good to see you, Hannah," Flynn said quietly.

He was a blur beside Tony—a grey blur in some grey outfit—and she kept him a blur. Tony was taller, broader-shouldered, physically a stronger male image that helped to blot out Flynn's, and his eyes were certainly just as sharply intelligent, boring into hers for answers that were buried under too many layers of pain to be dragged out into the open.

She forced herself to nod at Flynn but she wouldn't speak to him. Wouldn't look directly at him, either. She didn't care if Tony fired her on the spot. Her eyes challenged him to do it if he wanted to. Everything within her revolted against pretending this situation was acceptable in any shape or form.

"Right! Let's move," Tony said with firm authority, picking up the two cups of coffee, thrusting one at Jodie and one at Flynn so they were forced to take them. "Hannah has a lot to do preparing for lunch and it's a fine morning to be up on the bridge. Come and enjoy the view."

He literally herded them away, talking at them with so much dominant energy, any protest they might have made wilted under it. Even so, Hannah knew Jodie wouldn't be silenced for long. In no time flat she'd be spilling out to Tony that his new chef was a very *new* chef, her major work experience being in a completely different field. And then she'd pump him for all he knew about her—ammunition for her next visit to the galley.

"What a pushy bitch!" Megan commented.

Hannah took a deep breath to ease the painful tightness in her chest. The sense of being intolerably trapped was pressing in on her. The urge to run, to jump off the boat before it left dock, warred with the responsibility she had taken on. Impossible for Megan to handle all the work of the galley alone. The others had their duties. She'd be letting everyone down if she skipped out on them.

"Are you okay?" Megan asked, concern in her voice.

Hannah looked at her, desperation voicing a plea. "Could I ask a big favour of you, Megan?"

"Keep between you and them?"

She nodded. "They caused me a lot of grief in the past."

"Leave it to me. You just do your stuff, Hannah, and I'll spike their guns every time they front up to the bar."

"Thanks." She managed a wobbly smile. "I'd really appreciate it."

"Be a pleasure. Though I don't think you need worry too much. Tony caught the drift and he'll cut them out of the pack."

"Cut them...what do you mean?"

"Oh, he has a way of spotting trouble-makers and diverting trouble before it can develop. The guy is really smart, you know? Not just a pretty face?"

A nervous little laugh gurgled from Hannah's throat. "I haven't thought of Tony King as pretty."

Megan grinned. "You mean...more a knock-out hunk? Gotta say he's not bad for an older guy."

"Not bad," Hannah agreed, wondering precisely how old Tony was. Early thirties? The phrase, "older guy" hadn't even occurred to her. On the other hand, Megan was only nineteen, making the age gap bigger.

"Anyhow, you just relax now," the younger girl advised. "You won't see those two again until lunchtime, and you can bet your boots Tony will be right on their tails, making sure you don't get hassled out of focusing on cooking. *Duchess* is his baby, you know. Got to have the food and everything else for it just right."

"A hard boss?" Hannah queried, worrying now that she might not measure up under the stress of being accessible to Jodie and Flynn. Did they have to keep spoiling everything for her?

"No. He's very fair. You can count on that. He expects you to be fair to him, too. That's okay in my book."

Hannah nodded, though she bitterly wondered if

there was any fairness in this world. Why did Flynn and Jodie have to visit Port Douglas at this time and book a trip on *Duchess* today of all days? If they had any decency, they'd stay away from her. Just let her get on with this job since it was her choice. They'd certainly made their choice.

Amazingly that seemed to happen. Or Tony King made it happen. They made no re-appearance in the saloon at all, not even for lunch. Keith, the first mate, brought down an order for three lunches of barramundi and salad. Hannah cooked the fish, Megan served the salads, and the lunches were taken up to the upper deck, along with a chilled bottle of Chardonnay.

"See?" Megan commented smugly as she helped Keith stack the tray. "Tony's got those two eating out of his hands. No problem."

Except what they might be giving him in exchange, like personal information Hannah would prefer to keep private. She was utterly powerless to stop that and the thought of her past history being laid bare—especially to Tony King—made her feel vulnerable on too many levels.

It took considerable willpower to keep herself operating on a professional level, chatting to the passengers, ensuring what they ordered was cooked to perfection, delivering with a smile. Her inner tension eased somewhat once the lunch rush was over. No mishaps. No complaints. No problems apart from those in her head.

The afternoon wore on. *Duchess* left the outer reef at three o'clock for the run home. Most of the passengers trailed into the saloon, their scuba-diving and snorkelling finished for the day. Hannah forced herself to repeat the exotic fruit presentation which formed a pleasurable and refreshing wind-down during the ninety minutes it took to get back to Port Douglas. Tracy and Jai offered to man the bar and serve drinks, freeing Megan to take samples of the fruit to the upper deck.

Nothing was actually said, but Hannah sensed the whole staff had been worded up to shield her from the Lovetts. Ironically, this probably meant Flynn and Jodie had received five-star service all day, watched over and handled with kid gloves. All Tony King's doing, of course, though Hannah was under no delusions she'd be paying for it, one way or another.

If Jodie and Flynn didn't pounce on her the moment she walked off *Duchess,* Tony would, wanting to know what else in Hannah's background might raise an ugly head to disturb the smooth running of his ship. She tried not to think about it until she had to. Maybe everything could be avoided, relegated to the past where it belonged.

It was a vain hope.

They docked at the marina on schedule. The passengers streamed off, heading for transport back to their accommodation. The crew cleaned up after them. When there was nothing left to be done, they moved as a group onto the wharf, ready to report back to the office and be briefed on tomorrow's passenger list.

Predictably, Tony fell into step beside her, waving the others ahead to ensure a private conversation.

Hannah's nerves jangled an instant protest, but her head told her she owed this man for saving her from an unbearable situation today, regardless of whether it had been simply a pragmatic decision to avoid a bad scene that might upset people who'd paid for pleasure.

A grateful "thank you" pushed to be said, yet it was an admission that led straight into territory she didn't want to tread. An apology did the same thing. Better not to say anything. Let him lead into the raw area, if he had to.

"Are you planning to skip out on me, Hannah?"

The question startled her into halting. Her head jerked up as the realisation hit that the last previous sight he'd had of her today was the confrontation over the bar when she had been on the verge of bolting. She met a hard piercing gaze that was determined on nailing her down.

Her own sense of fairness forced a reply. "No. I'm sorry about today. Those people…" The heat of acute embarrassment burned up her neck and into her cheeks. "…they're not likely to book another trip on *Duchess.*"

"Right now they're sitting at a table out on the deck of the Fiorelli Bistro and Bar, which we'll be passing on the way to the office. You are being targeted, Hannah. I can keep them from getting to you but I'll need your co-operation. Are you willing to go along with me? Yes or no?"

"Yes." The word tumbled out, driven by an anguish of spirit that begged to be free of any further involvement with Flynn and Jodie.

"Then take my hand now and leave everything to me."

She didn't really take it. He took hers with a confident command that pulled her along with him. Another rescue mission, she thought, too shaken by the prospect of having to confront Jodie and Flynn by herself to even consider resisting Tony King's offer of support and protection.

It felt good, having him at her side.

She could feel his strength pumping up her arm, giving her wrung-out heart a much needed shot of adrenaline. Her frazzled mind didn't even begin to consider what Tony might do to ensure she wasn't harassed. He'd said to leave everything to him and her instincts had no trouble believing he would be master of the situation, whichever way it turned.

CHAPTER SEVEN

TONY liked the feel of Hannah's hand in his. He liked having her trust, too. What he didn't like was her reaction to the couple whose appearance on *Duchess* this morning had killed her natural exuberance stone-dead. Worse. She wouldn't even glance at the guy, and it had looked to Tony as though she'd been on the verge of quitting to escape the sense of entrapment with those two.

No need to be Einstein to work out the equation—*if he wanted to keep her, keep them out of her way.*

No need to consider his response, either. Losing Hannah O'Neill at this point was not acceptable. Not only would he be without a chef who had already won the approval of the crew, but he hadn't yet had the chance to explore what there could be between them on a personal level.

Nevertheless, this extreme stand from Hannah raised many questions that had Tony's mind buzzing, particularly since it hadn't softened one bit in the intervening hours of being free of the Lovett couple. Her current tension over their nearby presence was just as strong as it had been this morning. Which brought him to one firm decision. There was something going on here that *he* didn't want to walk away from.

It had been a very interesting day, observing the

interplay between the Lovetts. No love left in that marriage. Tony doubted there ever had been love. The woman was a man-eating sex-pot, mixing manipulative flirting with sly sniping, neither of which hit their mark with her husband who had maintained an air of arrogant boredom towards her malicious game-playing.

Tony had brushed off Jodie Lovett's questions about Hannah, stating only that she held the position of chef on *Duchess*. Flynn Lovett had bluntly told his wife to "put a gag on it" when she'd started claiming that Hannah's being a chef was ridiculous. He'd given Tony his full co-operation in diverting the conversation onto other subjects, much to his wife's chagrin. Yet Tony was convinced Flynn had been playing his own game—a waiting game—and the focus of all the games today was Hannah.

Why was the big question.

And why would she want to run away from them?

He could only think that old wounds had been re-opened. Bad wounds. Bad enough that re-visiting them was intolerable.

Tony didn't like that, either.

He wanted the butterfly flying free with him, not pulled away and hurt by these people.

"We won't take the usual route along the promenade deck to the office," he instructed. "We'll walk straight ahead into the shopping mall, bypassing the open-air table they've selected." Without pausing a beat he added, "For someone who's not a trained chef, I'd have to say you have a fine touch with barramundi."

She darted an apprehensive glance at him and he grinned at her. "You delivered. That's what counts. Now smile back at me. We're going to have a happy chat and not even notice the Lovetts."

Her smile flashed out, tinged with relief at his acceptance of her. "I have had training, Tony. Though not anything formal. More like an apprentice."

"Best training of all," he approved, pleased she could still say his name with that spine-tingling lilt. "What's more, everyone on the crew likes you. You're amongst friends, Hannah."

"They're a nice bunch of people."

"True. I picked them myself."

Her eyes flashed irony. "Except for me."

"You're certainly the surprise package but I'm not about to give you up. They're watching. Beam me another bright smile."

She did.

"You've got killer dimples, Hannah O'Neill, and I want to hear you laugh."

She managed it, chasing away the hunted look his warning had briefly evoked.

Having twigged that her quarry was heading towards the mall doors instead of the promenade, Jodie Lovett grabbed her husband's arm, urging action. Flynn unfolded himself from his chair, waving to catch attention. "Tony, come and have a drink with us. Hannah, too."

The fingers Tony held instantly scrunched up, nails biting. It was disturbing proof that Flynn got to her more than Jodie did—Flynn, the man! And this was not the past. This was here and now. The idea of any man having a strong effect on Hannah stirred all Tony's hackles.

He did not so much as slacken their pace towards the mall, though he acknowledged the call by raising his arm in a farewell salute. "More work to do. Enjoy yourselves."

Which brought Jodie to her feet, fighting against having their plans frustrated. "Join us when you're finished," she pressed.

"Other plans," he cheerfully excused.

The doors opened.

As they reached the relative safety of the mall, closing out the Lovetts who would make themselves ridiculous chasing after them at this point, Tony was acutely aware of Hannah's shoulders sagging in relief. He decided not to comment. He had a strong suspicion she was not home free yet. All his instincts were telling him she had become a strong focus of discontent between the Lovetts today and they were not the kind of people to accept having their own interests frustrated.

They were used to winning.

But they were on Tony's home ground. So was Hannah. And Tony had no intention of losing. He'd take the battle right up to them if he had to. The hand in his gave him the right to do it and he was not about to let that right slip. Not for a moment. Not while ever Flynn Lovett was in town!

Hannah's knees were like jelly. But any chance of a forced meeting with Jodie and Flynn was now behind her so at least she could breathe freely again. She took a big gulp of air and shot Tony King a genuine if somewhat wobbly smile.

"Thank you for escorting me."

His eyes lightly teased. "I quite enjoy the role of white knight to fair maiden in distress."

Very conscious that she had put him to considerable trouble on her account today she promised, "I'll be fine tomorrow."

He squeezed her hand. "Let's get through today first."

It reminded Hannah there was still work to be done and she had to get her mind focused on what needed to be ordered to cater for tomorrow's trip. She didn't think of extracting her hand from Tony's. He didn't release it, either, until they reached the office and they went about their separate responsibilities. Only then did she realise how deeply comforting that physical link with him had been.

Over the past two years she had become accustomed to conducting her life on her own. She hadn't minded being alone. It was easy enough to seek company when she wanted it. Strange to recall now how wary she had been of Tony King's effect on her this morning. It was different, feeling he *cared* about her. Or maybe it was just the job he cared about, making sure she didn't let him down.

Somehow that didn't matter. He had held her hand when she had needed it held and it had felt good. Better than anything she'd felt for a long time.

Having completed the salad and seafood orders for Sunday, and feeling more positive about her job now that Tony had been so decisive about keeping her

on—pleased by her cooking, too—Hannah set her
mind on tomorrow as she prepared to leave the office.
She didn't have to think about Jodie and Flynn anymore and she wouldn't. Tomorrow would not be
darkened by the past. Tomorrow she would see more
of Tony King who might be the man to blot Flynn
out of her memory on every level.

Mr Right...

Now there was a piece of whimsy, she thought,
given how wrong she'd been about Flynn wearing
that title. Still, one could but hope. Better than wal-
lowing in old mistakes.

"Hannah!"

Her heart jumped. Tony was coming out of his private office, obviously wanting some last word with
her. She paused, nervous tension gripping her again
at the thought of being queried on her connection to
Jodie and Flynn.

"I'll drive you home," he said with serious intent.
"See you safely to your door."

She stared at him, realising he thought there was a
possibility of her being accosted by the two people
she wished to avoid. It didn't seem likely to Hannah,
yet...they had been waiting for her to come off *Duchess*.

"It's only a ten-minute walk," she started to reason.

"A two-minute drive," he returned pointedly.
"And not out of my way. I have to drop by the castle.
My grandmother will want to know how you're do-
ing."

He didn't allow for any further argument, asking

Sally to lock up the office and sweeping Hannah out to the car-park with him. The reminder of his grandmother's part in her current situation was exercising Hannah's mind as they settled in his jeep.

"Sally said I have Monday and Tuesday off," she quickly mentioned, once they were on the road. "I'll find some accommodation for myself then."

"There's no big hurry," he said offhandedly, as though her staying in the Coral King apartment was of no concern to him.

Had she taken a completely wrong impression of his attitude last Wednesday? Needing the issue clarified, she said, "I thought you would prefer me out as soon as possible."

He slanted her a look that seemed to simmer with personal re-assessments, setting her pulse skittering and re-igniting a very strong sexual awareness of the physical attraction she'd tried to put at a sensible distance.

"I'd prefer you to feel settled in Port Douglas," he answered. "Take your time in finding what's right for you."

They were reasonable words, especially in the light of her urge for frantic flight this morning. On the surface of it, he simply wanted to remove sources of anxiety, give her a bit of space, yet she felt he was now closing the distance he had put between them at their first meeting.

On the other hand, maybe she was just being supersensitive, a nervous hangover from the stress of the encounter with Jodie and Flynn. "That's very kind of you," she said quickly, flushing self-consciously as she felt impelled to add, "You've been very kind all day. I do appreciate your help and…and consideration."

He pulled the jeep up on the verge of the road in front of the apartment block and Hannah rushed to alight. "Don't switch the engine off. I'll be fine from here. Many thanks again, Tony."

Her feet hit the ground.

He switched off the engine.

It thumped into her heart that the last word had not been said and this driving her home was meant to lead to something else. The plain truth was… Hannah wasn't ready for anything else. She recoiled from giving any explanation of her reactions today, and her feelings for Tony himself swirled in an ambivalent mess. She shot him a desperate look of appeal, only to find his focus not on her at all.

His gaze was on another jeep—a common form of transport in Port Douglas, particularly with the hire-car companies. It had just passed their parked vehicle and was moving slowly up the hill towards the castle. It came as a very severe jolt to Hannah to see that the male driver had chestnut hair and his female companion's long black locks fell over a red shirt.

"They followed us!" The shock of it spilled out the all-too-telling words.

"Yes!" Tony shot her a fiercely determined look. "No argument, Hannah. I'm coming in with you."

He was out of the jeep, his door banged shut in emphatic purpose before she could gather any wits at all. Her mind was in a ferment over the ramifications of Jodie and Flynn now knowing where she could be found in her private time.

As Tony rounded the jeep, she had the sense of a torrent of dynamic energy coming at her, encompassing her in his personal force-field. His eyes had the glitter of battle in them and his strong male face wore a hard aggression that was not about to countenance any denial of his intention.

Her knees had gone to jelly again. She felt helplessly caught by elements she had no control over and all her mind could do was bleat, *It's not fair…not fair…*

Tony scooped her along with him, an arm around her waist clamping her to his side. Somehow her legs kept up with his strides and they were at the front door of the apartment so fast, she then had to fumble in her handbag for the key. The moment it was produced, Tony took it, opened the door, and swept her inside. He was right behind her and she heard the door click shut, trapping her into what was now an inescapable situation.

"Okay!" he said with satisfaction. "When the Lovetts drive back down the hill, as they must, they'll see the empty jeep and conclude I'm here with you, so I don't anticipate they'll want to intrude because it's not me they want contact with."

It was impossible to refute his reasoning. Hannah felt sick at being pursued like this. What more did Jodie and Flynn want from her? Hadn't they taken enough, abusing everything she'd given them? She looked bleakly at the man who had appointed himself the safeguard between her and them. His eyes were ablaze with a demand for answers. The only words she could think of to say were, "It's not my fault."

His expression softened to sympathetic concern. "I think a stiff drink is in order. You go on out to the balcony and breathe in some fresh air while I raid the complimentary bar. What would you like?"

"I usually only drink water. It's good for you," she added so stiltedly, it brought an ironic smile to the grim set of Tony's mouth.

"Okay. A long glass of iced water coming up."

"Thank you."

Better to keep a clear head than fuzz it with alcohol. There was no possibility of drowning her sorrows in it anyway. She had a few minutes' respite before Tony's questions would start. With the feeling of having her privacy terribly violated and being helpless to stop it, she walked towards the setting sun outside, knowing it couldn't give her the sense of peace that this fraught day was finally over.

"Hannah…"

She paused, her spine tingling at the soft call. Not yet, she silently begged. Please…not yet. She couldn't bring herself to look back, to face what had to be faced. Not yet.

"I have to know the problem in order to fix it," came the quiet assertion. "Make up your mind to share it with me, Hannah, because it needs to be fixed. I'm not about to leave this apartment wondering if you'll still be here tomorrow."

How do you fix something that's unfixable? she wondered, moving on to unlock the glass door to the balcony and slide it open.

How do you handle people like Jodie and Flynn who won't recognise that the unfixable can't be fixed?

She stepped outside and wandered slowly over to the railing, leaning on it, gazing out over the water, the cane fields beyond it, the mountains beyond them, the reddening sky leaching colour from both sea and land.

Impossible to roll back the forces of nature, she thought. Everything moved to a pattern as old as time. Perhaps people did, too, and there was no stopping it.

Every female instinct in her entire body quivered as she heard Tony King step out on the balcony. He brought with him a force of nature that was far more immediate than those forming the landscape in front of her. It was coming right at her, and it was not about to be rolled back, either.

CHAPTER EIGHT

TONY set the drinks down on the glass top of the aluminium table on the balcony. There were six chairs around the table but Hannah hadn't chosen to sit. In fact, she'd distanced herself from him as far as she could, standing at the railing, her back still turned to him, shutting him out.

Was she brooding over Flynn Lovett, wishing…?

No, damn it! Whatever had gone on between them it was two years in the past and the guy was married. Not happily but that wasn't the point. Tony didn't want Hannah to be vulnerable to any move Flynn might make on her. He wanted that guy wiped right out of her mind. And talking about him wasn't going to do it. Her feelings about someone else was not what Tony wanted Hannah to share with him.

His instincts were raging at him to act.

Act now.

No waiting.

No weighing up rights and wrongs.

Talking, even thinking, was not the path to take here. Some things went beyond reason, he told himself, his legs already taking the path of their choice. Some things had to be pursued, known, taken in and processed. Some things could not be denied.

"Hannah…"

She turned her head towards him. The lost look in

her eyes caused an intolerable tightness in his chest. It was wrong. She wasn't alone, wasn't lost. He was here. He had to get through to her.

Her skin prickled at the way he said her name—like an intense claim on her that threatened any resistance with the power to smash it. It struck a compelling need to understand what drove Tony King and drew her into turning from the railing to face the oncoming force.

Before she had time to understand anything, his arms were around her and her hands were flat against his chest and her lower body was in vibrant contact with his, completely blowing all awareness of the rest of the world right out of her mind. Hard muscular thighs pressing, a broad hot chest heaving against her palms, strong arms maintaining possession, eyes blazing into hers, intent on burning away any defensive barrier she might fling up.

No time…

His mouth crashed down on hers, starting a passionate onslaught of kisses, and some fierce wild creature burst into life inside Hannah, exulting in the passion, feasting on it, and far from flinging up barriers, she wilfully and wantonly incited an escalation of this tumult of feeling, a totally reckless exploration of it, driving Hannah's hands up over wonderfully muscled shoulders which she fancied could bear any weight, carry any burden and make light of it, revelling in the strong column of his neck, the springy thickness of his hair, the sheer dominant manliness of him that was geared to fight any battle for her.

And her breasts were now crushed against the thump of a heart that cared about her, wanted her, his hands telling her so, his body telling her so, banishing the loneliness, bringing her in from the cold of not having anyone for herself, giving her the sense that nothing could come between her and this man. He wouldn't let it. No other woman. Her...only her.

A deep primitive satisfaction seized her as she felt his erection pressing its urgent need to join with her, proof of how much she was desired, and the desire to have him was exploding through her, pounding a need that screamed to have the emptiness of her inner world filled by him.

Thumbs hooking into her shorts and panties, hauling them down, her own hands attacking his shorts, wild to be rid of obstructions, hot for the feeling of flesh against flesh, and the fierce elation of finding how big he was, her fingers wrapping around him, loving his arousal, anticipation of how he would use it playing sweet havoc with her own sex, the yearning so intense, so overwhelmingly needful.

He hoisted her up on the railing, one arm supporting her there as he moved between her thighs. She threw her arms around his neck, instinctively hanging on to his strength as she felt him slide between her soft folds, stroking, seeking, teasing, building the wanting to fever-pitch. She felt herself convulsing in readiness and wrapped her legs around his hips, desperate to pull him inside her, to have him there.

The first plunge came—oh, such ecstatic pleasure—and stayed deep, the whole hard length of him so deliciously deep, like an integral part of her that she'd always missed and been waiting for and here it was, making her entire body pulse with joy. Then he drew her head back from where she'd rested it near his ear and kissed her, invading her mouth with the same deep intimacy, and he scooped her off the railing and carried her with him still inside her, making her feel an integral part of him *he* couldn't bear to let go.

He unclipped her bra, lowered her to the table surface, rolled up her T-shirt, bared her breasts and kissed them with an intensity that seemed to draw on all she was. Her body throbbed to the rhythm of his mouth, incredible sensations flooding through her, and when he raised his head and looked into her eyes, it was as though he was piercing her soul, demanding entry, forcing entry with a power that would not be denied.

"Come fly with me!"

Another command—ringing in her ears this time, like bells of jubilation—and a hand stroked her stomach, circling the butterfly she'd had tattooed around her navel as a symbol of freedom from all the stress of her life before she flew away from it. But the only freedom she wanted now was the freedom to fly with this man, to soar to heights that only they could share, and she felt him move inside her, a slow slide out, a fast slide in...pause...her muscles squeezing, holding.

Again...and again...her whole body instinctively fine-tuning itself to his rhythm...and the soaring began, like wings lifting through her, beating faster and faster, carried on currents that ebbed and flowed, lifting, floating, lifting higher to exquisite pinnacles of feeling, then flying higher still until it seemed the magical sky they were travelling shattered in a starburst of sensation and she lost herself in it.

But she didn't stay lost because Tony gathered her up again... Tony...cradling her against his lovely warm chest, taking her with him and she was kissing his neck, tasting his skin, breathing him in—such a wonderful, beautiful man who hadn't stopped wanting her.

He laid her on the bed and swiftly removed the rest of her clothes, and his, so they were both fully naked. She didn't think about how she looked to him. She was drinking in how utterly magnificent he was. To her eyes he had the perfect male physique, and when he stretched out on the bed beside her, her fingers thrilled to the sensual pleasure of touching him, the tight musculature, the satin-smooth skin, the whole shape of him.

It was probably wrong to make comparisons, but she couldn't help thinking he was more essentially masculine than Flynn, stronger, harder. Tony King... a king amongst men. She smiled at the thought and he smiled at her smile, lifting a hand to lightly trace the curve of her mouth with his index finger, making her lips tingle, just as he made her whole body tingle, though he could do that with only a look.

"Happier now?" he asked, his eyes simmering with pleasure in her.

"Yes," she answered simply. It was true, though she didn't want to look at why. Maybe she was in shock at arriving where she now was. Maybe she'd moved beyond shock to a place where normal things didn't matter. Her mind whispered, *Let it be. Even if it was only for now, just let it be.*

His smile turned slightly crooked. "I hope we haven't committed a totally rash act. I didn't think about protection."

She frowned over the health concerns that hadn't even entered her head. It was an intrusion of a reality that jarred on her, yet ignoring it wasn't right, either. "You don't have to worry about me," she answered quickly. It was embarrassing to ask but a risk had been taken. She searched his eyes anxiously. "I trust you're…"

"In tiptop condition, yes. But there is the pregnancy issue."

A fast calculation relieved her on that score. "Safe," she assured him.

"You're on the pill?"

"No." At his raised eyebrows, she added, "No need. I haven't had sex for two years."

His brows dipped into a dark frown. "Two years," he muttered, as though that length of time seemed very unnatural to him.

She shrugged. "I haven't wanted to."

A sharp look. "But you wanted to with me?"

"Yes."

Eyes probing hers. "And you're happy about it?"

"Yes." For now, she was. How could she not be with a man like him wanting her like this?

His face cleared into a wide grin. "Well, so am I, Hannah O'Neill. Got to say you've had me in knots from the first moment of meeting."

"*You*...in knots?" She shook her head incredulously. "I thought you didn't like me."

"Didn't like the situation of an employee getting under my skin. It's a good rule...never mix business with pleasure."

Understanding clicked in. "I won't take advantage of this in our work situation, Tony."

"No, I don't believe you will." He stroked her cheek, his eyes adding their own warm caress. "It's very clear you're not a user, Hannah."

He wasn't, either. She was sure of it. He was a man who took control, who wore a mantle of responsibility easily, as though born to it. "A fair man," Megan had said, and Hannah didn't doubt it for a moment. Clearly he had guessed, known, felt that the physical attraction was mutual, which, of course, had triggered this outcome.

She thought what an extraordinary day it had been—this morning, fretting over the disturbing strength of Tony's sexual impact on her, finding how amazingly real it was this afternoon, and in between... Jodie and Flynn with all the blighting memories of their betrayal of her trust in so many things.

Tony saw the happy light in her eyes dim just before her lashes lowered, veiling the clear green windows to her soul. He instantly sensed she'd gone to that bleak place she didn't want to share with him. Had he said anything to lead her down that road?

Not a user...

But Jodie Lovett was.

And two years of celibacy, feeling no need for sex.

Maybe a woman could hold back physical frustration that long without feeling too much stress. Women were certainly different to men. Nevertheless, it smacked to Tony of a deliberate disassociation from her own sexuality, and that spelled big hurt. Not physical or she wouldn't have responded to him as she had. No, this was emotional trauma so deep it had turned her off getting close to a guy, probably in every sense, and from her reaction to Flynn Lovett...

Was she thinking of him?

Comparing?

Primitive instincts surged to the fore again, demanding action that would spin his rival right out of her thoughts.

"Unbraid your hair!"

The command jolted Hannah out of her bitter memories. She was with Tony...Tony who was looking at her with such fierce desire in his eyes she was instantly flooded with the heat of his focus on her and the energy behind it—such powerful energy, pouring into her heart, making it leap with excitement.

"My hair?" she repeated in mesmerised wonder that he did desire her so much.

"I'm into unknotting everything right now," he declared with a challenging little smile. "I want to see it flowing free."

Free... It was a magic word, dispelling all the emotional baggage that had weighed her down today. The idea of being completely free with Tony was exhilarating. She sat up to have both hands free to undo the band that kept the braid fastened, then pulled the thick rope of hair over her shoulder so she could see to unknot it.

Tony clamped his hands around her waist and with seemingly effortless ease, lifted her to straddle him as he rolled onto his back, settling her in very intimate contact right over the apex of his thighs, which he raised enough to hold her precisely in that provocative position, grinning wickedly as he said, "I need you there so I can watch you properly."

She couldn't help laughing. There was absolutely nothing *proper* about this. It was definitely wicked, deliciously wicked, and the wanton creature who had emerged in Hannah when Tony had taken hold of her on the balcony, stirred into life again, urging the fun of teasing, the satisfaction of exciting Tony, watching him watching her.

Just a slight undulation of her hips and his semi-aroused state showed immediate interest in the stimulation, coming to full attention so quickly, the stimulation became highly mutual and so tantalising, Hannah could barely keep her fingers working on loosening the thick swathes of her braid, especially when Tony started caressing her breasts, lightly fanning her nipples with his thumbs, a totally absorbed expression on his face, his eyes simmering their pleasure in every aspect of her body.

It made her feel incredibly sexy, even more so when she shook her hair loose and he wound long rippling waves of it around his hands and pulled her down to him, kissing her with wildly erotic passion as the mass of her hair tumbled around both their faces, increasing the sense of intimacy, of diving headlong into a secret world of their own—just Hannah and Tony.

"Put me inside you."

Yes, she thought, yes…raising herself enough to do it, and even as she felt the exquisite sensation of him sliding into her, he was lifting her breasts to his mouth, taking them, drawing them in just as she was drawing him in, a deep, deep suction that tipped her into explosive action, wanting him to feel the same piercingly sweet sensations as strongly as she did…together…as one…more and more and more so…and the wild intensity of it glittered in their eyes, sharing the frenzy of feeling, exulting in it, loving it, loving each other for the sheer experience of it, driving it beyond all control to a climax so powerful, Hannah was a melting mass of quivering nerve-ends, awash in an ecstatic sea of sensory pleasure, and Tony was cradling her, stroking her, kissing her, making her feel she was wonderful and an endless delight to him, the wanting a continuous stream, not finished, not even diminished.

He was making love to her, she thought, and it didn't matter that they barely knew each other in any conventional sense. It felt so good…right…perfect… she didn't want to question it. Again her mind whispered, *Let it be, just let it be.*

All the conscious knowing she had believed in with Flynn hadn't proved true. All the planning she'd done towards their wedding…wasted in the worst possible way. Better to let life happen, not think too far ahead with this relationship. It would evolve into whatever it was meant to. Right now, all she wanted to think, to feel, was…Tony.

CHAPTER NINE

ISABELLA VALERI KING cast her eye around the grand ballroom, checking that all was as it should be for this wedding reception. King's Castle certainly provided a splendid venue for such happy functions and usually she took pleasure in seeing that everything was running perfectly, as it seemed to be this evening. However, the joy shining from the faces of the newly married couple at the bridal table was another reminder of Antonio's frustrating lack of co-operation in her plans for him.

She had specifically asked him to come by the castle this afternoon, ostensibly to reassure her she had chosen a good chef for *Duchess*—a perfectly reasonable request in the circumstances. Her main objective had been to gauge his interest in Hannah O'Neill, whether or not he had the good sense to see her as a possible partner for him in the journey of life.

They had definitely found each other attractive. Isabella had not missed the signs of a heightened physical awareness between them. *The chemistry,* as her very wise niece, Elizabeth, explained it, was there to draw them together. What Isabella wanted to know was what might keep them apart, and if she could play a hand in removing any problems.

She could do nothing without knowledge. Which made Antonio's failure to visit her, as he said he would, all the more vexing. On the other hand, it wasn't like him not to keep his word. Something must have prevented him from coming. Though he should have had the courtesy to call and let her know.

Feeling the need to talk over her discontent with Rosita, Isabella made a discreet departure from the ballroom, returning to the private quarters of the castle where she might make her own telephone call to her errant grandson. Or one to Hannah O'Neill, inviting her to afternoon tea on her day off.

A glance at her watch showed seven-fifteen. She had eaten earlier, but undoubtedly she would find Rosita in the kitchen, still half expecting Antonio to show up and maybe want something to eat. For over twenty years Rosita had been spoiling Isabella's three grandsons. It was high time they were more considerate of the woman who had served them all so well.

She entered the kitchen in a disgruntled mood and came to a startled halt when Antonio himself entered in a rush by the other door which led through the utility room to the grounds surrounding the castle. He was in his captain's uniform, as though he'd just come from *Duchess,* and he headed straight for the wall telephone, tossing apologetic words at her without so much as a pause in his step.

"Sorry I'm late, Nonna. Something came up and it hasn't gone away. Got to make a call. Only be a minute or two. Hi, Rosita. And no, I don't want anything to eat, thank you. I'll be dining out."

He was dialling even as he spoke. Isabella held her tongue. Antonio was emanating urgency and the fire of determination was in his eyes. She'd seen that look on his face many times, from when he was only a boy. It meant he was going into battle and nothing was going to turn him away from it, regardless of the odds against him.

She glanced at Rosita who was sitting at the island bench, paused in her self-appointed task of making pastry for whatever she planned to cook tomorrow. They exchanged a worried look, both of them aware of how Antonio acted when he was all stirred up.

In his determination not to lose, he could be dangerously reckless, taking risks that a less competitive person would never take. He counted on his force of will to carry him through and mostly it did. But this trait in Antonio's character always struck fear in Isabella's heart.

"Nautilis?" he said into the receiver.

Isabella frowned. The Nautilis was a very high-class restaurant, where President Clinton himself had chosen to dine when he had visited Port Douglas—certainly not the place for a battle.

"It's Tony King. There was a couple on *Duchess* today, name of Lovett. First names Flynn and Jodie. They mentioned they'd booked a table with you tonight. Would you be able to check that for me, please?"

His tone was pitched to a matter-of-fact enquiry, not suggesting any unpleasantness—simply one local business asking a small favour of another local business.

"Thank you. What time are you expecting them?"

He checked his watch, nodding at the reply.

"I'd like to dine there myself tonight. Can you fit

in another table for two? I realise this is late notice but I would appreciate it very much if…''

A grim look of satisfaction on his face indicated a positive reply. Isabella was anxiously wondering about the companion he intended to take with him. Was there some other woman entering the scene? Another one of his come-and-go relationships, wasting time and opportunity?

"Thank you. We'll be arriving at eight-thirty. One other favour… I'd rather not be placed on the same deck as the Lovetts' table. They caused me some trouble today…''

Trouble… So why go looking for more of it, Antonio? The restaurant had split-level dining areas but both levels were open to each other and all guests could be easily viewed.

"They're placed on the upper deck and you'll put us on the lower deck. Fine! Thank you very, very much.''

He replaced the receiver, his eyes glittering with triumph at having successfully made the arrangements he wanted. The battle ground was set. But what were the issues at stake?

"Antonio…'' Isabella started gravely.

He had the gall to grin at her. "Got to move it, Nonna. Shower, shave, change of clothes. I'll chat to you tomorrow. Promise.''

"Two minutes,'' she demanded. "You can give me two minutes. You're not due at the restaurant for another hour and it doesn't take you that long to get ready to go out.''

"Okay. What do you want to know in two minutes?"

He was tense underneath the token indulgence, wanting to go up to his room and get on with the plan he had in mind. He folded his arms with an air of patience, but Isabella read that piece of body language as sheer belligerence—nothing was going to stop him in any significant way.

"Hannah O'Neill," she said, and felt a spark of triumph herself when she saw his hands clench. He was certainly not indifferent to Hannah. Was the battle he intended to fight linked to her in some way? "Is she fitting in well?" Isabella pressed.

"Fine!" he answered tersely. "The crew like her. She can cook fish. I intend to keep her on. Satisfied?"

He started moving, assuming he'd said enough.

"I take it Hannah is still in the Coral King apartment Alessandro gave her?"

"Yes." He hesitated, frowning slightly. "Why do you ask? Monday is her first day off. She's too busy to look for a place before then."

"Oh, I was just thinking of giving her a friendly call. Now that you're finished with the telephone and too busy to chat with me yourself..."

"Don't!" The word was shot at her so fast it had the impact of a bullet being fired from a battle line.

Isabella drew herself up with straight-backed hauteur and gave him an arched look of reproof. "I beg your pardon?"

The aggression pumping from him was reined in. He made a curt, dismissive gesture, realising he had no authority whatsoever over her decisions or actions.

"Sorry, Nonna. I happen to have a situation with Hannah that needs careful handling. If you want to call her, please do it tomorrow, not tonight."

"You just told me everything was fine with her."

"It will be," he muttered darkly.

"But it isn't right now," Isabella claimed with utter certainty.

Another sharp, dismissive gesture. "Hannah almost walked out of the job today because of a couple who came on board. She doesn't want to talk about the past history they've obviously shared but they're not letting go, Nonna. They want to get their hooks into her again and I'm not about to stand for that."

"So…it's Hannah you're taking to the Nautilis tonight."

"Yes." His eyes narrowed with ruthless intent. "She needs to be free of that pair. One way or another I'm going to kill their games stone-dead."

Violent feeling shimmered from him. Without a doubt he was deeply engaged with Hannah O'Neill. But was he getting it right for her?

"Antonio, does Hannah know what you plan?" she asked pertinently.

"She'll be with me," he answered with such passionate emphasis Isabella knew instantly that Antonio was taking this fight into his own hands.

"You will throw her into the ring with these people she wishes to avoid?"

"You think running away solves anything, Nonna?" he flared back at her. "Two years she's been running from them and she would have run again if I hadn't acted fast this morning."

Isabella shook her head, having sensed none of this fear in Hannah O'Neill. She had seemed such a happy person, happy, confident, carefree...

"Are you sure this is so, Antonio?"

He nodded grimly. "It stops tonight. Hannah will stay with me."

The possessive ring in his voice should have warmed Isabella's heart, giving her hope that Antonio had at last found a woman he might come to love and cherish, but again she was lacking knowledge, crucial knowledge.

"You are doing what you want. But is it what Hannah wants? You say she hasn't talked of this past. You are taking on an enemy without knowing what it is."

"They're like a cancer on her soul," he retorted vehemently. "That's enough reason for me to get her to face them and choose to be rid of them."

"Ask her, Antonio," she urged. "Ask her if this is what she wants."

"Stay out of it, Nonna," he warned. "Just stay out of it. It will be how I want it to be."

He strode off, not prepared to listen to reason.

"He wants to rescue her," Rosita said quietly.

"He might be telling himself that, Rosita, but he is acting like a bull who is blindly intent on driving off another bull."

"You mean he is protecting his territory."

Isabella heaved a sigh of exasperation. "This could go badly."

"You don't think Antonio will win?"

"What makes a woman run from a married couple?

What if the cancer on Hannah O'Neill's soul is an unfulfilled love? A love that was forbidden to her?'' She shook her head, wishing she knew more. ''There is a reason why Hannah will not talk of these people.''

''If the man is married, then he is no good to her,'' Rosita argued, picking up the roll of pastry, slamming it down on the marble square and kneading it with far more energy than she needed to.

Antonio's energy making her jumpy, Isabella thought. The power of it was still hanging around, making them both feel highly unsettled. ''This Flynn Lovett cannot be happily married,'' she pointed out. ''Antonio sees him as a threat. A happily married man is no threat. If this man is considering a divorce…''

''Divorce is not good,'' Rosita declared firmly, giving the pastry a good punch. ''I think Antonio should save her from such bad things.''

Which was all very fine if she wanted to be saved, Isabella thought, but it was her experience that these days young women preferred to make their own independent choices.

Rosita was in her sixties and very Italian in her thinking. A man took care of such things. That was what a man was for—to fight for his woman and make the world a better place for her. A woman looked after the household and the children.

Isabella was wishing life could be that simple and people a lot less complicated when Rosita paused in her pummelling of the pastry and looked at her with all too knowing eyes. ''There is no stopping Antonio, Isabella. You know there isn't. What will be will be.''

This fatalistic view did not sit at all well. "He cannot make Hannah choose what he wants," she fretted. "It's all too fast. He should have moved her out of their way, taken the time to win her first. It's the wrong hand to play. He'll ruin everything."

"You thought Alessandro had ruined everything with Gina by acting too quickly," Rosita reminded her.

"Yes, but we knew Gina's background. We knew he could surmount her fears and objections."

"We know Hannah O'Neill's background, too. It is one of strong family. No divorce. That girl does not want a messy life. She ran away from it. Perhaps Antonio is right to make the stand and fight for her."

"It's a risk he didn't need to take."

"That is the man he is. If it is wrong for her, then *he* is wrong for her and they will not be happy together."

It was a line of logic Isabella could not refute.

Antonio was...Antonio. Totally elemental. No subtlety. All the polish she'd tried to give him...no more than a very thin veneer. His genes were probably a direct throwback to the genes from her husband, born and bred in the Outback, one of the Kings of the Kimberley.

Edward...

She remembered he'd taken one look at her—such a look it had made her toes curl—and said, "You are mine, Isabella Valeri."

And she was.

There had never been another man for her.

But that was sixty years ago and times had changed.

Whether Antonio was right or wrong for Hannah O'Neill...well, that was in the lap of the gods now.

CHAPTER TEN

TONY'S adrenaline was running high as he strode around the jeep to help Hannah out. She was wearing high-heels. Very sexy high-heels. Red, which looked great against her honey-tanned bare skin, with just thin little straps around her ankles and across her toes holding them onto her feet. She definitely needed help getting out and feeling steady in those shoes.

He opened the passenger door. Hannah swung her legs towards him. The filmy fabric of her dress slewed slightly, opening up the thigh-high side slit, semi-disguised by the soft ruffle that ran around the hem of the skirt. Very provocative, that ruffle. There was one around the V-neckline, too, forming filmy little sleeves over her shoulders and accentuating the soft swell of her cleavage. Fabulous dress, with big splashes of pink-red floppy poppies running down in a diagonal against a creamy background that was the exact same colour of some of the strands in her hair.

He loved her hair, rippling way out over her shoulders, a rioting mass of crinkly waves in an incredible array of blonde shades from cream to honey, all intermingled and looking great. It flowed towards him as she bent forward to stretch her legs down to the street. Shiny and soft from being freshly washed, it smelled of lemons, and he instantly thought how much he would enjoy burying his face in it later to-night.

She linked her arm around his, hugging it as she set her feet on the ground and straightened up. "Thanks, Tony." A slightly rueful smile was flashed at him. "I think I'll have to hang on to you. I haven't worn these shoes for a while."

He laughed, brimming over with pleasure in her as he clamped his other hand over the one resting on his arm. "When a man has a woman as beautiful as you are, hanging on his arm, he's not about to let her slip away. I want everyone to know you're mine, Hannah O'Neill."

Her lovely green eyes danced pleasure right back at him. "Well, I'm very happy to claim you as mine, too, Tony King."

"Just keep holding that thought," he advised.

She laughed, not realising he was deadly serious.

As they set off on the walk to the restaurant, Tony had a few moments' trepidation about what he was leading her into. She was happy with him. Right now all the vibrations between them were positive. Should he take her elsewhere and build on that happiness, making it a platform that would seal off the past for her? Was that possible?

Even if it was, could he live with not knowing what her choice would have been if Flynn Lovett made himself available to her?

Winning by avoidance…

No. The choice to run was wrong. It might have been right for Hannah two years ago, but not now. Not with him. He had to know…and she had to

know…just how much being with him counted. Talk
meant nothing. Action and reaction showed the truth.

The Lovetts were staying in Port Douglas for another three days. They'd told him so. Better to force
the connection between them and Hannah tonight and
break it, once and for all. Bury it so it never raised
its head again.

They reached the gate to the private path up to the
restaurant. He paused, knowing once they were past
this gate there'd be no turning back. Should he tell
Hannah what she was about to face? His grandmother's voice echoed through his mind. *Ask her if
this is what she wants.* But if she chose to run again…

No!

He couldn't bear for either Flynn or Jodie Lovett
to have that much power over her.

She was his. She wanted to be with him. She was
hanging on to his arm and no one was going to come
between them.

He opened the gate.

Hannah took a deep breath as Tony closed the gate
behind them. Her whole body was buzzing with excitement. It was such a beautiful evening…the balmy
atmosphere of this lovely laid-back tropical town
making any sense of turmoil absurd, plus being with
Tony, who not only made her *feel* beautiful, but was
so beautiful himself, incredibly sexy and wanting to
keep their pleasure in each other going, insisting she
dine with him at this top-line restaurant.

It was lucky she had held on to this dress and the
shoes that went with it so she had something decent

to wear. More than decent. She'd thought it wonderfully feminine and glamorous when she'd seen it modelled during the last fashion week she'd done, and it had been a gift of appreciation from its designer for her work on the show—a reminder of her other life, but she'd never worn it for Flynn. He'd never even seen it. She'd been keeping it to...

She shook her head free of the memory. Tony was turning back to her, taking her arm again, and she was glad she still had the dress to wear for him, to mark this evening as very special, because it was. *He* was special. Amazingly so. And stunningly handsome in his red sports shirt and fawn chinos. Even the colours they were wearing more or less matched. It seemed to reinforce the sense of being a couple, boosting her spirits even higher.

She happily hugged his arm as they started up a path that revealed how very special the Nautilis restaurant was, too. They were instantly plunged into a mini-rainforest which completely shut out the town behind them. Ahead and above them, seemingly just hanging there amongst the trees and ferns and beneath a canopy of towering palms, were open wooden decks where people were seated in high-backed cane chairs, dining under the light of candles set in huge black wrought-iron candelabras.

"Oh, this is wonderful!" Hannah breathed, thinking it was the epitome of tropical romance, placing an oasis of sophistication in the heart of a primeval setting.

"They do a great dish with mud crab, too," Tony dryly informed her.

She laughed, her eyes mischievously teasing as she asked, "You think I should pick up some pointers from the cuisine? Is this why you brought me here?"

"No." There was a touch of wryness in his smile. "This has nothing to do with your culinary expertise."

Her stomach contracted as memories of their physical intimacy flooded through her. "Well, I'd have to admit I've never cooked mud crabs so maybe I can learn something," she rattled out, wondering if he meant to spend all night with her and admitting to herself she wanted him to.

"They are a specialty of far North Queensland."

"Then I *will* have to learn. I love this part of Australia."

"Enough to live here?"

Her heart skipped as she looked into eyes that seemed to be seriously questioning. Could he mean he wanted her to? That perhaps they might make a future together?

Surely it was far too soon for such questions.

"I don't know yet," she answered lightly, shying from the inner tension of putting too much on the line.

The path had led them to a flight of steps that zig-zagged up to the reception deck above the two dining levels. Tony gestured for her to go ahead of him. "Better hold the banister as you go up," he advised, releasing her arm so she could.

Feeling extremely conscious of Tony following her and needing to lessen her physical awareness of him, not wanting her legs to suddenly turn to jelly when she was wearing such precarious shoes, Hannah rushed into more speech as she mounted the steps.

"You know, I had two marvellous weeks at Cape Tribulation before coming on down to Port Douglas. Was the tea plantation I saw there the one your grandmother said you manage?"

"Yes, though I manage two," he answered matter-of-factly. "The biggest one is near Innisfail."

"Plus the Kingtripper Company." No wonder he flew a helicopter to keep in touch with all his business interests.

"The Kingtripper line is my personal baby. The tea plantations are part of the family holdings," he explained.

Born and bred to responsibility, she thought, and probably thrived on the challenge of taking on more. He certainly shouldered it with an ease attained by very few people. "Your family must carry a lot of weight in these parts, Tony," she remarked. "A long history here. Property…"

"What about your own family, Hannah?" he inserted quietly.

"Oh, on the whole we're a productive lot. My father is an inventor. My mother is a writer. My brothers and sisters are all high achievers in one field or another." She slanted him a self-mocking little smile as they finally reached the top landing and he stepped up beside her. "I'm the only drop-out."

His eyebrows tilted. "Any regrets?"

She shook her head. "None."

It was true. She didn't want to go back to the frantic pace of a life that was driven by the demands of tight deadlines. Too many pressures had contributed to her ignoring things she should never have ignored, and neglecting her own needs in favour of getting the job done. She would never let work dominate her life again, not to that extent anyway.

Feeling very content just to be here at this marvellous place, she smiled at the woman who came forward to greet them.

"Tony, lovely to see you here."

"Glad you could fit us in," he answered warmly.

"And this is…?"

"Hannah." Tony took her arm again, smiling an appeal at the other woman as he added, "Hannah O'Neill, wanting to sample your mud crab. Not all gone, I hope."

"You are late-comers," the woman warned. "I'll have a word in the kitchen after I see you to your table. Or would you like a drink at the bar first?" She gave Tony a look of knowing sympathy and nodded towards the dining deck just below them. "The other party is settled."

What other party? Hannah wondered.

"We'll order drinks from the table," Tony decided.

"Fine! Let's go then."

She led off to the steps which took them down to the first dining level. As they followed, Hannah was still wondering about *the other party*. Tony hadn't mentioned meeting someone else here but there must have been talk of it when he'd made the booking. A little disappointed that he had some secondary motive for bringing her to this place, not just a special night out for the two of them, she glanced around the seated diners to see if anyone was signalling their presence to Tony.

Her heart stopped dead.

So did her feet.

Flynn!

Flynn staring at her, rising from his chair.

"Hannah?" Tony's voice, his hand clamping over hers, demanding her attention. "Just watch the steps," he instructed. "I won't let you fall."

The steps.

She wrenched her gaze from the man she would have married and looked down, made her feet move forward. Tony was holding her. He would guard her from any approach from Flynn. He'd done so this afternoon and he would do it again now. She had to concentrate on not letting her legs wobble from the shock of seeing him here, seeing him looking at her as he used to, eating her up with his eyes as though...

No! She wasn't going to remember that. Too late. Too long gone. Too wrong. He'd made his bed with Jodie.

"I booked a table on the next deck down," Tony said, telling her they were not staying on the same dining level as Flynn.

Relief.

Moving on.

No one calling out her name.

Nor Tony's.

Another set of steps.

Then to a table for two in the far corner of the lower deck, as far away as it was possible to get from Flynn's table, although he could undoubtedly see her from where he was, watch her if he wanted to. But he couldn't see much because Tony settled her in the chair that faced away from Flynn and the solidly woven cane of the high back rest gave her a large measure of privacy. Since he wasn't in her line of sight at all, she could pretend he wasn't here, except she knew he was. And Jodie had to be with him. The two of them together.

She dimly heard Tony order some recommended cocktails and a bottle of wine. They were handed menus. On some automatic level Hannah smiled and nodded at whatever was said. She couldn't concentrate her mind on the printed menu. When suggestions were made, it was easier to agree to them. Food was no longer of any interest to her.

They were left alone.

She took a deep breath, trying to put Flynn and Jodie behind her in every sense, and looked directly at Tony, needing him to keep her distracted from the couple she didn't want to think about. Her heart contracted as the watchful intensity in his eyes sent another shock wave through her system.

He knew what she was feeling.

He knew Flynn and Jodie were here.

He had known all along.

They were *the other party!*

"Why?" she blurted out.

He didn't try to pretend ignorance. His eyes blazed with determined purpose, and she felt the steel will behind them, ready to undercut any protest she might make. His reply was as direct as her demand.

"Because I don't like what's going on between you and the Lovetts and it's time it stopped."

Her hands fluttered an agitated appeal. "You don't understand…"

"Then try making me understand, Hannah."

It wasn't a request. It was a command. A flat-out challenge that he was not about to let her back away from. He leaned forward, reached across the table and took her hand, transmitting the warmth and strength of his touch, forcefully reminding her of how much they had shared of themselves with each other.

"You're with me. You have been *very intimately* with me this afternoon. Yet now you are letting them intrude on us. You are letting them impinge on our time together. What gives them the power to do that, Hannah?"

He was right. It was wrong to blight her present with Tony with painful memories of people who had nothing to do with him.

"I'm sorry. It's just…I haven't seen them for two years and they bring back…what was."

"So let's have *what was* out in the open so I know what I'm dealing with. You've held on to it too long. Share it with me."

"I'd rather not. I'd truly rather not, Tony. I'm sorry I let them distract me. Please…let's talk of other things. Tell me about the tea plantations. Please? I want to know more about you."

"And I want to know more about you. Why you run, Hannah. You dropped out and ran and you're still running. I don't want to be used as your escape route. And that's what you're doing right now."

He paused to let that sink in, his eyes deriding any other interpretation of her response to the situation. Hannah see-sawed between shame and panic, knowing what he said was true, yet feeling sick at the thought of revealing the worst moments of her life when the bottom had dropped out of her world and everything had turned black. It was too humiliating to talk about.

"Be fair to me, Hannah."

His voice was softly urging but it was another command. He was dictating how their relationship should go. And as much as she recoiled from baring her soul, an inner voice whispered she had already bared her body to him and that had felt good...right. Shouldn't she try trusting him with more?

He had stood by her today.

He was standing by her now.

But she would lose him if she wasn't fair. That was what was on the line. And suddenly the way forward was very clear, dictated by one vital, overriding factor.

She didn't want to lose Tony King.

CHAPTER ELEVEN

EVERY nerve in Tony's body was piano-wire tight as he waited for Hannah's decision. Her gaze lingered on their linked hands for what felt like aeons. He wanted to increase the strength of his hold on her, make withdrawal impossible, but he knew physical force would not win what he needed from her. This battle was for her heart and mind and soul and she had to give them up to him willingly.

He didn't stop to think why it meant so much to him. It just did. And he knew he would refuse to accept failure. She had to realise what he'd said was true. She had to realise he was on her side and would fight whatever demons plagued her memory, rendering them completely powerless...if that was possible.

He'd seen Flynn Lovett stand as he caught sight of Hannah, seen the stunned surprise on his face turn to an unmistakable lust for the Hannah who was dressed so desirably tonight, seen Jodie Lovett pull him down again, and the flash of angry frustration he'd shot at his wife as he submitted to her anger at his reaction.

There was trouble brewing at that table and Hannah was the focus of it. Tony didn't want to believe Flynn Lovett still resided in her heart, didn't want to believe that she wouldn't—couldn't—give him up. He hoped it was no more than a deep scar that could be erased and she would let him help her get rid of it.

Try me, he willed at her with all the energy he could harness.

Trust me.

"All right," she murmured, lifting her lashes to show him eyes that swam with vulnerability, stopping any triumph he might have felt stone-dead.

This was a bad journey for her. He'd pressed her into it and now he had to ease the way as best he could. He lightly squeezed her hand, wanting to impart reassurance as he quietly said, "I'm a good listener, Hannah. Don't worry about what you're telling me. Just spill it out and I'll still be here at the end of it, still wanting to be with you. Okay?"

She managed a wry little smile. Her hand slid away from his as she sat back, visibly gathering herself to re-visit the past. Tony sat back, too, careful not to make her feel crowded by him. Their cocktails arrived, giving her more time to find a starting point. She seized on hers, eagerly sipping it as though her mouth was very dry. He waited, sure in his own mind she would not backtrack on her decision to open up to him. It was important to keep his own reactions under control now.

"I used to be part of a very high-level team that organised events," she began. "We took on festivals, exhibitions, big money functions, fashion shows. We created themes to match the mood or personality of the event, organised the lighting, the music, the props, the seating—" a shrug "—whatever was required for the outcome to have maximum impact. It was also our job to ensure everything ran as planned."

"A lot of responsibility," Tony remarked encouragingly, thinking that making *an event* of presenting Matt's exotic tropical fruit was a piece of cake for someone with her background experience.

She nodded. "And pressure. The pressure was always on to perform, to deliver what we promised. We put in long hours. Travelled at the drop of a hat. It was exhilarating when we pulled off something big, but it was also a huge energy drain. Work sucked up most of my life. Even when I wasn't actively on the job, there were parties related to work, people to meet, contacts to make."

"The treadmill never stopped," Tony inserted, nodding his understanding.

A self-mocking smile tilted her mouth. "More like a roller-coaster. *I* never stopped to look where I was going or ask myself why, or even whether it was truly what I wanted. I didn't learn to do that until after I dropped out."

"Most people are carried along by the stream they're in, Hannah."

She shook her head. "That's no excuse for not making any effort to control it. Not choosing for myself." Her eyes dulled with painful reflection. "For the last two frenetic years of my high-flying career, I even considered Jodie my best friend. Mostly because I shared an apartment with her and she was a constant in my life."

They certainly weren't two of a kind, Tony thought.

"Actually, I was flattered that she asked me to share. Jodie is a few years older than I am and was— probably still is—a fashion buyer for a department store chain. Her flatmate had married and she was looking for someone who could afford half the rent on the apartment she'd leased at Bondi Beach. Very high-rental, very high-status place. I was earning big money and it was like another step up to me.''

Tony had little doubt Jodie Lovett would have manipulated that situation to her advantage. ''I guess you then found you had to fit in with her,'' he commented dryly.

Hannah looked surprised. ''Yes. She did want everything her way, but I didn't let it turn into open conflict because there were advantages to me, too. She used to get me fashion clothes on the cheap, and in lots of ways she was fun company, always full of in-crowd gossip. Our careers overlapped in areas like fashion week so we knew many of the same people.''

''And you would have extended her social network.''

''That went both ways. Jodie kept an A-list of eligible bachelors and used to wangle invitations to parties where they were likely to be. She dragged me along to them if she wanted a back-up woman in tow.''

''*Dragged* you?''

An ironic shrug. ''More often than not I was too tired to enjoy them but Jodie would insist that I not miss *an opportunity*.''

''But she was actually headhunting for herself.''

Slowly, reluctantly, miserably, she conceded, ''I think...the night I met Flynn...he was her target. Or maybe he became her target because he preferred me to her.'' She heaved a long ragged sigh. ''I don't know. At the time she pretended she was happy for me, and she kept up that pretence right up to the week before our wedding.''

Tony's stomach contracted at the shock punch of that information. She'd been on the verge of marrying the guy. Which had to mean she'd loved him. Might still love him. And Flynn Lovett sure as hell wasn't indifferent to her.

''I'd even chosen Jodie as my chief bridesmaid, ahead of my sisters,'' Hannah ran on. ''She was involved in all the plans. You could say it was to be—'' a sad grimace ''—the biggest event of my life. I'd organised everything down to the last meticulous little detail.''

Her eyes glazed, her focus turned inward, and Tony knew she was envisaging how it would have been if the wedding had taken place—*the event* on which she would have brought all her expertise to bear to make it the most perfect, the most memorable, the most magical day of her life.

Over the years, his grandmother's involvement in weddings at the castle had demonstrated how much planning went into them to produce exactly the desired result on the day itself. More so when it was personal family, as with Alex and Gina. The whole build-up, the anticipation…he could imagine how totally shattering it would have been for it not to go ahead, to learn just a week before…

What?

What had been the irrevocable turning point?

And was it still irrevocable?

Her eyes flickered out of their glaze, pain sharpening their focus as she took a deep breath and said, "I trusted her. I trusted her to liaise with Flynn on the wedding plans when I was too tied up with work to get any time free. I thought she was my best friend."

Betrayal...deep and unequivocal.

Jodie had wanted Flynn and she'd got him, probably using every chance she had to set up meetings with him when Hannah was otherwise occupied. And Flynn had succumbed to temptation. Had he cursed himself for a fool ever since?

Their starters arrived—a selection of seafood with a hot salad, an easily consumed dish if Hannah's stomach wasn't in too much of a twist. Wine was poured from the bottle he'd ordered. Tony had finished his cocktail. Hannah was still sipping hers.

"Would you prefer water?" he asked, remembering her insistence on it this afternoon.

"I'm fine with this, thank you." Another wry smile. "I don't have to guard myself with you anymore, do I?"

"No. And I hope that feels good. It's a lonely business, guarding yourself. I don't want you to feel lonely with me." He smiled encouragingly. "Let's eat. You should never let anything spoil your pleasure in good food."

Her eyes crinkled with dry amusement. "It would be an insult to the chef not to try."

"Absolutely."

They ate. With how much enjoyment on Hannah's part, Tony wasn't sure, but she did eat everything and commented on the delicate flavour of the sauce, which meant she had focused on the food. He waited until their emptied plates were removed before leading her back to the critical mass in her mind.

"Tell me about Flynn, Hannah…what drew you to him, what drew him to you?"

She heaved a deep sigh and sat back again, eyeing him almost curiously, giving Tony the uncomfortable sense she was measuring his attraction against her experience with the man she'd planned to marry.

Flynn had lost her, he fiercely reminded himself.

He occupied the box seat now and he was not about to take any backward steps in the winning of Hannah O'Neill.

"I wasn't attracted to him at first," she said musingly. "Jodie pointed him out to me at the party and he certainly had a kind of commanding presence, but my initial impression was he was a bit too full of himself, and I didn't feel inclined to compete for his attention."

A blow to the ego of an A-list bachelor? Tony wondered cynically. A woman as beautiful as Hannah ignoring him?

"Why he chose to come after me, I don't know."

A challenge to be taken up and won, Tony thought.

"It was like he suddenly channelled all his energy into capturing my interest. It was very flattering and after a while, quite mesmerising. He was fascinating, very intelligent, witty, clever, and he exuded the kind of arrogant confidence that comes with knowing he dared more than most men and was on top of his game, which was trading commodities and manipulating international currencies. Somehow it gave him an exciting power.''

Her lashes lowered, veiling how much it had affected her. ''Anyhow, I fell for it.'' She took a deep breath and raised her gaze to his, her eyes hard with bitter mockery. ''I fell for the whole package. The black Porsche convertible, the apartment at Miller's Point with views of Sydney Harbour, the cupboards full of Armani suits, the glamorous courtship with champagne and roses and being whirled off to luxurious places. I loved it. I loved him. And when he asked me to marry him, I felt I was the luckiest woman in the whole world.''

A haunting disillusionment crept in as she added, ''And I believed he loved me. I never had any doubt about it. Not about anything. He said he liked the fact that I had such a full-on exciting career. It made me an extraordinary person to him, the kind of woman he wanted as his partner in life. There was never, never any criticism about the hours I had to put in. He worked long hours himself. I thought we were perfect for each other.''

''You didn't ever live with him?'' Tony asked, thinking that would have been a pertinent test of reality.

She shook her head. ''The question never came up. It wasn't as though we had a really long relationship. Only ten months in all. Short in today's terms.''

The length of time was irrelevant to Tony's mind. Impact could be immediate and lasting.

''So what happened a week before the wedding, Hannah?'' he asked softly.

Her head jerked in anguish. Then her chin set with the determination to finish it for him. The bleakness in her eyes echoed through her voice. "I was bringing home my wedding dress. I'd had it made to my own design. I met up with my three sisters after work. They were picking up their bridesmaid dresses from the seamstress, too. I collected Jodie's as well as mine and invited my sisters back to the apartment to have a bit of a hens' night, spreading out the dresses, trying them on, making sure we all looked right. It was exciting…"

Her voice trailed off for a moment. Then she scooped in a deep breath and continued. "My sisters were right on my heels when I reached the front door. We were all in high spirits, chatting, laughing. I guess I burst into the apartment and…" She shuddered, reliving the shock, the horror of it draining her voice of any colour as she forced herself to go on. "There they were, on the floor in the living room, in open view…"

"Jodie and Flynn."

She nodded. "Obviously, it had all been too urgent for them to make it to the bedroom, though there must have been some foreplay. Her blouse was hanging apart and…" She swallowed convulsively. "His trousers were down around his ankles…"

"Caught in the act," Tony murmured.

"And no…no hiding it…from any of us. I remember Jodie crying out that they couldn't help themselves. They were mad for each other and just couldn't help it. And Flynn blaming me, yelling if I hadn't been so caught up in my bloody work…and there I was, holding my wedding dress, with my sisters looking on. It was…unbearable. I threw the dress at Flynn and Jodie and bolted.''

"Did he follow you?"

"Yes, but by that time I was back in my car. He tried to stop me from driving off. I think I would have run him over if he hadn't leapt out of the way."

"What about later?" The scene smacked of a deliberate set-up by Jodie, who must have known Hannah was due home with the dress.

"There was no later. I neither saw nor spoke to either of them again until today."

No real closure, Tony thought, and that was dangerous. If talking had been done then, she wouldn't be so much on edge now.

"I drove to my parents' home, told them the wedding was off, collected some clothes I'd stacked there, then kept on driving," she went on, her voice gathering the same grim, shut-out purpose that had been activated this morning. "The next day I made the calls I had to make to cancel the wedding, assure my family I was okay, resign from my job which was no great drama since I'd been about to take time off for my honeymoon anyway. I simply…dropped out of the whole scene and left Jodie and Flynn to it."

It wasn't simple. It was trauma on an extreme level—a double betrayal completely blowing her mind and everything else it had touched and tainted. She had survived it in her own fashion and Tony admired the way she had gradually restructured her life along different lines. No regrets about it, either. But the clean slate had ghosts that had never been confronted nor exorcised…ghosts that had to be dealt with and banished.

Nothing was ever totally black and white and Tony suspected it was the greys that haunted her, the greys that had never been allowed a voice. They had to be talked about. He had to know how much power Flynn Lovett still held over her heart, and it was better she face it now with him than continue to repress it.

"If Flynn begged your forgiveness, begged for another chance, could you love him again, Hannah?"

"No!" Sharp and emphatic, her eyes flashing instant recoil from the idea.

"You don't feel…he might have been entrapped by Jodie?" Tony probed carefully.

"Oh, I'm sure Jodie would have played her cards artfully but Flynn chose to pick them up," came the bitter truth. "He may well have enjoyed the kick of daring to, right under my nose." Her chin lifted in determined rejection. "I would never be able to trust either of them again."

"So you wouldn't accept any excuse."

"Would you, given the same circumstances?" she flared at him. "Would you forgive and forget, Tony?"

Anger…from deeply wounded pride. But pride could be a shield for far deeper feelings.

"I can't imagine myself doing so, no," he answered truthfully. "But I know from observing other people's relationships that the heart does find ways of accepting the unacceptable, especially if the offender is very persuasive and the injured party is still vulnerable to the love that was given. Infidelities do get forgiven, Hannah, even though they may not be for-gotten.''

A tide of heat washed up her neck and burned into her cheeks, making the flare of pride in her eyes very green. ''I guess I'm no good at swallowing humilia-tion.''

Humiliation beyond bearing…and nothing done—nothing allowed to be done—to alleviate it by the parties who had inflicted it, so it was still as strong as it had ever been.

Tony nodded, fully understanding now why she had wanted to walk off *Duchess* this morning and not have any contact whatsoever with the Lovetts. But by Hannah's extreme action of *dropping out,* both Jodie and Flynn had been robbed of any real closure with her, as well. That left the wound still tantalisingly, tormentingly *open,* perhaps more so to them than it was to Hannah—a running sore in their marriage.

Flynn might not have any chance with her but he was arrogant enough to give it a try, and if he was prepared to humble himself enough…would Hannah's pride crack?

Jodie would certainly do whatever she thought would queer Flynn's pitch.

The Lovetts had three more days in Port Douglas…time enough to find an opportunity to tackle Hannah on her own…unless they were stopped in their tracks tonight.

''Well, I'm sure this will be much sweeter to swal-low,'' he said, smiling to lighten the mood as their waitress delivered the mud crabs to their table.

The business of serving gave Hannah time to recover some equanimity after the stress of her revelations.

"Enjoy," the waitress said as she left them.

"We will," Tony answered, shooting an appealing look at Hannah. "Let me get this straight now. You want Jodie and Flynn to go away and stay away. You want nothing more to do with either of them, regardless of how they might explain their actions, regardless of any appeal for your forgiveness or understanding. Is that where you stand, Hannah?"

"Yes." Her face was still flushed, eyes feverishly bright. "Do you think that's too mean of me, Tony?"

"No. It would be better, for your own sake, if you could feel indifferent to them, and I hope that will happen in time, but since I now understand where you're coming from, I'll simply get rid of them for you."

"Get rid of them?"

He grinned at her shock. "There used to be an Italian Mafia operating up here, extorting money from all the canefarmers. It was called *The Black Hand.* They cut off people's ears and hands..."

"Tony..." she pleaded frantically.

He laughed. "Relax. I was only teasing. My great-grandfather assisted in driving out *The Black Hand* decades ago. My family has always stood up to help people who couldn't find help anywhere else, Hannah."

Her tension eased. Her eyes softened. "That's a fine family tradition, Tony."

"Imbued in us from the old pioneering days. You have to look after your own. Which also covers feeding them. So please taste the mud crab. It's delicious.''

She laughed.

It might only be from nervous relief but it sounded good to Tony. The weight on his heart lifted. He'd get her over this hump with the Lovetts. He wanted to hear much more of her laughter. He wanted to see her face light up for him and know the shadows of her past were completely gone.

Before they left this restaurant, Hannah O'Neill would be his.

That was the hand he intended to play.

CHAPTER TWELVE

AMAZINGLY, Hannah did enjoy the mud crab. Her stomach had stopped churning once Tony had teased her into laughing. The dreadful tightness in her chest had eased, too, and she found herself wanting to please him, to share his pleasure in the gourmet dish he'd ordered for both of them.

Somehow his sympathetic interest and calmly considered comments had drained away the angst of telling him about Jodie and Flynn. Or talking the whole miserable story through had unloaded the burden of all the bad feelings their presence here had stirred up again.

Tony was probably right in his judgement that keeping those memories bottled up gave them a power they shouldn't have any more. In any event, she was glad now she had shared them with him. And it was very heart-warming that he wanted to help her, though how he intended *to get rid of* Flynn and Jodie was a tantalising question.

He could hardly hound a couple of tourists out of Port Douglas...could he? How much influence did the King family have in this town? Clearly they had a long history here, and Tony had pressed to have this table tonight, precisely as he wanted it. That kind of manipulation made her feel uneasy. On the other hand, Flynn and Jodie had hardly been fair to her.

It suddenly struck her that what Jodie had said might have been true—that she and Flynn had been mad for each other and couldn't help themselves. Hadn't it been like that with Tony and herself this afternoon? What if they had fought against it, trying to be fair to her, and then with the wedding so close...

It might have happened that way. Though it seemed highly dishonest to her. How could a wildly strong mutual attraction be denied for so long? She looked at Tony and the desire that had swamped her earlier was instantly re-kindled. He really was the perfect man; beautiful, strong, kind, caring...*the white knight.* And very, very sexy.

He caught her look and his eyes zapped desire straight back at her, an electric current that linked them to the exclusion of everyone else. ''Hello again,'' he said with a slow sensual smile that warmed her all over.

''Hello to you, too. I'm sorry for being distracted from us. Will you tell me about the tea plantations now?''

He laughed and she thought how brilliantly handsome he was with his face lit up with pleasure. ''Better if I show you, Hannah,'' he said, his eyes sparkling with happy anticipation. ''Come fly with me up to Cape Tribulation on Monday morning. I'll give you a tour.''

''Fly? In your helicopter?''

''Quickest way to get there. Then on Tuesday we can fly to Innisfail and you'll see the whole picture.''

''I'd love to do that, but have you forgotten?

Mondays and Tuesdays are my only days off and I should look for a place of my own, Tony.''

He waved dismissively. ''That can wait. The apartment you're using isn't required for anyone else right now.''

''But…''

''I'll square it with my brother and my grandmother. Okay?''

''No. I won't feel right about it. It's like…like sponging on your generosity. I can afford to be independent.''

''Fine! Then this week you can pay Alex the rental you've figured out you can afford, and I'll explain to him it's my fault you haven't moved out yet because I took up your free days. How's that?''

She sighed, feeling she was being bull-dozed but immensely tempted to give in to his persuasion. It was an exciting prospect, flying with Tony to whatever he wanted to share with her. ''You're sure your family won't think badly of me?''

''Definitely not.'' He grinned. ''Any thinking they might do will be centred on me. My grandmother will say…'' He gestured exasperation and mimicked her voice, ''Antonio…always in a rush. He cannot wait for anything.''

Hannah couldn't help laughing.

''And Alex will say…'' A roll of the eyes. ''…A waste of time and breath arguing with Tony. He's like a bull at a gate.''

''Are you?''

''Depends on the gate.''

"And what will Matt say?" she asked, amused by this insight into their family relationships.

"Ha! That upstart brother of mine, trying to steal you right under my nose..." A dark lowering of his brows. "Matt will loudly complain that I'm deliberately taking up all your free time so he can't get a chance with you."

"And would that be true?"

The eyebrows lifted. "Does he have a chance with you?"

"No."

He grinned, a triumphant delight dancing in his eyes. "Then we have nothing to worry about, do we? You'll come with me."

Hannah's resistance to the plan melted away. Nothing to worry about was a wonderful state of mind. She wanted to have it. And she suddenly realised Tony was giving it to her, taking her out of Port Douglas on her days off so there could be no chance of further contact with Jodie and Flynn. This was his way of *getting rid of them*, as well as giving her something positive to occupy her mind.

She smiled at him, the smile going right down to her heart with this understanding of how he was taking care of her. Tony King...truly a king compared to all the other men she had known. "Thank you, Tony," she said warmly.

Their waitress arrived to clear the table and take their orders for sweets. Hannah read down the selections on the menu, for the first time tonight actively interested in what was being offered. Having made her decision, she looked at Tony to query what he fancied. His gaze was not trained on the menu. His attention was intensely engaged by something on the upper dining level.

Hannah instantly tensed.

He was watching Jodie and Flynn. She didn't have to look to know that. The direction of his gaze, the hard set of his face, the sudden tautness of his body emanating a readiness to tackle trouble head-on.

"Tony?" The appeal spilled from her lips, anxiety surging at the prospect of being confronted by them again. They had married. Why couldn't they just get on with it and leave her alone?

"Ah!" His head swung to face her, the hardness wiped out by a quick smile. "Made your decision?"

"I thought…the soufflé…"

"Two," he said to the waitress, handing up his copy of the menu.

Hannah's was collected and the waitress departed.

"We're about to have company," Tony announced, his smile turning sardonic, his eyes glittering a challenge he expected her to meet. "Are you with me, Hannah?" The words transmitted strong vibrations of feeling that demanded a positive response.

"Yes," she forced from a throat that was choking up.

"Then show Flynn Lovett you are, very much so, by putting on a happy face and agreeing with everything I say."

"Just…Flynn?"

"Jodie left their table a couple of minutes ago. She walked off in high dudgeon, probably expecting him to follow. Flynn has not followed. On the contrary, he is now making his way towards us and I have no doubt his destination is this table. Now give me your hand and smile.''

His hand was already reaching out. She met it without hesitation, wanting the physical connection with Tony and also needing to show Flynn she was now attached to a man who could not only match him in strong self-assurance, but beat him hands-down in the qualities that mattered more to her than material possessions and successes in the paper world of money markets.

There was a solidity to Tony King that Flynn would never have. She was proud to be with him—fiercely proud—and if there was any humiliation to be felt at this meeting, it would be Flynn's, not hers. She would not let him get to her.

"I won't let you down, Tony," she promised, gritting her teeth into a very determined smile.

"You will have to look at him, Hannah," he warned. "Treat him as you would any old acquaintance who's just passing by and stopping to say hello. Can you do that?"

Her nerves quivered at the pressure to perform as Tony wanted. His eyes blazed into hers, commanding her assent. She nodded, not knowing if she could deliver a semblance of social politeness but resolving to do her best.

"Mostly, you can look besottedly at me," he instructed, and grinned to make it easy for her.

Even so her heart skittered nervously as Flynn made a very aggressive arrival, drawing a chair from the vacated table next to them and placing it at theirs with the clear intention of seating himself with them. "Sorry to interrupt your twosome, but I'll only take up a few minutes," he tossed out, arrogantly assuming that neither of them would want to make a public scene by forcibly ejecting him from their company once he sat down, which he promptly did.

"You're not welcome, Flynn," Tony stated bluntly. "This is a very special night for us and you're intruding."

"Well, I'm sure you feel any night with Hannah is special, Tony. I certainly did," he claimed in a tone that raised Hannah's hackles so fast she had no problem at all in facing him with a look of arch surprise.

"Don't you think that line is a bit *off*, Flynn?"

His gaze locked onto hers, his brilliant brown eyes shooting their magnetism straight at her. "I self-destructed with you and have regretted it ever since. To me you were and always will be uniquely special, Hannah. I want you to know that."

Ashes...and strangely enough they weren't even bitter ashes. Not with Tony holding her hand. "It's a waste of time having regrets, Flynn," she said with a dismissive shrug. "You're married to Jodie..."

"We're getting a divorce."

"And Hannah is marrying me," Tony declared, shattering Flynn's shock announcement with his own and snapping their heads towards him.

"What?" shot out of Flynn's mouth.

It almost shot out of Hannah's mouth, as well. Her hand started to jerk up in a startled reaction, hitting against Tony's hold on it. He swiftly tightened his grip, squeezing to warn her off any further show of agitation, while smiling so besottedly at her, her heart did the startled leaping.

"This is the woman I love and will love till my dying day," he further declared. "And the miracle is, she feels the same way about me."

His tone of voice, the look in his eyes...it was so convincing Hannah's skin tingled all over.

"So you see, Flynn, your presence here is quite hopelessly out of place," he ran on, not bothering to even glance at the man who had tried to come between them. "We're not interested in your feelings. We're not interested in your marital problems. We're here, planning a future together, aren't we, Hannah?"

Another squeeze of her hand. "Yes. Yes, we are," she responded, smiling back at him in the same besotted fashion with no effort at all.

"Hannah..." It was a cry of exasperation, protesting the situation.

"Go away, Flynn," she said dreamily, still looking into Tony's eyes. "Your time was up a long time ago."

Which was the absolute truth! And it felt really really good to be able to say it with no angst whatsoever.

"Yes. Go away, Flynn. You are distinctly *de trop*," Tony said, his gaze locked on Hannah's as he lifted her hand to his mouth and grazed his lips warmly over her knuckles. "Would you like an emerald ring to match your eyes, my darling?"

"You'll waste your life in this hick town, Hannah," Flynn jeered, rising to his feet.

She ignored him. In fact, she took immense satisfaction in ignoring him. He deserved it for so rudely trying to cut out Tony who was definitely worth ten of him. More. Flynn wasn't even in the same category as Tony King.

Steaming with frustration, he virtually flung the chair he'd collected back to where it belonged and strode off.

"If that bastard gave you an emerald, I'll have to get you something else," Tony said mock seriously.

"No, it was a diamond. An emerald would be all yours," she informed him in the same vein.

His eyes grew properly serious. "You are well rid of him, Hannah."

"I know. And thank you very, very much for helping me. I don't know how you thought up that marriage line so fast but it sure was effective in cutting Flynn dead." She shook her head admiringly. "I almost died myself."

"You recovered superbly."

"You made it easy for me."

"It *was* easy." He cocked his head to one side assessingly. "And what does that say about us, Hannah?"

Her heart skittered. He couldn't mean…he wasn't really applying the idea of marriage to them. She shied away from any thought of rushing into a commitment. Having been so sure of Flynn…even though Tony was different…she instinctively recoiled from counting too much on a relationship, especially one that had barely begun. It was a big mistake to fall into fantasy. But what was *real* right now could be acknowledged.

"I think what it says about us, is that there are moments when we're very closely attuned to each other."

He nodded, seeming to weigh up her answer against some measure he had in his mind. Feeling she had short-changed him, and highly aware of how much he had come to her rescue, she fervently added, "And I also think you're quite wonderful, Tony King."

It sparked a wicked look. "Well, the night is young and I think you're quite wonderful, too, Hannah O'Neill. Can I take it that the past is past and the future is ours to make of it whatever we want?"

"Mmm...if that means I still get to fly with you," she answered lightly.

He laughed and kissed her hand again. "It certainly does. I fancy we may do quite a lot of flying together."

She heaved a happy sigh. What either of them would make of the future—together or apart—she had no idea. For so long now she had taken one day at a time, never planning too far ahead because then you started counting on the plans and they could go badly astray. It was better to simply take life as it came and hug all the spontaneous joys it brought.

Joy was bubbling up in her right now.

The night was young.

And she was with Tony King.

CHAPTER THIRTEEN

TONY had the emerald ring in his pocket. It was burning a hole in his pocket. He wanted it on Hannah's finger. The big question was whether she would accept it and she'd given him no solid encouragement to believe she would.

Yet she *was* happy with him. He was certain in his own mind that she loved him. It couldn't be otherwise. In the month since he'd got rid of Flynn Lovett they had spent all their spare time together and every minute of it had proved his instincts right. Hannah O'Neill was the woman for him in every sense and on every level. And he was right for her. He knew it in his bones.

So it was highly frustrating the way she shied from any talk of marriage. Just the mention of it and her gaze would slide away from his and she'd quickly fasten on some other line of conversation that led away from any talk of *the future*. It was almost as though she didn't want to think in any terms of permanence.

A butterfly…

Tony was beginning to feel haunted by the tattoo that just might symbolise Hannah's attitude to life, taking pleasure in a place and its people for a while, then flitting on. Was he simply part of her sojourn in Port Douglas? When it came to the end of the tourist season, did she intend to kiss him goodbye and move on?

She had her own apartment now, clearly deter- mined on maintaining an independent situation, and she was always careful not to take any advantage of their intimacy on board *Duchess*. The chef was the chef and she did the job with such good cheer and appealing flair, the crew and passengers invariably re- sponded positively to her. No one could ever say she hadn't given value in the position she held.

But was she really content, just being a chef? It hardly stretched the skills he knew she had. And while this part of far North Queensland was and al- ways would be his home, she might come to view Port Douglas as *a hick town,* and start hankering for a more sophisticated city life again. Like Chris's part- ner, Johnny, who'd been happy enough to while away a year up here. But only a year.

He wanted to give her the ring. He wanted her to want what it symbolised. Impatience surged through him as he landed the helicopter in the castle grounds. Pressure of business had forced him to stay in Innisfail last night but today was Saturday, and a whole weekend with Hannah lay ahead of him—time to settle his doubts.

Regardless of any evasive tactic she tried to use he was going to propose marriage. What was the point of waiting any longer? The need to know where he stood with her was eating at him. Maybe he was being like a bull at a gate, but he'd either open the gate this weekend or smash it down.

He drove his jeep down to the marina in a very

determined frame of mind. *Duchess* had been chartered for a family party today, only twenty-four passengers, so he might be able to snatch some private time with Hannah while they were anchored at the reef. One way or another, he had to pin down how she was thinking.

"So, how's it going with Tony?"

Hannah threw a startled glance at Megan. They were putting the salads away in the galley and such a direct personal question from her younger workmate caught her by surprise.

Megan laughed. "We all *know,* Hannah. Just because you don't talk about it or throw it in our faces, you can't hide the vibes between you two. We're betting that Tony's down for the count this time."

"The count?" Hannah echoed.

"Fallen hard." A waggle of eyebrows emphasised the point. "And since you light up like a Christmas tree every time he's around..."

"Do I?"

"All smiles and sparkles. Gotta be love, I've decided."

"Well, since you're the expert," Hannah drawled teasingly. "Is it the great-while-it-lasts kind of love or the forever kind?"

"You mean...is Tony likely to walk you down the aisle?"

Hannah sighed. "Marriage isn't really the question. Divorce is so very common these days." Flynn and Jodie hadn't even lasted two years, and before that,

Flynn hadn't lasted ten months before being unfaithful.

"Well, I can tell you one thing," Megan said, nodding seriously. "When the King family makes a commitment, it's rock-solid, providing you keep your side of the bargain. They're renowned for it. If any agreement with them falls through, you can be dead certain it's the other party who's broken trust. That's how they operate. So if Tony King asked you to marry him, he'd mean to make it work, Hannah. And he sure wouldn't like it if you were thinking of divorce as an option."

"How do you know this, Megan?"

She shrugged. "Lived here all my life. The Kings are like legends all up and down the far north. They go way back, you know? There are so many stories about that family standing by its word, playing fair, making things stick…that's just the way they are. Everybody knows that."

Megan had said something about Tony being a very fair boss the day Jodie and Flynn had come on board *Duchess,* and he'd certainly made getting rid of them stick. As for standing by his word, he certainly hadn't let her down on anything yet, but it was still early days. The problem was, it was so easy to be in love with him, she couldn't quite bring herself to believe something so easy and wonderful would last. Just seeing him made her bubble with joy…but bubbles did break.

"Good morning!"

They both swung to face Tony who had just stepped into the saloon, bringing with him his own special charge of energy that instantly set Hannah's pulse racing and made her feel vibrantly alive.

"Morning!" Megan chimed back at him.

"Hi!" Hannah breathed, her mouth already breaking into a smile that precluded forming more words.

His smile, as always, illuminated how very handsome he was, and again Hannah could hardly believe her luck that he found her so attractive and their desire for each other was so blissfully mutual. At least her work couldn't come between them, she thought, happy to hold a relatively simple job that left her with plenty of hours for them to be together.

"The family party is streaming down the wharf now," he informed them. "I've forgotten their name."

"Anderson," Hannah replied.

"Is it some celebration? Birthday? Anniversary?"

"Family reunion."

"Then they should be happy just talking to each other," he said with satisfaction, his eyes simmering with some private intent that definitely included Hannah.

The sound of voices moved him into his usual position to greet the incoming passengers who were always directed into the saloon by the dive team inviting them to get their coffee or tea and meet the captain.

Hannah quickly carried two cups to the coffee machine, ready for the first requests. She heard Tony say, "Ah! Mr and Mrs Anderson, welcome aboard *Duchess*. I'm Tony King, your..."

"So you're Tony King," a voice she instantly recognised cut into Tony's spiel.

Shock speared through her. It was lucky she'd just put the cups down or they probably would have dropped from her hands. She stared disbelievingly at *her parents* who were eyeing Tony up and down as though they wanted to take in and assess every detail of his appearance and character.

"Yes, I am," Tony confirmed, looking somewhat perplexed at being the focus of such pointed interest.

"The man who's going to marry my daughter," her father ran on in his booming voice, galvanising stunned attention even from Megan.

"What?" spilled from her lips.

Hannah was speechless.

"I beg your pardon?" Tony queried, heavily frowning, as well he might, being faced with such an outrageous assumption.

"The name is not Anderson. It's O'Neill," her father corrected. "Connor O'Neill. My accountant booked the charter for me."

"O'Neill," Tony repeated dazedly.

"Hannah's father," came the pointed assertion. "This is her mother, Maureen. And may I say right here and now, we are not about to let you marry our daughter without her entire family present and we've come to make that known. Do I have your hand on that, Tony King?"

A hand was aggressively offered for Tony to take and shake on this man-to-man agreement. He shot a piercing look at Hannah, loaded with questions she couldn't answer. She was still speechless. Her stunned mind couldn't find any clue to how her father—her family—had arrived at the idea that she and Tony were getting married. It hadn't come from her. She hadn't even mentioned Tony to them in her e-mails. Not one word about their relationship.

A flood of heat rushed up her neck and scorched her cheeks. This was so embarrassing! He had to be thinking she had, at the very least, speculated to her parents about marrying him. His eyes glittered, undoubtedly from the electric activity in his mind. Then, apparently deciding the only way to rescue the situation and save her and her family major embarrassment, he seized her father's hand, pumping it vigorously and said what her father wanted to hear.

"You certainly have my agreement on that, Mr O'Neill. And may I say I'm delighted to meet you and Mrs O'Neill. I look forward to getting acquainted with the rest of Hannah's family today."

A masterly piece of diplomacy. Hannah didn't know if she appreciated it or not. Didn't it perpetuate a terrible mistake which should be corrected?

Her mother then grabbed his hand with both of hers, pressing anxiously. "You mustn't let Hannah talk you into some quick little register office wedding, Tony. I may call you Tony?"

"Of course."

"I told her father we had to get up here in time to stop that. Thank God we could get this trip arranged before the month was up."

"The month?" Tony queried.

It completely blew Hannah's mind. They'd been worrying about a marriage between her and Tony for a whole month? She'd barely been with him that long! Only since the day Jodie and Flynn... understanding crashed through her confusion like a thunderclap.

"You can't get married under a month without a special licence," her mother rattled on. "Which was a worry, knowing how good Hannah is at organising things, but I hoped..."

"Mrs O'Neill..."

"You can call me Maureen, dear." Patting his hand in approval now.

Hannah opened her mouth to rush out an explanation for the situation that had brewed up because of Tony's tactic for getting rid of Flynn. Before she could manage to form sensible words, he plunged on, compounding the whole problem a thousandfold.

"Maureen, I can assure you Hannah and I will have a very proper wedding with all the trimmings and all family present. My grandmother would never speak to me again if we did anything else."

Hannah choked. It was one diplomatic step too far, letting her parents think there would be a wedding. She had to stop this. But how was it to be done without making Tony feel like a fool for coming to her rescue so gallantly in front of her parents?

Weddings could be cancelled, she thought wildly.

Who knew that better than she did?

"How long will you be staying in Port Douglas?" Tony went on charmingly, probably wondering how long he had to keep up the pretence. "I know my grandmother would love to meet you."

No, no, no! screamed through Hannah's mind.

Isabella King might think it was real. They had to contain the damage, not spread it.

"Only the weekend," her father answered, much to Hannah's relief. She and Tony worked Sundays so...

"In that case, I'll re-arrange the crew roster for tomorrow so Hannah and I are free to be with you," Tony declared, ruining everything again.

Her mother beamed at him. "That will be wonderful! I can see why Hannah..."

"Mum!" Enough was enough! "You, too, Dad!"

That snapped their attention away from Tony and their faces lit up with triumphant delight at sight of her behind the galley counter. Hannah still gave them both barrels of her displeasure at their gross assumptions.

"What on earth do you think you're doing, dragging the whole family up here and expecting..."

"If Mohammed won't come to the mountain..." her father rolled out.

Her mother hastily broke in. "Hannah, we waited and waited for you to tell us about Tony yourself, and when you didn't..."

"I've got a right to my own private life!" Hannah hurled at them.

"Now that's enough, young lady," her father boomed, marching up to the galley counter to dress her down. He was a big barrel-chested man who made a habit of mowing down any opposition and he went straight into attack mode, wagging his finger at her.

"We respected your need to flit off and find some new direction for yourself, never mind how much your mother worried about you. For two years you've deserted your family." His fist slammed onto the counter for emphasis. "Two years!"

"I kept in touch," she fiercely retorted, her eyes every bit as battle-green as his as they locked in challenge. "You always knew where I was and what I was doing."

"Travelogue stuff!" her father scoffed.

"Connor, stop scolding!" her mother cried, ranging up beside him, her slender build and the rather scatty mop of grey curls that framed a face full of friendly appeal belying the strength she wielded in the O'Neill household. "We're here to build bridges and don't you forget it."

Behind them, Hannah's sisters and brothers were spilling into the saloon, introducing themselves to Tony, closely followed by wives, partners, children, all creating a distracting hub-bub as they made happy comments about the forthcoming mythical marriage. The whole scene was hopelessly out of control, absolute chaos and getting worse by the second.

"Please don't be angry with us, Hannah," her mother was pleading.

"Maureen, she has no reason to be angry with us," her father instantly argued.

"I'm not angry," Hannah put in helplessly. "Just... surprised."

"Of course you are!" her mother agreed indulgently. "That was what it was meant to be. A lovely surprise!"

Twenty-four O'Neills descending on her—the whole family pressure-pack—with Tony haplessly cornered by their belief in a marriage that hadn't really been proposed or accepted. And she could see he was actually beginning to enjoy the act, egged on by her rather boisterous family. She hoped he realised this was all his own fault, using the getting-married line to torpedo Flynn's arrogant attempt to chat her up again.

"He's certainly a fine figure of a man, Hannah," her mother said admiringly.

"I like him much better than Flynn already," her father declared, intent on mending fences.

"Connor, we are not going to mention Flynn," her mother chided.

"And why not when *he's* to blame for Hannah playing this secret hand?" he growled. "Here she is, too uptight to tell us anything in case something goes wrong this time."

"That's not true, Dad." Hannah took a deep breath, feeling more and more wrong about letting this deception run on. Tony didn't have to save her face in front of her family. As for bringing his grandmother into it, that was just way over the top. Her family would simply have to understand that their information had been deliberately planted on a person who wasn't supposed to be in contact with them. Which reminded her... "Who told you about this?" she demanded.

Her mother grimaced apologetically as she replied, "Our Trish ran into Jodie Lovett at a fashion parade three weeks ago. Jodie made some catty remark about you and Tony King and your sister promptly dug her heels in and wouldn't let Jodie go until she had explained herself…'' Her eyes telegraphed knowledge of highly suggestive intimacy as she added, ''…very fully.''

Hannah flushed, recalling that Jodie had seen Tony enter the Coral King apartment with her, as well as being witness to the dinner for two at Nautilis. No doubt Jodie had painted a vivid picture, and Trish, eager to believe her jilted sister did have a new fiancé, had probably elaborated on it to the rest of the family.

She could see them all speculating like crazy, especially when there had been no news from her about an engagement. Tony had never encountered the O'Neill clannishness—the networking that never stopped. It was one of the reasons Hannah had run two years ago. She couldn't have stood their overwhelming sympathy and caring, endlessly turning the knife in the wound of what had happened in their attempts to cosset and comfort.

''So when do you and Tony plan to marry?'' her father demanded to know.

''Dad…'' She heaved a sigh and gathered herself to lay out the truth. ''…we haven't even…''

''The ring!'' Trish called out excitedly, breaking from the pack around Tony, the lovely auburn hair she'd inherited from their father—although his was now white—being flipped over her shoulder as she rushed forward, completely forgetting the sinuous grace she used on the catwalk as a top-line model. ''Show us the ring, Hannah!''

It was the last straw of this whole ridiculous mess! Hannah glared at her busybody younger sister, opened her mouth and began to say, ''I haven't got…''

"She hasn't got it on," Tony loudly overrode her, drawing her gaze to his as he parted the cluster of O'Neills and strode towards her, his eyes transmitting an unmistakable command that Hannah let things be.

Which threw her into more turmoil. She didn't want to let Tony down, but couldn't he see how much out of hand this could get if they kept feeding the misunderstanding?

"Hannah doesn't like to wear the ring when she's working—preparing food, cooking fish, wiping up, using her hands all the time," he explained.

All very reasonable. Hannah's heart was sinking at his persistence with the story. He was pinning her to it instead of...

"So I keep it in my pocket for her."

All eyes turned to him as he pulled out a small jewellery box from his shorts pocket and held it out on the palm of his hand for everyone to see. It was like a conjuring trick. Hannah couldn't believe it. Her parents moved aside to give him room to reach the galley counter directly in front of her and he placed the black velvet box on it—unmistakably a ring box. Even Hannah's eyes were glued to it now and it certainly wasn't disappearing in a puff of smoke.

"Give me your hand, Hannah."

She did. It seemed to her that her left hand lifted of its own accord. Tony opened the box, plucked out the ring, held her hand steady, and slid a fabulous emerald ring onto her third finger. The brilliant green gem winked up at her as if to say, "Here I am, as promised, all yours."

"Well, the cat's out of the bag now," Megan muttered smugly.

And it was! Everyone was oohing and aahing over the ring Tony had put on her hand, on her engagement finger, a very real, very serious ring that spoke more convincingly than any words could. If she tried to deny it…no, that option was gone. They would all think she was mad, treat her as mad, not realising that Tony had swept away her right to choose.

Her heart quivered at the sheer boldness of his move. He had to have ordered this ring for her, planned a proposal of marriage. How could he have made up his mind so fast?

Panic welled up in her.

It was too fast.

Much too fast.

"Take it back, Tony," More panic…did she really want him to? "Keep it for later," she hastily tagged on.

Later…when they were alone together…when this madhouse with her family was behind them…and she had time to think. All she knew now was she couldn't hand out a public rejection. The emerald ring was too serious. It forced her to look at what could be…*if* she truly was the only woman in the world for Tony King.

CHAPTER FOURTEEN

AT LAST they were in the jeep, driving away from the marina, away from her meddling family who had piled into a minibus for the trip back to their hotel, away from her fellow crew members and their happy grins exulting in how right they'd been about her and Tony.

Hannah didn't know what was right.

She simply felt intense relief that the barrage of well-meaning remarks and advice was over and she didn't have to smile anymore. Her face ached. Her head ached. And her heart ached, because it was torn between accepting the picture Tony had painted all day, and the fear there were too many flaws in it.

"Are you stressed out by your family...or by me, Hannah?" he asked quietly.

"Both," she answered on a heavy sigh.

He took one hand from the driving wheel and reached across to make physical contact with her, his fingers closing around her hand and gently squeezing. "I didn't plan this, though I did intend to propose to you tonight."

"I realise you were catapulted into it by my family thinking it was already a done deal, but...there was no deal between us, Tony, and..." She shook her head, finding it difficult to articulate exactly how she felt about it.

"I pre-empted your choice."

"Yes. Yes, you did."

"Is that so bad, Hannah? Would you have chosen otherwise if we'd been alone together?"

"I don't know. You didn't give me the chance to think…to consider…to…to talk about it."

"Then I guess we need to talk about it now."

He squeezed her hand again before releasing it to bring the jeep to a halt outside her apartment. His calmness actually increased Hannah's anxiety. She didn't hop out of the jeep when he did.

She sat staring at the big white wooden house that had been divided into four separate living quarters— not exactly flash apartments although they were completely private and she usually felt comfortable in hers. Her own space. Sharing it with Tony had been good, so why did she now feel he was invading it? Her heart was pounding so hard she couldn't think.

He opened the passenger door for her and still she didn't move, paralysed by a confusion she couldn't sort out. Wild doubts whirled through her mind as she stared at him. Was he Mr Right for her? Would he love her to her dying day and never look at another woman with desire? Was that an impossible dream?

Without a word, Tony stepped forward, scooped her off the passenger seat, and proceeded to carry her towards her front door, taking any decision out of her hands…again!

"Why are you doing this?" It was more a plea than a protest. Her arms wound themselves around his neck and hung on, hardly a reaction that would deter him in his purpose.

"You look very fragile," he answered gruffly.

It was how she felt. And it was so easy to rest her head on his lovely broad shoulder and close her eyes and let the whole fraught day drift away, just breathe in his comforting maleness, feel his strong arms supporting her, the steady pumping of his heart within the warm wall of his chest.

He stood her on her feet to open the door to her apartment, but he was right behind her, his arms encircling her waist, his body like a protective shield she could lean against, his head bent to hers, his mouth softly grazing her ear.

"I'm sorry today was hard for you. I can't take it back, Hannah."

"I know," she murmured, unlocking the door, letting him in because she wanted him, needed him, and instinct was stronger than reason.

He closed the door and drew her into his embrace, face-to-face this time, and his eyes burned into hers as he spoke what had never been spoken between them. "I love you, Hannah. You must know that, too."

Her heart contracted. Why did those words hurt so much? They shouldn't hurt. They should be filling her with joy and happiness. Yet the shadows of pain and betrayal were flitting through her mind.

"Kiss me, Tony," she pleaded. "Make me feel it."

He kissed her with a fierce passion that flooded through her bloodstream and revitalised every cell in her body. It ignited a blaze of desire that obliterated shadows and the only thought pulsing through her mind was *yes, yes, yes*. She was so much *with him,* it was a jolt when he wrenched his mouth from hers and savagely muttered, "No, no, no...this is wrong!"

"Why is it wrong?" she asked, totally befuddled.

"You don't want to be stormed."

"Yes, I do."

"No...that's a quick fix. You want to feel loved. That's different."

He rained soft kisses around her face and took her mouth with a sensual tenderness that sent sweet shivers down her spine. He unbraided her hair and gently massaged her scalp as he kissed her some more, warmly, lovingly. It was so nice, relaxing, caring, Hannah basked in the pleasure of it, all her tensions melting away.

"I love the silkiness of your hair," he murmured, rubbing his cheek against it. "I love burying my face in it, breathing in its scent."

"I like smelling you, too," she whispered.

"And your breasts..." He started undressing her, stroking her clothes away, caressing her flesh as though it was a source of endless wonder. "You have beautiful breasts, Hannah. All of you is beautiful. I love looking at you, touching you..."

"I feel the same way about you. You're so completely perfect to me," she confessed, eagerly undressing him, wanting to see, to feel, and her heart was beating the refrain... Tony, Tony, Tony...

"Let me make love to you as I want to," he said, sweeping her off her feet again and carrying her to the bed. "Just lie here, Hannah, and feel me loving you."

It was always enthralling to her, being naked with him, the blissful intimacy of it, the freedom, revelling in his very masculine beauty, the innate power of his body. She never really thought of herself, except how lucky she was to have such a man as her lover.

Yet now, letting him do as he willed, focusing only on what he was doing to her, every erotic caress, every sensuous kiss, feeling her body responding—ripples of delight, quivers of excitement—it dawned on her that Tony *was* giving her the sense of every part of her being loved. More than loved…adored, cherished…and when he moved to give her the most intimate kiss of all, she was on fire to have him inside her, to show him how deeply she welcomed this loving, wishing it could go on forever.

It was utterly glorious when he finally surged into her. She embraced him with all she was—body, heart, mind, soul—and soared with him to one exquisite climax after another until they were both spent and lay tangled together in the sweet ecstasy of feeling completely fulfilled by each other.

"Marry me, Hannah," he murmured, pressing warm kisses over her hair. "Nothing could feel more right than this."

She sighed, wanting to agree with him. But it had only been a month. Maybe it was so wonderful because it was still new. "Can't we wait awhile, Tony? Make sure it's going to last?" she softly pleaded.

His chest rose and fell under her cheek and she sensed he was gathering himself to argue with her, yet when he spoke it was with a quiet calmness. "Why do you think it might not, Hannah?"

That was so hard to answer. How could she say she didn't trust him? That wasn't true. She did trust Tony. He had given her no reason not to trust him.

"Are you worried about the constancy of my feelings…or yours?" he asked when her silence had gone on too long.

"There…there hasn't been much time…to test them," she got out, struggling for words that wouldn't hurt.

"Hannah, I'm thirty-two years old. I've been with many women. Attractive women whom I've liked very much, whose company I've enjoyed. Not once in all that time, in all that experience, did I ever feel…this is the woman I want to share my life with. Until I met you. I can tell you unequivocally…that's not going to change for me."

Was it true? Could she believe it?

He gently rolled her onto her back and hitched himself up on his elbow to look down at her. Panic welled up in Hannah at the thought he was going to demand a decision from her. She was actually frightened to meet his gaze, knowing how compelling it could be. Yet his eyes were soft, kind, and a huge wave of grateful relief washed away the panic. He smiled, and her heart swelled with love for him.

"You knocked me out the day we met, Hannah O'Neill. And the very next time I saw you, the message started beating through my brain—this woman is mine. Since then, everything that's happened between us has confirmed that message, over and over again."

He traced her lips with feather-light fingertips, reminding her of the tenderness he'd shown. "Is it asking too much, wanting you to wear my ring? You can always hand it back to me if you decide I'm not the right man for you, Hannah." His smile turned into a tilted appeal. "I can't force you to marry me, you know. That choice is very definitely yours."

Tony…her husband…her partner for life…always loving her…the dream swam before her eyes, tantalisingly reachable…almost convincing…

"Let me put my ring back on your finger, as a promise from me. It doesn't lock you in. It simply says I love you and I want to marry you, and every time you look at it you can think about it."

In a flash he was off the bed, fetching the ring box from his shorts pocket.

Hannah's mind was in a whirl. Was it all right to wear the ring, on the clear understanding she would hand it back if their relationship started feeling wrong, or less than what she felt was needed for a marriage to work? They were expected to have dinner with her family tonight. Everyone would expect to see it on her finger. If it wasn't…how was she to explain? But if it was there…they would expect more…and more…

Tony bounced back onto the bed, grabbed her left hand and slid the emerald onto her third finger. "Made for you," he declared triumphantly. "Fits perfectly."

It did. "How did you manage that?" she asked, staring down at the ring which was stirring a storm of turmoil. There were consequences if she fell in with Tony's plan. Much as she wanted to please him, make him happy with her, wearing this ring would start a train of events she wasn't ready to face.

"I waited until you fell asleep in my arms, then measured your finger," he answered, his tone rich with the pleasure he had taken in his forethought, pleasure she would take away if she refused to go along with him. "You didn't even stir," he went on. "Very peaceful sleep. Which just goes to show how good I am for you."

"You have been good for me, Tony," she acknowledged, and didn't want it to stop. But what if it did?

"And *will* be good for you."

His confident claim stirred the turmoil further. He'd chosen an emerald because Flynn had given her a diamond and Tony wanted to give her something different. But the words weren't different. Flynn had said he'd be good for her, too. It was too much to take on board right now. She couldn't do it.

A surge of desperate determination lifted her gaze to his. "If I wear this ring, everyone—my family, your family, all the people we know—will expect me to start planning our wedding." She shuddered from the sheer violence of feeling ripping through her. "I won't do it, Tony."

He frowned, his eyes probing hers with sharp intensity. "Do you mean...you don't want to wear my ring...or you don't want to get involved in planning a wedding?"

"They'll start it. They'll start it tonight. And you'll involve your grandmother tomorrow. They'll all look to me to do things..."

Her chest tightened at the mere thought of it. She could see Tony didn't understand. After all, wasn't it every woman's dream to plan her wedding? Except striving to produce that perfect day turned into an obsession, an obsession fed by the wedding merchants and the bride's family, claiming this had to be done and that had to be done if everything was to be *perfect*.

The groom was largely left out of it.

The bride was very busy.

So busy, the groom had time to look elsewhere, to start wondering if he'd made a mistake and some other woman might fill his needs better.

"I won't do it." She shook her head, feeling the whole destructive pressure of it and needing to break free of it, stay free of it. Her eyes begged understanding as she tried to explain. "It becomes an event that takes on a life of its own and it gobbles up too much. It…it consumes love instead of giving it room to grow strong and unbreakable. I'll get trapped into it because that's a bride's job. Not the groom's. And I won't be available when you want me…"

"You think I'll do what Flynn did."

His eyes accused her of misjudging him on totally unfair grounds.

"It's only been a month, Tony," she shot back at him, rebelling against his *certainty*. "You buy me a ring while everything's red-hot between us, when there's nothing getting in the way of doing whatever we like together…"

"You think it's going to cool?"

"I don't know. All I know is it has only been a

month, and I will not be bull-dozed into planning a wedding that I end up having to cancel. I've been there, done that, and just the thought of it happening again freezes me up.''

"What if it's still red-hot after six months, Hannah? Would you marry me then?''

She took a deep breath, trying to calm herself enough to consider. Six months. Any cracks in their relationship should be showing by then. If it was still the same, still as wonderful as it had been this past month... "Yes,'' she decided. "I'd feel more sure of everything being right for us if it lasted six months.''

"Okay. On that basis, will you make a bargain with me?''

"What bargain?''

"You wear my ring, which you can give back at any time in the next five months if you don't feel right about us. At the end of that five months, if you're still wearing my ring, you will turn up as my bride at a wedding which I will arrange.''

"You...arrange?'' Sheer astonishment glazed her mind.

"I'll do all the planning, make all the arrangements. I'll buy what has to be bought, hire what has to be hired, book what has to be booked. All you'll need do is to turn up at the church at the specified time in the wedding dress which I'll supply. Five months from now.''

She stared at him in amazement. "You'd take on all that...to marry me?''

He nodded, his eyes serious, absolute commitment written on his face. "I would like very much for us to have a wedding to remember, one we can look back on as a wonderful celebration of our marriage.''

Tears swam into her eyes. He was making it sound so real. And didn't it prove he loved her, being prepared to arrange a wedding himself? He wasn't even considering there was a risk in putting so much of himself on the line. Was he so sure they were right together?

"I want to give you that, Hannah," he said softly. "But I do need something from you."

Need...he had answered so many of her needs. The urge to give was instant and strong. She nodded for him to go on, too choked up to speak.

"Give me your word...there'll be no running away at the last minute."

She swallowed hard and fervently replied, "I wouldn't do that to you, Tony." Never would she deal out such painful humiliation...jilting him at the altar.

"Then...do we have a bargain?"

A shiver ran through her as she recalled Megan's words. *When the King family makes a commitment, it's rock-solid, providing you keep your side of the bargain.* Her eyes searched his as she asked, "Are you really sure about this, Tony?"

There was not so much as a flicker of uncertainty. "I'm sure," he said with a blaze of conviction that poured warmth into the cold places in her soul.

It felt good.

It was fair.

More than fair.

"Then yes. We have a bargain."

CHAPTER FIFTEEN

ISABELLA VALERI KING sat by the fountain in the loggia, waiting for Antonio to fly in from Innisfail. It was Friday, and on Sunday there would be a family luncheon here at the castle to celebrate his engagement to Hannah O'Neill, but he wanted this private meeting with her first.

His request had not surprised her. All was not as it should be. Isabella had reflected on the events of last weekend many times—the shock announcement on Saturday evening that the O'Neill family had arrived in Port Douglas—all twenty-four members—and he was going to marry Hannah. She was wearing his ring. No time to talk then. They were to dine with the O'Neill family and could he bring them all up to the castle for afternoon tea on Sunday?

Isabella had gone to bed that night filled with joy. Choosing Hannah O'Neill as the chef for *Duchess* had been the right move. Antonio had fallen in love with her—such a suitable young woman for him—and she would soon have a second grandson married.

She had enjoyed meeting the very large O'Neill family on Sunday—all of them so clever and talented—good stock—but she had felt uneasy at the way Antonio had been very protective of Hannah in front of them, fending off any questions directed at her about their future, answering them himself.

169

It was charmingly done. Isabella doubted the O'Neills had found anything amiss. When Antonio *performed,* he gave out so much dynamic energy, people didn't really notice anybody else and he had been in dazzling form that afternoon. No one seemed to notice that Hannah was being passive, letting him take control. No one except Isabella.

It didn't feel right to her. At the job interview, and on two subsequent meetings with her, Hannah had shown herself to be very active and enterprising, not at all backward in taking the initiative, confident in expressing herself—a delightful personality. Yet all that had been subdued on Sunday afternoon. Maybe she had wanted Antonio to shine in front of her family, but surely not as much as he had, even handling all the questions about wedding plans.

Tony had declared they would be married in Port Douglas—a decisive announcement with no input from Hannah, no excuse to her family why she did not choose to marry in Sydney from her parental home, which was the bride's prerogative. Oddly enough none of the O'Neills had protested this although Hannah's mother had looked sadly wistful for several moments before putting a cheerful face over her private feelings.

Antonio had gone on to state that the wedding ceremony would be held in the local church, *St. Mary's by the sea,* and the reception would be here at the castle. Then he had asked Isabella to show the older family members the ballroom while he and Hannah took the younger children up to the tower. Which was, perhaps, a reasonable arrangement, but why wouldn't Hannah want to check out the ballroom personally with her mother? This was not normal behaviour from a happy bride-to-be.

Two years of running away...that was what Antonio had said the night he had taken Hannah to Nautilis, intent on confronting the couple who had distressed her. Was she still *running away?* What did this mean in the context of consenting to marry Antonio?

The sound of the helicopter coming in broke into her disturbing thoughts.

Soon she would know the truth.

As much as she wanted Antonio married, it was so important to get it right. She remembered sitting here with Elizabeth whose three sons—the Kings of the Kimberley—had all made good marriages. Elizabeth had understood her need for the family to go on, building on what had been built. She had also understood it couldn't be done without the right women. Partners for life. Absolute commitment. No running away.

I have lived for eighty years, Isabella thought, *years that have brought many joys and many sorrows.* She wanted to see her grandsons settled in good marriages with families of their own before she died...the last achievement that would make sense of all the rest. But time was getting shorter and shorter. It went so fast now. Even so, it would be bad if Antonio rushed into a marriage that was wrong. Such a mistake would be very costly.

''Nonna...'' He emerged from the castle foyer,

closing one of the big entrance doors behind him. "…I thought you'd be inside."

"I like sitting here, Antonio. I find it…harmonious."

It was eminently clear all was not harmonious in his world. He brought tension with him like an ill wind, as well as the battle energy that signalled a problem he was determined on facing and beating.

"I told Rosita not to bring us anything. I hope you don't mind," he said as he took the chair at the opposite end of the table to hers.

"You want to talk about Hannah without interruption," she surmised, her eyes informing him she was well aware of the sensitivity of this conversation. "I suspect you have moved too fast for her, Antonio."

A wry little smile acknowledged her perception. "One has to move fast to catch a butterfly, Nonna."

A butterfly? The fanciful allusion worried Isabella. A beautiful creature, yes, but… "It is wrong to pin one down," she pointed out, thinking such a fluttery characteristic was not what she had envisaged in a wife for Antonio.

"Hannah wants to fly with me. It's a matter of proving I won't stray from her side."

"You…stray?" Isabella shook her head, frowning over such a doubt. Hannah could not know him well enough. Once Antonio made up his mind, nothing could shift him from his course. "She needs more time with you."

"I've bought enough time," he claimed with confidence. "Hannah will wear my ring as long as it keeps feeling right. I've made a bargain with her and I need your help to carry it through, Nonna.''

"Then you had best explain it to me."

He gave her the knowledge she was lacking, painting the backdrop to the current situation with all the shades she'd been missing. Hannah's previous high-pressure career as a top-line events organiser did not really surprise her. A useful talent to have in any walk of life, Isabella thought.

The story of her relationships with Flynn and Jodie Lovett was illuminating. That betrayal and the humiliation in front of her family explained much. It was relatively easy to piece together the problem. Hannah had suffered a massive loss of trust, not only in her own judgement of people, but also in planning for any future at all.

It took time to build trust, time to be convinced it would never be abused. Antonio had rushed in, knowing what his word was worth and expecting, as usual, to carry all before him, only to discover that winning his own way was not so simple.

Still, the bridal bargain he had made with Hannah was clever, possibly a masterstroke, though it laid him open to public humiliation should she cancel the wedding. He was taking all the risks, leaving Hannah free to walk away without any cost at all from their relationship.

The gift of love...

Did Hannah recognise it for what it was?

"So you see, Nonna, I need your help. You know how to go about planning a wedding. If you'll tell me what I have to do and when to do it..."

"Are you absolutely certain it will be right for both of you in the end, Antonio?" she asked, not wanting to see him hurt.

"Nonna, I have never felt anything more right," he answered with quiet gravity. "In my heart, I know Hannah loves me. And in her heart, she knows I love her. She is simply afraid to believe it."

Was it true?

Or was it blind faith?

Five months...

Isabella gathered herself and stood up, knowing she had to trust Antonio's instincts. "Come. We will go to the library so I can look up available dates for a wedding in my work diary. We must set a day. All planning begins with that."

Antonio heaved a huge sigh of relief as he rose from his chair. A few quick steps and he was hugging her in an emotional overflow of gratitude. "Thank you. I want the very best for Hannah, Nonna. It has to be the best."

"The choices must be yours, Antonio. I will put them to you. I will see that your decisions are carried out. But this wedding must be your gift to Hannah, not mine. You do understand this?"

"Yes." He drew back to meet the challenge in her eyes with the fire in his soul. "I took the responsibility. I'll see it through. When Hannah walks down the aisle as my bride, Nonna, you'll see that it's right. She needs me to do this. It's the proof of my love for her."

A quest...that was what it was, and Hannah needed him to fulfil it.

Isabella smiled.

Getting his teeth into a quest was so Antonio. Did Hannah know instinctively it would bind him to her more effectively than anything else? She had agreed to the bargain. That alone had to mean she valued this relationship very highly. The butterfly might not yet be caught but it seemed she wanted to be caught. And to Antonio, failure was inconceivable.

Isabella hoped she would see Hannah O'Neill walk down the aisle to him as his bride. If she did...then it would be right.

CHAPTER SIXTEEN

THEY were all in the church…waiting. At least, all those who could fit into the small white church—the two families and the people closest to them—were jammed in…waiting.

The old wooden building, constructed in the traditional Queenslander style with its studs exposed on the outside, weatherboard cladding on the inside, was virtually a historic landmark in Port Douglas, positioned near the shoreline of Anzac Park, overlooking Dickenson Inlet. *St. Mary's by the sea* did not hold a big congregation. But outside, the whole park was filled with people…waiting.

Alex checked his watch.

Beside him, Matt muttered, "She's running late."

Tony's nerves tightened another notch.

"Only five minutes," Alex murmured.

But Hannah was always, always punctual. It must be someone else's fault, Tony fiercely reasoned. She wouldn't leave him standing here today. She'd promised. No running away at the last minute. His ring had still been on her finger yesterday. There was no need to worry.

He stared out the big picture window at the back of the church. It was a brilliant sunny afternoon yet there were no boats out on the inlet. No boats and no business being done in Port Douglas. Everything had stopped for *the wedding*.

It was like a festival day out there in the park. Marquees had been set up to serve food and drinks. Local bands were entertaining the crowd. An Aboriginal dance troupe had come down from Kuranda, adding their primitive colour to the celebratory atmosphere. People had flocked here from up and down the whole far north to witness the occasion. Even the ferals who shunned all society had left their shelters in the hills and come into town today.

Tony King was getting married.

If his bride turned up.

Did Hannah realise this was not like a city wedding where only those directly involved in it would be affected if it was cancelled? This was a community event and the King family always delivered what it promised. It wasn't just his pride at stake here. Almost a hundred years of tradition was riding on his judgement that Hannah loved him enough to be his bride.

His heart said she did.

His mind said she had to or there was no sense to what he felt with her.

His soul yearned for her to join him.

"Listen!" Alex nudged him, a huge grin breaking across his face. "She's on her way."

Cheers rising from the crowd outside. It had to mean they could see the horse-drawn buggies coming down Wharf Street from the Coral King Apartments where the O'Neill family had been housed for the wedding.

His grandmother and her great-grandson, Marco, would be in the first one, having come from the castle to head the procession. Alex's four-year-old son was to carry in the grey-velvet cushion on which lay the wedding rings. No doubt he was jiggling with excitement at being part of this grand occasion.

Alex's lovely wife, Gina, and Hannah's sister, Trish, would be riding in the second, wearing the emerald-green gowns he'd chosen for them.

Behind them would be Hannah with her father. Tony hoped she felt his love for her in everything she wore today—the bride of his choice. The wedding gown was relatively simple, a slim silky ankle-length dress which would hug her lovely curves, its low square-cut neckline and shoulder straps beaded with white pearls. Most meaningful of all to him was the headdress that would hold her veil.

Picard pearls—the best in the world from Broome at the coastal edge of the Kimberly. He'd contacted Jared King whom he'd met at Alex's wedding. The Kings of the Kimberly were descended from the same paternal line as his grandfather, and Jared ran the Picard Pearl Company.

His wife, Christabel, had requested photographs of Hannah and had created a special design for her from the ideas Tony had wanted expressed. It was his special gift to his bride on their wedding day. He hoped she loved it…was wearing it with love for him. She might not understand what it symbolised but he would tell her tonight—tonight when he made love to *his wife*.

Outside the noise of cheering and clapping increased. The jazz band broke into a joyous rendition of "When The Saints Come Marching In." The crowd started singing.

"What's the betting the band is leading the procession in?" Matt remarked, happy now that activity was in the air.

Everyone in the church started buzzing with anticipation. The waiting was almost over. Peter Owen handed his god-daughter, Alex's and Gina's new baby girl, to Rosita and moved to sit at the electronic keyboard, ready to play. His white grand piano could not fit into this church, but it was waiting for him in the ballroom at the castle. For *this* wedding, he would do anything asked of him. Gina was to sing and he always accompanied Gina when she sang, joining in the duets with her.

The band's jazz playing stopped just outside the church. The crowd hushed. Tony took a deep breath to relax himself. In his mind's eye he could see the drivers of the buggies helping their passengers step down. A little shiver ran down his spine as the deep haunting throb of didgeridoos began.

The Aborigines who'd gathered were calling up the spirits of the dreamtime to wish this union well. It brought an eerie sense of ancient rites to this moment, reminding Tony that he belonged to this land which had proved fruitful for four generations of his family. The nature of it had to be respected and one had to work in harmony with it. That was the way of everything and the same had to be applied to marriage. Respect, harmony…

Silence.

Footsteps in the vestibule.

Alex and Matt, half turning to look.

Tony took another deep breath and followed suit. His grandmother was entering the church, walking up to the front pew. She was smiling at him. It was a smile that promised all was well.

Behind her he could see Marco and Gina and Trish lined up to make their entrance, but not Hannah as yet. No amount of sensible willpower could get rid of the butterflies in Tony's stomach. The moment his grandmother reached her place, Peter Owen started playing, the electronic keyboard producing quite a wonderful rendition of Mendelssohn's wedding march. There were speakers outside the church transmitting the ceremony to all who wanted to listen and the music seemed to swirl everywhere.

Marco started up the aisle, carefully carrying his cushion and grinning delightedly at his father who stood beside Tony, undoubtedly encouraging his little son. Gina came next. Then Trish. Tony forgot about breathing altogether when finally Hannah and her father moved into position to start their procession towards him.

His heart stopped.

She was here… Hannah…his bride…so radiantly beautiful…smiling at him…her green eyes sparkling…and holding the long white bridal veil was the plait of pearls, looping over the top of her head, each end fastened by exquisite gold and pearl butterflies, below them the long unplaited strands of pearls falling down beside her ears, mingling with the wavy tresses of her hair.

Two butterflies—one for him, one for her, joined by a bond that would intertwine them for the rest of their lives—and that was how it would be because she was here, willing to marry him, wanting to share the future with him, and she walked towards him, not one shadow of doubt dimming the happiness that shone from her and beamed straight into his heart, kick-starting it into a thunderous beat, a joyous drumming of love for this woman—*his* woman.

He held out his hand to her.

She took it.

The bargain was complete.

This was the time for them.

The link was unbreakable.

CHAPTER SEVENTEEN

DEAR Elizabeth,

It was a great pleasure to have you and your family attending Antonio's and Hannah's wedding. I feel very strongly that now we have forged these ties which reach back to the past, they must be carried into the future. Heritage should be valued, not forgotten. Which brings me to your very good advice at the wedding.

You are right. I carry so many memories with me that no one else has. And there are the stories—almost legends now—of all my father achieved from when he first landed in this country. These things should be written down so that future generations can read the family history and know what has brought them to where they are—perhaps even making them what they are as people. The genes are passed on. I see the similarities in your sons and my grandsons. I think the King bloodline must be very strong. But then, so is my father's. It is a good mix.

I shall advertise for a person who is skilled in family research, someone who will know what questions to ask of the older members of the Italian community here, and who can assist me in organising all the accessible information. I must hunt up all the old photographs from the early days, although it is a shame they were always posed in a stiff fashion, not like those taken of Antonio and his bride.

I sit here, looking at a photograph of them taken on their wedding day, and it captures all the joy and love that shone from them. I remember the moment well. The photographer was trying to arrange some formal photographs by the fountain, but Antonio would have none of it.

''Take one of this!'' he demanded and scooped Hannah off her feet. ''Come fly with me!'' he said and whirled her around, her feet kicking through droplets of water, and they laughed at each other, so light-hearted and happy.

A wonderful photograph! I will enclose it with this letter. I'm sure it will bring a smile to your face. Although there is another one I like just as well. When Antonio set Hannah on her feet again, her arms were still around his neck and she looked up at him and said, ''I love you, Tony King.'' You cannot see the words but their faces show the depth of feeling between them. It is beautiful. I shall enclose it, too.

So my dear Elizabeth, another year has almost passed, but I am well satisfied with this one. Hannah told me she wants at least four children and I am sure Antonio will oblige her. Next year perhaps I will have another great-grandchild. I have much to look forward to.

Thank you again for your company at the wedding, and for your very good advice. I shall definitely proceed with recording a family history and it will be most interesting to see what eventuates from this worthwhile enterprise.

Perhaps I will have photographs of Matteo and his bride by the time it is ready for print. For me, it would make the story complete. I know you will understand this, Elizabeth. It is the women who give birth, who nurture families. I must find the right woman for Matteo. Then I can rest in peace.

With sincere respect and affection,
Isabella Valeri King

The Honeymoon
Contract

CHAPTER ONE

MATT KING had spent a highly satisfying day, whitewater rafting on the Tully River with his friends. It was good to be single and unattached, free to enjoy fun and games anytime he liked. At thirty, Matt figured he had a few more carefree bachelor years up his sleeve before marriage became a serious item on his agenda and he was not about to fall victim to any plans his grandmother might have to get him wed.

Today's activity had been the perfect excuse not to turn up at the Sunday luncheon she had organized for the purpose of introducing her latest female protégée to the family. Matt knew it was only delaying the inevitable. Sooner or later he would have to meet this Nicole Redman. He could hardly avoid her for the whole six months she was under contract to write the family history, especially as she was staying as *a guest* at King's Castle for the duration. Nevertheless, he was determined not to dance to his grandmother's tune.

The telephone rang just as he was about to settle down and watch a bit of television before going to bed. Feeling at peace with his world, and pleased with the neat little sidestep he'd performed today, Matt even smiled indulgently when he heard his grandmother's voice on the other end of the line.

5

"Ah! You are safely home, Matteo," she said, letting him know she disapproved of dangerous pursuits that risked life and limb for no good reason.

"Yes, Nonna. I managed not to drown or break any bones," he answered cheerfully.

"More good luck than good management," she muttered darkly before moving to the real point of her call. "Will you be in your bus depot office in the morning?"

No ducking out of this one, Matt thought. Business was business and his grandmother knew his work routine. Midweek he moved around the tropical fruit plantations but Mondays and Fridays were spent with the transport company he'd developed himself, picking up the tourist dollar in a big way.

"Yes," he replied to the lead-in question, waiting for the crunch.

"Good! I'll send Nicole along to you. I want you to give her a gold pass so she can travel freely on any of your bus tours."

"Doesn't she have a car?" Matt asked very dryly, knowing he was about to be outmanoeuvred but putting in a token protest anyway.

"Yes. But the bus tours will give her a general feel of the area she will have to cover in her research and your drivers do give potted histories as they go."

"More gossip than fact, Nonna. The aim is to entertain, not cram with information."

"It adds a certain flavour that is distinctive to far North Queensland, Matteo. Since Nicole is not familiar with Port Douglas or its environs, I don't see it as a waste of time.''

''A pity you didn't employ someone local who wouldn't have to start from scratch,'' he remarked.

''Nicole Redman had the qualifications I wanted for this project,'' came the definitive reply.

''Nothing beats local knowledge,'' he argued, strongly suspecting *the qualifications* had very little to do with writing a family history.

He was awake to his grandmother's matchmaking game. His two older brothers hadn't twigged to it and here they were, neatly married off to brides of their choice, or so they thought. Not that Matt had any quarrel with the women they'd wed. Gina and Hannah were beautiful people. It was just that he now knew they'd been Nonna's choices for Alex and Tony before his brothers had even met them.

Good thing he'd overheard her triumphant conversation with Elizabeth King at Tony's wedding, plus the voiced hope that she would be able to find a suitable wife for her third grandson. Matt had little doubt that Nicole Redman was the selected candidate.

She probably didn't know it, any more than he was supposed to know it, but that didn't change the game. Her arrival on the family scene repeated the previous pattern of his grandmother employing a young woman who ended up married to one of her grandsons. Since *he* was the only one left unmarried...

''Many people can do research and write down a list of facts, Matteo,'' his grandmother declared in a tone of arch disdain, applying her authority in no uncertain terms. "Having the skill to tell a story well is something else. I do not want an amateurish publication. This is important to me."

It was pure Isabella Valeri King…not to be denied. Even at eighty years of age she was still a formidable character and Matt loved and respected her far too much not to give in…a little.

"Sorry, Nonna. Of course it is," he quickly conceded. "You know best what you want and if a gold bus pass will help the project, I'm only too happy to assist."

It would only take a minute of his time. A brief meeting during business hours—no social obligation attached to it—would serve to satisfy his curiosity about what made Nicole Redman *suitable* for him in his grandmother's eyes.

"I thought you could also supply the road maps she will need when she does venture out by herself. Explain the various areas of particular family interest to her and how best to get there."

Matt could see the minute stretching to half an hour but there was no way he could refuse this reasonable request. "Okay. I'll have them ready for her." With all the plantations marked on them from Cape Tribulation to Innisfail. That would save time and evade the cosy togetherness his grandmother was undoubtedly plotting.

"Thank you, Matteo. When would be most convenient for Nicole to call by?"

Never. He suppressed the telling word and answered, "Oh, let's say ten-thirty."

The call ended on that agreement and for quite some time afterwards, Matt mused on how very clever his grandmother was, keeping strictly to business, no hint of trying to push any personal interest, not even a comment on Nicole Redman as a person, simply pressing a meeting which was reasonably justified.

Could he be wrong about this plot?

No, it still fitted the modus operandi.

His grandmother had produced Gina Terlizzi, a wedding singer, just as Alex was planning his wedding to a woman his grandmother didn't like. With good reason, Matt had to concede. He hadn't liked Michelle Banks, either, and was glad Alex had married Gina instead. Nevertheless, it was definitely his grandmother's guiding hand behind the meetings which had brought the desired result.

Then she had trapped Tony very neatly, choosing Hannah O'Neill to be the new chef on his prized catamaran, *Duchess*. Never mind about her highly questionable qualifications to be a cook. Tony had made the mistake of giving their grandmother the task of interviewing the applicants and making the choice, which had allowed her to present him with a *fait accompli* which sealed his fate. Impossible to ignore Hannah's other qualifications when they were inescapably right in his face. Tony had been down for the count in no time flat.

Two protégées married to his brothers.

Third one coming up.

Nicole Redman had to be aimed at him. The only question was…what ammunition did she have to shoot him into the marriage stakes? It certainly added a piquant interest to tomorrow morning's meeting.

He grinned with easy confidence as he switched on the television.

Didn't matter what it was, he was proofed against it. There was not going to be a honeymoon contract attached to the contract Nicole Redman had with his grandmother. No way was *he* ready to get married!

CHAPTER TWO

NICOLE paused at the head of the steps that led down to Wharf Street and looked back at King's Castle, marvelling that such a place had been built here back in the pioneering days. Tropical North Queensland was a long way from Rome, yet Frederico Stefano Valeri, Isabella's father, had certainly stuck to his Italian heritage when constructing this amazing villa on top of the hill overlooking Port Douglas.

The locals had come to call it a castle because of the tesselated tower that provided the perfect lookout in every direction, but the loggia and the fountain had definitely been inspired by Roman villas. And all of it built with poured concrete, a massive feat in those early times, although no doubt Frederico, having seen the timber buildings of Port Douglas destroyed in the 1911 cyclone, had been intent on having his home stand against anything.

Home and family, Nicole thought, her mind turning to the two great-grandsons she had met yesterday, both of them exuding the kind of strength that would tackle any problem and come out on top. The sense of family heritage and tradition was very much alive in them, nurtured no doubt by their extraordinary grandmother. It

11

would be interesting to see if their younger brother fitted the same mould.

Three brothers—Alessandro, Antonio, Matteo—carrying the past into the future, adding to the levels of enterprise that had been started by Frederico when he had left Italy to start a new life in Australia in 1906. A fascinating family with a fascinating history and an equally fascinating present, Nicole decided, turning away from the castle to continue her walk to the KingTours head office.

It was only ten o'clock in the morning but already the heat was beating through her wide-brimmed straw hat. All too easy to get sunstroke up here in the tropics, she'd been warned, so she kept to the shade of the trees bordering the road on her leisurely stroll down the hill to the main business centre. Given her very fair skin, she had to protect herself against sunburn, as well. It was to be hoped the block-out cream she'd lavished on her arms and legs would do the job.

Being a redhead did have drawbacks in a country devoted to sunshine and outdoor pursuits. It was lucky she had always loved books, reading and writing being her dearest pleasures. Staying indoors had never really been a hardship, plus living with her father for the last few years of his life had left her with the habit of being a night owl—a habit she had to change while working with Isabella Valeri King.

Still, that was no real hardship, either. There was a special brilliancy to the days in Port Douglas; the magic of sunrise over the ocean, the kind of sharp daylight that made colours more vibrant. One never saw green this *green* in Sydney, and the reds and oranges and yellows of the tropical flowers were quite wonderful.

Everything was different; the whole laid-back pace of the town, no sense of hustle and bustle, the heat of the day followed by a downpour of incredibly heavy rain most afternoons. It spurred an awareness of nature and the need to live in harmony with it. She felt a long long way from city life, as though she'd moved to another world that worked within parameters all its own. It was a very attractive world that could easily become addictive.

Here she was, swinging along at a very leisurely pace, flat sandals on her feet, no stockings, wearing a yellow sleeveless button-through dress that loosely skimmed her body, minimal underclothing, a straw hat featuring a big yellow sunflower on her head, and it didn't matter what anyone thought of her. No students to teach, no fellow academics pushing their political agendas at her, no back-biting about the book she'd written on her father's life.

Freedom...

She grinned, happy with the feeling. It was like starting a new life even though she'd be researching old lives for the next six months, writing a history. But it was a history *she* hadn't lived and it was about a family who had endured and survived and was still thriving, the kind of family she didn't have and had never known. Another attraction...finding out first-hand what it was like to actually belong to a place, deep roots and long lines of growth.

She reached Macrossan Street and strolled along it until she found the King building where Alessandro—Alex, as he was called by everyone except his grandmother and Rosita, the very motherly Italian housekeeper at the castle—managed investments and property development, as well as handling all the business attached to the sugarcane plantations.

Further down Wharf Street was the marina where Antonio/Tony operated the Kingtripper line of catamarans, taking tourists out to the Great Barrier Reef. That was his personal enterprise, apart from managing the tea plantations which was his family responsibility. Nicole intended to check out the Kingtripper company office after her meeting with Matteo/Matt.

She turned into Owen Street which led down to the bus depot and the KingTours main office. The transport company was Matt's brainchild and one of the tours he ran was to his exotic fruit farm, an extension of the tropical fruit plantations that came under his umbrella of family responsibility.

It was interesting that none of the three brothers had simply accepted their inheritances and been content to live off them. Which they could have done, given the current prosperity of all the plantations. Of course, diversity was always a healthier situation in any financial sense, but Nicole suspected the pioneering blood ran strongly in these men. Perhaps it was the challenge of going for more that drove them. Or a *male* thing, wanting to conquer new territories.

Certainly Alex and Tony King were different to all the city men she'd known. They were very civilised, very polished in their manners, yet they had a masculinity that was somehow more aggressive. In her mind's eye she could see the two of them going into battle, shoulder to shoulder, emanating the attitude that nothing was going to beat them. Perhaps it was fanciful imagination but that was how they had impressed her.

Would the third brother measure up to the other two?

It was with a very lively anticipation that Nicole stepped into the KingTours main office. A fresh-faced boy, possibly in his late teens, was manning a large L-shaped desk. He looked up from his paperwork, gave her a quick once-over, then a welcoming grin.

"You Miss Redman?"

"Yes."

He waved to a door in the back wall to the side of his desk. "Just step this way to the boss's office. He's got all the maps ready for you." His blue eyes twinkled as though that statement reflected some private joke. "I marked out the main locations of interest myself so you can't possibly miss them," he added, making Nicole wonder if he'd been told to assume she was the most hopeless navigator in the world.

He already had the door open for her so there was no time to chat with him. "Miss Redman," he was announcing, even before she thought to remove her hat.

Indeed, the ushering was effected so quickly, Nicole

found herself inside Matt King's office with her hat still on and her wits completely scattered at being confronted by the man himself. Not like Alex. Not like Tony. This brother was wickedly handsome. If the devil was rolling out every sexual temptation he could load into a male body, Matt King had to be his masterpiece.

His hair was very black, very shiny and an absolute riot of tight curls, a tantalising invitation to be touched. It didn't soften the strong masculine cast of his face. Somehow the contrast added a wildly mischievous attraction, as did the long, thick, curly eyelashes to the dark chocolate eyes. And his olive skin had such a smooth sheen, the pads of Nicole's fingers actually prickled with the desire to stroke it. All that on top of a physique that seemed to pulse manpower at her.

He came out from behind his desk, tall, big, dressed in a blue sports shirt and navy chinos, white teeth flashing at her, and Nicole felt as though every bit of oxygen had been punched out of her lungs. Her heart catapulted around a chest that had suddenly become hollow. It was purely a defensive instinct that lifted her hands to grab her hat and bring it down in front of her like a shield against the impact of his approach.

The action startled him into pausing and Nicole's cheeks flamed with embarrassment. Such a clumsy thing to do, no grace at all in this foolish fluster. And she'd probably mussed her hair. He was staring at it. A slight frown drew his brows together as his gaze dropped to hers, his eyes brilliantly sharp now, seemingly as black as his hair and with a penetrating power that felt so invasive it made her toes curl.

She had the weird sense he was searching for some sign of recognition. It forced her to collect her wits and speak, though her tongue moved sluggishly and she had to push the words out. "Your grandmother sent me. I'm Nicole Redman."

"Red..." he said with an ironic twist, then appeared to recover himself. "Forgive me for staring. That shade of hair is not exactly common. It surprised me." He stepped forward and offered his hand. "Matt King."

She unlatched the fingers of her right hand from the hat and gingerly met his grasp. "I'm pleased to meet you," she managed stiltedly, absorbing the shock wave of his engulfing touch with as much control as she could muster. A bolt of warm, tingling vitality shot up her arm and caused her heart to pump harder.

His gaze dropped to her mouth, studying it as though it held secrets she was not revealing. Her throat constricted, making further speech impossible.

"Nicole Redman..." He rolled her name out slowly, as though tasting it for flavour and texture. His gaze flicked back to hers, his eyes having gathered a mocking gleam. "This meeting is overdue but no doubt we'll soon get acquainted."

He had to be referring to his absence from the family luncheon yesterday, yet that look in his eyes was implying more. Mental confusion added to her physical tension and it was a blessed relief when he withdrew his hand and turned aside to fetch a chair for her, placing it to face his on the other side of the executive desk.

"Have a seat," he invited, and Nicole was intensely grateful for it.

Her knees felt like jelly. Her thighs were quivering, too. She found the presence of mind to say, "Thank you," and sank onto the chair, fiercely telling herself to construct some composure fast.

It wasn't as though she hadn't been given a hint of what Matt King might be like, having met his brothers yesterday, both very handsome men who carried an aura of power. She had been able to view them objectively. Why not this one? Why did she feel so personally affected by this one?

It was crazy. She was twenty-eight years old and had met hundreds of men. Probably thousands. Not one of them had scrambled her insides like this. Maybe she was suffering sunstroke and just didn't know it. Come to think of it, she did feel slightly dizzy. And very hot. Hot all over. If she just sat quietly for a minute or two, she'd be fine.

She slid her shoulder-bag off and propped it against the leg of the chair, then set her hat on her lap and focused on the sunflower. By the time Matt King reached his chair and settled himself to chat with her, she'd be ready to look at him and act normally.

All she needed from him was the gold pass for the bus tours and the road maps which his assistant had helpfully marked. It shouldn't take hardly any time at all. A bit of polite to-and-fro and she'd be out of here.

Her hands were trembling.

She willed them to be still.

Her heart persisted with hops, skips and jumps, but it had to steady soon. Clearly she had to be more careful in this tropical heat. Drive, not walk. That was the answer. When Matt King spoke to her she would look up and smile and everything would be all right.

CHAPTER THREE

NO MISTAKE, Matt grimly assured himself as he walked slowly around his desk to his chair, his mind working at hyper-speed to reason out what the hell this woman was doing here, supposedly assisting his grandmother on the family history project.

The flaming red hair had instantly jolted his memory, spinning it back ten years to a night in New Orleans, the night before Halloween in that extraordinary city. The delicately featured face, the white porcelain-perfect skin, the big expressive sherry-brown eyes, the full sensual curves of her mobile mouth…all of it like a video clip coming at him in a flash. A tall slender young woman, swathed in a black cloak lined with purple satin, long red hair flowing free, not rolled back at the sides and clipped away from her face as it was today.

He'd seen her lecturing the tour group outside Reverend Zombie's Voodoo Shop. He'd watched her, listened to her, appreciating the theatrical appearance of her as she captivated the group with her opening spiel for the Haunted History Walking Tour. Just to hear her speaking in an Australian accent added to her allure.

He'd even tagged along for a while, fascinated by the look of her and her performance. He would probably have stayed with it but the novelty appeal of the tour soon wore thin for the friends he was with and they'd moved on to one of the colourful bars in the French Quarter.

Nevertheless, he remembered her very clearly...the hair, the face, the pale, pale skin adding its impact to her ghostly tales. Which raised the question...what tale had she spun his grandmother to get this job? Had she faked qualifications...a con-woman getting her hooks in for a six months' free ride? Had his grandmother checked them out? Or hadn't they mattered, given that her prime objective was finding him a bride?

A spurt of anger put an extra edge on the tension this meeting had sparked. His grandmother had struck out badly on this candidate for marital bliss, being fooled by what he could only think of as a fly-by-night operator, though undoubtedly a very clever and convincing one, calling on her experience with *haunted history,* plus a liberal dash of entertainment.

He slung himself into his chair, barely resisting the urge to give it a twirl as a derisive tribute to the marriage merry-go-round his grandmother was intent upon. Highly disgruntled with this absurd situation, he glowered at the woman sitting opposite to him. *Why her?* What did his grandmother see as the special attributes that made *her* suitable as his wife?

Red hair?

It certainly suited the exotic night-life in New Orleans, but here in the tropics? That pale skin would fry in Port Douglas. Utter madness!

Though he had to concede her dramatic colouring and

the delicacy of her fine skin and features did have a certain unique beauty. He'd thought so ten years ago and it still held true. But it was perfectly plain she didn't belong in this environment. As to there being any possibility of her spending a lifetime here…that was definitely beyond the pale.

She sat very still, very primly with her knees pressed together, the hat held on her lap, eyes downcast, projecting a modesty that was at ridiculous odds with the role she had played ten years ago. Uncloaked, she had small but neatly rounded breasts. Her arms were neatly rounded, too, slender like the rest of her but not skinny. Interesting that she wore yellow, which wasn't a modest colour.

She was playing some game with him, Matt decided, and the temptation to winkle it out of her overrode his previous intention to send her on her way as quickly as possible. He leaned back in his chair and consciously relaxed, knowing he had the upper hand since there was no chance of her remembering him. He and his friends had been wearing masks that night, part of the wild revelry leading up to Halloween.

''I understand this is your first visit to the far north,'' he started.

She nodded and slowly raised her gaze to his. ''I did fly up a month ago for the interview with Mrs. King.''

Her eyes were wary and he instantly sensed her guard was up against him. He wondered why. A need to hide the truth about herself? Did she see him as a danger spot, a threat to her cosy sinecure at the castle?

Curiosity further piqued, he smiled to put her more at ease as he teasingly asked, "Six months at the castle didn't sound like a prison sentence to you?"

The idea seemed to startle her. "Not at all. Why would you think so?"

"Oh, you'll be stuck mostly with my grandmother for company and the novelty of living in a rather romantic old place won't make up for the things you'll miss or the things you'll have to tolerate," he drawled, watching her reaction to his words.

Her head tilted to one side as though she was critically assessing him. "Don't *you* enjoy your grandmother's company?"

"That's not exactly relevant," he dryly countered.

A slight frown. "You didn't come to the family luncheon yesterday."

"True. I don't allow my grandmother to rule my life. I had another activity booked and I saw no reason to cancel it." He paused, wanting to probe her character. "Were you offended that I didn't roll up on command?"

"Me? Of course not."

"Then why do you think I should have come?"

"I don't. I just thought…you said…" She stopped in some confusion.

"I was simply suggesting that six months under the same roof with an eighty-year-old lady might make King's Castle a prison for a young woman used to all the attractions of city life."

A wry little smile. "Actually I find older people more interesting than younger ones. They've lived longer and some of them have had amazing lives. I can't imagine ever being bored in Mrs. King's company.''

Her eyes flashed a look that suggested she could very easily be bored in his, which spurred him into derisively commenting, ''So you're prepared to bury yourself in the past and let your own life slide by for the duration of this project.''

Her chin tilted in challenge. ''I've always found history fascinating. I think there's much to be learnt from it. I don't consider any form of learning a waste of my time.''

''A very academic view,'' he pointed out, wondering what she'd *learnt* from ghost stories. ''They say history repeats itself, so what really is gleaned from it?'' he challenged right back. ''Human nature doesn't change.''

She didn't reply. For several moments she looked directly at him in a silence loaded with antagonism. She wanted to attack. So did he. But his grandmother stood between them, a force that demanded a stay of any open hostilities.

''Are you against this project, Matt?''

The question was put quietly, calmly, a straight request to know where he stood.

''Not in the slightest. I think such a publication will be of interest to future generations of our family,'' he answered easily. ''I think it's also meaningful to my grandmother to have a record of her life put into print. A last testament, which she richly deserves.''

''Are you against me doing it?''

Right on target! He had to hand it to Nicole Redman.

She certainly had balls to lay the cards right out on the table. "Why should I be?" he asked, wondering if she'd let anything slip.

"I don't know." Another wry little smile. "You'll need to tell me."

Clever, throwing the question back onto him. "How old are you Nicole?" he tossed at her.

"Twenty-eight."

"Are you coming out of a bad relationship?"

"No."

"Not engaged with one at the moment?"

"No."

"Not looking for one?"

"No."

"Why not?"

"Why should I be?"

"I would have thought it was a normal pastime for a woman of your age."

Hot colour stained her cheeks. Her eyes burned with pride as she replied, "Then I guess I don't fit your idea of normal."

Which neatly left him nothing to say...on the surface of it. He was not about to fire his hidden ammunition until he knew some facts about her more recent circumstances. A lot could happen in ten years. If she was telling the truth about her age, she'd only been eighteen in New Orleans. A wild youth could have been followed by a more sober settling down.

As it was, she had obviously notched up qualifications in his grandmother's wedding plans; single, unattached, of a mature enough age to find marriage an acceptable idea, and certainly physically attractive if one fancied red hair.

Not everybody did.

So why had his grandmother chosen a redhead for him? Why not a blonde or brunette? He'd never even…

The answer suddenly clicked in. Trish at Tony's wedding. Hannah's sister had long auburn hair and he'd been matched with her in the wedding party, bridesmaid and groomsman. Being a professional model, she was tall and slender, too, and they'd had a lot of fun together at the reception. No serious connection, just light happy flirting, enjoyed by both of them. Had his grandmother read more into it, perceiving Trish as his type of woman?

He shook his head and Nicole took the exasperated action as directed at her.

"This is a project I want to do," she stated, her eyes mocking his assertion that looking for a man should be her top priority. "I understand from Mrs. King that you started this tour company because you wanted to do it. You've also developed a market for exotic fruit, which I assume you wanted to do, as well. I'm sure you had your reasons for taking those directions in your life and I bet they had nothing to do with your lack of, or desire for, a relationship with a woman."

She had him there. This was one smart chick. If he so much as suggested it might be different for a woman, he'd be marked as a sexist pig. Besides, he didn't believe it was different. He'd simply been checking what his grandmother had undoubtedly checked before entering Nicole Redman in her matchmaking game.

"Well, I hope you find as much satisfaction in pursuing the past as I've found in setting up a future," he said with a grin designed to disarm.

She returned an overly sweet smile. "You're very fortunate to have a past that can be built upon."

The slip! It was in her eyes, a bleak emptiness that had escaped her guard. His instincts instantly seized upon it and threw up a quick interpretation. She'd come from nothing and had no future direction. She moved on the wings of opportunity, not having any roots to ground her anywhere. Perhaps she even felt like a ghost, having no family to give her any real solidity. Or was he assuming too much from one fleeting expression?

"What about your own family?" he shot out.

"I don't have one," she answered flatly, confirming his impression.

"You're an orphan?"

A momentary gritting of teeth, then a terse dismissal of that description of her. "I'm an adult, responsible for myself, and I've taken the responsibility of seeing this project through with Mrs. King. A six-month contract has been signed to that effect. If you have a problem with my appointment to this job…"

"It's purely my grandmother's business and I have no intention of interfering with it," he assured her, though whether his grandmother would get value for her choice on the history side of things was yet to be seen.

Nevertheless, that was not his problem and he wasn't about to make it his problem.

"I don't want to interfere with your business, either." She surged up from her chair with the clear intention of making a brisk departure. "Your assistant said you had road maps already marked for me..."

Damn! He'd torpedoed any reason for keeping her with him. Had to go with the flow now. He killed the stab of frustration and rose to his feet, telling himself he had six months to get to the bottom of this woman, so no sweat about letting her off the hook this morning.

He picked up the bundle of maps stacked on his side of the desk and set them on her side. "Here they are," he said obligingly. "Using these, you should be able to find your way to every point of historical interest."

"Thank you." She scooped her bag from the floor and rested it on the desk to load the maps into it, her face closed to everything but the purpose that had brought her to him.

Matt didn't like the sense of being put out of Nicole Redman's picture. He wasn't ready to let her go...*to let her win.* He snatched up the gold bus pass he'd laid beside the maps and strolled around the desk, intent on forcing another passage of play.

"And this gives you free travel on any of the tours," he said, holding it out to her.

She jerked towards him, a couple of the maps spilling out of her hand. In her quick fumble to catch them, she dropped her hat. They both bent to pick it up, their heads almost bumping. She reared back, leaving Matt to retrieve it, which he did, straightening up to find her breathing fast and very flustered by the near collision.

Her mouth was slightly open, her eyes wide in alarm, and this close to her, Matt had the weird sensation of being sucked in by the storm of feeling coming straight at him from the highly luminous windows to her soul. He stared back, momentarily transfixed by a connection that threw him completely out of kilter.

He wanted to kiss her, wanted to draw from her mouth all the secrets she was hiding from him, wanted to bind her to him until she gave up everything she was. The need to know pounded through his mind. Adrenaline was rushing through him, making his heart beat faster, tightening his muscles, driving a fierce urge for satisfaction. An intensely *sexual* urge for satisfaction.

''Thank you.''

The words whispered from her lips.

They forced a realisation of what he was supposed to be doing. Shock pummelled the madness out of his mind. This was the woman his grandmother had lined up for him. He was *not* going to fall into her trap.

He thrust out the gold pass.

Her hand was trembling as she took it from him. He tried to rein in the wild burst of energy that had escaped from him. Was she aware of it, affected by it? One part of him savagely hoped so, even as another part just as savagely wanted to deny there was any power of attraction in operation here, on her side or his.

He watched her shove the pass and the maps into the bag, lashes lowered, head bowed, the red of her hair so vibrant he had to clench his hands to stop them from reaching out to touch it. They clenched over the straw brim of her hat. He still had the hat. But it was crazy even thinking he could hold her hostage with a hat. Her haste in packing her bag, slinging it over her shoulder, said she wanted to go. And he should let her go. Any other action would put him well and truly in the loser's seat.

She managed a step away, increasing the distance between them as she turned to face him, her gaze flicking up in frazzled appeal. "My hat…"

He could have handed it to her. It was the simplest response. But some perverse aggressive streak goaded him into setting the hat on that taunting hair himself, as though covering up the temptation would make it go away. He stepped forward and did precisely that, fitting the crown of the hat on her head, focusing on the sunflower to position it as she'd had it positioned when she came in, an unknown woman he'd intended to remain unknown to him in any close personal sense.

Except his whole body was suddenly electrically aware of hers, her height against his, the slightness of her figure, the almost fragile femininity of it, the yellow of the sunflower reminding her of her dress—a button-through dress that could be easily opened—and she was standing so still, submissively still.

"Thank you."

A gush of breath. Had she been holding it?

The thought excited him. He'd won something from

her. On a heady wave of triumph he stepped back, smiling. "Got to be careful of the heat up here."

Her cheeks were reflecting an inner heat that put him on a high as he moved to open the office door for her exit. She walked forward with the stiff gait of someone willing her legs into action. Her gaze was fixed on the doorway. She gave him a nod of acknowledgment as she passed by.

Matt grinned as he closed the door behind her.

He'd definitely rattled Nicole Redman's cage.

And he certainly felt a zing of interest in opening the door to it.

Not to marry her, he assured himself as he headed back to his desk. Marriage was not on his agenda. But a few hot nights with Miss Exotic New Orleans would not go amiss. Why not…if she fancied a taste of the tropics? Not under the nose of his grandmother, of course, but if Nicole was doing all the bus tours, sooner or later she would take the trip to Kauri King Park where the exotic fruit was grown.

He would make a point of being there that day.

And see how he felt about her then.

CHAPTER FOUR

As was her habit, Isabella Valeri King took afternoon tea in the loggia by the fountain. The sound of flowing water was soothing. There was always a sea-breeze at this time of day to alleviate the heat. She liked being outside with so much of her world to view, its changing colours, changing light, the sense of being part of it, still alive, though not with as much life left to live as the young woman sitting with her.

Nicole Redman...

So different to Gina and Hannah both in looks and nature, yet she shared with them the quality Isabella most admired—the inner strength to make hard life decisions and follow them through. The book about her father had revealed much about herself—a child who had shouldered the responsibility of an adult, seeing the gain, setting aside the loss—a very mature view for one so young.

Though she had suffered loss.

Just as Isabella had.

The past two hours in the library, reliving the years of the Second World War through old photographs and letters, had left her feeling heavy-hearted. She'd lost both her husband and only brother to that dreadful conflict in Europe, and there'd been other troubles, many of the Italian immigrants in far North Queensland interned because they had not taken out Australian citizenship as her parents had.

Her father had done his best to ease that pain in the Italian community, making a deal with the government, offering land he owned as a suitable camp for *his people,* then talking the forestry department into supplying the plants and trees to construct a rainforest park there, arguing the conservation of tropical species as well as keeping the internees occupied by the work. Better than useless imprisonment. Something good would come of it for everyone.

''After the war, you and Edward can build a home up there, Isabella,'' he'd told her.

But Edward hadn't come back from the war and Kauri King Park, as it came to be known, had never been her home. It was now Matteo's, and Nicole had not yet been there. Which brought Isabella's focus back to the young woman who had been with her for almost three weeks now.

Only the one meeting with Matteo.

A pity she had been unable to observe it.

Perhaps there would have been nothing to observe. The beauty she saw in Nicole may not have appealed to Matteo. He had made no attempt to pursue an acquaintance with her. Nor had Nicole made any comments that would have revealed a personal interest in him.

Isabella silently conceded the undeniable truth that one could not order mutual attraction. Physical chemistry was ordained by nature and no amount of wanting it to happen could *make* it happen. However, it was curious that Nicole had soaked in the background information from many of Matteo's bus tours, yet had not so far chosen to take the one tour which might bring her into contact with him. Since it was also the one tour most closely connected to the family history, why was she putting it off?

To Isabella's mind it smacked of avoidance. Which could mean something about Matteo moved Nicole out of her comfort zone. A negative reaction? Had Matteo offended her in some way?

Her youngest grandson was not normally an abrasive person. He had a happy, fun-loving personality, very agreeable company to most people. He carried his passions lightly although they ran every bit as deeply as his two older brothers'. The lightness was his way of carving a different niche in the family.

Alessandro…the strong pillar of responsibility.

Antonio…the fierce competitor.

Matteo…the nimble dancer between the other two, pretending to skate through life as though it was a game to be played, but he did care about his responsibilities and he was every bit as competitive as Antonio. He just expressed it differently.

Maybe something had happened between Matteo and Nicole that neither of them wanted to acknowledge. An unexpected chemistry could be uncomfortable, disturbing their sense of control over their lives. Matteo liked to stir things along for other people but he was very much in charge of himself. As for Nicole…she sat with an air of tranquility which was probably hard-won, given all she'd been through. A storm of feeling might tear at nerves that craved peace.

Wishful thinking, Isabella chided herself. Whatever the situation, the history project had to stay on track and it was time for Nicole to see what they had just been talking about.

"Tomorrow I must spend on the organisation of a wedding," she stated. "The bride and her mother are coming to decide on all the details for the reception in the ballroom."

Nicole smiled. "I can't imagine a more romantic setting, having a wedding here at the castle."

"In the old days we held dances and showed movies in the ballroom. I did not want it to fall into disuse so I turned it into a function centre many years ago. Weddings are so popular here, it is used for little else now."

"I'm sure it adds very much to the sense of occasion for the couples getting married."

"I think so. The feeling of longevity is good. It makes something solid of the passage of time. As you'll see when you visit Kauri King Park. Tomorrow would be a good day for you to do that tour, Nicole, since I've just been telling you how it came to be."

The tour that would take her to Matteo's home.

There were instant signs of tension—Nicole's shoulders jerking into a straighter line, hands clenching in her lap, chin jutting slightly, and most interesting of all, a tide of heat rushing up her neck and flooding her cheeks.

It could not be the prospect of walking through a rain-forest park and an exotic fruit plantation causing such a reaction. If it was the prospect of encountering Matteo...well, perhaps more meetings should be planned.

Isabella waited for Nicole's response.

A fine hand had to be played here.

But her heart was already lifting with hope.

"Tomorrow..." Nicole struggled to hold back a protest against the proposed arrangement. None was justifiable. She had delayed the inevitable as long as she could. There simply was no acceptable excuse for getting out of going to Matt King's territory this time, but everything within her recoiled from being near him again. "Yes," she forced herself to say, then clutched at a dubious lifeline. "Though the tour could be all booked up. It's late to be calling."

"If so, you could drive up and join it at the gate. It's not far. Just above Mossman. A half hour drive at most. You won't miss much of the background chat from the bus driver," came the dismissal of any possible objection.

Nicole's stomach contracted. She had to do it. No escape. All she could hope for was Matt King's absence.

"Tomorrow is a good day," Mrs. King ran on. "Matteo is always there on Thursdays. He can help out with anything you'd like to know."

It was the worst possible day and she'd now been trapped into it. Her own stupid fault for not going before when she could have avoided meeting him. She knew he was in the tour company office on Mondays and Fridays. The problem was, she hadn't felt safe about going on any day.

If Matt King checked the tour bookings—and she'd had an uneasy feeling he would check on what she was up to—he could waylay her on his home ground whenever she went. Why, she wasn't sure, but everything about him put her on edge. And he knew it, played on it, getting under her skin. She didn't like it, didn't want it.

"I wouldn't want to take him away from his work, Mrs. King," she said quickly, trying to quell the panicky sense of being cornered. "I'm sure the tour guide…"

"Matteo can make the time to oblige you with his more intimate family knowledge of the park."

Intimate. A convulsive little shiver ran down Nicole's spine. Matt King literally radiated male sexuality. Even at that one brief meeting in his office she'd been sucked in by it twice, her whole body mesmerised by the attraction of his, wanting the most primitive of intimacies. She'd never felt anything so *physical.* It even messed up her mind, making it impossible to hang on to any logical thought.

"I'll call him tonight and tell him you're coming so he can watch out for you," her employer said decisively, sealing a totally unavoidable meeting.

The only question left was bus or car. Nicole didn't know which was better; trying to cling to a tour group which might diffuse Matt King's impact on her, or having her car handy so she could leave at a time of her choosing. Either way, she couldn't ignore her job which entailed gathering all the historical information she could from this trip. Somehow she would have to keep her focus on that.

"I'll go and call the tour office and see if there's a seat available on the bus," she said, rising from her chair.

Isabella Valeri King smiled her satisfaction as she nodded approval of the move. Apart from that regal nod, she didn't move herself, remaining where she sat with the quiet dignity which Nicole associated with an inner discipline that would never crack.

There was something about the smile that made her look more sharply at her rather aristocratic employer before going. She had an eerie impression of power shimmering from her...a soft but indomitable power that would not be thwarted by time or circumstance.

Again a little shiver ran down her spine.

Dark shiny eyes...almost black...like Matt's.

This family...she'd known from the beginning it wasn't ordinary...but how extraordinary was it...and where did the power come from?

She walked towards the great entrance doors to the castle, knowing she was entering their world, and finally acknowledging that running away from it wasn't really an option she wanted to take. It intrigued her. It fascinated her. Even what frightened her was also compelling.

Matt King...tomorrow.

CHAPTER FIVE

MATT stood on the balustraded roof of the pavilion café, watching the tour passengers emerge from the bus at the other end of the kauri pine avenue. Phase two of the match-making plot, he thought in amusement. Little did his grandmother know, when she'd called last night, he'd already been informed that Nicole Redman was booked to be on this bus today. He would have been waiting for her any day she chose to come.

But she hadn't chosen.

Which put a highly interesting twist on this visit. It was almost three weeks since he'd decided to keep tabs on Nicole's bus tours. She'd done almost every one of them but this, and it was clear from his conversation with his grandmother that the resident family historian had been put under pressure to come today—*his* day for this plantation.

It wouldn't have been a command. No, more a subtle manipulation, shaped in a way that undoubtedly made refusal impossible. Matt was alert to his grandmother's little tricks. But was *she* alert to the fact that Nicole Redman was very reluctant to meet him again.

What was she hiding in the cage he'd rattled?

The question had been teasing Matt's mind ever since he realised that her delay in coming here had to be deliberate. Kauri King Park was prime material for the family history. Anyone eager to research the past would have been drawn to this place within days, not weeks. So how good was Nicole Redman at the job she had taken on? How genuine? Was his grandmother being fooled? His very astute grandmother?

Unlikely, Matt decided. She might have been fooled at the beginning, but not after three weeks. Unless she was blinded by her other agenda. Was that possible? Surely she wouldn't want him to marry a con artist. She might have been beguiled by Nicole's looks, but what about character? How good an actress was this woman?

There she was! Same broad-brimmed straw hat with the sunflower. Even at this distance she stood out amongst the other tourists. She was the only woman in a skirt. The others were in shorts or light cotton slacks, teamed with loose T-shirts or skimpy tops, the usual garb for the tropics. Nicole had chosen to wear a long-sleeved blouse, the same forest green as her skirt which swung almost to her ankles.

Protecting her skin, Matt thought, but on her tall, slender figure, the effect of the outfit was very feminine. Elegantly feminine. Magnetically feminine in that crowd, especially with the hat. Others wore caps or fabric hats which were easily packed. The sunflower hat was well out of that category. It hid her hair but somehow it made an equally dramatic statement. It stood out, as everything about Nicole Redman stood out. Not one of the pack.

Matt felt his body tightening with the desire to have

her. He'd lain awake many nights, fantasising her naked on his bed, her long pale body subtly inviting him to experience every pleasure it could give him, her silky hair flaming across the pillow, a provocative promise of the fiery passion he was sure would blaze between them.

Her reluctance to meet him again had actually fuelled an urge to pursue her, but he'd restrained it, not wanting to give her any sense of power over him. Besides, there was no need to pursue when a further meeting was guaranteed, given his grandmother's game plan. Patience was the better play.

But he didn't have to be patient any longer.

She was here.

And for all she knew, he was only doing his grandmother's bidding in personally accompanying her on this tour. Which put him very neatly in control of what happened with Nicole Redman today.

Nicole stared up at the amazing kauri pines as the guide spoke about their planting, sixty years ago. They had such huge trunks running straight up to the sky, no branches at all until the very top and even the foliage they supported seemed dwarfed by the towering height of the trees. The giants of the rainforest, the guide said.

She was reminded of the giant redwoods she'd seen in Muir Woods, just outside San Francisco, but these trees were very different, a mottled bark on the trunks, not stringy, and somehow they looked more primitive. Just as majestic but...her gaze travelled slowly up the avenue as she tried to formulate her impression in words…and caught Matt King striding down it, coming straight at her.

She stood like a paralysed bunny, watching him, feeling the primitive power of him attacking her and charging every nerve in her body with a sizzling awareness of it. Her mind tried to argue he was just a man on a family mission that had been requested of him. It made no difference to his impact on her.

Her eyes registered his casual clothes, dark blue jeans and a red sports shirt. Both garments hugged his big male muscular physique, destroying any sense of security in the normality of how he was dressed. He emitted an animal-like force that could not be tamed or turned away. And the really stunning part was Nicole knew it excited her. Something uncontrollable inside her was wildly thrilled by it.

"Good morning," he called to her while he was still some metres away.

Even his voice seemed to put an extra thrum in her bloodstream. She took a deep breath as she fiercely willed herself to respond in a natural fashion. The purpose of her visit here was to see and understand what had been achieved with this park, and the exotic fruit plantation beyond it.

"Hello," she said, more awkwardly than she would have liked. "It's good of you to come and greet me but please…if you should be doing something else…"

He grinned, his dark eyes twinkling at her obvious discomfort. "I don't mind obliging my grandmother, adding my bit to the history of this place."

"The tour…"

"Has moved on while you waited for me."

The realisation he spoke the truth brought an instant flush of embarrassment. She hadn't even noticed, hadn't heard the guide directing everyone elsewhere, hadn't been aware she'd been left standing alone. A babble of voices drew her gaze to the left-hand side of the kauri pine avenue. The group had been diverted down a path bordered by electric-blue ferns.

"Shall we follow or…?"

"Yes," she quickly decided, choosing the safety of numbers and hopefully a dilution of the effect Matt King had on her.

She started off after them and he fell into step beside her, making her extremely conscious of how tall he was. She was above average height for a woman but she was only on eye level with his shoulder, and walking side by side, the broad brim of her hat was a barrier to looking directly at him and vice versa, which gave her time to regain some composure.

"So how's it all going for you?" he asked, reminding her of his sceptical view of her staying power at the castle with his grandmother.

"Fine!" she answered lightly.

"Not feeling swamped?"

"By what?"

"By all the information you'll have to fit into a coherent story."

"It's a big story. Big in every sense. But not overwhelming. There's an innate order to it."

"As there is to any life," he dryly commented. "I assume there's a logic to yours."

"Yes, I guess there is. Though I haven't really reflected on it in that light."

"Perhaps you prefer a haphazard pattern."

"I don't think so."

"But you *are* willing to take on new experiences, despite obvious drawbacks. You're committed to being in Port Douglas for six months although the climate here can't be kind to you."

He was digging at her again, just as he had in his office. Why did he want her to admit she'd made a mistake in taking on this project? Was she some kind of thorn in his side?

"I think it's a wonderful climate," she asserted with a sense of perverse satisfaction in flouting his opinion. "No cold," she added pointedly. "I hate the cold."

"You don't find the heat oppressive?"

"It can be if I'm outside in the middle of the day," she conceded.

"Particularly when you have to cover up to protect your fair skin."

"I'm done that all my life. It doesn't bother me."

"Well, you don't need your hat on now. We're in total shade. And I prefer not to talk to a straw brim."

She had a stubborn impulse to deny him her bare face. On the other hand, he might have the gall to lift her hat off himself, just as he'd taken the liberty of putting it on her head in his office. Better to avoid that kind of familiar contact. She was barely hanging on to a semblance of control as it was. Besides which, it was true the rainforest canopy had now blocked out the sun. It was unreasonable and probably offensive to stick to wearing the hat so she reached up and removed it.

"There! Doesn't that feel better?"

She looked up into wickedly teasing eyes and the strong impression thumped into her heart that he would very much enjoy stripping her of all her coverings. It triggered the thought that he was as sexually attracted to her as she was to him. Which completely blew her mind.

Instinctively she sought time out by attaching herself to the tour group and focusing fiercely on the official guide who was naming ferns and vines. It reminded her she should be paying attention, taking notes, keeping an eye out for what might make good photographs to illustrate what had been achieved here. Determined to get on with her job and not let *this thing* with Matt King throw her completely off course, she fumbled in her carry-bag for her notebook and biro...and dropped her hat.

In a trice Matt scooped it up. "I'll carry it for you."

Heat whooshed into her cheeks. She just knew he'd put it back on her head himself when they emerged into sunshine and he'd reduce her to a quivering mess of jangling nerve-ends. "Thanks," she mumbled, wishing she hadn't clipped back her hair, wishing it was veiling her face as she hunted in her bag for the elusive objects. "I do need my hands free to take notes," she added, finally producing the evidence of this intention, taking out her camera, as well, and hanging it around her neck for easy access.

He reached out, slid his hand around the nape of her neck and lifted her hair out from under the camera strap. Nicole stood stock-still, her heart hammering, her face burning. "Just freeing your hair," he excused, but his fingers stroked down its length before he dropped the uninvited contact.

She didn't know what to do. She'd never felt like this before, so super-conscious of touch, of *who* was touching and the shivery intimacy of it, *the wanting* she could feel lingering on her skin and her own physical response so vibrant it swallowed up any possibility of making even a token protest.

She found herself gripping the notebook and biro with knuckle-white intensity and tried to concentrate on hearing what the guide was saying, jotting down snatches of words which would probably never make sense to her later. It simply gave her some purpose beyond being aware of Matt King beside her, Matt King watching her. Her mind shied from thinking about what he was thinking.

Maybe her imagination was running riot anyway. Let him speak, she decided. If he truly was interested in her as a woman, let him spell that out in no uncertain terms so no mistake could be made on her side. If he didn't, she could conclude that attraction was one thing, pursuing it quite another. He might very well think a relationship with her could end up with more problems than pleasure.

The last thing she wanted was to make a fool of herself over her employer's grandson. It would put her in a dreadfully embarrassing position with no easy escape from it. She had to stay at the castle for five more months and in that length of time there would undoubtedly be family occasions involving him. Caution had to be maintained here. Her own pride and self-respect demanded it. Yet the desire for some verbal rapport with him kept her very much on edge, waiting, listening.

To her intense frustration, Matt King said nothing out of the ordinary. He simply adopted the role of casual companion. They strolled along at the tail end of the tour group, stopping when the group stopped, looking at whatever was being pointed out to them. Nicole took photographs when others were taking photographs, regardless of whether they might be usable for the project or not. It used up otherwise idle time—time which might have led into dangerous ground with Matt King.

As it was, he commented on her prolific use of the camera. ''Are these photos for your own private pleasure of do you imagine they'll provide some kind of pictorial history?'' he said with a mocking amusement that needled her into justifying the activity.

''I don't know yet what will best illustrate this place when I come to writing about it. It will be good to have all these shots to choose from.''

One black eyebrow arched quizzically. ''Have you done much writing so far?''

''I'm still taking notes.''

''So I see.''

The dry tone and a flash of scepticism in his eyes implied he doubted she would ever get around to serious writing. It ruffled Nicole's feathers on a professional level. He had no right to judge her ability to produce what was required. Though she had to concede her erratic note-taking today might not have impressed him.

"I think you'll find the photographs in my home of more pertinent interest—historically speaking—than any you've taken today," he drawled. "They show stages of the park from its inception to its completed state."

"Why didn't you tell me before?"

"Oh, it was interesting observing what you thought was important. Besides which, you could have asked me." He slanted her a sardonic smile. "I didn't really make myself available to you just to carry your hat."

Nicole could have died on the spot. She'd been so flustered by his physical presence, so caught up in her own response to it, she hadn't *used* him as she should have done as a source of information on this part of the family history.

"I'm sorry. I was so carried away by the park as it is now…" She shook her head in obvious self-chiding and managed an apologetic grimace. "You must think I'm some kind of fraud."

It was a toss-off line, one she expected him to deny, letting her off the hook. Instead, he delivered another blow to her self-esteem.

"Are you?"

She stopped, shocked that he could actually be thinking that. Her gaze whipped up to his and found his dark eyes glittering with a very sharp intensity.

"No, I'm not," she stated with considerable heat.

He cocked his head assessingly. "Then is there some reason you must cling to this public tour?"

"I…I came with it."

"And I'll see you return to it before it leaves. Failing that, I'll drive you back to Port Douglas myself."

Her heart was catapulting around her chest at the thought of spending the next few hours alone with Matt King. She could feel the force of his will pressing on her, commanding surrender, and once again feeling under attack, she struggled to retain her independence from him.

"We're heading for the pavilion now," she rushed out. "I'd like to walk around it."

"Of course." A taunting little smile curved his lips as he waved her into trailing after the group again. "It was built as a recreation centre for the internees. It gives a fine focal point to the kauri pine avenue and it overlooks the tennis courts on the other side. People can sit on the roof of the pavilion and watch tournaments being played."

"And your great-grandfather designed it all," Nicole quickly slipped in to show her mind *was* on family history.

"Yes. No doubt you've already noticed the touch of old Rome in the construction of the building," he returned dryly.

The central block was surrounded by colonnades and the balustrade enclosing the flat roof was cast in a Roman style. "All that's missing is a fountain," she commented.

He laughed. "There's a row of fountains in a long rectangular pond on the other side." He grinned at her. "Nothing was missed. Frederico Stefano Valeri was very thorough in everything he took on."

Impulse spilled the question, "Are you?"

His eyes danced teasingly. "I guess history will be the judge of that."

"The tour carries on to your exotic fruit plantation after refreshments in the pavilion."

"Just feeding a curiosity. You can pick up all the information you might need on that from the pamphlets in the pavilion. You won't miss anything important." Again he grinned. "A detour to my home will save you a long walk in the heat."

There really was no choice but to go with him. Trying to postpone it longer than she already had would only feed his suspicions she was not up to the job she'd been employed to do. She could hardly explain that *he* was the problem.

"I'll even give you a personal sampling of the exotic fruit I grow," he added, piling on the pressure. "Along with any other refreshment you'd like."

Sheer wickedness in his eyes.

He knew she didn't want to accompany him.

He was playing a game with her—trap Nicole Redman.

But for what purpose?

Was he about to get...very personal...once they were alone together?

Her pulse drummed in her temples. Her whole body

was seized with a chaotically wanton urge to experience this man, but she didn't trust it to lead anywhere good. The sexual pull was very strong—very, very strong— yet other instincts were screaming something was wrong about Matt King's game.

And that meant she had to stay alert and somehow keep a safety door open so she could walk out of the trap with her personal integrity intact.

CHAPTER SIX

DESPITE Matt King's unnerving company, Nicole loved his house. He ushered her into a large open living area which was instantly inviting, full of colour and casual comfort. The floor was of blue-green slate, cool underfoot. The room was cool, too, no doubt kept that way by an air-conditioner—blissful relief from the late-morning heat.

At one side, three green leather chesterfields formed a U to face a huge television screen. A long wooden table with eight chairs balanced it on the other side. A kitchen with a big island bench was accessible to both areas, and beyond them a wall of glass led out to a veranda.

Other walls held paintings of the rainforest and scenes of the Great Barrier Reef with its fabulous coral and tropical fish. It was very clear Matt King loved his environment and was very much at home in it. Even the outside of the house was painted green to merge with its surroundings and the approach to it was beautifully land-scaped with palms and shrubs exhibiting exotic flowers or foliage.

''I'll get some refreshments,'' Matt said, heading into the kitchen. ''Leave your things on the table and go on out to the veranda. It overhangs a creek so you'll find it cool enough. Nice place to relax with the sound of water adding to the view.''

Any place she could relax was a good idea, Nicole thought, following Matt's instructions. At least he had given her back her hat to put on herself, and he wasn't crowding her now as she took it off again and set it on the table with her bag. Maybe it was stupid to feel so tense. Directing her onto his veranda surely indicated he was not about to pounce on her.

A sliding-glass door led onto it and Nicole moved straight over to the railing, drawn by the sound of rushing water. The creek below ran over clumps of boulders in a series of small cascades. It sparkled with a crystal-like clarity and the view was so pretty with the banks covered with ferns, she momentarily forgot all her troubles.

Birds flitted amongst the trees, their calls adding a special music to the scene—soft warbles, sharp staccatos, tinkling trills. She caught glimpses of beautiful plumage; gold, purple, scarlet. This was a magical place and she thought how lucky Matt King was that he could lay claim to it. To live here with all this…the sheer natural beauty of it, the tranquility…absolute Eden.

"Don't move," came the quietly voiced command from behind her. "Butterflies have landed on your hair. Just let them be until I get a flower and move them off."

She stood very still, entranced by the idea of butterflies being drawn to her, not frightened by her foreign presence. There was the sound of a tray being set on a table, Matt's footsteps as he walked to the end of the veranda and returned. Out of the corner of her eye she glimpsed a bright red hibiscus bloom in his hand, a long yellow stamen at its centre. She felt a light brushing on her hair, then suddenly two vivid blue butterflies were fluttering in front of her, poised over the flower which Matt was now holding out over the railing.

"Oh!" she breathed in sheer wonder. "What a brilliant blue they are!"

"Ulysses butterflies. Lots of them around here," Matt murmured. "The bright colour of your hair attracted them."

"Really?" She looked at him in surprise, still captivated by the pleasure of the experience.

He smiled, even with his eyes, and he was standing so close, it was like being bathed in tingling warmth. For a few heart-lifting moments, it seemed they shared the same vision of the marvels of nature, felt the same appreciation. Then the warmth simmered to a far less comfortable level and Nicole could feel herself tensing again.

"Drawn to the flame," he said in a soft musing tone that set her skin prickling. "I wonder how many it has consumed?"

"I beg your pardon?" she said stiffly.

"Moths…men…your hair is a magnet."

"It doesn't consume things."

"It has the allure of a *femme fatale*."

"I don't see you falling at my feet."

He laughed and teasingly drew the soft petals of the hibiscus flower down her cheek. It was a shockingly sensual action and he enjoyed every second of it while she lost the ability to breathe, let alone speak.

"Life is full of surprises," he said enigmatically. "Let me surprise your tastebuds with many exotic flavours."

He stepped back and gestured to the table where he'd left the tray. It was a table for two, cane with a glass top, and two cane chairs with green cushions on their seats stood waiting for them. The tray held a platter containing an array of sliced fruit, two small plates with knives and forks and two elegant flute glasses filled with what looked like...

"Champagne?" The word slipped out, bringing home to Nicole how far out of control she was.

"The best complement for the fruit," Matt said with an authority that seemed to make protesting the alcoholic drink too mean-spirited to try. He smiled encouragingly. "It's chilled, which I'm sure you'll appreciate."

He was waiting for her to take her chair. Nicole took a deep breath, needing to collect her scattered wits, and pushed her jelly-like legs into action. As she seated herself, Matt unloaded the tray and placed the scarlet hibiscus flower beside her glass of champagne, a taunting reminder of how easily she could lose her head with this man. She vowed to sip the champagne sparingly.

He sat down and grinned at her, anticipation of pleasure dancing in his eyes, making her heart contract with the thought that it was not the prospect of eating fruit exhilarating him. She was the target and he was lining her up for the kill. Although her mind was hopelessly woolly on what *kill* meant.

"I think we should start with what is commonly regarded as the king and queen of all tropical fruit." He forked two pieces of fruit onto her plate, pointing each one out as he named them. "The king is durian. The queen is mangosteen."

The durian was similar to a custard apple, only much richer in flavour. Nicole preferred the more delicate taste of the sweet-acid segment of mangosteen. "I like the queen better," she declared.

"Perhaps the king is more of an acquired taste. The more you eat it the more addictive it becomes."

Was he subtly promising this about himself?

"Now here we have the black sapote. It's like chocolate pudding."

He watched her taste it, making her acutely conscious of her mouth and the sensual pleasure of the fruit.

"You'll need to clean your palate after that one," he advised, picking up his glass of champagne and nodding to hers.

She followed suit as he sipped, her own gaze drawn to his mouth, wondering what it would taste like if he kissed her.

"Try a longan. It's originally from China and similar to a lychee."

So it went on—exotic names, exotic tastes—but more and more Nicole was thinking erotic, not exotic. There was a very sexy intimacy in sharing this feast of oral sensations, the conscious sorting out of flavours on the tongue, mouths moving in matching action, relishing delicious juices, trying to define interesting textures, watching each other's response, the telling expressions to each different experience...like an exciting journey of discovery...exciting on many levels.

Matt King...he stirred needs and desires in her that wanted answering. He embodied so much of all she had missed out on in her own life and the craving to know if he could fill that emptiness was growing stronger and stronger. It wasn't just that he was the sexiest man she'd ever met. It felt like...he was a complete person...and she wasn't.

Perhaps it had to do with having a firm foundation of family, a sense of roots, a clear continuity. She felt she was still looking for *her place,* both in a physical and spiritual sense. She wished this was her home, wished she could belong here, wished Matt King would invite her into more of his world.

"Would you like some more champagne?"

It jolted her into the realisation that she'd drained her glass without even noticing the fact. "No," she said quickly. "It was lovely, thank you. It's all been lovely...the park, your home, the fruit, sitting out here with this wonderful view..."

"And you haven't even minded my company," he slid in, his eyes telegraphing the certain knowledge of what had been shared in the past half hour.

Nicole shied from acknowledging too much, telling herself she still had to be careful of consequences. "You've been very generous."

"A pleasure." His smile seemed to mock her caution. "Would you like to see the photographs now?"

"Yes, please."

He laughed as he rose from his chair. "You sound like a little girl. Which makes me wonder how full of contradictions you are, Nicole Redman."

"I'm not aware of any," she retorted lightly, standing to accompany him.

"You're very definitely a tantalising mix." He slanted her a mocking look as he ushered her back into the house. "I'd find it interesting to delve into your history, but that's not why you're here, is it?"

"No." What else could she say? This wasn't a *social* visit. But if he really wanted to know more about her...or was he testing her again? Challenging her? Why did he make her feel uneasy about what should be straightforward?

They walked through the living room. At one end of the kitchen he opened a door which led into a very workman-like office. The far wall had a picture window with a spectacular view of the rainforest park. A long L-shaped desk held a computer, printer, fax machine, telephone, photocopier—all the modern equipment necessary for running a home business. File cabinets lined the other wall. Above them was a series of large framed photographs, depicting various stages of the park.

Nicole was instantly fascinated by them. Matt drew her attention to a framed drawing above the printer. "You should look at this first. It's the original plan, sketched by my great-grandfather. This is what the internees worked from."

It was amazing…the thought, the detail, the vision of the man. "Do you have a photocopy of this?"

"Yes, I can give you one. Now if you look over here…" He directed her to the first photograph by the door. "The first thing planted was this fast-growing bamboo, all around the perimeter of the camp to block out the fences which represented emprisonment."

Understanding and caring, Nicole thought, again marvelling at what a remarkable person Frederico Stefano Valeri had been. As they moved from one photograph to the next, with Matt explaining the story behind each stage of the park, giving it all a very human purpose, she couldn't help wondering if goodness was inherited, as well as strength and the will to meet and beat any adversity.

There was no doubting the strength, both physical and mental, in the man beside her, but what was in Matt King's heart? Was it as big as his great-grandfather's? Did it hold kindness, tenderness? What moved him to act? Would he stand up for others?

Most people, Nicole reflected, were little people, wrapped up in their own self-interest. They didn't stride through life, shaping it in new ways for the benefit of others. Yet from all she'd learnt of the Valeri/King family, they did just that, certainly profiting themselves, but never at the cost of others. They were *big* people, in every sense.

Her gaze was drawn to the muscular arm pointing to the last photograph, tanned skin gleaming over tensile strength. Her own skin looked white next to his, white and soft, unweathered by time or place. Perhaps it was the contrast that made him so compellingly attractive.

His arm dropped.

The deep rich timbre of his voice was no longer thrumming in her ears.

She looked up to find him observing her with heart-squeezing intensity. Having completely lost track of what he'd been saying, she held her tongue rather than make some embarrassing *faux pas*.

"I have the original photos filed if you want to make use of them," he said, but she knew intuitively that wasn't on his mind.

She shook her head. "I'd rather not have the originals. They're precious. If you could have copies made for me…"

"As you like. I'll bring them to the castle when they're done."

"Thank you."

"It *is* too much for you, isn't it?"

"What?"

"It would be fairer to my grandmother if you admit it now."

"I don't know what you mean."

"Do I have to shake it out of you?" His hands closed around her upper arms, giving substance to the threat.

Alarm screeched around her nerves. "I think you've got something terribly wrong here. Please let me go."

He released her, throwing up his hands in a gesture of angry impatience. His eyes blazed with accusation. "You might have been able to swan through God knows what else on your looks and your ability to adopt a role convincingly, but let me tell you your performance on this project today has been too damned shallow for me to swallow.''

"It's your fault!" she hurled back at him. "Making me nervous and..."

"And why do you suppose that is, Nicole?" he savagely mocked. "Because I recognise you for what you are?"

She stepped back, confused by the violence of feeling coming from him. It was like a body blow, shattering any possible sense of togetherness with him, shrivelling the desire he'd aroused in her.

"What am I:...to you?" she asked, needing some reason for this attack.

His mouth curled sardonically. "The same bewitching woman I watched in New Orleans ten years ago.''

"New Orleans?" He was there...when she was there with her father?

"Don't tell me it's some mistake. The image of you is burned on my memory. Indelibly.''

"I don't remember you."

"You wouldn't. I was masked that night.''

"What night?"

"You must have spent many nights spinning your ghostly tales on the haunted history tour. You were very good at it.''

"Yes, I was.'' Her chin lifted with defiant pride. "So what? That was ten years ago." And she wasn't ashamed of raking in the tourist dollar then, any more than he'd be of doing it now.

A black cynicism glittered in his eyes. "Still spinning tales, Nicole? Drawing people in? Getting them to shell out money with clever fabrications and exaggerations? Pulling the wool over their eyes? Eyes already dazzled by the striking combination of pearly skin and flame-red hair?"

Shock spilled into outrage at his interpretation of her character. He had no cause at all to think she was some kind of confidence trickster. Even if she had embellished those old tales a bit, it was only to add to the fun of the tour, giving people more for their money.

"I was doing a job," she cried emphatically. "The only job I could get at the time. I followed a script I was given. I certainly didn't fleece anyone. Everyone got good value on the haunted history."

"And now you're fully qualified to research and write a family history." Scepticism laced every word. "Except you haven't quite demonstrated a fine nose for it today."

"You're right!" she snapped, feeling more and more brittle. "I'm much better at it when there's no hostile force muddling my mind."

"Hostile?" he derided. "I gave you every chance to prove you were on top of this job. You even lost track of what I was telling you right here."

"I was thinking."

"Sure you were! And maybe you were thinking what I was thinking…" His eyes raked her from head to foot and up again. "...how well we might go together in bed."

Her skin was burning. Her insides were quivering. She was in a total mess. For a few soul-destroying seconds she stared at him, knowing at least she hadn't been wrong about the mutual sexual attraction but there was nothing to feel good about in that. No way in the world could she stomach any physical intimacy with him now.

"Please excuse me," she said with icy dignity. "I'll go and rejoin the tour."

A fierce pride gave her the power to walk out of his office and cross the living area to the table where she'd left her hat and bag. She was shaking as she picked them up.

"Running away won't resolve anything."

The mocking drawl flicked her on the raw. She turned her head to give him one last blistering look. He was leaning against the doorjamb, the loose-limbed pose denying any tension on his part. An ironic little smile played on his lips.

"Better to face up to the situation and try to make it more workable," he advised. "I could get you some help."

Her jaw clenched at this offer. She managed to unclench it enough to say, "Provided I satisfy you in bed?"

That wiped the smile off his face. "I don't trade in sexual favours, Nicole."

"Neither do I. And I've always found prejudice quite impossible for resolving anything. Please check my pro-

fessional credentials with your grandmother before we
have to meet again. I'd prefer not to feel under fire from
you in future.''

She didn't run, but she swept out of his house as fast
as she could at a walking pace. He didn't come after her,
for which she was intensely grateful because she was
right on the edge of bursting into tears. Anger, frustration, disappointment…all of them were churning
through her, and she hated herself for having given him
any reason to think what he did.

She would not be vulnerable to his…his aggressive
maleness…ever again.

Just let him come near her.

Just let him.

She would freeze him into eternity!

CHAPTER SEVEN

THREE hours, Matt told himself, as he drove to the Sunday luncheon he couldn't avoid. Four at most. He should easily manage to pass that length of time with his family without putting a foot wrong with Nicole Redman. He could do a show of polite interest in her work, enough to satisfy his grandmother's standard of good manners, and spend the rest of the time chatting to his brothers.

He was not about to make any judgments today. Let Nicole Redman stew in her inadequacies as far as the family history was concerned. He'd brought the photographs and the photocopied plan she'd requested. He'd hand them over to her and that was his bit done. She wasn't about to seek him out for anything more and be damned if he'd chase her for anything, either.

What was it…ten days since he'd called her bluff? The gall of her to blame *him* for *her* lack of professionalism on the project! Sheer amateursville taking all those tourist photos in the park. No theme, no purpose, just click, click, click. And calling him a hostile force…huh! She hadn't thought he was hostile while they shared the fruit platter on the veranda.

A pity he hadn't taken his chance then and there.

It was well and truly gone now.

Though it was better he hadn't got sexually involved with her. She probably cheated on that level, too, promising more than she'd ever deliver. Visual pleasure definitely wasn't everything. And reality rarely lived up to fantasy.

His grandmother could have Nicole Redman all to herself from now on. She would just have to accept that her matchmaking scheme had bombed out and live with the consequences of her choice. It wasn't paramount that the family history be published at the end of Nicole's contract. Another person could be brought in to get it right. This was not a full-scale disaster, more a minor mess they could all sweep under the carpet.

On the marriage front, she had ready consolation for her disappointment with him. This luncheon...Tony's pressure for him to be there...reading between the lines, Tony was bursting to celebrate with the family the fact that he and Hannah were expecting their first baby. Had to be. Hannah wanted a whole pack of children, having come from a big family herself, and Tony had declared himself happy to oblige her. Three months married...time enough for Hannah to get pregnant.

So today was bound to be happy families day for Nonna. She'd have Alex's and Gina's two children to cluck over and Tony and Hannah promising another great-grandchild. Plenty of good stuff for her to focus on. She could count her blessings and forget about him for a while. A *long* while. He'd get married in his own good time to his own choice of wife.

He drove in to the private parking area behind the

castle, noting that Alex's Mercedes was already there and Tony's helicopter was sitting on the pad. He was the last to arrive, which was good. Easier to lose Nicole Redman in a crowd, although if his grandmother parked him with her at the dining table... Matt gritted his teeth, knowing he couldn't completely ignore her. He hated being boxed into a corner. Hated it!

Using the back entrance, he strode along to the kitchen where he was bound to find Rosita, who knew everything there was to know about what went on in the castle. She'd not only been the cook and housekeeper here for over twenty years, she was his grandmother's closest confidante, sharing the same Italian heritage and always sympathetic to her plans.

She was at the island bench, tasting a salad with an air of testing its ingredients for the correct balance. Matt grinned at her. Rosita loved food and didn't mind being plump because of it. He and his brothers had been fed many great feasts in this kitchen.

"Have you got it right?" he teased.

"This is Hannah's special salad. An interesting combination...cabbage, noodles, walnuts...but you do not want to know these things." She gestured expansively. "It is good to see you, Matteo!"

"You, too, Rosita." He gave her a quick hug. "How's everything going here?"

"Oh, busy, busy, busy. You will find everyone in the billiard room."

That surprised him. "Why the billiard room?" He couldn't imagine Alex and Tony wanting to play today.

"It is where Nicole has her work on the family history. Your grandmother is showing them what's been done so far.''

''Well, that should be interesting,'' Matt said dryly, wondering how Nicole was managing to convince them that anything had been done.

''She works too hard, that girl.'' Rosita shook her head disapprovingly. ''Up all hours of the night. I make a supper for her but more times than not she forgets to eat.''

''Definitely a crime,'' Matt commented with mock gravity.

''Oh, go on with you!'' She shooed him away. ''And do not leave it so long again before visiting your grandmother. Over a month.''

''Busy, busy, busy,'' he tossed back as he left the kitchen.

''Young people,'' he heard her mutter disparagingly. ''Rush, rush, rush.''

But Matt didn't *rush* to the billiard room. He was considerably bemused by the picture painted of Nicole Redman by Rosita. Hardworking? And why was such a large room being taken up for this project? How did she justify it?

The door was open. The rest of the family didn't even notice his arrival. Their attention was fixed on the billiard table which was still wearing its protective cover. A quick sweeping glance told Matt Nicole Redman was not present, which made his greeting much more relaxed.

''Hi!'' he said, strolling forward. ''What's the big deal here?''

Everyone answered at once, saying hello and urging him into their midst to look at what was fascinating them. The surface of the billiard table held a pictorial history of the family, a massed display of old photographs, arranged in sequential decades, with a typed annotation of who, where and why underneath each one. Some of them Matt had never seen, or if he had, he didn't remember them.

"This is great, Nonna," he couldn't help remarking.

"Nicole and I have been sorting them for weeks. These are the best from a store of old albums and boxes."

Probably more his grandmother's work than Nicole's, Matt decided.

"Have a look at this time line, Matt." Tony waved him over to a whiteboard which he was now studying. "All the big dates lined up—the wars, the mafia interference, the cyclones, the whole progress of the sugar industry, when the other plantations became viable...and on this side of the line, notes on what the family was doing through these critical times. Just the bare bones but it gets the history in perspective, doesn't it?"

It did. In fact, Matt had to concede it was quite an impressive summary. And a very logical method of getting the whole story in order. He was beginning to have a nasty niggly feeling he might have misjudged Nicole Redman. Yet if she really could do this job, why had she been so inept during her visit to Kauri King Park?

Which reminded him of the bag he was carrying. He turned to his grandmother. "I've got more photographs here. Shots of the park being built. Nicole asked me to get copies of the originals and a photocopy of the plan. Where should I put them?"

"On her desk. Thank you, Matteo."

Following the direction of his grandmother's nod, Matt saw that a large desk had been brought in and positioned under the window at the far end of the room. It held a laptop computer, piles of manila folders, a tape-player and a stack of cassettes which Alex was sorting through, picking up each cassette and reading the label.

"So what's Nicole Redman's taste in music?" Matt asked as he put the bag next to the computer.

"It's not music. They're interviews with the old families in the Italian community. Nonna said she's off doing another one today."

"Not joining us for lunch then?" Matt now had mixed feelings about whether he wanted her there or not. Easier for him if she wasn't, but if he was guilty of prejudice—and the evidence was stacking up against the assumptions he'd made—an apology was due.

"No. She's gone down to the Johnstone Shire. A couple of hours' drive. Won't be back until late afternoon, I should think."

Free of her.

Except she sat uncomfortably on his conscience.

"She's certainly compiled a lot of material this past month," Alex remarked admiringly.

"Yes, but can she write?" Matt snapped, part of him needing to justify his stance with her.

Alex gave him a startled look. "Don't you know...?" He stopped, frowned. "That's right. You weren't at the lunch when Nonna introduced Nicole to the rest of us. One of the reasons Nonna chose her to do this was the biography she'd written of her father."

"A biography," Matt repeated, stunned by this new information.

"Mmm... It's called *Ollie's Drum*. Her father was a jazz musician."

Jazz... New Orleans...

"Have *you* read it?" he shot at his oldest brother, whose opinion he'd always respected.

"No." Alex gave him a droll look. "But biographies don't get published unless the author can write, Matt. Besides, Nonna has read it and it satisfied her."

Ollie's Drum. Matt fixed the title in his mind. He needed to get hold of that book, read it for himself. The ferocity of that thought gave him pause to examine it more rationally. What was the point of pursuing more information about her? If he'd blotted his copybook with Nicole Redman, so what? Hadn't he already decided any kind of relationship with her was not on?

Though he didn't like feeling he hadn't been fair.

Injustice of any kind was anathema to him.

On the other hand, she'd given him every reason to think what he had, and accusing him of being a hostile force, making her nervous...absolute hogwash!

"You're right off base if you're thinking Nicole Redman isn't up to this job," Alex remarked, eyeing him curiously.

"I didn't say that."

An eyebrow was cocked, challenging any doubt at all. "She's got a swag of degrees. History, genealogy, literature..."

Degrees could be forged. With today's computers almost anything could be made to look genuine.

"She's taught various courses at a tafe college, too," Alex went on. "Very highly qualified. Nonna was lucky to get her."

Not even a hint of suspicion that Nicole was not as she had presented herself. If Alex was sold on her…and Alex certainly didn't have a matchmaking agenda…then it had to be conceded Nicole did have the ability to do this job.

Which meant he should apologise.

The sooner, the better, in fact. She couldn't be feeling good about a member of the family casting aspersions on her integrity. She might very well have gone out today to avoid the unpleasantness of his presence. And working on a Sunday could be taken as a slap in the face to him for doubting her commitment to the project.

Her absence suddenly felt very personal.

Matt didn't like it one bit. He'd never been painted as a hostile ogre before. He wished he hadn't brought up the sexual angle with her. It made the situation doubly awkward when it came to back-pedalling on the stance he'd taken. Nevertheless, he couldn't just walk away from it. She had another five months left on this project and leaving her under a black cloud where he was concerned, was not right.

This *blot* had to be confronted and dealt with.

Today.

Even if he had to wait hours for her to return to the castle.

CHAPTER EIGHT

NICOLE glanced at her watch as she drove into the castle grounds, heading for the family parking area at the back. Almost five o'clock. Late enough for everyone to have gone home. Not that she would have minded saying hello to Matt King's older brothers and she really liked their wives. Gina was genuinely warm-hearted and Hannah literally bubbled with the joy of life. Probably more so now if she was expecting a baby, as Mrs. King suspected.

No doubt she would hear all the family news over dinner tonight, though it was a shame she had missed out on Hannah's excitement. Nicole instantly argued that Matt King's presence at the luncheon would have dampened it for her anyway. And if he'd been seated next to her at the dining table…she shuddered at the thought. An utterly intolerable situation.

It was reassuring to see that the helipad was empty. Clearly Tony and Hannah had flown back to their home on the tea plantation at Cape Tribulation. Alex's Mercedes was not in the parking lot, but the one car sitting by itself gave Nicole's heart a nasty lurch—a forest-green Saab convertible, a typical choice for a wealthy, sexy bachelor like Matt King.

She brought her own modest little Toyota to a halt

beside it and sat, fighting a sickening rise of tension. She couldn't be certain the sporty convertible was his since she'd never seen him driving a vehicle. Nevertheless, any hope that it belonged to someone else didn't feel very feasible.

Best to assume he had stayed behind with his grandmother and stay clear of where they might be. If she could scoot upstairs to the privacy of her bedroom…no, that would mean passing the library. Maybe she could slink into the billiard room without being seen.

Nicole thumped the driving wheel in disgust at these *fugitive* thoughts. Why should she let herself be intimidated by Matt King? It was wrong. *He* was wrong. While she certainly didn't want to meet him again, it was absurd to shrink from doing so when she was absolutely entitled to hold her ground.

Determined on acting normally, she alighted from her car and walked into the castle, intent on heading openly to the billiard room where she would take her briefcase and empty it of the material collected today. This meant passing through the kitchen and predictably Rosita was there. It was a considerable relief to find the motherly housekeeper alone.

"Ah! You are back!" she said in a satisfied tone, as though Nicole was some recalcitrant chick who had finally returned to the nest.

"Yes, I'm back. Is Hannah expecting a baby, Rosita?"

A triumphant clap of the hands. "Two months pregnant! It is very happy news."

"How lovely!"

"And Matteo is still here, talking to his grandmother. If you would like to go on out to the loggia and join them, I will bring some fresh drinks."

"I'd rather let them enjoy each other's company, Rosita," she quickly excused. "I have some work to get into my computer while it's still fresh in my mind."

This announcement earned a disapproving tut but Nicole was off before Rosita could gear up for her argument that there was more to life than work, especially for a young woman who had not yet been fortunate enough to find a husband to take care of her.

As Nicole walked down the hall to the billiard room, she darkly decided that if Rosita was fondly casting her employer's third grandson in that role, she was doomed to disappointment. No way was matrimonial bliss on that horizon!

In fact, the thought of joining Matt King in any sense raised hackles that might have drawn blood had she gone out to the loggia, despite her respect for her employer. She closed the door of the billiard room very firmly behind her, willing her antagonist to keep his distance because she was not prepared to suffer any more slights on her integrity.

And if he had checked out her qualifications today, she hoped he was stewing in guilt over his rotten accusations. Not that it was likely. He was too arrogantly sure of himself to think he might have been mistaken. Just because he'd been right about the sexual attraction... Nicole heaved a big sigh to relieve the mounting anger in her chest as she marched over to her desk.

Enough was enough!

How many nights had she lain awake, seething over their last encounter? It was such a foolish waste of time and energy. The man was not worth thinking about. To let him get under her skin as far as he had was just plain stupid.

She switched on the computer with more force than was needed. Work was the answer to blocking out unpleasant connections from her consciousness. Her gaze fell on a bag that didn't belong on her desk. A long cardboard cylinder protruded from it. Frowning over the Kauri Pine Park logo on the bag, she set her briefcase on the floor, uncomfortably aware that she had asked Matt King for copies of photographs and the original plan of the park. Was this his delivery?

Her hands clenched, not wanting to touch anything he had touched. Had he brought this bag in here himself, invading her private space, spying on what work she'd done? She shot a quick glance around the room, looking for anything out of place. Only the bag. Yet somehow the very air felt charged with his presence.

It was unnerving, inhibiting. She stared at the bag, telling herself its contents were completely harmless. It didn't matter if they were meant to mock her position here at the castle. She would use them effectively and show Matt King how very professional she was. Even if he never backed down from his insulting judgment of her, she'd know that he had to know he was wrong once the history was published. There could be no refuting that evidence. In the end, she would triumph.

The only problem was…it didn't take away the hurt.

A knock on the door sent wild tremors through her heart. *Not him…please…not him,* her mind begged as she heard the door open.

"Nicole?"

His voice.

She wanted to keep her back turned to him but what good would that do? *He* would have no compunction about walking in and doing whatever he wanted. She could feel his forceful energy hitting her, commanding an acknowledgment of him. If he didn't get it, he would engineer a confrontation one way or another.

"May I come in?"

The polite query cut into the fierce flow of resentment in her mind. It was just a sham of good manners, she swiftly told herself. The predatory nature of the man simply would not accept a negative reply. Nevertheless, pride in her own good manners demanded he be faced and answered.

Instinctively she squared her shoulders, stiffened her spine, armouring herself against his impact. Impossible to calm her heart. She half turned, enough to see him, watch him, while giving him the least possible target to fire at.

"What do you want?" Blunt words, but she didn't care. Why wait for his attack? Better to get it over with quickly.

He closed the door behind him, ensuring privacy. His

face wore a grimly determined look, causing Nicole's stomach to contract in apprehension. The sense of his presence was now magnified a hundredfold. She forced her gaze to rake him from head to toe, as he had done to her at their last meeting, but there was no sexual intent behind the action, more a need to reduce him to just a body without the power behind his eyes.

Except it wasn't just a body.

It had power, too.

And it struck her as hopelessly perverse that she could still feel attracted to it, everything that was female in her responding with treacherous excitement to the aggressive masculinity of his perfectly sculpted physique.

''I want to apologise.''

The words wafted quietly across the room and slid soothingly into ears that were clogged by the clamouring of her heart. Nicole wondered if she had imagined them. She saw his hands lift in an open gesture of appeal, giving some credibility to what she'd heard. Her gaze lifted to his mouth, waiting for it to move, to say more, to mitigate the deep offence he'd given.

''I'm sorry I suggested you were not what you portrayed yourself to be. In part, I was influenced by a memory which coloured my judgment.''

It was like pressing the trigger on a shotgun loaded with bitter pellets. ''A *memory!*'' she fired at him, her eyes meeting his in a raging blaze of feeling. ''You didn't even stop to ask why I was there in New Orleans, doing what I was doing. You know nothing about me except...'' Her teeth were bared in savage scorn. ''...you happened to see me one night, leading a haunted history tour.''

He winced.

She kept on blasting. ''And for that you decide I'm little better than a whore, pulling tricks, fleecing people, using whatever sex appeal I have to get out of trouble…''

''I didn't say that,'' he whipped back, frowning at the vehemence of her attack.

''You *thought* it. And you had no right to think it, no reason to think it. It was you…you…who took liberties with me. Touching and…and suggesting…'' A tide of heat was rushing up her neck, flooding into her cheeks, making her wish she hadn't brought up any reminder of how he had mused over how well they might go in bed together.

He took a deep breath and calmly said, ''I'm sorry if any action of mine made you feel uncomfortable.''

''If…if?'' His calmness incensed her. ''You set out to do it. You know you did,'' she wildly accused. ''Even in your office. Why didn't you just hand me back my hat instead of…''

''It wasn't deliberate. It was pure impulse.''

''I didn't invite it.''

''No, you didn't.'' His mouth curved ironically. ''Except by being an exceptionally attractive woman.''

She shook her head not accepting this excuse. ''It showed a lack of proper respect for me.''

''Oh, come on, Nicole!'' he chided, impatience with her argument slipping through the reins of his control.

He started walking towards her, gesturing a mocking dismissal of her case against him. "You can hardly call putting your hat on your head and touching your cheek major violations. You didn't protest. Didn't flinch away. In fact…"

"Well, please take note of my evasive action right now, Matt King," she flung at him, marching pointedly to the other side of the billiard table to put it between them. "I don't want you near me," she stated bitingly.

"Fine!" he snapped, having already halted. Black derision glittered from his eyes. "I'd have to give you full marks for the drama queen performance."

"So much for your apology!" she mocked.

"A pity you weren't gracious enough to accept it," he shot back at her.

Her chin tilted in defiant challenge. "What's it worth when you're still casting me in a false light and not admitting to any fault yourself?"

"I might have cast you in a false light, lady, but you helped me do it, floundering around as you did in the park."

"And before that? Your *memory* from New Orleans?"

"Yes," he admitted.

From no more than a superficial look at her.

While her memories…the sadness of them still gutted her…although she was glad she had them.

"And just what were you doing there ten years ago?" she asked, still fiercely resenting his interpretation of one brief view of her.

"Seeing some of the world before settling down to family business," he answered with a dismissive shrug.

A wild youthful spree. Totally carefree.

The contrast between them could not have been wider.

Emotion welled as she remembered the heavy weight of her responsibility that year. Impossible to keep it out of her voice. She looked directly at Matt King, wanting to nail home how very mistaken he was about her, but even he faded from her mind as she spoke, the memories sharpening, taking over.

"Well, I *was on* family business. My father was dying of cancer and his last wish was to go back to New Orleans. He was a jazz musician and to him it was his soul city. We had very little money but I took him there and got what work I could to help support us. Every night he sat in Preservation Hall, right across the street from Reverend Zombie's Voodoo Shop, where the haunted history tours started and ended. In case you don't know, Preservation Hall is revered by jazz musicians all around the world. It's where…"

"I know," he broke in. "I dropped in there one evening."

She stared at him, wondering if he'd seen or met her father, heard him perform. A lump rose in her throat. She had to swallow hard to make her voice work and even then it came out huskily.

"Some nights when my father wasn't too ill, he'd be invited to play the drums. He was a great jazz drummer."

"Ollie's Drum," he murmured.

"You know? You heard him play?"

He shook his head. "I only know about the book you wrote."

"The book…" Tears blurred her eyes. "He was a genius on the drums. Everybody said so. A legend. There were so many stories…"

"Did he die over there?"

She nodded, trying to blink back the tears, but she could see the jazz bands playing in the streets behind the coffin and the tears kept gathering, building up.

"I'm sorry, Nicole. I really am sorry."

She nodded. The quiet voice sounded sincere. Though somehow it wasn't important anymore.

"Please…go," she choked out, not wanting to cry in front of him.

He hesitated a moment then gruffly said, "Believe me. You do have my respect."

Without pressing anything else he left the room, closing the door quickly to give her the privacy she needed. Her chest was so tight it felt like a dam about to burst. She felt her way around the billiard table, reached the chair in front of her desk and sagged onto it. She didn't see the plastic bag with the Kauri Pine Park logo this time. She wasn't seeing anything.

It was ten years since she had buried her father.

It felt like yesterday.

And the loneliness of not having anyone to love, or anyone to love her, was overwhelming.

CHAPTER NINE

ONCE Matteo had headed off to the billiard room, Isabella Valeri King moved from the loggia to the library. She sat at her desk, her work diary in front of her, giving some semblance of purpose. She'd opened it to the one date she wanted to discuss with Matteo when he came to say goodbye to her, but work was not on her mind.

There was trouble between Matteo and Nicole—a sure sign they had connected on a personal level, but not a good result so far.

Nicole stiffened up every time his name was mentioned. Even more so since her visit to the park. And there had been no need for her to work today. Even her argument that Sundays were best for chatting to the old Italian families held no weight since the current members of the family she was writing about had all been gathered here—an easy opportunity to get their input on any facet of the history.

Nicole's choice—her very determined choice against the much-pressed invitation to stay and join them for the luncheon—spelled out a resolution to avoid Matteo at all costs. Quite clearly he had been just as resolved on forcing a meeting, staying on at the castle as long as he had and acting like a cat on hot bricks when Rosita had informed them of Nicole's return.

Such strong resolution had to have passion behind it, Isabella decided. Indifference did not give rise to such behaviour. The trick was to channel the passion into a positive direction. She hoped whatever was going on in the billiard room right now was getting rid of the negatives.

Pride could play the very devil in trying to get two people together. Isabella suspected that pride was a big factor here. It was a pity she didn't know what had caused a conflict to erupt between them, but neither of them would welcome interference on her part, anyway. Though, of course, she could stage-manage opportunities for them to reach out to each other…if they wanted to.

Desire…

It had to be there.

Matteo had clearly been distracted today, not his usual cheerful self at all. Brooding over Nicole's absence, Isabella had concluded. Not even celebrating Hannah's pregnancy had kept his spirits lifted for long. The jokey chatting with his brothers had seemed forced, and his conversation with her after everyone else had gone, had been peppered with silences. But he'd come very briskly to life at Rosita's further announcement that Nicole had gone to the billiard room to work.

"I'll just check that Ms. Redman has everything she needs from me before I leave," he'd said.

Which could have been done by telephone anytime.

The desire for physical confrontation had been paramount.

Desire…passion…surely it was the right mix.

Isabella was clinging to this hope when Matteo appeared in the doorway to the library. Her mind instantly dictated acute observation.

"I'm off, Nonna. Great luncheon. Happy news about the baby. You must be pleased."

Short staccato sentences, his mouth stretched into a smile but not a twinkle of it in his eyes, tension emanating from him as he quickly crossed the room to drop a goodbye kiss on her cheek.

"Yes, I am. Pleased for Antonio and Hannah, too. It's what they wanted," she replied, wishing Matteo would confide what *he* wanted.

He hadn't won whatever he'd gone to win from Nicole Redman. His kiss had no feeling in it, a quick performance of what was expected of him before he left. His mind was clearly preoccupied, and not with happy thoughts. Isabella spoke quickly to hold him with her long enough to ascertain his mood towards Nicole.

"I was just looking through my diary."

"Mmm…" No interest. Mental and physical withdrawal under way.

"I trust you have marked Gina's premiere night on your calendar."

He halted beside her desk, frowning at the reminder of his sister-in-law's debut on the stage of the Galaxy Theatre in Brisbane. "When is it again?"

"Two weeks from this coming Thursday. I've booked six seats on a flight to Brisbane that afternoon."

"Six? Won't Alex and Gina be down there already?"

"Naturally. In fact, Alex will have the children there, too, during the last week of rehearsals. He doesn't want Gina worrying about them when she has to concentrate on her singing. Such a big role, playing Maria in *West Side Story*."

"She's got the voice for it," Matteo said dismissively. He gave her a hooded look. "So who are the six seats for? Tony, Hannah, you, me…"

"Rosita and Nicole."

A pause. Then in a voice stripped of any telltale expression he asked, "Nicole will be going?"

Not *Ms. Redman* this time, Isabella noted. "Yes. She's very keen to hear Gina sing. And see Peter Owen's production of the show. Such a charming man, Peter. He flew up last weekend to iron out some production details with Gina and dropped in to visit me. Gave Nicole a personal invitation to the post-premiere party he's throwing and she was very happy to accept."

Matteo's jaw tightened.

Peter Owen had a very *colourful* reputation as a latter-day Casanova. Alex had once been quite jealous of his professional association with Gina. It had spurred him to declare his love for her very publicly. Isabella reflected that a highly competitive streak ran through each of her grandsons' characters. Perhaps the threat of Peter Owen's winning charm would sort out Matteo's feelings towards Nicole.

"I've also booked hotel accommodation for all of us that night," she went on. "Does that suit you or do you want to make alternative plans?"

His brow was lowered broodingly. His silence went on so long, Isabella was drawn into a terse command. "You can't miss the premiere, Matteo. If only to support Gina, you must go."

His hand sliced the air. "No question, Nonna. Alex would kill me if I didn't turn up."

"Well, what is the problem? You seem...very distracted."

He grimaced. "Sorry. I'll go along with the arrangements you've made. I suppose it will be red carpet at the theatre. Limousines. Formal dress."

"You can count on it. Peter Owen wouldn't have it any other way."

"The ultimate showman. Well, we'll see, won't we?" he muttered darkly and headed for the door, holding up a hand in a last salute. "'Bye, Nonna. Fax a schedule to my company office and I'll toe the line like a good little boy."

He flashed a mocking smile and was gone.

Definitely not a happy man, Isabella thought.

However, she had achieved the setting for the next scene between Matteo and Nicole, and put in a clever little needle by throwing Peter Owen into the ring. Control of the seating in the plane and in the theatre was hers. As long as neither of the antagonists found some rock-solid excuse for not following through on their given word, they'd have to bear each other's company for many hours.

Isabella smiled to herself.

There was nothing like enforced time together to wear down barriers.

CHAPTER TEN

MATT arrived at Cairns Airport twenty minutes before their flight to Brisbane was scheduled to take off. He didn't have to check any luggage through. A suit bag encased the formal clothes he had to wear to the premiere tonight and a small carry-on bag held the rest of his needs.

Tony met him in the entrance hall, handing over his ticket and seat allocation. "The others have gone through to the departure lounge. Ready to join them?"

"Sure! I guess I'll be sitting next to Nicole Redman on the flight," he commented casually, trying to feel relaxed about it as they strolled towards the security barrier.

"No. Nicole took off early this morning. Nonna said she wanted to spend the day in Brisbane, going through newspaper archives."

Anger blazed through him. She was using the excuse of work to avoid him again. Okay the first time. He had cast slurs on her integrity. But he'd gone out of his way to admit he was wrong and apologise for the offence given. It was definitely not okay a second time. This was a deliberate snub.

"What does she hope to find there?" he asked, barely

keeping his anger in check. Some show of interest was called for since he'd brought up her name.

"Well, you know Nonna's husband and brother were on the same boat that sailed from Brisbane when they went off to the Second World War. Nicole wanted some background stuff on how it was for them."

Naturally it *sounded* reasonable, using the plane ticket to serve two purposes. Very conscientious, too, saving Nonna the expense of funding an extra research trip to Brisbane. Except saving dollars was not what this family history project was about and Nonna would not have blinked an eye at any expense it incurred anywhere along the line. So there was no doubt in Matt's mind that Nicole Redman had deliberately engineered this arrangement to thumb her nose at him and his apology.

"Tough luck, Matt! You'll have to put up with your own company for the next two hours," Tony tossed at him teasingly.

"No problem." He laid his bags on the roller table and they stepped through the security gate without setting off any bells.

"Got to hand it to Nicole," Tony rambled on. "Not leaving a stone unturned to do a thorough job on our family history."

"Seems that way," Matt answered non-committally, collecting his bags and glancing around the departure lounge to spot where the others were seated.

"Over there..." Tony pointed, then grinned at him. "You must be losing your touch, Matt. Gorgeous girl more interested in her work than getting acquainted with you.''

He shrugged. ''I'm probably not her type.''

''Can I take it that's mutual? She's not your type?''

Matt rolled his eyes at him. ''Give it a rest, Tony. I know you're a happily married man but I don't need any matches made for me.''

Certainly not with a fiery little number who wasn't reasonable enough to let her rage go. No, she had to keep rubbing in how offensive he'd been, despite his complete backdown and apology. And to think he'd actually bought the book about her father's life and read it to see where she was coming from, just so he could make his peace with her on this trip, even lying awake half of last night, working out what to say…all for nothing!

He greeted his grandmother, Rosita and Hannah just as the boarding call for their flight was announced. No need to make conversation, which suited him very well because he wasn't in the mood for social chitchat. On the plane he had a window seat with no one next to him. The stewardess handed him a newspaper and he used it to close out everyone else.

His eyes skimmed the print but nothing sank into his consciousness. The empty seat beside him was a constant taunting reminder of Nicole Redman's deliberate absence from it. No truce from her. She'd probably arrange for her seat in the theatre tonight to be the furthest from him. And no doubt she'd ride in the limousine transporting his grandmother and Rosita and he'd be directed to ride with Hannah and Tony and Alex.

Which was fine by him.

He didn't care what she did.

She could flirt her head off with Peter Owen at the post-premiere party, too, and he wouldn't turn a hair. In fact, he'd feel utter contempt for it because it would be an act of blatant dishonesty, pretending she fancied Peter Owen. He hadn't been wrong about the sexual attraction she'd felt with him. She could deny it as much as she liked. He knew better.

She would have let him kiss her out on the veranda, after he'd removed the butterflies from her hair. She had not recoiled from his touch one bit. What did she expect a man to do, anyway? Hold back until she gave verbal permission to come close? Ignore the body language that was telling him he was welcome and wanted?

Just let her try that fruit-tasting exercise with Peter Owen and Casanova Pete would be dragging her under the table to take what she was offering. Given the desire she had aroused, Matt figured he'd been a positive gentleman. And what had he got for his restraint? Lies and abuse.

His fault that she hadn't been able to concentrate on the job!

What absolute rot!

She'd had sex on her mind, same as he had, and he hadn't made one suggestive remark to feed her fantasies all the time they'd been walking through the park. It was totally perverse to blame her thoughts on him. She'd made them up all by herself. So why the hell couldn't she admit it instead of scuttling behind a defence of *his fault?*

She might not like wanting him.

He didn't like wanting her.

That didn't change the truth.

Matt seethed over this truth all the way to Brisbane. He was still seething over it when they booked into the hotel, more so when he reached his room and tossed his things on the queen-size bed, which reminded him how open he'd been in laying out what he'd felt to Nicole Redman, stating an obvious desire when wondering out loud how they might be together in bed.

He'd been wrong about her ability to do the job, wrong about her trading on her looks and being unfair to his grandmother, but even with all his wrong assumptions, he'd offered to smooth the situation over by getting whatever extra help she needed. But did she appreciate he'd been bending over backwards to keep her in Port Douglas? To get rid of the deceit and set up a platform of trust so they could move forward into a relationship that he wouldn't feel bad about?

No!

She couldn't even admit he was right about the mutual lust.

He snatched up the bedside telephone, pressed the button for reception and asked for her room number. He glanced at his watch as the information was given to him. Five-thirty. Everyone in their party was to meet in the hotel lobby at seven-fifteen, ready to be transported to the theatre, and be damned if he was going to be snubbed by Nicole Redman again!

He'd sort this out right now.

She had to be in her room. Women always took forever getting ready for a big night out and tonight was *big* for the family. She'd be aware of when his grandmother was arriving at the hotel, aware that she should be on hand to assure her employer that time was not a problem. Work would definitely be over for today. No one of any sensibility would mess with tonight.

No point in trying to talk to her over the telephone. No way would he give her the satisfaction of hanging up on him. This had to be face to face. And there wasn't one bit of guilt she could throw at him this time. With a burning sense of righteousness, Matt left his room and strode towards Nicole Redman's.

Nicole was luxuriating in a bubble bath. Some sensual pampering was precisely what she needed to relax the tension that had made her feel edgy all day. It was impossible to completely avoid Matt King tonight. She simply had to accept that and keep as much distance between them as she could.

Though she still couldn't stop her mind from circling around him, especially knowing she would be seeing him soon. No doubt he would look even more handsome in formal dress. Every man did. It wasn't fair that *he* was so *physically* attractive. It made her feel she might be missing out on some extra-special experience with such a powerhouse of masculinity.

And she wasn't sure she liked the entirely feline instinct that had drawn her into buying a dress she didn't really need. She'd brought one with her that would do for tonight. This afternoon's wild rush of blood to the head had resulted in sheer unnecessary extravagance. She shouldn't have gone into the shopping mall that housed such an alluring range of designer boutiques, courting temptation. The moment she'd seen the black dress, her mind was consumed by one burning thought...

I'll show him.

Show him what? That she could look attractive, too? Or were her claws out, wanting to get under his skin as much as he got under hers. From afar, of course, so he'd sizzle with frustration...if he still fancied a session in bed with her. Justice, she'd told herself, turning the insults he'd handed out into savage regret on his part. After all, he'd savaged her with his outrageously false reading of her character.

Though he had apologised.

Far too late.

Such a late apology couldn't begin to make up for how he'd made her feel for over a week of miserable days and even more miserable nights.

All the same, maybe she shouldn't wear the dress. Maybe she should return it to the boutique and get her money back. Being vengeful wasn't about to result in anything good. It just kept her thinking about him and his response to her.

Was that a knock on her door?

Yes.

Nicole hauled herself out of the bubble bath, thinking it might be Hannah dropping by for a little chat before they had to dress, probably unable to contain her excitement over Gina's premiere, wanting to share it. She had raved to Nicole about Gina's voice, certain that her sister-in-law was going to be a star in tonight's show, but first-night nerves might have got to her.

Nicole gave herself a quick towelling, then wrapped herself in the big white bathrobe supplied by the hotel as she hurried through the bedroom. Another knock urged her into faster action. Without pausing to check the identity of the caller, she opened the door and stood in paralysed shock at being confronted by Matt King.

With him standing right in front of her, barely an arm's length away, she was swamped by how big he was, how male he was, and all of him bristling with aggression, sending an electric charge through every nerve of her body. She was instantly and acutely conscious of her nakedness under the bathrobe, and the blistering force of his glittering dark gaze reminded her that her hair was piled carelessly on top of her head, pinned there to keep it out of the bathwater.

"Let's talk, shall we?" he said in belligerent challenge, stepping forward, driving her back from the door and the intimidating power of his advancing presence.

She was hopelessly unprepared for this. It didn't even occur to her to try and stop him as he entered her room and closed the door behind him. She was too busy back-pedalling to put some distance between them, checking that the tie-belt was tied, clutching the lapels of the robe together to prevent any gap from opening, catching her breath enough to speak.

"What do you want to talk about?"

He looked at her mouth. Was it quivering? She had no make-up on, no armour at all in place to give her any confidence in maintaining some personal dignity against the raw onslaught of his sexuality.

His gaze dropped to the hollow in her throat. She could feel the dampness there that she hadn't had time to wipe away. He took in the clutching position of her hands on the hotel robe, an obvious pointer to how vulnerable she felt. His eyes missed nothing. He probably saw her toes curling as he looked at her bare feet, and he surely absorbed every curve of her body as his gaze slowly travelled back up to her face, her mussed hair, her eyes.

"Maybe talking isn't what either of us want," he said gruffly, his deep voice furred with the desire for a more primitive means of man/woman communication.

Sheer panic galloped through her heart, contracted her stomach, shot tremulous waves down her thighs. "I don't know what you mean," she gabbled, her mind totally seized up with a clash of fear and excitement.

"Yes, you do." His eyes mocked her denial as he moved forward and cupped her chin, fingers lightly fanning the line of her cheek. "You know exactly what I mean, Nicole Redman. The only question is…will you give an honest response?"

He was going to kiss her.

And she just stood there, mesmerised by the blazing

purpose in his eyes, mesmerised by the tingling warmth of the feather-light caress on her cheek, allowing his cupping thumb to tilt her chin to a higher angle, a readily kissable angle, and when his mouth covered hers, it wasn't just her lips yearning to know what his kiss would be like. Her whole body was zinging with antic-ipation, vibrantly alive to whatever sensations this man would impart.

It wasn't a gentle kiss. She hadn't expected it to be. Didn't want it to be. He'd churned her up so much, the need for some outlet for all the pent-up feelings crashed through her, urging answers from him. His mouth was hotly demanding and hers demanded right back, no holds barred as they merged in a rage of passion that craved satisfaction.

An arm clamped around her back, slamming her against him. The hand that had been holding her face to his, raked through her hair, dislodging pins, exulting in freeing the long tresses, and she exulted in it, too. She revelled in being pinned to the hard surging strength of his powerful physique, loved the feel of his hand in her hair, its aggressive need to tangle in the long soft silki-ness of it.

Somehow it freed her to touch him as she liked; the muscular breadth of his shoulders, the wiry curls at the back of his neck. Every contact with him was intensely exciting, the squash of her breasts against the firm hot wall of his chest, the pulsating sense of their hearts drumming to the same fierce escalation of desire for each other, thighs rubbing, pressing, wanting flesh against flesh.

She felt the tie-belt on the robe being yanked, pulled apart. Matt wrenched his mouth from hers, dragging in air as he lifted his head back. His eyes glittered an intense challenge as he moved his hands to hook under the collar of the robe, intent on sliding it from her shoulders. He didn't speak. He didn't have to. The words zapped straight into her mind.

Stop me now if you want to stop.

Her mouth throbbed with the passion he'd fired. Her breasts ached to be touched, kissed, taken by him. Her whole body was aroused, screaming for the ultimate intimacy with this man, uncaring of any moment beyond the experience he was holding out to her.

She didn't speak.

As her hands slid down from his shoulders to make the disrobing easy, her eyes told him there'd be no stopping from her and it wasn't a surrender to his will. It was her choice. And it was up to him to prove the choice was worth taking.

He eased back from her to let the robe slither to the floor. He didn't look down at the nakedness revealed. His gaze remained fastened on hers, the challenge still very much in force as he brought her hands up to his chest, resting them beside the buttons on his shirt.

"Don't give me passive," he growled. "Show me. Get rid of my shirt."

He released her hands. He stood there, inviting her touch but not forcing it. She could feel the burning pride behind his stance, the tension of not knowing whether she might refuse, the determination not to leave himself open to any accusation that he'd taken unfair advantage of her, yet the wanting was not in any way diminished. The heat of it was sizzling around her, bringing tingles to her bare skin and the sense of partnership he was demanding acted like a heady intoxicant to the cocktail of excitement already stirred.

Her hands moved with eager purpose. He'd stripped her naked. He had to be naked, too. She wanted him to be, wanted to feast her eyes on all that made him so masculine, wanted to touch, to absorb the power of him, to experience exactly what it was that compelled such a strong sexual response in her, even against her will, against her reason. She didn't want to fight it now. She had to know.

The shirt was open. She slid it from his shoulders. Warm, satin-smooth skin, tightly stretched over firm muscles. His chest was magnificent. She couldn't resist grazing her fingers through the little nest of black curls below his throat, gliding her palms down towards his flat stomach.

It spurred him out of his tense immobility. It was *his* hands that unfastened his trousers, got rid of the rest of his clothes, stripping with a speed that was breath-taking in its effect of instantly revealing more than she had let herself imagine. He was a big man, big all over, and a little shiver ran through her at the thought of mating with him.

Too late to back off now.

Besides, she didn't want to.

Her heart was thundering in her ears. Her whole body was at fever-pitch anticipation. And there was a wanton primitive streak inside her that was wildly elated when his strong hands gripped her waist, lifted her off her feet and swung her onto the bed.

He loomed over her, all dominant male, and there was a fierce elation in his eyes at having won what he wanted. Though she knew it wasn't true. She was the one taking him. And her eyes beamed that straight back at him. No surrender. A searing challenge to complete what had been started, complete it to *her* satisfaction.

It was like a battle of minds...a battle of hearts... intensely exhilarating...all-consuming...concentration totally focused. There was no foreplay...none needed... none wanted...just this apocalyptic coming together... the ultimate revelation of all the uncontrollable feelings they had struck in each other.

Every nerve in her body seemed to be clustered in that one intimate place, highly sensitised, waiting, poised to react to his entry. There was a tantalisingly gentle probing, a teasing test of how welcome he was. Instinctively, needfully, she clasped him with her legs, urging him on. He plunged forward and her whole body arched up in ecstatic pleasure at the sense of him filling her with his power. It was glorious, having him so deeply inside her, then feeling him thrust there over and over again. Her own muscles joyously adjusted to his rhythm, revelling in the exquisite sensations, craving more and more peaks of pleasure.

Her whole being was centred on how it was with him. She'd never felt anything like it in her entire life, hadn't known what was possible. She lost all sense of self. This was fusion on such an intense level there was no room for any other reality and even when she reached the first incredibly sweet climax, it simply set her afloat on a sea of pleasure that kept on rolling with waves that crested even more deliciously.

How he held his climax back for so long she didn't know, but when it came it was wondrous, too, the fast friction, the powerful surge of energy, the explosion of heat spilling deeply inside her...and a feeling of overwhelming love burst through her, tingling right to her scalp, her fingertips, her toes. And she found herself hugging him to her, hugging him with every ounce of strength she had left in her arms and legs.

His arms burrowed under her and hugged her right back, and there was no letting go, even when he rolled onto his side. He carried her with him, as blindly and compulsively intent as she was on holding on to the togetherness. Time had no meaning. Nothing had any meaning but this.

Until the telephone rang.

CHAPTER ELEVEN

THE telephone!

The realisation of where she was and what she was supposed to be doing came like a thunderclap, jerking Nicole up from Matt King's embrace. Eyes wide open with the shock of having lost track of everything, her gaze instantly targeted the radio clock on the bedside table: 18:33. Only forty minutes left to get ready for tonight's premiere and be down in the lobby for the trip to the theatre!

"Look at the time! We've got to move!" she shot at Matt, heaving herself off him and rolling to the side of the bed to pick up the receiver.

"Right!"

The quick agreement helped to get her mind focused on dealing with the situation. First the call, which was probably from her employer to ask about today's research—her employer who was footing the bill for this hotel accommodation which had just been used for...nothing at all to do with the agenda Isabella Valeri King had approved for today and tonight!

It was some relief to feel Matt moving off the other side of the bed, going straight into action. Nicole swung her legs onto the floor, sat up straight, took a deep breath, lifted the receiver to her ear, and spoke in a reasonably even tone.

The caller *was* Mrs. King.

Nicole quickly expressed satisfaction in the information she'd collected from newspaper archives, replied to various other queries about her day, gave assurances that her hotel room was fine and she hadn't forgotten the seven-fifteen deadline in the lobby, lied about having had something to eat, and every second that ticked by increased the tension of losing more time.

She had her back turned to Matt but she could hear him moving around, pulling on clothes. No sound of his exit, though. Which doubled her tension as she managed to conclude the call. Bad enough that she'd had no option but to remain naked while he dressed. What was he waiting for? Didn't he understand there was no acceptable excuse for not being punctual tonight? And it would be dreadfully inappropriate not to be properly dressed and groomed, as well.

Her heart pitter-pattered nervously. What was his reaction now to what had transpired between them? Had it been as world-shaking for him as it had been for her? Suddenly feeling intensely vulnerable, she forced herself to look at him over her shoulder, needing some reassurance that he had been deeply affected, too.

He stood near the short passageway to the door, his gaze trained very intently on her. He was fully dressed, looking every bit as respectable as when he'd entered, ready to meet anything or anyone.

"Don't try skipping out on me tonight, Nicole," he

fired at her, his eyes blazing a command that promised she would rue any deviation from what was planned. "You *be* in the hotel lobby at seven-fifteen. We'll take it from there."

He was gone before Nicole could even catch her breath. He'd brought an electrifying wave of aggression into her room and his exit left her with the same sense of force which would not be denied, no matter what ensued from this moment.

It stunned her into losing a few more moments.

Her mind rallied to examine what he'd said since it had to be a lead to what he was feeling. *Skipping out on him...* Was that how he viewed her choice to take an earlier flight today? Perhaps even further back, a reference to the family luncheon she'd deliberately missed.

He must have taken both absences as very personal slights. Which they were. But this had to mean he'd been thinking about her as much as she'd been thinking about him, and getting highly riled about it. And he wasn't about to walk away from what had just happened.

Be there!

The command of a very determined man to have her with him. He certainly hadn't had enough of her. Which was fine by Nicole. She hadn't had enough of him, either. Which brought a crooked little smile to her face. She'd leapt in at the deep end with Matt King and didn't know if she'd be able to keep her head above these turbulent waters. But she wasn't about to drown yet.

The black taffeta dress.

Yes, she'd be there in the lobby at seven-fifteen, but

not as a woman submissive to his will. In fact, she'd do her absolute utmost to knock his eyes out. Teach him not to take anything about her for granted.

Matt was the first down. He was early. Eight minutes past seven. He hoped to catch his grandmother before Nicole appeared and ensure the *right* seating in the limousines and at the theatre. He didn't care if this raised her eyebrows or gave her satisfaction. Nicole Redman had certainly proved his match in bed but that didn't mean marriage was on the line.

Ten past seven. Matt breathed a sigh of relief as he saw Rosita, Alex and his grandmother emerge from an elevator. Alex, as always, looked impressive and totally in control of himself. Nonna was in royal-blue silk, very regal with her head of white hair held high and all her best jewellery on. Rosita wore burgundy lace and was beaming with excitement. They all smiled at him.

Matt forced a smile he didn't feel, knowing he should be sharing their anticipation of pleasure in the show and a triumphant night for Gina. All he could think of was getting Nicole Redman to himself again. As the others joined him in the middle of the lobby, he directly addressed his grandmother.

"So what's the arrangement, Nonna? You three go in the first limousine, the rest of us to follow?"

She appeared to consider, then slowly answered, "Nicole may want to ride with us."

"Won't look good for the red carpet arrival at the theatre," he argued. "I think Alex should take both your arm and Rosita's for the walk in. Which would make Nicole the odd woman out. Better that she be accompanied by me, stepping out of the second limousine.''

"Matt has a point there, Nonna," Alex remarked supportively. "Peter has lined up media coverage. Bound to be cameras on us."

Was that a smug little smile flitting across her lips? Certainly there was a twinkle in her eyes as she answered, "Then we will do it Matteo's way."

Inwardly he bridled against seeming to fall into her matchmaking trap. He didn't pursue the issue of seating at the theatre, deciding he'd hold on to Nicole's arm so that any separation would not occur, unless she made a point of it. Unlikely that she would carry out a public snub in these circumstances.

The problem was Matt didn't feel sure of her, despite the intimacy they had just shared. Giving in to mutual lust behind closed doors didn't guarantee a positive response in other areas. They hadn't talked, hadn't reached any kind of understanding he could feel comfortable with.

Maybe she'd just been satisfying a sexual curiosity, an itch that needed scratching, and she'd back right off him again now. He found his hands clenching and forced himself to relax. She had to stay beside him for the next few hours. At least that much was assured.

Tony and Hannah emerged from another elevator, Hannah looking absolutely fantastic in a beaded green gown, her long crinkly blond hair billowing around her shoulders. Pregnancy not showing yet.

Matt checked the time on his watch again. Thirteen minutes past seven. If Nicole wasn't here in the next two minutes he'd go up to her room and haul her down. No way was he going to let her call in sick or make some other lame excuse for not joining him tonight. If she thought she could take him for sexual pleasure, then turn her back on him... Matt seethed over the possibility, vowing he'd set her straight in no uncertain terms.

He caught his grandmother observing him and tried to adopt a nonchalant air, glancing around the lobby in a pretence of careless patience for their party to be complete. An image of red and black caught his eye, high in his normal field of vision. His gaze jerked up. There, at the top of the staircase, leading down to the lobby from the mezzanine floor.

She stood looking straight at him.

Checking him out?

Matt neither knew nor cared. His heart turned over as he slipped back in time to the night he'd first seen her in New Orleans. Red and black. And her skin glowing pearly white. Stunning. Fascinating. Compelling him to follow, to watch her, listen to her. Not the time nor place to get to know her then, but now...

"Oh, there's Nicole on the mezzanine level," he heard his grandmother say. "She must have pressed the wrong button in the elevator."

No, Matt thought. It was deliberate.

Her gaze didn't so much as waver from his as she began her descent to the lobby. He wasn't someone in a mask at the back of a crowd of tourists tonight. She knew who he was and was challenging his interest in her, refiring the desire he'd driven to its ultimate expression earlier, desire she'd conceded herself.

He'd called her a *femme fatale*.

Mockingly.

He could feel her flaunting it in his face with every step she took down the staircase. Her black dress was the sexiest he'd ever seen, its heart-shaped neckline cut wide on the shoulders to little cap sleeves that virtually left her slender white arms bare. The décolletage was low enough to show the valley between her breasts and the upper swell of them on either side. More provocative than blatant. The bodice was moulded to her curves and the whole gown hugged her figure to knee-length. He could see a fishtail train slithering down the steps behind her. The shiny fabric added to the whole sensual effect.

Matt belatedly realised he was moving to meet her. She'd drawn him like a magnet. Too late to stop, to deny her that power. Better to make the action seem perfectly natural, her escort doing the polite thing. He waited at the foot of the stairs, ready to offer his arm, which she'd take if he had to forcibly hook hers around it.

Her hair gleamed like liquid fire, a smooth fall forward over one shoulder, brushed back behind the other. That was provocative, too. Her mouth the same colour red. Her lashes were lowered to make it appear her gaze was focused on the steps, but it wasn't. Through the semi-veil, her eyes were simmering with satisfaction at having him waiting on her.

Matt had to quell a wild surge of caveman instincts.

His family was watching and be damned if he'd give his grandmother the satisfaction of knowing *her choice* was making him burn more than any other woman he'd ever known. Now was the time for very polished manners and Nicole Redman had better match him in that.

He offered his arm as she took the last step, his own eyes hooded to prevent her from seeing the inner conflagration of rampant desire and angry frustration with the situation he found himself in. Control was needed. He hated not having it. He would not let this woman take it from him.

The tightness in his chest eased as she slid her arm smoothly around his, no hesitation at all. "Thank you," she said huskily.

"My pleasure," he replied, darting a sharp look at her, surprised by the furred tone.

Her gaze fluttered away from the quick probe, but he was left with an impression of uncertainty. No triumph. No confidence, either. She wasn't claiming him. In fact, the hand resting on his coat sleeve was actually tremulous. He quickly covered it with his own, holding it in place. If she was having second thoughts about linking herself to him, no way would he allow her to flit off and leave him standing like a fool.

"You look quite superb tonight," he said, determined on appearing outwardly calm and collected as he led her towards the family group.

"So do you," she muttered, then took a deep breath as though she needed it to steady herself.

Was she regretting having had sex with him? Worried

about it? Afraid he might now take some advantage from it she didn't want? Did her appearance have more to do with bravado than deliberate allure?

Alex was ushering his grandmother and Rosita towards the door. Tony and Hannah were hanging back, waiting. Matt waved them on, wanting them to go ahead and give him a few private moments with Nicole.

"We need to do some talking," he shot at her.

Red battle flags in her cheeks. "I thought you'd done all the talking you wanted to do with me."

What was this? Blaming him for what she'd wanted to do herself? "Nowhere near," he mocked. "You could say we now have a basis for a beginning."

"I thought it was an end in itself," came her snippy reply.

"Rubbish! If circumstances were different, we'd still be on that bed."

Her mouth compressed. No reply. She didn't want to admit it and denial would be a lie. He hadn't actually meant sexual communication. Why was she being difficult? Talking had to be the next step. He tried again.

"We don't have the time now but after the show…"

"There's a party and I intend to go to it." She turned her head to direct a blaze of defiance at him. "With you or without you. Please yourself. I will not be dictated to by you, Matt King."

"I had mutual interests in mind," he grated out.

"Above the sexual level?"

It goaded him into retorting, "Something wrong with the sexual level?"

"No. But there's more to me than that."

"You think I don't know it?"

"You haven't shown it."

Her head snapped forward, pride stamped on her tilted profile.

Matt fumed at her intransigence. "Precisely how was I supposed to show it when you've been avoiding me like the plague?"

"You *were* a plague."

"Well, well, progress," he drawled mockingly. "Thank you for the past tense. Satisfying our mutual lust was of some benefit."

Her chin tilted higher, emphasising her long graceful neck. Matt wondered how long it would stay extended if he planted a few hot kisses on it. Going to see *West Side Story* had no appeal to him tonight, even with Gina singing. *The Taming of the Shrew* would have suited him much better.

Ahead of them, Alex was stepping into the first limousine after his grandmother and Rosita. Tony and Hannah were outside the lobby, waiting for the second limousine to slide into place. The hotel doors were being kept open for his and Nicole's imminent passage to the pick-up point.

At least Nicole hadn't queried arrangements. Matt figured he'd won that much from her. And she'd accepted him as her escort. No overt attempt to avoid his physical presence. She might be burning over the fact he hadn't left her with honeyed words after their intimacy, but given the way she'd treated him previously, what could she expect?

He'd been entirely reasonable.

So what the hell was her problem?

"Well, I hope *you* enjoy the show tonight," he said with a twist of irony.

She looked at him, obviously confused by his line of thought. "What do you mean by that?" she asked, her tone wary, suspicious.

"It's about star-crossed lovers, ending unhappily. Which is what you seem determined on for us."

The comment sharpened her eyes into a fine glitter. "You're very fast at assumptions."

"You could try giving me more to work on," he retaliated.

"And you could try asking instead of making up your own scenarios and thinking you can force me into them," she flashed back at him.

"Fine! After the show tonight..."

"I'm going to the party," she said stubbornly.

"So am I," he snapped, having run out of time to say any more.

The first limousine had pulled away, Hannah and Tony were climbing into the second, and he and Nicole were now on their heels, poised to follow. A few seconds later they were all settled inside it and the chauffeur was closing the door on them.

Matt sat facing Tony, almost hating his brother for looking so happy. And there was Hannah next to him, holding his hand, glowing as though all her Christmases had just come. In contrast, he filled the space beside the red-haired witch who kept stirring cauldrons of boiling oil to hang him over them.

But he'd get her tonight.

If she thought she could give him the slip at the post-premiere party, she could think again. He'd be there at every turn, making his presence felt. And she'd feel it all right. He wasn't making any wrong assumptions about the sexual spark between them.

Absolute dynamite.

And the fuse was burning.

CHAPTER TWELVE

THEY had a box at the theatre. Nicole was placed next to Matt in the second row of seats behind Alex and Rosita and Mrs. King, but at least she had Hannah on her other side and the arrangement made for easy conversation amongst the family. She wasn't isolated with Matt, which was an enormous relief since she couldn't trust herself to speak civilly with him.

Not that her inner tension eased much. She was hopelessly aware of him. Their physical intimacy had heightened it a hundredfold, making her acutely conscious of her sexuality and his. It played on her mind so much she could barely think of anything else. Back in the hotel lobby, she'd ended up snapping at him out of her own resentment that it could be so overwhelming.

Other things should be more important. Respect, love, trust, understanding…what about them? And he was so arrogant, confident of claiming her whenever he wanted, and the worst part was she was quivering inside, yearning for what he'd given her to be given again. How was she going to handle this? How? What was the best way? Was there a best way?

Star-crossed lovers…ending unhappily.

Those insidious words lingered in her mind as the show started but she was soon caught up in the Romeo and Juliet story being played out on the stage. The production was vibrant and intensely emotional with its continual overtone of tragedy looming, the inevitable outcome of irreversible conflict.

Every time Gina sang there was an almost breathless silence throughout the theatre, the poignant power of her voice and the empathy she drew from the audience made her a wonderful Maria. The rest of the cast put in very good performances but she shone, and at interval the buzz of excitement and pride in the family box put irrepressible smiles on everyone's faces, even Matt's and Nicole's.

The second half of the show was even more heart-wringing. With tears pricking her eyes, Nicole fumbled around her feet for her evening bag, needing tissues. Matt offered a clean white handkerchief. Rather than make any noise, unclicking her bag, she took it, nodding her thanks. It was very handy when Maria's lover was shot and lay dying with Maria kneeling beside him as they sang a last plea of hope for the world to come right—*"Somewhere…"*

Tears gushed.

Nicole mopped frantically, struggling to stop a sob from erupting.

"Hold my hand…" The words were so terribly moving, and when Matt's hand covered hers, squeezing sympathetically, she gripped it and squeezed back as though it were a lifeline to stop her from falling apart.

The curtain came down.

The only sounds in the theatre were sniffles being

smothered and throats being cleared. The applause was slow in coming, a sprinkle of handclaps quickly joined by more, building like a huge wave to a crescendo that urged more and more clapping. Nicole wanted to use her hands but one of them was still entangled with Matt's and she was suddenly acutely conscious of having hung on to it.

His hand.

The warmth and strength of it zinged up her arm. Her heart skipped a beat. She didn't want to let the comforting contact go but was there really any comfort for her in this attraction to Matt King? Embarrassed, she darted him a look of appeal as she wriggled her fingers within his grip. He returned an ironic little smile and released her hand, moving his straight into a long round of applause.

There was an absolute ovation for Gina, many shouts of "Bravo!" She was presented with a huge bouquet of red roses and she smiled directly up at Alex who leaned on the railing of the box and blew a kiss to her. She blew one back to him. Their obvious love for each other gave Nicole a stab of envy.

Why couldn't it… Her head turned to Matt King even before the thought was completed. *…be like that for them?*

He caught her glance and cocked a quizzical eyebrow.

Heat whooshed into her cheeks and she jerked her attention back to the stage. The thought certainly hadn't occurred to him. The expression lingering on his face from having watched the interplay between his brother and sister-in-law was amusement. Did he find real love between a man and a woman a joke? Was sex all he considered?

Or was it all he was considering with *her?*

Nicole found herself pressing her thighs tightly together, a silent, vehement protest against such a limitation, especially when a relationship could be so much more. Surely such strong sexual chemistry had to be linked to some special selective process. It made no sense otherwise.

She was still battling the feelings Matt aroused when Peter Owen, the director of the show, was called on stage to another loud burst of applause. She couldn't help smiling at his air of elated triumph as he took the microphone and made a short speech, thanking the audience for their acclaim, which of course, was richly deserved, and it demonstrated how magnificently perceptive they all were to recognise and acknowledge it.

As always, he was so charmingly over-the-top he drew laughter and more applause, leaving everyone in high spirits as the final curtain came down. *He's still Peter Pan,* Nicole thought fondly, remembering how he'd brought an effervescent lightness to some of her darker hours in the old days, a kindness that felt more like fun than kindness.

Alex stood and spoke to his grandmother. "I'll just slip backstage while the theatre is emptying. I won't be long."

"Take your time, Alessandro. We're in no hurry."

She turned around to smile at Nicole and comment, "Peter made it work wonderfully well, didn't he?"

"A brilliant production," she agreed. "I didn't know he had this in him but he really did pull it off."

The old lady's gaze shifted to Matt. "The ultimate showman," she said with a nod, as though repeating a remark he'd made. Then in a whimsical tone, she added, "Nicole knew Peter when he was just starting out as a pianist, getting the occasional gig with jazz bands."

Matt turned a frown on her. "In the same bands your father played in?"

"Sometimes," she answered evenly, vowing to watch her wayward tongue and invite more normal conversation between them. "He was more a fill-in than a regular. Though I must say I missed him when he dropped out of the Sydney jazz scene. He took a job as a pianist/singer on a cruise ship and sailed out of our lives."

The frown deepened. "You made no mention of him in your book."

He'd read her book?

Her mind scrambled to fit this stunning news into her picture of Matt King. Her heart lifted at the realisation he had to be interested in her as a person to put the time into reading a biography which revealed her background. It couldn't be just sex on his mind!

"You didn't tell me you'd read *Ollie's Drum,* Matteo," his grandmother half queried, one eyebrow arched in surprise.

Nicole stared at him, still processing her own surprise. He sat back, jawline tightening as though he'd just been smacked on the chin. "Since you've contracted Nicole to write our family history, Nonna, it seemed a good idea to see how she'd dealt with her own," he drawled, deliberately eliminating any *personal* interest in the content.

"I trust you were satisfied," Nicole bit out, anger rising at the lengths he'd gone to, checking that she wasn't cheating his grandmother.

"Very much so," he conceded. "The book was very well written and held my interest."

She burned. He'd probably been flipping through it to see if it contained any evidence of her whoring or fleecing people of their money. Her tongue wanted to whip him for thinking so badly of her, but she restrained it, remembering her outburst in the billiard room when he had apologised for misjudging her.

He had apologised.

He'd even said he respected her.

But then he'd bedded her with only the barest pause for her consent. Nothing to make her feel appreciated or valued. Just straight into sex, since her book had proved she was okay and there probably wouldn't be any nasty comebacks. She hated him for it, hated herself for having been a willing party to it, but in this company she had to appear civil.

"Thank you," she aimed at him, then forced a smile at his grandmother. "To get back to the show, I do think the staging was excellent, but Peter obviously knew what he had in Gina and she certainly delivered it for him."

"Oh, yes!" came the ready agreement. "From the

time he first heard her sing, he was determined on show-casing her talent.''

"Well, he sure did it tonight," Hannah chimed in, giving Nicole the opening to turn to her and chat on until Alex returned.

This was the signal for them to start making their exit from the box. Alex reported on all the excitement back-stage as they milled out into the corridor. Inevitably Nicole was coupled with Matt again for the walk down the stairs to the foyer of the theatre.

As reluctant as she was to take his arm, common sense argued the stairs could be tricky in her long gown and high heels, and it would be too impolite if she ignored his offer and used the banister instead. Better to suffer his rock-steady support than risk losing her dignity by wobbling or tripping, though she inwardly bridled at having to be close to him, feeling the whole length of his body next to hers.

They trailed after the others and she wished he would quicken his pace to catch up, but if anything he slowed it, frustrating her wish not to be alone with him, not to be reminded of how he had felt naked, how she had felt...

"How old were you when Peter Owen featured in your life?" he asked, thankfully pouring cold water on her feverish thoughts.

"Ten and eleven," she answered, relieved that he wasn't dwelling on the same hot memories.

"Just a kid then," he muttered dismissively.

It goaded her into adding, "I might have been *just a*

kid, but Peter always went out of his way to make me feel welcome in his company.''

''Couldn't resist charming even little girls,'' came the sardonic comment.

''Charm is often in very short supply,'' she returned tartly. ''And I appreciated it very much at the time.''

''No doubt you did. Not much charm in waiting around hotels and nightclubs, watching over an alcoholic father and getting him safely home after his gigs.''

The soft derision in his voice piqued her into glancing at him. He caught her gaze and his dark eyes were hard and penetrating as he added, ''Was he really worth all you gave him of your life, Nicole?''

''You don't understand...''

''No, I don't. He should have been looking after you. What kind of man puts a set of drums and a bottle of whisky ahead of the welfare of a child? You were nine when your mother died. Nine...''

''He was my father,'' she answered fiercely.

''Yes, and being a father should mean something,'' he retorted just as fiercely. ''Do you imagine that Alex or Tony would ever neglect their responsibility to their children? That they'd let themselves wallow in depression or find oblivion in a bottle, robbing their children of the sense of security they should have?''

''They occupy a different world,'' she cried defensively.

''They're men.''

''All men aren't the same.''

''True. But you're a woman now, not a child, and you

should see things how they really were. From the story you've written it's obvious your father could charm birds out of trees when he wasn't completely in his cups. But charm doesn't make up for the rest."

"You're making judgments again about things you don't know," she seethed at him.

His eyes glittered a black challenge back at her. "Well, I do know Peter Owen has been married and divorced twice, and I'm sure his ex-wives were thoroughly charmed by him to begin with. You might keep that in mind at the party."

She sought to explain the difficulties in living with people who were passionately absorbed in creating a unique form of magic. "It's hard...living with musicians. If you don't understand how important it is to them..."

"So important that your needs always have to take a back seat to their kind of self-expression?" He cocked a mocking eyebrow at her. "You've had a long taste of that, Nicole. Was it so sweet?"

It finally dawned on her that he might be jealous of her interest in Peter. Possibly because she'd made such a firm stand about going to the party where she would inevitably meet her old friend again. Now that he knew of their personal connection, was he imagining she wanted to revive it?

She shook her head, dazed at the convoluted way he had used her life with her father to undermine any chance of her being charmed by Peter. The arm holding hers suddenly felt very possessive, as though it wasn't about to let her stray from his side.

They'd reached the foyer and were trailing the rest of the family group out to the street where the limousines were waiting. In a few minutes they'd be on their way back to the hotel where the party was to be held in a private function room. But Matt King wasn't quite finished pressing his point of view.

"You're free now," he went on in a low intense voice. "Free to pursue what *you* want. *Have* what you want. I gave you a choice up in your room, and you chose me. What do you think that says, Nicole? About your needs?"

She didn't know.

She'd been trying to work out what was happening between them and why. It was confusing, disturbing, and she wasn't acting like her normal self at all. There was no time for a reply, which was just as well, because her mind couldn't fasten on one. She followed Tony and Hannah into their limousine and put on a congenial mask for the ride back to the hotel.

Behind it she silently acknowledged Matt King was right about one thing. She was free to pursue whatever she wanted. No personal attachments. Her only responsibilities applied to whatever work she took on, and she no longer accepted a job that didn't appeal to her.

Free...

Was it a deliberate choice not to tie herself to anyone in all these years since her father's death? At first, she'd felt emptied of anything to give to a relationship. Easier to keep associations superficial. Nothing could be demanded of her. The need to become a whole person, by herself, for herself, had probably been more instinctive than thought out, but Nicole now recognised it was what she'd been doing throughout her years at university.

After that, well maybe she'd got into the habit of being alone. But she had felt lonely and there'd been a few men she'd dated for a while. Until the balance of what they'd enjoyed together got heavier and heavier on their side and she simply didn't want to be the one doing the majority of the giving and the understanding to keep the involvement going.

It was like a line drawn in her mind. This much I'll do. No more. But Matt King blurred all the lines, smashing every perception she'd ever had about men. The Kings, she decided, were a different breed. Their family history was telling her so with everything she learnt about them. Strong compelling men. Family men. Men who held what they had, looked after it and built on it.

Was that what she needed?

Was this why Matt King drew such an instinctive response from her, bypassing any rational thought?

She looked down at the hand he'd held.

Did he mean to keep holding it…if she let him?

Or was she a passing fancy?

CHAPTER THIRTEEN

"Nicky!"

Matt gritted his teeth as Peter Owen headed towards them, arms outstretched.

"You look wonderful!"

His bedroom-blue eyes might just get socked out if they kept gobbling her up.

"Who'd have thought that skinny little red-haired kid would bloom into such a beauty?" he raved on, grabbing her upper arms and planting a kiss on both cheeks.

She laughed and bantered, "Who'd have thought Peter Pan would become such a maestro of the theatre?"

Peter Pan was right, Matt thought darkly. The man was forty and still sparkled with the exuberance of a boy who'd never grow up.

"What a premiere! Are you proud of me?" he preened.

Again she laughed. "Immensely. You're Superman tonight."

"That's exactly how I feel. I could leap off tall buildings…"

Pity he didn't do it!

"Well, don't go faster than a speeding bullet," she teasingly advised. "Enjoy the moment."

"Ah…you always were a sweetheart, Nicky dear.

Good to see you! Got to go and mix now but I'll claim a dance from you later."

Over my dead body!

He shot a grin at Matt. "Look after her. She's very special."

I don't need you to tell me that.

Matt forced a smile. "Great night, Peter! Well done!"

He paused, lifting a hand in salute to the real star. "Gina sang like the angel she is," he said with sincere fervour before moving on to spread himself around.

It made Matt feel mean about his more violent thoughts. He knew there was real affection between Gina and Peter. Even Alex had grown to like the man. Peter was godfather to their baby daughter. But he did have a reputation for being a world-class womaniser.

Matt turned to the woman beside him, taking some encouragement from the fact that she hadn't tried to drift away in the crowd of people at the party. On the other hand, she probably didn't know anyone here, apart from Peter and the King family. Mostly she'd been silent, filling the time by sampling the gourmet finger food being carried around and offered by numerous waiters.

Had his words as they'd left the theatre got through to her?

Her gaze was following Peter's progress through the crowd. Did she want him back in her life? He'd made her laugh. Matt hadn't heard her laugh before. Usually he did share lots of laughter with the women he spent time with. Why was everything so intense with this one?

He was getting obsessed with her, thinking of little

else. Having sex with her hadn't given him any relief from it, either. If anything, it had locked him into a deeper pursuit of the woman she was. He wanted to know how her mind worked, what she felt, how she saw things.

"Do you like being called Nicky?"

She shrugged, not looking directly at him as she flatly answered, "It's a name from a different life."

"One you've moved on from," he pressed, wanting it to be so.

"Yes and no." Her gaze slowly lifted to his, the rich brown of her eyes somehow reflecting a depth of feeling that put him instantly on alert. "Do we ever really leave our past behind? Aren't we the sum of all our years?" A wistful smile flitted across her very kissable lips. "Perhaps even more. Look at you…"

"What about me?"

"You have a heritage to live up to, as well. Don't you feel that?"

"No. I am who I am."

"One of the Kings. Like Alex and Tony whom you invoked earlier as examples of what a father should be. And I'm sure you consider yourself in the same mould. The King mould."

He frowned over this assertion. Pride in his own individuality wanted to deny he was like his brothers, yet they did all have the same background, the same upbringing. There were common factors. And they lived by the same principles, principles that had been hammered into them by their grandmother. Their heritage…

A waiter came by with a tray of drinks, diverting Nicole's attention to it. She picked up a glass of champagne and sipped as though she needed the kick of alcohol. Matt swiped a glass, too, before the waiter moved on. He thought about Nicole's heritage as he sipped.

Her mother had been Irish. She'd met and fallen in love with Ollie Redman when he'd been touring Dublin, married him and came to Australia. There'd been no maternal family in Sydney for Nicole to fall back on when her mother had died. No paternal family, either. Ollie Redman had spent most of his young life in an orphanage. He probably hadn't known what a father should be, having had no role model himself.

People were the sum of their lives...

So what did that make Nicole?

"Why did you take on this project?" he asked, a sixth sense telling him the answer would be enlightening.

She slanted him a half-mocking look. "To find out what a different life was like."

The life of a long-rooted family. That he was part of. Shock stiffened his whole body. Was this why she'd had sex with him? An intimate experience with one of the Kings? The only one who wasn't married?

His mind went into a ferment. She might have been thinking about it ever since they'd met in his office. Certainly when she'd come up to the park, she'd been considering it, wanting it. She'd been eyeing him off as he'd shown her the photographs in his home. If he hadn't put her professionalism on the line, stung her pride...

But they were past that now and tonight she'd taken

what he'd offered without so much as a hesitation. Taken it and revelled in it every bit as much as he had. So she would want more. One taste wasn't enough. It certainly wasn't enough for him. They'd barely begun to explore...*what it was like.*

Her head was slightly bowed as though she was contemplating the contents of her glass. His gaze drifted down the gleaming flame-red fall of her hair, the fine silk of it caressing the bare white skin of her back above the dip of her gown, a dip that revealed the sensual curve of her spine. Below it, her delectable bottom jutted out, begging to be touched. Matt felt himself getting aroused, thighs tightening, sex stirring. He wanted this woman again. Again and again and again.

She was rubbing her index finger idly around the rim of her glass. The urge to snatch it away, force her to look at him and admit what she wanted was strong. Then they could get out of this party, go to his room or hers, and...

"What you said about charm..." She lifted her head and there was sadness in her eyes, making a savage mockery of the desire running rampant through him. "Neither my father nor Peter had family behind them. The charm is a defence against that emptiness, and a reaching out to be liked. A need for everyone to like them, even if it is only on a superficial level."

She paused, her eyes begging some understanding from him. "You don't have that need, Matt. You're very secure in the life you were born into. It makes a difference."

He felt chastened. He *was* more fortunate than others with his family. No denying it. Yet he couldn't imagine himself not making his own way to a life he could be proud of, in every sense. Having to be propped up by others, dependent on what they did for him…no, that was not a situation he'd ever want or accept.

"Maybe it does," he grudgingly conceded. "But in the end, everybody is responsible for what they make of their own lives. There are choices."

And she'd chosen to have sex with him!

She must have read his thought. A tide of heat rushed into her cheeks. He wondered if she cursed her white skin for being such a telltale barometer of her feelings. It gave him a kick, just watching it, though he'd prefer to touch. His hands itched to touch.

"I think choices are shaped by what's gone before," she argued. "People fall into them because…" She stopped, floundering in the face of what she saw in his eyes.

Matt wasn't hiding what he was thinking, what he was wanting. "Because a need pushed them that way?" he finished for her.

"Yes," she whispered.

"And when there's a mutual need, it's even easier to go with it," he pushed, all his energy pumping into drawing her with him. "And why not? Why not see where it leads?"

She stood absolutely still, her gaze fastened on his, her lips slightly parted as though she needed to suck in air, but if she did it was imperceptible. Matt suspected her lungs weren't working at all, seized up with tension, as his were, waiting for the line to be crossed. The fire in her cheeks did not abate. She didn't speak but Matt knew in his bones she wanted what he wanted. An exhilarating recklessness zinged through him.

A waiter approached, offering another tray of fancy canapes. Matt plucked the glass from Nicole's hold, her fingers sliding from it, not clutching. He put both his and her glass on the tray, uncaring that it was carrying food. The action jerked her gaze towards the tray. Matt wasn't about to give her time to regroup. The wave was going his way and ride it he would.

He grabbed her hand, winding his own firmly around it. "Come with me," he commanded and set off, making a path through the partying crowd, pulling her with him.

She didn't try to pull back.

Her acquiescence put a surge of power into his sense of rightness. Nothing was going to stop him. They had to pass by his grandmother and Rosita. He didn't care if they saw or what they thought of him and Nicole leaving together. Let them wonder. It didn't matter.

A phrase from the old *Star Wars* movie clicked into his mind—*The force be with you!* It was with him all right, pounding through his bloodstream, invigorating every muscle in his body, making his skin tingle with electric vitality.

They were finally free of the function room, out in the corridor, heading for the elevators. There was a tug on his hand, a breathless cry, "Where are you taking me?"

"Where we can be alone together." He paused long enough to release her hand and put his arm around her waist, wanting her clasped close to him, inseparable. He scooped her with him the last few steps to the bank of elevators and pressed the button to give them access to one of them.

"This isn't right," she gasped, still out of breath.

"Oh, yes it is!"

"I think…"

"That's the problem." His eyes blazed his inner certainty at her. "You've been thinking too much since we were interrupted."

Doors slid open.

He swept her into the empty compartment and pressed the button for the floor where his room was situated.

"This is not a grey issue," he stated as the doors slid shut. "It's black and white…" He turned her fully into his embrace, sliding one hand into her glorious hair to hold her head tilted up to his. "…and red," he added with deep satisfaction, loving the feel of her hair and craving the taste of her red mouth.

He kissed her. Her lips felt soft under his, infinitely seductive. Her mouth was far more intoxicating than champagne. It fizzed with passion, exciting all the primitive instincts she stirred in him.

When the elevator doors opened, it triggered the urge to pick her up, keep hold of her. He bent, hooking his arm around her thighs, and sweeping her up against his chest where his heart was beating like a wild tom-tom, drumming him forward.

He was out of the elevator and striding towards his room, his whole being focused on one outcome, when unbelievably, her hand slammed against his shoulder and she began struggling.

"Let me go! Put me down!" Fierce cries, ringing in his ears.

He stopped, looked his puzzlement at her, realised she was in earnest, wanting to be released, so he set her on her feet, still not understanding what the fuss was about.

She wrenched herself out of his hold, whirling to put distance between, then backing towards the elevator, her hands up in a warding-off action, her face blazing with passionate protest.

"I won't let you do this again!"

"Do what?" He was completely perplexed by her reaction. She'd responded to his kiss…

Her breasts heaved as she drew breath to hurl more words at him. "Just taking me when you feel like it."

"Now hold on a minute. You…" He stepped towards her.

"Stop right there!" Her voice cracked out like a whip. "Don't you dare grab me again!"

He stopped, clenching his hands in frustration at this unreasonable outburst. "You came with me, Nicole," he grated out.

"Yes," she snapped. "But I've come to my senses now and I will not come with you any further, Matt King."

"Why not?"

"Because I don't like myself for…for letting your sex

appeal...override everything else. I won't let what happened earlier tonight happen again.''

"It was good. It was great," he argued vehemently.

"That's all you want from me, isn't it? More sexual satisfaction."

"You get it from me, too," he countered hotly knowing full well she'd not gone short on pleasure with him.

Heat scorched her cheeks. "So we're supposed to service each other, are we?"

He could feel his chin jutting out at this crude description, but pride wouldn't let him back down. "Seems like a good idea to me."

She shook her head. "That's not who I am."

"What do you mean?"

"I mean..." Her eyes flashed with scornful pride. "...find someone else to take to your bed. I don't want that kind of relationship."

She turned and jabbed the button to summon an elevator. Matt had the sinking feeling he'd just dug his own grave with her. But how could that be? The wanting *was* mutual. What was wrong with being honest? She'd kissed him back in the elevator. Her body had clung yearningly to his.

"What *do* you want?" he shot at her.

She shook her head. "I'm going back to the party."

Her gaze was fixed on the arrow indicating an elevator rising to this floor.

"Nicole!"

She wouldn't look at him.

"The least you can do is answer me."

"Just…leave me alone…please."

Her voice wobbled. It struck Matt that she was in acute distress, possibly crying. What had he done? Before he could begin to figure out how to fix the situation, an elevator opened and she moved in a frantic flurry, rushing into it and jabbing at the control panel inside the compartment, her head dipped, her hair swishing forward, curtaining her white face. No colour in her cheeks now.

The doors started to slide shut. Matt moved instinctively to block their closure, the urge to fight any closure with Nicole Redman screaming through him.

"Don't! Please, don't! Let me go!" she cried despairingly, flapping her hands at him in wild agitation as she backed up against the rear wall of the small compartment, her eyes swimming with tears, lashes blinking frantically but unable to stop the moist stream from trickling down her cheeks.

"Just tell me what you do want. Whatever it is you think I won't give you," he demanded hoarsely, churned up by her turbulent emotion. "I need an answer."

"*You* need…" Her throat choked up.

She bent her head and wrapped her arms around herself in a protective hug. He could see her swallowing convulsively and wanted to offer comfort, wanted to hold her and soothe her distress away, but her rejection of him made it impossible.

Her head slowly lifted, lifted high, her chin raised in a proud lonely stand, her eyes bleakly haunted by needs that were part of her world, not his.

"I want to be loved," she said in a raw husky voice. "I want someone to care about me. Look after me. My life is empty of that. Empty..."

It was an instantly recognisable truth. No family, no attachments. And from what he'd read in her book, she'd done all the loving and caring and looking after her father. Not much coming back her way.

Her mouth twisted into a mocking grimace as she added, "And sex doesn't fill that space. It never will."

It shamed him, made him realise how blinded he'd been by his own desire for her, blinded every which way from his initial prejudice against her job with his grandmother to her physical response to the sexual attraction between them.

"Please...will you let me go now?"

What could he do?

He stepped back and let her go, watching the doors slide shut, knowing there was nothing he could say that would change her mind about him. No power in the world would force her to see him differently, not at this point. Besides, it was plain she wanted what he was not prepared to give.

Love...marriage...family.

It was not on his agenda.

But he hated leaving her...so empty.

It made him feel empty himself.

CHAPTER FOURTEEN

ISABELLA VALERI KING sighed in contentment and smiled at her long-trusted confidante. "What a splendid night, Rosita!"

They were comfortably seated in armchairs in a corner at the back of the function room. The band's music was not so loud here and it was possible to converse without shouting. On the table in front of them was a selection of sweets—little fruit tarts, cheesecake, apple slices, florentines—which Rosita was sampling one by one, checking out the quality of the catering.

"Everything is good," came the ready agreement. Rosita's dark eyes twinkled. "But I'm thinking you're especially pleased by the absence of people rather than the presence of people."

Isabella allowed herself a smug little smile. "Matteo is definitely taking the initiative. He made himself Nicole's escort tonight, and from my observation before they left this room, they are very caught up with each other."

"The history may suffer," Rosita archly remarked. "When Matteo decides on something he does not let the grass grow under his feet. Nicole will be distracted."

"I would rather have a another good milestone in our

family to write about, Rosita. The words can be written when all is resolved.''

''You are so sure they will be right together?''

''Did you not see the way they looked at each other when Nicole was coming down the stairs to the lobby?''

''I saw that she looked very striking, very beautiful. Any man would admire her.''

''No. It was more than that. I am certain of it.''

''Then let us hope it is so. She is too much alone, that one. And immersing herself in other people's lives...'' A sad shake of the head. ''She should have a life of her own. A husband. Babies.''

Isabella couldn't agree more. And Nicole was perfect for Matteo, very strong in her own right, but with much love to give and a sense of loyalty that ran very deep, a woman who would always stand by her man through any hardship.

Her gaze skimmed around the crowd, picking out her other two grandsons and their wives—two couples glowing with happiness. A sense of triumph warmed her heart. If Matteo married Nicole...

There she was!

Isabella sat very upright in her armchair, her back stiffening at a most unwelcome sight.

Nicole was alone.

Where was Matteo?

Most of the people who were not seated as she and Rosita were, had drifted towards the dance floor, either standing in groups around it or gyrating on it in their modern way. Nicole had obviously just re-entered the function room and was in open view as her gaze anxiously searched the more crowded area.

Looking for Matteo?

He was not here.

She looked stressed. Her hands were fretting at the small evening bag she held in front of her at waist level. This was not right to Isabella's mind. What had happened to put Nicole in such a state? Where was Matteo?

"Rosita…" Isabella grasped her arm to draw her attention to Nicole. "…things are not going as they should. Quickly now. Pretend you are going to the powder room. As you pass by Nicole, direct her to me."

"It is not good to meddle," she protested.

"Go! Go!" Isabella commanded, out of patience with holding back and not knowing what was wrong.

Rosita heaved herself up and made her rather ponderous way across the room. Isabella composed herself, hiding her chagrin and making sure an inviting smile was hovering on her lips. Nicole gave Rosita a nervous acknowledgment, too uptight to manage the usual warmth between them. Rosita played her part well, a wave of her arm forcing Nicole to look at Isabella who instantly applied the smile, forcing her wish to talk. As her employee, Nicole would feel bound to oblige, whatever her private inclinations were.

Isabella felt no guilt whatsoever about flexing her power as she watched the young woman tread a slow and reluctant path to pay her respect. It was important to know what was going on now. The tension she had noted between Matteo and Nicole at the theatre should have eased. They had seemed very much together once they'd arrived at the party, clearly attuned to each other.

How long had they been out of the function room? Twenty minutes? Half an hour? Some conflict must have erupted between them. Who was at fault? Could it be fixed? Time for a more propitious encounter was running out tonight and if barriers were set in place again…oh, this was so frustrating!

"Mrs. King…" Nicole greeted her in a flat voice.

Isabella patted the armrest of the vacated chair. "Come sit with me while Rosita's gone," she invited, thinking that time limit shouldn't strain Nicole's nerves too much and any other choice of action would seem impolite.

She moved around the table and sat down without any attempt at small talk. The passive obedience worried Isabella all the more. "I thought Matteo was looking after you tonight," she probed, keeping her tone lightly interested.

Nicole visibly bridled. "He was with me earlier," she said in a corrective tone, glancing around the room again to evade looking directly at Isabella. "I don't know where he is now."

"Didn't I see you leave the party together?"

"We…parted. I went to the powder room."

"How very ungallant of him not to have waited for you! I must speak to that boy."

Red splotches on her cheeks. "It's not his job to look after me, Mrs. King, and I certainly don't want him to feel obliged to do so.'' A low ferocity underlined those words.

Pride, Isabella thought. She frowned for Nicole's benefit. ''You don't like my youngest grandson? Matteo has done something to offend you?''

Instant agitation. ''Please don't think that. It was... kind of him to escort me to and from the theatre. Perhaps he wanted an early night. I am perfectly happy by myself, Mrs. King.''

Perfectly miserable!

''He should not have deserted you,'' she pressed.

''He didn't. Really...'' Pleading eyes begging her to desist. ''...your grandson is free to do whatever he wishes. Just as I am.''

Free...

Freedom was highly overrated in Isabella's opinion. There was Matteo going off doing ridiculously dangerous things like whitewater rafting and bungy-jumping because he didn't have the responsibility of a wife and family. As for Nicole, what was she free for? Books and more books?

She wished she could knock their heads together, get some sense into them. It was clear they had come to the parting of the ways, and Isabella was so annoyed by it, she threw discretion to the winds and bored straight into the heart of the matter.

''I do not like this. I have been aware for some time there is friction between you and Matteo. You were unhappy after your visit to Kauri Pine Park and you have made a point of evading his company since.''

This observation startled Nicole but she bit her lips, offering no comment.

"This cannot be pleasant for you, given your situation in our family circle," Isabella went on. "I was hoping it would sort itself out tonight. If it hasn't, Nicole, I feel bound to step in and…"

"No! There is nothing…" Her eyes flashed a wild vehemence. "…nothing between us." Realising that statement didn't answer the questions raised, she hastily added, "There were…differences…which we've cleared. Truly…there is no need for you to say anything, Mrs. King. I'm sorry that you've been worried."

"So everything is fine now?"

Nicole hesitated, hunting for words that would paper over the problem. "We both know where we stand. That makes it easier."

"There was a misunderstanding?"

"Yes. But no more. So it's all right. Truly."

She jerked her focus away from Isabella, fastening her gaze on the crowd around the dance floor. The agitated dismissal of all concern made it too unkind to continue probing. Indeed, Isabella was allowed no time for it.

"There's Peter!" Nicole cried, leaping to her feet. She shot a pleading glance at Isabella. "Please excuse me, Mrs. King. He said he'd dance with me and I'd like to spend some time with him."

"Of course." She managed a benevolent smile. "Go and enjoy yourself."

"Thank you." Intense relief.

Isabella shook her head as she watched Nicole make

her way to Peter Owen's side. Matteo was a fool to let this woman go. There was Peter welcoming her company, only too happy to draw her onto the dance floor and give her whatever pleasure she sought with him.

Disheartened by the talk which had revealed, at best, that Nicole and Matteo had established a neutral zone; at worst, they were poles apart in what they wanted from each other. But *the wanting* was very real. Nicole would not be so distressed if it wasn't. As for Matteo…where was he? Why was he turning his back on *the wanting* that had pulled Nicole out of this room with him?

Totally exasperated with the situation and wanting to discuss her thoughts on it, Isabella looked to see if Rosita was on her way back from the powder room. Her heart skipped a beat as her gaze found Matteo standing just inside the entrance to the function room, his face tight as though it had just been soundly smacked, his eyes projecting a glowering intensity as they watched the occupants of the dance floor, notably Peter and Nicole, no doubt.

His hands clenched.

But he didn't move to get closer or cut in on Peter.

In two minds about what his next action should be? Isabella wondered.

Rosita appeared behind him. Isabella instantly signalled for her to grab Matteo and bring him over to her. Rosita heaved a reproachful sigh but went ahead and touched his arm to draw his attention. Matteo turned a frown on her, then cleared his face as he saw who it was. They conversed for a few moments. Rosita gestured towards their table and Isabella gave her grandson a bright look of expectation, which sealed his reluctant acquiescence as deftly as she had sealed Nicole's.

He hooked Rosita's arm around his and escorted her back to her chair, acting the gentleman Isabella had trained him to be. "Nonna…" He nodded to her. "…I take it you're still enjoying yourself? Not ready to retire yet?"

"Such wonderful nights do not come very often, Matteo. At my age, who knows how many more I will have?" Which was a fine piece of emotional blackmail. She smiled an appeal. "Do draw up another chair and share a few minutes with me."

A slight wince as he bowed to her pressure, taking a chair from another table and placing it next to hers. He dropped into it with an air of resignation. He aimed a dry smile at Rosita. "Fine selection of sweets you've got on the table in front of you."

"Help yourself, Matteo," she invited effusively. "The cheesecake is very good."

"No, thanks. Not hungry. I'm glad you're enjoying them."

"And you, Matteo?" Isabella broke in. "Have you been enjoying yourself?"

He shrugged. "The show was great. Certainly a night to celebrate."

"Perhaps you would like to dance now. Am I keeping you from it?"

"It can wait," he answered in a careless tone.

Isabella put the needle in. "I see Nicole dancing with

Peter. It must be nice for her to renew their old acquaintance."

"No doubt. A shared background is always congenial."

Was that the problem? He'd read *Ollie's Drum*. Did he think Nicole's background precluded her from making a life up here? Didn't he know that if a love was strong enough, place didn't matter? Her own mother had sailed halfway around the world to be with her father in a very foreign land. She herself would have gone to the Kimberly Outback if her husband had survived the war. Was Matteo nursing some woolly-headed prejudice?

"I do not think those memories are ones Nicole cherishes," she said. "They were hard years for her. She has said many times how much she likes the life around Port Douglas. I think she may stay after she finishes the project."

"Doing what?" came the mocking question. "She's bound to head back to Sydney once her contract is over. There's nothing for her up here."

"What is in Sydney for her?" Isabella countered. "She has no family to draw her back. No permanent home. Nicole plans to take time off and try her hand at writing fiction. One can write anywhere, Matteo."

He frowned and muttered, "The heat will get to her. Six months in the tropics will be long enough for the novelty to wear off."

"Many people love the tropical climate. Look at Hannah. She was from Sydney."

"Hannah doesn't have red hair and white skin," he retorted tersely.

Isabella looked at him in astonishment. "What has that got to do with anything?"

He grimaced and made a sharp, dismissive gesture. "Nicole will get burnt. Or suffer sunstroke. She's obviously not suited to…"

"You've met the King family from the Kimberly," Isabella cut in, exasperated by this superficial judgment. "Tommy King's wife, Samantha, has carrot-red hair and very fair skin. She was born and bred in the Outback, with heat and sun that's even more blistering than what we get in Port Douglas."

"That's always been her life," he argued.

"And you think Nicole Redman can't manage it?" Isabella tossed back, barely able to keep the scorn from her voice. "Didn't you say you'd read her book about her father, Matteo?"

"Yes, I did," he snapped, not wanting to be reminded of it.

"Then didn't it occur to you that Nicole is a survivor?" Isabella bored in, relentless in her mission to pull the wool from her blind grandson's eyes. "Given some of the worst circumstances a child could face, that girl came through everything with a strength I can only admire. With a grit and determination that would have served some of the leaders in this country well. With amazing and fearless enterprise, she coped with enormous difficulties and…"

"In my opinion, she wasted her young life on a man

who didn't deserve what she did for him," Matteo flashed at her, a black resentment in his eyes.

"He was her father," Isabella retorted, outraged by this view. "Would you not have rescued your own father if you could have done so?"

"Yes, I would have braved the cyclone that killed him if I'd been anywhere near him, but..."

"A child does not think of the cost to themselves. We are talking blood family here. Sticking to family. It is a quality all too lacking in modern day society. It is a quality I value very highly. I am disappointed that you do not, Matteo."

"Nonna..." Sheer fury looked at her. He jerked his head away, took a deep breath, expelled it slowly, then rose to his feet and looked down at her with hooded eyes. "I really don't wish to discuss Nicole Redman any further," he stated flatly. "I have an early flight in the morning so please excuse me. Goodnight, Nonna... Rosita..."

He strode off with stiff-necked pride, not glancing at the dance floor, intent on denying any interest whatsoever in Nicole Redman. But Isabella was not in any doubt that he had been trying to justify a view which he was using as an excuse not to commit himself to a serious relationship with Nicole. Why he wanted an excuse was beyond her.

Did *freedom* mean so much to him?

"He is very angry," Rosita murmured.

Isabella sighed. "I lost my temper." She turned to her

old friend. "But have you ever heard such nonsense, Rosita?"

She made one of her very expressive Italian gestures. "I think he is hurting badly but he doesn't like to say so. Matteo has always been like that. He jokes to make little of things that hurt."

"He wasn't joking tonight."

"Which means it is a very bad hurt."

"They are both hurting." Isabella shook her head worriedly. "The question is…can they get past it? I may have smashed the barriers in Matteo's mind tonight, but is he prepared to smash the barriers he put in Nicole's?" Her eyes flared her deep frustration. "That is beyond my power. Only Matteo can do it, Rosita. Only he…if he wants to enough."

CHAPTER FIFTEEN

PREGNANT!

Oh, God! Oh, God! Oh, God!

What was she to do?

With shaking hands, Nicole piled all the evidence of the pregnancy test into a plastic bag to dispose of somewhere away from the castle when she felt up to a walk. She couldn't leave it lying around for Rosita to find. The motherly Italian housekeeper was very thorough in her cleaning.

Still in shock, Nicole tottered from her ensuite bathroom, stowed the incriminating packaging in her straw carry-bag, then crawled onto her bed and buried her face in a pillow. It was Sunday morning. She was not expected to work on Sundays. It didn't matter if she was late down for breakfast. In fact, Sunday was a good excuse to miss it altogether. Even the thought of food sickened her, especially first thing in the morning.

Now she knew why.

The punishment for her madness with Matt King.

She couldn't even blame him, knowing she'd been equally responsible. Though *irresponsible* was the correct word. Wild stupid recklessness, not even thinking of the possibility of getting pregnant. Only when she'd gone to bed—alone—after the premiere party had she wondered and worried, and decided there was a good chance she was safe. It simply wouldn't be fair to end up paying even more than the intense emotional letdown from that one experience.

A baby.

No more hiding her head in the sand, finding excuses for her period to be late—the heat, stress, anything but the truth. The truth had just stared her in the face. She was undeniably pregnant. And somehow she now had to plan a future with a baby…a child…a child of her own.

She vividly recalled Matt King spouting off about the responsibilities of fatherhood, but did she want him to be connected to her and their child for the rest of their lives? A man who'd only wanted sex with her? A man who raised turbulent feelings every time she saw him?

Only a few days ago he had dropped in at the castle, stopping to join his grandmother for afternoon tea. He'd breezed out to the loggia where Nicole had been sitting with her employer, cheerfully announcing, ''I just left a box of exotic fruit with Rosita in the kitchen.'' Then with a dazzling grin aimed at her, he'd added, ''I brought some mangosteen especially for you, Nicole. It was your favourite, wasn't it?''

''Yes. Thank you,'' she'd managed to get out as she'd tried to quell the flush erupting from his reminder of their fruit-tasting.

Luckily he'd chatted to his grandmother for a while, giving her time to adjust to his presence. Not that it helped much. Her mind kept fretting over why he'd come and the mention of the fruit seemed like an indication that he still wanted sex with her. Was he scouting his chances?

She'd kept her eyes downcast. It was disturbing enough, hearing his voice, feeling his energy swirling around her. When he'd asked about her progress on the family history, forcing her to look at him, she'd had to concentrate very hard on giving appropriate replies. He'd been quite charming about it, not critical at all, no dubious comments, yet his half-hour visit had left her completely drained.

Even if he remained simply polite to her, she didn't want to be near him. It was too much of a strain, fighting his sexual attraction. And she certainly didn't want him to feel honour-bound to offer marriage because of becoming an accidental father. That would be totally humiliating, knowing he hadn't considered her in the light of a possible wife for him.

No love.

At least, by having a baby, her life wouldn't be empty of love anymore. That was one positive to comfort her. Though how she would manage as a single mother…she would have to start thinking about it, planning.

Four hours later, Nicole was feeling considerably better. She'd walked down to the marina, got rid of the pregnancy test in a large waste bin, idled away some time watching activity on the boats, wandered around the market stalls set up in Anzac Park, lingering at those offering baby clothes and toys, finally buying a gift for Hannah's baby, telling herself it was far too soon to start acquiring anything for her own. Better to wait until she was settled somewhere.

Not here in Port Douglas.

She couldn't live anywhere near Matt King.

The rest of his family she liked very much. Alex and Gina had taken an apartment in Brisbane for the duration of the show, with Alex commuting to Port Douglas as business demanded. Mrs. King missed having them close, especially the children, but today Tony and Hannah had come to lunch at the castle and their company always cheered her.

Usually Nicole enjoyed being with them, too. They were happy people. But today, as they sat around a table near the fountain in the loggia, their happiness made her feel sad. This is how it should be, she kept thinking, a man and a woman loving each other, getting married, having a baby because they both wanted it. Hannah seemed to glow with good health. Nicole wondered if she had suffered morning sickness earlier on in her pregnancy, but she couldn't ask.

"Matt!"

Tony's cry of surprise sent a shock through her heart. Her head dizzied as her gaze jerked to the man coming out of the castle, brandishing cutlery and serviette.

"Knew you'd be here, Tony, so I thought I'd join you," he announced. "Rosita said you were lunching outside so I've come armed for the feast."

"There's such a nice breeze," Hannah explained. "We didn't want to be inside."

"Good thinking," Matt approved. "I'll just move you

up a place, Hannah, so I can sit next to Nonna." He smiled at his grandmother. "I trust I'm welcome?"

She returned his smile. "Always, Matteo."

"Nicole…" He nodded to her as he rearranged the seating. "…how are you?"

"Fine, thank you," she managed to reply, though her stomach was now in knots.

He was seating himself almost directly opposite her, which meant she'd be facing him all through lunch, the man who'd fathered a child with her and didn't know it.

Fortunately, Tony claimed his brother's attention, chatting on about the tourist business which was of vital interest to both of them. They were coming out of the wet season, which meant the influx of visitors to Port Douglas was rapidly increasing, people wanting a vacation in the sun and trips to the Great Barrier Reef and other wonders of the tropical far north.

Rosita wheeled out a traymobile loaded with a variety of salads and a huge coral trout that she'd baked with a herb and pinenut crust. She placed the platter containing the fish in front of Tony to carve into servings and the smell of the herbs wafted down the table, instantly making Nicole feel nauseous. Trying to counter the effect, she sipped her iced juice, desperately breathing in the scent of its tropical fruit.

"Only a very small portion for me please, Tony," she requested when he was about to serve her.

"Don't stint yourself because I'm an unexpected guest," Matt quickly threw in, his gaze targeting her with persuasive intent. "There's more than enough to go around."

"I'm not really hungry," she excused, savagely wishing he wouldn't look directly at her. He was so wickedly handsome, it screwed up her heart, making it hop, skip and jump in a highly erratic fashion.

"But you missed breakfast this morning," Mrs. King remarked, surprised by Nicole's lack of appetite.

She sought wildly for a reasonable explanation. "While I was wandering around the market stalls…"

"You succumbed to the famous prawn sandwich?" Matt supplied, his brilliant dark eyes twinkling teasingly.

She nodded, robbed of speech. He was putting out magnetic sex appeal again, reducing her to a quivering mess inside. Thankfully Hannah rescued her.

"And look what she bought the baby at the markets, Matt!" She leaned down beside her chair, took the cleverly crafted caterpillar from the plastic bag and demonstrated how the multi-coloured segments could be stretched out and when released, they'd bunch together again. "Isn't it gorgeous?"

Hannah was beaming pleasure at her brother-in-law and he beamed pleasure right back at her. "Fantastic! I can see little hands having a fun time with that."

Tears pricked Nicole's eyes at the thought of her own baby's little hands, reaching out for a father who wasn't there, a father who'd never watch him or her having fun.

"Well bought, Nicole," Matt declared with warm approval, turning her to absolute mush.

Why was he doing this?

Why was he here?

Hadn't she made it clear that she would not have an affair with him? She wanted what Tony and Hannah had, not just a physical thing that went nowhere but bed.

Distractedly she helped herself to salads, hoping to smother the herb smell on the plate Tony had passed to her. The result was a heap of food she couldn't possibly eat, which made her feel even worse. She picked up her knife and fork, telling herself she had to get through this, had to act normally and not draw any attention to her state of helpless torment.

"Did you try one of the exotic fruit ices while you were down in Anzac Park?" Matt asked her, forcing further conversation with him.

Nicole gave him a fleeting glance as she answered, "No, I didn't."

"Then you missed out on a treat," he cheerfully persisted. "They're very flavoursome and refreshing. The people who run the stall buy their fruit from me. They do well with it."

Wishing she could ignore him but knowing it would be perceived as impolite by Mrs. King, Nicole forced her gaze up from her plate and managed a quick smile. "I'm sure they do. I did notice they had quite long queues at that stall, people waiting to be served."

Her eyes didn't quite meet his but only he would notice, and hopefully he would get the message that she wasn't interested and would prefer to be left alone. She picked doggedly at the salads she'd chosen, determined on closing him out as much as she could. He chatted to his grandmother, apparently not having noticed anything untoward in Nicole's behaviour. It was as though he wasn't aware of any tension, or was consciously ignoring it, hoping it would go away.

It didn't go away for Nicole. She had the strong sense of Matt King biding his time, waiting to pounce when the opportunity presented itself, planning how to manoeuvre her away from the others. He'd given no notice of his coming and his arrival had coincided with the serving of lunch, which meant she couldn't easily absent herself. She was sure this was planned, not an impulse. Behind it all was a relentless will beating at her, not letting go.

It made her head ache. Her stomach started to revolt against the food she was doing her best to eat. She sipped her juice, desperate to control the waves of nausea. It was no use. The added stress of Matt King's presence was just too much to bear on top of everything else. The casual cheerfulness of his voice, the confident way he was dealing with his meal, the sheer power of the man…it all made her feel weak and miserable.

She set down her cutlery, placed her serviette by her plate and pushed up from her chair. "Please excuse me." She swept an apologetic look around the table, then directly addressed her employer. "I must have walked too long in the heat this morning." She rubbed her forehead which was definitely clammy. "I'm just not well."

Mrs. King frowned in concern. "Go and lie down, my dear. I'll check on you later."

"Thank you."

"If it's an upset stomach, could be the prawn sandwich," Hannah suggested as Nicole made her way around the table. "Takeaway food can be tricky."

"Yes," Nicole agreed weakly.

"Or is it sunstroke?" Matt queried. "Do you feel feverish, Nicole?"

"Only a headache," she answered, wishing they'd just let her go without fuss, fixing her gaze on the double entrance doors to the castle to deflect any further inquiries about her health.

A chair scraped on the cobblestones. Matt spoke, *not letting her go.* "I'll accompany you up to your room. Make sure you're all right."

"No!"

She spun to face the man she most wanted to escape, her hand flying out in a warding-off protest. He was on his feet, so big and tall he seemed to tower over her, filling her vision with multiple images. Which was wrong. She was dizzy from having whirled on him so fast, the shock of his action draining the blood from her face.

The next thing she knew was finding herself clamped to Matt King's chest, then being set in his chair, head down between her knees, his arm around her supportively, his voice ringing in her ears as he crouched to her level.

"Deep breaths. Get some oxygen back in your brain."

Had she fainted?

Embarrassment churned through her. Having so much

attention focused on her was dreadful. "I'm all right," she gasped, intensely distressed at having made this spectacle of herself.

"You were blacking out, Nicole. Take your time now," Matt advised. He felt her forehead. "Not overly hot. A bit clammy."

"Perhaps I should call a doctor," Mrs. King said worriedly.

"No!" Nicole cried, alarmed by what a doctor might tell her employer. She had to keep the pregnancy a secret. "I just need to lie down for a while. Truly…"

"I'll carry her up to her room, Nonna. Make sure she's okay," Matt said.

"You do that, Matteo, and I'll go and speak to Rosita. She has remedies for everything."

"Oh, please…" Nicole barely got those words out before she was lifted off the chair and cradled across the same broad masculine chest she had struggled against at the Brisbane hotel.

"I'll get the doors open for you," Tony chimed in, already out of his chair and striding ahead of them.

Fighting them all seemed like fighting an unstoppable juggernaut. Nicole felt too weak to do it. She let herself be carried into the castle, hating the enforced awareness of the man who was carrying her, his strength, the sense of once more being enveloped by him. She refused to put her arms around his neck to make the carrying easier. It would bring her into even closer contact with him, possibly encouraging whatever devious plan he had in mind.

Tony didn't follow them in. Mrs. King left them at the staircase, pursuing her own path to the kitchen and Rosita. This left Nicole alone with Matt King as he started up the stairs.

"Put me down. I can walk," she pleaded.

"It's not far. I can manage," he stated firmly, as though she was worrying about being too heavy a burden.

She closed her eyes and took a deep breath, which was a mistake because she breathed in the warm male scent of him and her head swam again. "Why are you doing this?" she hissed, angry at her own vulnerability to an attraction she didn't want to feel.

"You need help."

"I don't want you holding me."

"You surely don't imagine I'm taking you up to your bedroom to seduce you when you're obviously sick."

She was too agitated to think straight.

"Seduction wasn't what we were about anyway," he added dryly. "You know that, Nicole."

"I'm not going to change my mind," she blurted out, desperate for him to understand her position.

"I didn't expect you to."

"Then why are you here?"

"Was I supposed to be banned from the castle?"

She floundered, knowing it was absurd to try to cut him off from his grandmother for the duration of the project. "You know what I mean," she muttered helplessly.

"You wanted enough notice so you could avoid me?"

She bit her lips, knowing to concede that also conceded how deeply he affected her. But he knew it already, she wildly reasoned. Nothing would have happened between them if she hadn't wanted it to.

"You made your point, Nicole," he went on quietly. "I'm not going to push anything else."

He didn't have to, she thought miserably. She was a mess around him anyway. He'd reached the top of the staircase, seemingly without any effort at all, and headed down the corridor towards the guest suites.

"Which door?" he asked.

"Please...put me down now," she begged. "I'll be fine. The dizziness has gone."

"Which door?" he repeated.

"I don't want you coming into my private room," she cried. "It's *private*... to *me!*"

He stopped. His chest rose as he sucked in a deep breath and fell as he expelled it. Slowly, carefully, he set her on her feet, still holding her as he waited to see if she really was steady enough to be safely released.

"I was only trying to look after you, Nicole, not take some...some crass advantage," he said quietly. "I'm sorry I left you thinking so badly of me. Next time we meet..." Another deep sigh. "There's no need for you to feel stressed in my company. Okay?"

"Yes. Thank you. May I go now?" she rushed out, unable to look at him with tears pricking her eyes again.

"As you wish," he murmured, dropping his hands.

She made it to her room in a blind dash, conscious he was waiting, watching. It was an enormous relief to close the door on him. She stood against it, letting the tears roll, swallowing the sobs that threatened to erupt.

Trying to look after her...

I want someone to care about me. Look after me.

Those were the words she'd hurled at him in the elevator. Did he remember them or was he just reacting to her being ill in front of his family? Nothing really personal. Except he wanted to call at the castle without her being stressed. Which was totally impossible now she was pregnant with his child.

Oh, God! Oh, God! Oh, God!

What was she to do?

CHAPTER SIXTEEN

ISABELLA VALERI KING decided this was no time for sensitivities. There was very little time left for anything. If she was wrong, Matteo could soon set her right. However, if the situation was what she suspected it to be, action had to be taken before Nicole drove back to Sydney. Once in her home city, it would be all too easy for an enterprising and determined woman to make herself uncontactable in any direct sense.

The contract to write the family history would not be broken. Isabella had no doubt about Nicole's integrity on that promise. The research had been thorough with everything recorded for easy reference. The argument that the writing could be done anywhere was irrefutable. Nicole Redman was going and Isabella knew in her heart there'd be no coming back to Port Douglas. An irrevocable decision had been made.

Unless Matteo stopped it.

If he had reason to stop it.

With all this churning through her mind, Isabella entered the KingTours main office, intent on a face-to-face confrontation with her youngest grandson.

"Mrs. King!" the boy behind the desk cried in surprise, this being a rare and unheralded visitation by a woman of legendary stature in the community.

"Is my grandson in his office?" she demanded. He ought to be. It was Friday morning. And she didn't want to hear any excuses for not meeting with her.

"Yes," the boy informed, not seeing any reason to check with his employer.

"Good! You need not announce me," she instructed, leaving him staring after her as she marched into Matteo's office and closed the door firmly behind her.

Matteo looked up from the paperwork on his desk with the same air of stunned surprise. "Nonna! What are you doing here?"

She paused, for the first time wondering if she was about to do him an injustice. Giving herself more time to think, she moved slowly to the vacant chair on this side of his desk and sat down.

"Is something wrong?" he asked in quick concern, rising from his chair.

She held up a hand to stop him. "I only wish to talk, Matteo."

He frowned, sinking back onto his seat. "What about?"

"It's Friday. I thought perhaps you might intend to visit me this afternoon."

He nodded, his brow still creased, more in puzzlement now. "I had planned to drop by. Is there a problem?"

"Nicole is leaving us. She begins the long drive back to Sydney tomorrow."

His frown deepened again. "Do you mean she is breaking her contract with you?"

"No. She will write the family history. But she will not remain at the castle to do so."

"Did she give a reason?"

"She says the heat is getting to her. And it is true that she has been unwell all this week."

He grimaced. "I did say…"

"It is nonsense, Matteo," Isabella cut in. "She has been here three months, through the hottest time of the year, with no ill effect whatsoever. Until very recently."

"Last Sunday…"

"Yes. That was the most noticeable."

"Since then?"

"She has not been…herself."

"Maybe the heat has gradually worn her down, Nonna."

"No. It is not logical."

His eyes narrowed. "So what do you think? Why come to me?" he rapped out.

"I may be old but I'm not blind, Matteo. There has been something between you and Nicole. She is tense in your presence and you are certainly not indifferent to her."

"Are you blaming *me* for this choice she's made?" he challenged tersely.

"Are you to blame?" she fired straight at him.

His hands lifted in an impatient gesture. "I have tried to put Nicole more at ease with me. If she cannot accept that…"

"Maybe it is not possible, Matteo," Isabella said sadly. "Rosita says Nicole is pregnant."

"What?"

His shock was patent.

Again Isabella paused, not certain that he was responsible. She sat silently, watching him deal with what was obviously news to him.

He shook his head incredulously. Then his face tightened as though he'd been hit by some truth he recognised. He shot an intense look at her. "How does Rosita know this?"

Isabella shrugged. "I have never known Rosita to be wrong on the matter of pregnancy. She says there is a look about a woman. She told me Hannah was pregnant weeks before Antonio announced it. I don't doubt Rosita's judgment, Matteo. And as much as Nicole tries to hide it, her morning sickness..."

"She's been sick every morning?"

"For over a week now."

"Before last Sunday?"

"Yes."

Clenched fists crashed down on the desk. "She knew." He erupted from his chair. "She knew!" He paced around the desk, his hands flying out in violent agitation. "Why didn't she tell me? She had the chance."

All doubt was now erased. Isabella took a deep breath and said, "Nicole must have felt she had good reason not to tell you, Matteo."

"But..." He sliced the air in angry dismissal. "...I told her how I feel about fatherhood."

"How *you* feel. Perhaps you should consider how Nicole feels."

"It's my child!" he protested. "She can't just ignore that, Nonna."

"If you want any part in your child's life, I advise you to proceed with great care, Matteo. With great care."

She stood with all the dignity at her command, bringing to a halt the wild tempest of energy emanating from her grandson.

"In this matter Nicole has all the rights," she said to sober him. "And if she leaves tomorrow, your child will be gone with her. This is not a time for rash action or anger, Matteo. It is a time for caring, for kindness, for understanding."

She walked to the door. Matteo did not move to open it for her. She looked back at him, saw conflict raging across his face, tension gripping his entire body, the need to act almost explosive.

Was this turbulence they struck in each other the cause of all the problems?

Isabella shook her head.

What more could she do?

"It is not the heat nor the pregnancy that has made Nicole Redman sick to her soul," she said sadly. "You would do well to think on that today, Matteo. Whatever you decide to do...you will live with this for the rest of your life."

She opened the door and left him.

The decisions were his now.

She could only hope he made the right ones.

CHAPTER SEVENTEEN

EVEN at the last moment, Nicole hesitated, the sealed and addressed envelope still clamped between her finger and thumb as it hovered over the slot in the postal box. It had to be done, she told herself. It wasn't right to deny Matt King knowledge of a child he'd fathered. By the time he received the letter she'd be long gone, although once the baby was born, she would notify him again. Then if he wanted contact...their child had the right to know its father.

That was the really important truth.

She could not turn her back on her child's rights.

Whatever happened with Matt King in the future she would learn to cope with it...somehow. This had to be done. Her finger and thumb lifted apart. The envelope dropped.

Nicole hurried back to her car. No turning back on this course now. All week she had fretted over it. A weight seemed to shift from her shoulders as she settled herself in the driver's seat. There was nothing more that had to be done.

It was almost five o'clock. She'd bought a packet of barley sugar to suck on the trip tomorrow in the hope it would keep any sickness at bay, plus bottles of mineral water to stop dehydration. Only one more night at the castle…

She drove around the town one last time, knowing she would miss this place, wanting to remember everything about it. Maybe, sometime in the future, her child would come here for visits, if Matt King wanted that. It was a heart-wrenching thought. Tears pricked her eyes. She blinked them away and drove up to the castle, wanting to catch the sunset from the tower.

Rosita was in the kitchen when Nicole carried in the bottles of water to put in the refrigerator overnight. "I have made my special lasagna for your dinner," the motherly housekeeper announced.

Nicole didn't feel like eating anything heavy but she smiled, knowing Rosita wanted to give her a last treat. "I'm sure I'll enjoy it."

"I will pack a picnic box for you to take in the morning." Her kind eyes searched Nicole's in hopeful concern. "Is there anything else I can do for you?"

"No, thank you, Rosita. You've been marvellous to me. I'm just going up to the tower now to watch the sunset."

"Ah, yes. It is a fine view from the tower. Take care not to fall on the steps. They are very old and worn."

Nicole took away the strong impression that Rosita knew what she'd tried to keep hidden. Or at least suspected it. All the fussing over her, the admonitions to *take care*… but nothing had been said. Sadness dragged on her heart as she climbed the steps to the tower. She would miss Rosita's motherliness. Having been motherless for so many years, it had been nice to be fussed over, cared about.

There was so much she would miss.

Many times she had come up here to the topmost level of the castle, having finished work for the day and needing a relaxing break before dinner. The view was fantastic to every horizon, the sea, the mountains, the endless sky, all the colours beginning to change as the sun lowered.

She walked around the tessellated wall, taking in the many vistas one last time, stopping finally at her favourite view over Dickenson Inlet where the boats came into the marina, the cane fields on the other side of it stretching out to sea, and beyond them the darkening hills behind which the sun would sink.

It was so calming, peaceful, beautiful. She thought of her employer's mother, Marguerita Valeri, standing here in the old days, watching the ships come in from the sea, watching the cane fields burn at harvest time, watching the sun set, and for the first time it occurred to Nicole that her child—Matt King's child—was part of the same pioneering bloodline that had built this castle and so much else up here in the far north.

She herself might never belong anywhere but her child had deep family roots. A real history. A history she would write so it would always be known. It was something good she could give. And maybe Matt—if he truly felt the responsibilities of fatherhood—would provide their child with a solid sense of belonging.

*　*　*

Matt reached the top of the tower and halted, gathering himself to do what had to be done. Nicole was standing at the far wall, her back turned to him, her gaze seemingly fixed on the view his grandmother liked best. Her tall slender figure was completely still, wrapped in a loneliness he knew he had to break.

The setting sun gave the frame of her fiery hair a glowing aura. The shining of inner strength, he thought, though the rest of her looked fragile. The urge to simply take her in his arms was strong, but he sternly reminded himself that taking was not keeping and Nicole would resist force.

Only the truth would serve him now.

His anger at her keeping everything to herself had dissipated hours ago. His pride was worth nothing in the face of losing this woman and the child she was carrying. If Rosita was right about the pregnancy, he had to win both of them. He had to reach Nicole with the truth, make it speak for him, make it count.

One chance.

He couldn't afford to mess it up.

Matt took a deep, deep breath and called to her.

"Nicole…"

Her heart leapt.

His voice.

She turned with a sense of disbelief, having already relegated him to the past, and the far future. He wasn't supposed to appear in the here and now. Yet he was striding towards her, large as life, the force of his vital energy making her pulse flutter and spreading a buzz of confusion through her entire body.

"What are you doing here?" she cried, her mind struggling to accept a reality she didn't want to face.

He slowed his step, his hands lifting in an appeal, his dark eyes begging her forbearance. "Sorry if I startled you. I came by after work to see my grandmother. She mentioned you were leaving us tomorrow."

"Yes. Yes, I am. I don't need to stay here to do the writing," she gabbled out, belatedly remembering he worked in the KingTours offices on Fridays and cursing herself for not foreseeing the possibility of a casual visit to the castle. Although why he had to come up here, seeking her out...

"Is it because of me?" he asked, coming to a halt at the tessellated wall right beside her, barely an arm's length away, and turned to face her, an urgent intensity in the eyes searching hers.

Her heart thumped wildly. "Why would you think that? I told Mrs. King..."

"There are more kinds of heat than the weather," he said with savage irony, "and I know I'm guilty of subjecting you to them, Nicole."

He was doing it again right now.

She turned her face to the sunset, hoping the red glow in the sky would somehow hide the tide of heat rushing up her neck, scorching her cheeks. Her mind literally could not come up with a dismissive reply. It was drowning in the truth he'd just spoken, a whirlpool of truth that had swept her around in tormenting circles ever since she had met Matt King.

"I've been very wrong about you," he went on quietly. "And I regret, very deeply, making you feel...threatened by me. I wish I could take it all back and we could start again."

Impossible. What was done couldn't be undone. The new life she carried forced her to move on. And regrets didn't change anything. Though at least his admission of being wrong about her might make a rapprochement between them easier in the future.

"I'm glad you don't think badly of me anymore," she said, steeling herself to look directly at him one more time. "Let's leave it at that."

His gaze locked onto hers with compelling strength. "I can't. I don't want you to go, Nicole."

She shook her head, pained by the raw desire in his eyes, in his voice. Her stomach was curling in protest. She placed her hand over it, instinctively protective. "Please...it's no good."

"It can be good," he argued vehemently. "The two of us together...it *was* good. Better than anything I've known with any other woman."

Sex!

She recoiled from him.

"Wait!" His arm lifted in urgent intent to halt her retreat. "I know I've messed up everything. It was stupid, trying to negate the truth of what I felt, trying to sidetrack it. I didn't want to get...*hooked* on you."

"I'm not…not…*bait!*" she cried, horrified at the image his words conjured up.

"I thought my grandmother…" He broke off, venting a sigh that carried a wealth of exasperation.

"What about your grandmother?"

He grimaced. "Nonna is into matchmaking. She found Gina for Alex, inviting her to the castle as a wedding singer. And she hired Hannah as the cook for Tony's prized catamaran, *Duchess,* putting her right under his nose. I know she wants all three of us married, having families. I thought she'd picked you for me."

She stared at him in total disbelief. "That's…that's crazy!"

Another grimace. "Not as crazy as it sounds."

"You don't think *I* might have a say in whom I marry?"

"I'm trying to explain…" He looked harassed, raking a hand through the tight curls above his ear, frowning, gesturing an appeal for patience. "I wanted her to be wrong. And when I remembered you from New Orleans…"

"You concocted a scenario that put me in the light of a totally unsuitable wife," she hotly accused.

"Yes," he admitted fiercely. "And grabbed at every other reason I could think of, too. Anything to stop me from even thinking of pursuing the attraction I felt. I was pig-headedly determined not to fall into Nonna's marriage trap, even though…" He shook his head self-mockingly. "…she had nothing to do with the attraction I felt for you ten years ago."

"You mean…in New Orleans?" she asked, confused by his previous interpretation of her work there.

"I tagged on to your tour that night, just to watch you, listen to you. If I hadn't been a tourist…if I could have met you in some appropriate way…but my time there was at an end and I told myself it was fantasy."

Amazed at this turnabout in his view of her, she ruefully murmured, "I wouldn't have had time for you anyway."

"Our paths were at cross-purposes, but does it have to be like that now, Nicole?"

Pain washed through her. The cross-purposes couldn't be worse. Pregnancy was the oldest marriage trap in the world. It was too late to simply pursue an attraction to see where it might lead and he'd just made it impossible for her to admit the truth. He didn't want to be *trapped*.

She stared at him, hopelessly torn by the possibility he offered, wishing time could be turned back, wishing it was just the two of them, a man and a woman, free to start out on a promising journey…but it wasn't so. It just wasn't so.

Her silence pressed him into more speech, his eagerness to convince her of his sincerity permeating every word. "When I read your book, I realised what a fool I'd been to even question your integrity and your ability to do anything you set out to do. I hadn't meant to hurt you. I'm sorry I did. Genuinely sorry."

The passion in his voice stormed around her heart, squeezing. She wrenched her gaze from his, afraid of being swayed into clutching at some way to have another chance with him. But the idea of deception was sickening. The truth about her pregnancy would have to come out. No choice at all. And she couldn't bear him to feel bound to her because of their baby. This nerve-tearing impasse had to be ended.

"I forgive you that hurt," she said flatly, staring at the long red streaks in the sky, the bleeding tatters of a dying day. "You don't have to worry about it anymore."

"That night in Brisbane..."

She tensed, instinctively armouring herself against letting that memory invade and undermine her resolution.

"...you wanted me, too, Nicole," he said softly.

"Yes, I did. You have nothing to blame yourself for on that account," she clipped out as coldly as she could.

"Can you forget it?"

It was a biting challenge, determined on getting to her, arousing all the feelings they had shared in the heat of the moment. No cold then. And he wanted to remove the chill now, reminding her...

She closed her eyes, determined on sealing off all vulnerability to him. If she didn't see, didn't feel...

"I can't. I don't think I ever will," he said with skin-prickling conviction. "It was as though we were meant for each other. Perfectly matched. You tapped things in me I've never felt before."

Nicole gritted her teeth. Just sex, she savagely reminded herself. Great sex, admittedly, but still only sex.

"It was like...all of me reaching for all of you...and finding a togetherness which went beyond the merely physical. And because it was so...so incredible...I was impatient to experience it again, not taking the time to..."

"It's okay!" she choked out, unable to bear his recollections. "I didn't anticipate what happened, either. We didn't plan it. We didn't...*choose* it."

In a spurt of almost-frenzied energy she turned on him, desperate to finish it. "That's the one right we hold unassailable in our lives...to choose for ourselves. You didn't want your grandmother's choice thrust upon you. I understand that. And I don't want a...a fling with you."

"That's not what I want, either," he shot back.

"Then what do you want?" she cried helplessly, her hands flapping a frantic protest. "What's all this about? Why try to stop me from leaving?"

"Because I love you!" he retorted vehemently, stunning her, stunning himself with the force of feeling he'd hurled into the maelstrom of need that was tearing at both of them.

They stared at each other, a mountain of emotion churning between them. He scaled it first, charging ahead with all the pent-up ferocity of a warrior committed to battle.

"I just need the time to give you every reason to love me. I know I haven't done that yet, but I will. *I will!*"

Still she couldn't believe her ears. "You...love... me?"

He drew in a deep breath, but his gaze did not waver even slightly from the incredulity in hers. "I do. I love you," he stated again. "You're in my mind, night and day. If you'll just stop pushing me away, I'll show you I can and will look after you, that I do care about the person you are. Whatever your needs are, I'll answer them. I want to answer them."

She stared mutely at him, feeling as though her whole world had just shifted on its axis. "You hardly know me." The words spilled from a swirling abyss of doubts.

"Nicole, I've read parts of your book over and over again." He stepped forward and gently cupped her cheek, his eyes burning into hers as his tenderly stroking fingers burnt into her skin, seeking every path to the torment in her soul. "I love the child who had the courage to lead her father away from the darkness he was in danger of falling into. I love the young woman who gave the end of his life as much meaning as she could. You shine through the whole story…"

"It's not about me," she protested, her voice reduced to a husky whisper.

"It reveals the heart of you. The kind of heart a man would be a fool not to love."

"Maybe…" She swallowed hard, trying to work some moisture into her mouth. "Maybe you…you think that. But feeling it is something different."

"How does this feel?"

He tilted her chin and she was too stunned to take any evasive action before his mouth claimed hers, not with blitzing passion but with a tantalisingly seductive sensuality that wooed her into accepting the kiss, testing it for herself, feeling the electric tingle of his restraint, letting it happen because she needed to know *his* truth beyond any niggle of doubt before she could surrender her own.

"I love you," he murmured, feathering her lips with the feeling words, then drawing back to look into her eyes with mesmerising fervour. "I love everything about you."

He smiled whimsically as his fingers softly nudged her hair behind her ears. "Your hair is like a brilliant beacon calling to me."

A moth to a flame, he'd said before.

His hands trailed down to her shoulders. "I love the way you hold yourself. It shouts—*I am a woman and proud of it.* And so you should be proud of who you are, all you are, Nicole."

I am, she thought, ashamed of nothing, not even the slip in sensible caution that had made her vulnerable to falling pregnant. Maybe it was meant to be because he was *the man,* she thought dizzily, and as though he could read her mind, his next words melted the armour she'd tried to hold around her heart.

"It excites me simply to look at you. It's like all my instincts immediately start clamouring—*this is the woman…the woman for me.* It happens every time I see you, and it's so powerful I have no control over it. You can call it primitive. I don't care. It's there…and I believe it's there for you, too, Nicole."

He shook his head at her, negating any denial she might make. "You wouldn't have let us come together in Brisbane if you didn't feel the same way," he pressed on. "You would have shot me out of your room. It was right for us. It was how it was meant to be between us, and would have been all along if I hadn't put up barriers to keep you at a distance."

Was that true? If she hadn't sensed antagonism in him at their first meeting, if he hadn't been so cynically challenging, if he'd been welcoming, charming…she probably would have fallen in love with him on the spot, dazzled right out of her mind. As it was, she'd resented his sexual impact on her, hated it. Yet when she'd surrendered to the intense desires he stirred, it had felt right, beautifully wonderfully right. Could it be that way again if…but there was still the baby.

"All I'm asking is that you stay on here," he said earnestly. "Let me show you…"

"I'm pregnant!" she blurted out, then instantly averted her gaze from his, frightened of the effect of such a stark statement on his plans for whatever relationship he wanted with her. Only a golden rim of the sun was left shimmering above the dark hills. Twilight hovered above it, a purpling sky that signalled the end of this day. The night would come. And then tomorrow…

"I wrote you a letter. It's posted to KingTours. It says we…we made a baby…when we came together," she said in a desperate rush, needing him to understand the emotional dilemma of a future neither of them had planned or even foreseen. "I would have written again when the baby was born. In case…in case you wanted to be a real father. Like you said…"

Silence.

Silence so fraught she couldn't breathe.

The trap, she thought. He's seeing the trap now.

It was no longer a case of winning her over with a promise of love. It wasn't about today or tomorrow or her staying on at the castle for the last three months of the history project. It was about being bonded by a child for the rest of their lives.

CHAPTER EIGHTEEN

"So it's true. You *are* pregnant."

His words fell strangely on Nicole's ears. She had expected shock. The lack of it was mind-jolting.

"I didn't want to believe you'd go without telling me," he went on, hurt gathering momentum. "Without giving me the chance to…"

"You *knew?*" Her own shock spun her around to face him.

He gestured dismissively as though it didn't matter. "Rosita told my grandmother. She thought I should be informed."

"You knew before you came up here and said all those things to me?" Her voice climbed at the shattering of all she'd wanted to believe.

He frowned at her. "How could you do that? Leaving me *a letter?*"

"You don't have to feel responsible. I don't want you spinning me a whole pack of lies to…"

"A letter!" he thundered, cutting her off. "Letting me know so I could stew about it for the next eight months, wondering how you were, worrying if all was well with the baby, while you took care of everything by yourself, shutting me out of both your lives. Was that the plan?"

"Yes!" she snapped. "I couldn't bear you to feel trapped into something you wouldn't have chosen with me."

"You didn't give me the choice. You chose to give me the hell of being shoved aside. Rendered useless. I wasn't to help you through the pregnancy. I wasn't to be at your side when you gave birth to our child. You were going to cheat me of holding our son or our daughter when it came into this world." He threw up his hands, his whole body expressing a towering rage. "How could you do that? How?"

"It's all about possession to you, isn't it?" she fired back at him, defying his stand on what he considered his paternal rights. "Possession, not love. You didn't want to let me go because you knew I had something you wanted."

"Let you go? Not in a million years." Fierce purpose glared at her. "I'm not taking any more nonsense from you, Nicole Redman. We are going to get married. We're going to get married so fast, it'll put Nonna in a total tailspin getting it arranged in time."

She backed away from him. "You can't make me marry you."

"Give me one good reason why you won't," he challenged, his eyes glittering with wild certainty in his cause.

"No one should marry for the sake of a child. It doesn't work," she cried vehemently.

"Marrying for love does."

"You're just saying that."

"No. Don't speak for me, Nicole."

"You *said* you didn't want to be trapped into marriage."

"I'm walking right into it with my eyes wide open." He stepped towards her. She retreated. He kept coming as he pressed his view. "No trap. This is precisely what I want. My woman. My child. A home we share. A future we make together."

His aggressive confidence came at her like a tidal wave, swallowing up everything in its path, crashing past barriers as though they were nothing. Nicole struggled to hold on to the sense of the decisions she'd made.

"If I hadn't fallen pregnant..."

"You would have stayed at the castle long enough for me to show you we belonged with each other."

"How can I know that?" She stretched out her hands, pleading her uncertainty. "How can I believe anything?"

"Listen to your heart." He was all command now, brushing aside any equivocation. "You don't want to be alone in this. You want to be with me. I'm the man who'll look after you. I'm the man who'll always be there for you. The provider. The protector. But most of all, the one who loves you."

"Love..." she repeated, her voice wobbling over the tantalising word, her head reeling from the overwhelming force of arguments which were sweeping into all the empty places of her life and setting up unshakable occupation.

She forgot about backing away from him. He kept

coming—big, tall, powerfully built, sinfully handsome, intensely sexy, with a mind that saw obstacles as something to beat, nothing to stop him. And the truth was she loved him. She loved everything about him—this king amongst men.

He seized her upper arms. His eyes blazed with an indomitable will to win. "Stop all this destructive resistance, Nicole," he commanded in a voice that drummed through her heart. "Stop and remember what we felt when we came together. When we made our baby...yours and mine...together. It was right. Admit it!"

The intense blast of his passion poured a sizzling sense of rightness through every cell of her body. And wasn't he promising everything she had ever ached for? *Admit it!*

She wanted to be Matt King's wife...wanted to become part of his extraordinary family...wanted their child to belong here.

His fingers pressed urgent persuasion. "Give us a chance, Nicole. Please...just give us a chance."

CHAPTER NINETEEN

Dear Elizabeth,

I write this with great joy. Yesterday Nicole gave birth to a beautiful baby boy. He is to be called Stephen, after my father. Nicole insisted on it. She has a very strong sense of family tradition, which is very comforting to me. I know when I am gone, she will be the keeper of all I have tried to set in place. It is meaningful to her.

Every day I leaf through the family history she wrote for us and I can feel her love of it on every page, even to the way she placed the photographs. I hope she will add to it in the years to come, especially the photograph I am enclosing with this letter. Ah, the love and pride on Matteo's face, looking down at his wife and newborn son, and Nicole glowing the same feelings right back at him. It brings happy tears to my eyes.

This was a match truly made in heaven, though God knows they were difficult people to bring together. It was so fortunate they were blessed with a child to make them come to their senses and acknowledge what they were to each other. Well, you saw them at their wedding. Such strong passion between them. There will never be anyone else for those two.

I can rest content now. Alessandro, Antonio, Matteo…they have the right partners. And here I am with four great-grandchildren, two boys, two girls. Antonio and Hannah adore their darling daughter and no doubt she and Stephen will be splendid company for each other, born so closely together.

There is nothing like family. To me it is the keystone of our lives—our past, our present, our future. I know you feel this, too. I enjoy our correspondence very much, and I want to thank you once again for all your wise advice. Each night I lie in bed and I think of our family lines—yours in the Kimberly, mine here in the far north—and I see them thriving for a long, long time, Elizabeth. I go to sleep with a smile.

I am sure it is a smile we share.

With love,
Isabella Valeri King

MILLS & BOON®

Live the emotion

Tender romance™

THEIR NEW-FOUND FAMILY *by Rebecca Winters*

As a single mum, Rachel Marsden has always tried to do her
best by her daughter. So when Natalie's long-lost father, Tris
Monbrisson, shows up, Rachel swallows her feelings and moves
to Tris's beautiful home in Switzerland. But as she and Tris
fall into the role of mother and father, the secrets of the past
unravel…

THE BILLIONAIRE'S BRIDE *by Jackie Braun*

Marnie LaRue has come to Mexico for relaxation – but the
man in the neighbouring hacienda makes her laugh, and *feel*
more than she has in a long time. Mysterious JT doesn't know
Marnie is a grieving widow – and she doesn't have any clue that
he's a billionaire…

CONTRACTED: CORPORATE WIFE *by Jessica Hart*

Patrick Farr is happy with his bachelor life, dating beautiful
women – but how can he make them understand that he'll
never marry for love? A marriage of convenience! Lou
Dennison is his cool and calm PA – she's also a single mum, so
when Patrick proposes her answer's definitely no. Or is it?

IMPOSSIBLY PREGNANT *by Nicola Marsh* (Office Gossip)

Keely Rhodes has a new work project – to get up close and
personal with the famous Lachlan Brant! He's invited her to
spend a weekend away with him – but she's sure he has more
than business on his mind… Keely's friends think Lachlan's
her perfect man – and tell her to go for it. But after her trip,
she discovers the impossible has happened…

On sale 2nd September 2005

*Available at most branches of WHSmith, Tesco, ASDA,
Borders, Eason, Sainsbury's and most bookshops*

Visit www.millsandboon.co.uk

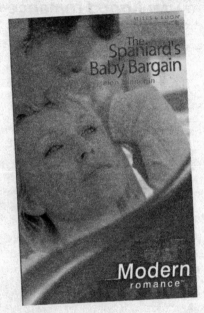

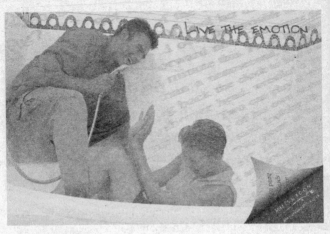